The Journeyman
An Irish Story

W.A. PATTERSON

CHAPTER 1

L iam Flynn was a journeyman carpenter. He hoped this would be his last journey.

The August afternoon was yielding to evening and the warm summer wind was already stale. A youthful, but bedraggled, figure trudged wearily down a dusty Tipperary road, pulling a cart behind him. On it, packed neatly in a trunk, were his few worldly possessions, the tools of his trade. He had underestimated the 20 mile journey from Thurles to Nenagh and now he cursed himself for not having bought a donkey.

Liam was an ordinary looking young fellow, the kind you might see every day and give no more than a passing glance to. His hair was tied back, and rivulets of sweat traced furrows through the dust that covered his face, before disappearing into his shirt at the neck. His hands were already hardened by years of manual labour and his muscles were sinewy. His face was grim and determined.

Every now and then, he would lift his gaze from the dusty track. The shadows had begun to grow longer and the low sun stared him in the face, making him squint as he took in his surroundings. The year was 1704 and Ireland was still swathed in expanses of primeval oak forest. The farmland which had dominated the landscape in South Tipperary now gave way to tracts of forbidding, dark woodland as the young man trekked westwards. His sweeping glance took in the trees, his expert eyes considering them as potential sources of material, with which to ply his trade, rather than the vestiges of what was once Ireland. As he travelled further westward, the land climbed, the uphill stretches growing longer, the downhill slopes shorter.

Liam had listened to the stories his mother had told him of growing up on a farm in County Cork and it was these idealised fantasies, heard at her knee, that spurred him on today. The River Shannon and the shores of Lough Derg were his destination. He had heard there was still land in West Tipperary that had never known a plough. He was a determined man, some would even say stubborn and, when he set himself a goal, he would allow nothing and no one to deter him. Liam knew little about farming but he was a dreamer and this was his dream. If he had one attribute, it was that he was a keen observer and could adapt himself to whatever the situation dictated.

Now and then, he glanced behind him. The very fabric of society in Ireland had been torn asunder by a hundred years of war, and was just beginning to re-establish itself anew, but the rule of law still did not extend much past the borders of the townships. These were times of outlawry and a man travelling alone would be an easy target for thieves. Some plied banditry as a means to feed their pitifully poor families; many had been evicted from the homes their families had lived in for hundreds of years and now, out of desperation, had turned to a life of crime. Some were ex-soldiers who had fought for a lost cause and had returned to find nothing.

For others, it was easier to rob than it was to find work.

Liam resolved not to be on the road after dark. If he passed a monastery, he would spend the night there, and he would be assured safety, at least, perhaps even a bite to eat. If not, he would pull off the road and camp under a tree, cover himself with his worn felt blanket and sleep lightly, ever watchful for danger, listening for sounds that didn't belong to the night. He had done this many times before.

The ruins of a castle came into view up ahead and, for a moment, Liam considered making it his resting place for the night, but it was still too early and he decided to carry on for another mile or so.

The Williamite Wars had ended in Ireland little more than 10 years ago and, with it, any hopes of Irish independence. The ruins of Cromwell's legacy, less than 50 years before, had left the countryside strewn with the bones of Ireland's ancient, proud castles and the skeletons of its once grand cathedrals. Here and there, he saw farms which still thrived, in contrast with others, whose farmhouse roofs had been burned and their stone walls breached. Liam thought momentarily of the displaced families who once dwelled there but put them out of his mind. He had his own troubles and could do nothing to help them. He forged onwards, his feet sore, his hands blistered from hauling the wagon.

He had been on the road for four days now and his clothes were caked in dirt and dust. His yellow leine, the long linen shirt he wore, cinched by a woven belt, was no longer its faded saffron colour but was now the colour of the road. He wore short trews as britches, ending just above his ankles, and his old leather brogues barely protected his feet.

His head hung low as he pulled the heavy cart, one

weary step following another, bringing him closer to Nenagh town. Each hill seemed higher than the last and he hoped that before tomorrow was old, he would find lodgings and a proper bed. He thought a decent meal wouldn't go amiss either, and his stomach growled in response to the idea. He had eaten nothing since dawn, his breakfast a cold potato and a draught of water warmed over a small fire. At his waist was a pouch containing a piece of brown flatbread and a lump of cheese. His mouth watered, right now it sounded like a feast to him.

The shadows grew longer still and, as Liam scanned the horizon, he saw the unmistakable outline of the Silvermine Mountains in the distance. He knew that Nenagh lay at the foot of the Silvermines and that they signalled the last leg of his journey. His spirits lifted, his stride lengthened and he made up his mind to forge ahead for another hour or so before pulling his cart off the road for the night. He peered up at the sky and hoped the clouds that were gathering overhead would not bring a change in weather. He had been fortunate so far on his mission.

The countryside that surrounded him now was lush and green, and Liam allowed himself the luxury of stopping for a few moments to admire it. He thought about lighting his clay pipe and having a smoke. Later perhaps, his twist of tobacco was getting small and there was no prospect of purchasing more until he reached his destination. He looked out over the land. A patchwork of green and yellow fields stretched over the rolling hills like a blanket, with dark green forests and hedge rows embroidered into the view. Sheep grazed contentedly in meadows carpeted with wild summer flowers and cows chewed placidly on their cud, waiting to be milked. A raven flew overhead, his raucous cry momentarily disrupting the idyllic scene. Liam wished he could cover his distance with the ease of a bird but, putting the thought aside, he took up the shafts of his cart again and continued his journey.

He had been concentrating on the road immediately in front of him, in an effort to prevent any of the larger stones from upsetting his cart and its contents, but as he crested a hill, he looked up, eager to gauge how much progress he had gained.

What he saw, was three strangers on the road up ahead. They were walking in his direction and they had seen him too. Liam's first thought was that it was too late to seek cover, so he would have to brazen it out. He became more apprehensive as the strangers approached and fanned themselves out across the road in what seemed like a well-practiced manoeuvre, designed to impede his progress. Liam brought his cart to a halt. The largest of the three strangers took the lead, a handsome, dark haired fellow and, as he approached Liam, he smiled. It was not a friendly smile, however, but rather one of a predator, confident of his advantage. His two cohorts wasted no time and circled around to the back of the wagon, eyeing up his belongings. Liam shot them a glance but they ignored him and began to rifle through the contents. As he turned back to face their leader, he was struck a mighty blow on his forehead by a shillelagh. He felt his knees buckle and a darkness descended upon him.

When consciousness returned, night had fallen but Liam had no concept of what time it could be. The sun had long descended and a crescent moon skipped in and out between the clouds. He tried to lift his head, but groaned and laid it back down on the dirt, it pulsated with a dull throb. He opened his eyes and tried to focus on the scythe-shaped moon overhead. He couldn't see out of his right eye and he wiped it with the heel of his hand. As he pulled his hand away, he saw it was covered with blood. It was wet and sticky and, in the darkness, it looked black. He managed to haul himself up into a sitting position, the stones on the road beneath him adding to his discomfort. As he tried to clear the haze that had descended on him, he realised his wagon had gone and so had all his belongings, along with his shoes and his felt cloak. The bastards had even stolen his pipe, and the sack with his bread and cheese in it.

The memory of the three bandits, and the events that had taken place, came tumbling back into his mind and a sudden dread gripped him. His life savings… He had tied his purse around his waist and slipped it into the back of his trews. His hands instinctively moved to where his money should be and he momentarily forgot his aching head and his bloodied eye as he let out a sigh of relief. Thank God, it was still there.

Liam sat on the dusty road in the moonlight long enough to gather himself. Further examination revealed that the blood had come from a gash on his forehead which, although still bleeding, had subsided a little. Before long, he got to his feet and slowly began to walk in the direction he had been travelling, stumbling at first. The stones on the road hurt his now bare feet, but his mind was otherwise occupied. He needed a new plan. His head throbbed with each step and occasionally he wiped the blood away from his eye with his sleeve.

A welcome freshness had come with the night and the cooler air helped to clear his mind. Liam possessed a characteristic Irish philosophy. Things could be worse, he thought. I'm not dead, or at least I don't think am. My head hurts so I can't be. I still have my money and the tools can be replaced. Sure things could be a lot worse.

He lurched on as best he could down the dark, winding road and, after about a mile, he saw the glimmer of lights in the distance. As he drew nearer, he realised the light came from candles which flickered from inside the windows of an inn. He could hear the sounds of revelry and, as he neared, the soft glow of the inn's lights grew more welcoming.

The moon broke free of the clouds and momentarily illuminated the scene ahead. Liam's jaw dropped and his eyes widened. Some twenty feet away from him stood his cart, with what seemed like all his belongings intact. With grateful disbelief, he stealthily approached the wagon, stopping in the shadows whenever the raucous noise from within changed its pitch. When he had convinced himself that those inside were preoccupied, he grasped the shafts of his cart and, furtively at first, pulled it away.

Once on the road, his pounding head forgotten, he quickened his pace to put as much distance as possible between him and his assailants.

CHAPTER 2

To describe Gortalocca as a village was perhaps an exaggeration. It was a small cluster of simple dwellings, grouped together where two roads met, near the town of Nenagh. At the village crossroads was a well, and the pure clear water which sprang from it was the source of water for the residents of the village. It was a holy well too, a place of pilgrimage, and beside it grew a rag tree, an ancient holly whose branches were festooned with scraps of cloth. The belief was that if you tied a piece of cloth belonging to someone who was sick or in distress to a branch of the tree, it would invoke God's intervention, making that person well or granting their wish. This had been the custom well before Christianity had arrived in Ireland, only the benefactor had changed.

Across from the well was a small general store. Whitewashed and thatched, it was the social center of Gortalocca. Here, you could buy everything from nails to flour whilst supping a pint and catching up on the latest village gossip. It was customary for the local farmers to gather here for a drink of beer after a long day in the fields and trade news of goings-on in the parish. On occasion, a stronger beverage was called for, poteen, a locally-produced distilled whiskey made from rye, potatoes or whatever corn was available.

The store had a rough, but sturdy, wooden sign beside the door which read M. HOGAN. Hogan's wasn't much bigger than the other cottages in the village, except for a small addition on the side, where the owner lived with his daughter. Michael Hogan was a widower, his daughter was Roisin. Michael had bought the small cottage some 30 years before, when he and his wife, Marie, came up from Ballina. He wasn't much of a farmer and so, to support himself and his wife, he began to transport small goods from Nenagh to sell in the village. Marie had a sound business head and together, they expanded the small cottage into a general store with a little counter at the front and, towards the back, an oak bar with four stools. As business increased, they put in two small coach tables with a pair of chairs at each one.

Michael was a quiet but good-natured man in his late 50's, not very tall and a little on the thin side. He had long since lost any hair he'd had on top of his head and flecks of grey had begun to pepper what remained wrapped around his head from ear to ear.

He was the perfect host. He listened intently to his customers, nodded solemnly when it was expected of him and laughed heartily at their jokes. He would launch a new topic if the conversation lagged and, as soon as a tankard was emptied, he would refill it immediately until the drinker waved him away. Michael knew the words to every song and, although he couldn't play an instrument, he led the singing every night.

Roisin was Michael's pride and his joy. She had taken on the role of 'woman of the house' eight years before, at the age of eleven, when her mother had died of consumption. She could read and write, a rare accomplishment for rural Irish women of the day. She had attended a convent school for 5 years and, although the nuns had groomed her for a life of poverty, chastity and obedience, Roisin was headstrong and had quickly formed her own ideas and opinions. When her mother died, Roisin's formal education had ceased.

She was taller than average and physically strong, with the right curves in the right places. Her features were full-faced, her expression direct, her eyes her most striking feature. They were pale blue-grey and expressed every emotion as sure as if she had voiced it. In them was a wisdom beyond her age and a compassion, but they could flash without warning and change their very shape when she was angered. Her hair was long and golden, the colour of ripened wheat. She wore it tied back out of the way with string, but often a tendril would escape its incarceration and spring into her eyes. She would sweep it back with her hand, only to have it return.

Roisin was strong, as only an Irishwoman could be. She held her own opinions, defended them tenaciously and only changed them for good reason. One night in the bar, one of the young local farmers had drunk a little too much of the strong poteen and, in a moment of lapsed judgement, had slapped Roisin on her arse in front of the other farmers. A gasp went through the bar as she spun on her heels to confront him. She grabbed him by the front of his shirt with both hands and dragged him out of his chair.

'So you think you can treat me like one of your strumpets, do you?' she snarled. She pushed him backwards and he fell over his chair onto the floor. 'Get yer good-fer-nothing arse outta here, and keep it out!'

The young man scrambled to his feet and out the

door, to the raucous delight of the small assembled crowd. He knew better than to venture back to Hogan's for a good while after that. Roisin's temper was legendary and she stubbornly bore a grudge when she believed herself justified. She had grown up in a man's environment and had quickly learned how to handle them. She'd also seen enough to know that she would never wed if it meant compromising herself by marrying a man she didn't love. Now, at the age of 19, Roisin was a spinster.

The usual regulars were gathered at Hogan's bar on this Friday evening, with the exception of three.

'Where d' ya suppose dat young rogue, Sean Reilly, and 'is two lick-spittles are tonight?' asked Clancy.

'Agh, who knows or cares — sure, aren't we better off widdout dem,' responded Shevlin.

'Yer right fer once,' replied Clancy. 'At least we have a bit o' peace fer a change. I wouldn't be at all surprised if dey're up t' some divilment or udder down around Nenagh, d' blaggards. Some poor fella'll probably wake up widdout his purse … if indeed he wakes up at all.'

Shevlin saw an opening for a bit of banter. 'The father's not a bad fella, mind, auld Mick Reilly. How do ya suppose he bred a wolf like dat only son of his?'

'I heard d' Mammy's family come from a long line o' Galway pirates,' was Clancy's offering.

'Her family are from Clare,' retorted Shevlin, 'ya ignorant sheep.'

'Agh sure, Clare, Galway, 'tis all d' same,' said Clancy. 'T'ank God we don't have pirates here in Tipperary. No ocean, sure, just loughs an' rivers.'

'What about land pirates?' replied Shevlin. 'I heard dey have land pirates down d'ere in South Tipp.'

Clancy had just taken a glug of beer and sprayed the

contents of his mouth back out. He wiped his chin with the back of his hand and spluttered, 'Dere's no pirates on land, ya daft pig farmer!'

Michael Hogan had been listening with amusement to his two regulars.

'The two of ye gossip like old women over a garden fence,' he said. 'Land pirates indeed. And don't go accusin' young Sean Reilly of t'ings you have no proof of.'

'Agh, ya would say dat, Michael Hogan. Sure don't we know dat young thug's yer best customer,' said Clancy. 'He'd drink dis place dry if Roisin didn't t'row him out on occasion.'

Roisin had been making her way from the back room and heard her name mentioned. As she appeared through the door, she put her hands on her hips and addressed Clancy.

'I heard that, Ben Clancy,' she said. 'You don't talk about womenfolk in a bar, so if you don't want to get thrown out on your ear too, you'll be wise to leave me out of your conversations.' Everyone laughed and Clancy blushed. Roisin laughed too and reached across the counter to pinch Clancy's cheeks. She had just been teasing him, everyone liked Clancy, he was a good man. That caused him to blush all the more and everyone else to laugh louder.

Ben Clancy raised sheep, Paddy Shevlin - pigs. They often indulged in lively banter in which they would passionately defend the merits of their own beasts whilst wholeheartedly denouncing the other's. Despite this, and the many other differences between them, they were the best of friends and lived in neighbouring cottages in the village. Clancy was in his thirties. No sooner had his wife given birth to one child, it seemed she was expecting again. They had nine already and a new baby was on the way. Paddy Shevlin was an old widower who always smelled of pig. While Clancy had his wife to keep his clothes clean and mended, Shevlin always looked as if he'd thrown his into the air and run underneath them. They differed physically too. Clancy was tall and rail thin. Shevlin not only smelled like his pigs but he also bore a striking resemblance to them. He was short and wide but his arms and legs were thin. Clancy regularly observed that the more time Shevlin spent around his swine, the more he came to resemble them. Shevlin's response was always that the longer Clancy herded sheep with those collie dogs of his, the more he bred like one.

The evening wore on uneventfully and the men trickled away from the bar one by one as their money ran out or they reached their capacity. Finally, just Roisin and her father remained so, as she washed the clay tankards, Michael swept the floor. When they had everything clean and tidy, Michael blew out all the paraffin lamps except the one on the bar and said to his daughter,

'It's bin a nice quiet evening, Macushla. It's time t' call it a day.'

'You go on ahead, Da. I just want to check the shelf stock.'

'Alright but don't stay late, mind,' smiled Michael. 'It's market day tomorra and we have t' make an early start. G'night now.'

'I won't,' she said, 'G'night yerself.' Roisin allowed herself an indulgent smile as she watched her father disappear through the door to their living quarters. She knew she had been the centre of his world since Marie died and she knew he still missed his wife dreadfully. Roisin missed her mother too. She missed her good heart and her kind face. She missed her sound advice and her guiding hand and, perhaps most of all, she missed her soft embrace. Roisin hadn't touched or been touched since her mother died. She hadn't cried since the day her mother died either but now, the memory brought the unfamiliar sting of tears behind her eyes. She immediately shook off the feeling, there was no room for sentiment in her life now. She counted the bottles, made a mental note of what stock needed to be replenished the next day and blew out the lamp, leaving the bar in darkness except for the meager light from a sliver that was the moon.

CHAPTER 3

L iam reached Nenagh just before noon the next day. When he had finally pulled his cart off the road to get some rest the night before, a violent storm had broken and wet him to the bone. Now, the dust which had accumulated on his ragged clothes from the four day journey, had dried into a plaster-like coating. His head still ached from the blow delivered by the thief and his eye was now partially swollen shut. At least the blood had been washed off but, even so, he knew he looked like a vagabond and not what he was, a man of the yeoman class.

Just outside town, he spotted an inn and drew his cart up to it. The door was open and a stout, middle-aged woman was sweeping the front step. Her hair was scraped back severely and tied, and she wore an apron with a few flowers embroidered on it around her thick waist. She looked up and stopped sweeping as Liam approached. She took in his appearance with one glance, then eyed him suspiciously.

He spoke first. 'Do you have a room to let, missus?'

'D' ya have money?' she asked.

'I do, o'course,' said Liam indignantly, 'and I need a hot bath too.'

'You're not settin' foot in my clean house in dat state!' she snapped. 'I run a respectable establishment here an' dat bruise on yer eye tells me you're a fightin' man.'

Liam was exhausted and didn't want to stand there being berated any longer than he had to. 'I had a run-in with a welcoming committee on the road into town last evening and they saw fit to give me an extra lump on my head.'

Her face softened slightly, then she scowled. 'Agh! Feckin' highwaymen!' she spat, 'It's lucky y'are t' be standin' and even more fortunate t' have yer purse an' belongin's. Ya must've put up quite a fight.'

Liam managed a weak smile and she returned it. 'It wasn't much of a fight,' he said. 'The big feller hit me with his stick and I fell.'

'You can tell me all about it later. C'mon now, pull yer cart aroun' to d' back. You'll find a big tub o' clean water dere. It's cold but it'll do d' job. I'll bring some soap an' we'll see what kind o' fella lies under all dat mud. Dat'll be thruppence-ha'penny.' She held out her hand. 'In advance.' Liam counted the coins out into her hand from a small purse at his waist and did as she instructed.

His clothes made a sorry-looking pile where he had discarded them at the side of the wooden tub and, as Liam gingerly lowered himself into the icy water, it occurred to him that thruppence-ha'penny was costly for a cold bath and a bed. In his present condition though, he would have paid a whole shilling just to get some sleep and a good scrub. His head still ached.

He had just begun to scrape the mud off, when the

woman showed up with a rough chunk of lye soap and a piece of coarse hessian cloth to dry himself with. Liam tried to duck down behind the side of the tub, in a vain attempt at modesty, knocking off the scab which had formed over the wound on his forehead. The blood began to run down his face again, turning the now muddy water pink.

She ignored his embarrassment and said. 'C'mere,' she said briskly. 'Let me look at dat cut.' Liam opened his mouth to protest but, before he could speak,she said, 'Hold yer whisht! I'll get a needle and some thread and put a stitch or two in it. I can't have you bleeding all over my nice clean house. They call me Ma Daley, by the way. Do you have a name?'

'Flynn,' he said.

'Is that it?' she asked.

'Liam, missus' he said. 'My name's Liam Flynn.' She bustled away into the house. He relaxed a little when she had gone. This is going to hurt, he thought, I hope the needle's small. Before he could anticipate it any longer, Ma Daley had returned with a needle and thread and deftly placed a couple of stitches in his forehead. Liam clamped his eyes shut and tried not to wince.

'Dat t'ick Irish skull o' yours mighta just've saved yer life,' she said. She nipped the thread with her teeth when she had finished suturing his wound and stood back to admire her handiwork. Liam blushed under her open scrutiny.

'Flynn, is it?' she said. 'I knew a Flynn once … a scalawag from out Borrisokane way.'

'No relation,' said Liam. 'I'm from South Tipperary. Thurles.'

'What brings ya t' North Tipp, so?' Her questions were beginning to make him uncomfortable. He considered telling her to mind her own business and leave him to his bath but, in his present state of vulnerability, decided against it.

'I'm looking to buy a piece of land.' he answered truthfully.

She opened her eyes wide in disbelief. 'Are ya mad?' she said, 'Ya look like a tradesman o' some sort t' me, yeoman class anyway. Now why would ya wanta go floggin' yerself from dusk to dawn on an auld farm?'

'I can't answer that,' said Liam, 'at least not in a way that anyone but me would understand.'

She shook her head in bewilderment, then bent down to sweep up his shirt and trousers in her arms and took them over to a smaller wooden tub filled with water. She picked up one of two wooden brushes that lay beside it and began to scrub Liam's filthy clothes against a corrugated metal wash board. She stopped for a moment to pick up the other brush and lobbed it at Liam.

'Here,' she said. 'Scrub dat filth off yerself. A farm, is it? Sure dere's already enough Tipperary dirt on ya t' grow a crop o' spuds.' Liam's arm shot out instinctively to catch the brush but it landed in the water and splashed his face. The lye soap stung his eyes.

Ma Daley finished washing Liam's clothes about the same time Liam finished scrubbing his body. He stayed in the tub and his vain attempt at modesty amused her. As she hung his clothes to dry on a rope, stretched across the yard, she said with a wry smile,

'Mr Flynn, I've buried two husbands and the third is in the house as we speak, tryin' to dodge the work I've asked him to do. You've nothing I've not seen before. Now get yerself dried off an' put the cloth around you. I'll show ya your room.' Her tone was so matter-of-fact and authoritative that Liam obeyed without a word. He wrapped the scant towel around himself as best he could and held it with one hand, clutched his purse to him with the other and followed Ma Daley into the house.

She led him to a room at the top of a steep, narrow staircase. It was tiny, with just enough space for a bed and a roughly built chair. Clean but tattered lace curtains covered the tiny window, letting in just enough of the bright sunlight to see his surroundings, and the paint on the frame was peeling. It didn't matter. Liam was transfixed by the bed and the prospect of a few hours of sleep. Ma Daley told him she would leave his clothes outside the door when they were dry. She said she would expect him to present himself in the kitchen in a few hours and she left the room, closing the door behind her.

Liam collapsed gratefully onto the bed and, although he was exhausted, sleep didn't come as easily as he thought it would. He tossed this way and that, while his mind raced like a runaway horse. Perhaps Ma Daley was right, perhaps he *was* mad. Maybe this whole idea of his was just a deluded dream. Why would anyone give up a relatively secure future for something so intangible? Sometimes he even baffled himself. But he had dreamed about this for more years than he could remember and his mind was made up. Nothing would deter him.

He had just begun to slip into the twilight that comes between consciousness and sleep when Ma Daley opened the door and came into the room carrying a mug of hot buttermilk. He snapped into alertness and quickly pulled the cloth back over himself. Could a man get no privacy around here? Ma Daley looked pleased with herself. Liam hated buttermilk, he always had, but he knew that to refuse it would be an insult to her so he drank it down like a man dying of thirst. She waited until he had finished and, satisfied that he had drunk every drop, she took the mug away and left Liam to his thoughts. He drifted off into a dreamless sleep.

When he woke, the sun no longer streamed into the room. He didn't know how long he had slept but there was still some light out, and he thought it must be late afternoon or early evening. As he descended the narrow wooden staircase, the last tread groaned loudly and the noise was responded to by a man's voice,

'In here, Mr. Flynn, we're in the kitchen, come through.' He followed the direction the voice had come from, and it brought him from the small hallway into a large but cosy kitchen. A substantial wooden table stood at its centre and, sitting at it, were two old fellows and Ma Daley. One of the men was dressed in common clothes and Liam assumed this was Ma Daley's work-shy husband. Indeed, Dan Daley had spent the day finding the means to shirk the tasks his wife had given him to do. Judging by his attire, the other fellow was a gentleman. He wore a top coat and waistcoat and beside him, on the table next to a tankard of beer, was a tall felt hat.

Although his clothes were showing signs of wear, they were undoubtedly those of lower level gentry. Liam knew how to conduct himself in company. He greeted the older men with a nod of acknowledgement and waited for Ma Daley to make the introductions. Both returned his nod with polite indifference.

'Dis is Mr. Johnson,' said Ma. 'He has a small farm about 5 miles north, in Gortalocca, an' he might be willin' to sell it fer d' right price. Dere's no dwelling on it an' d' land hasn't been tilled fer a fair few years.' The gentleman cast her a withering glance, she had already revealed too much information to this unkempt young stranger. Ma Daley was pleased with herself because she had begun negotiations even before the proper introductions were made. Johnson was abrupt, as only a man who is used to giving orders and having them obeyed without question can be.

'Have you got money or am I wasting my time?' he asked.

'I have money,' responded Liam. The man relaxed slightly but his eyes remained narrow.

'How much?' Now it was Liam's turn to assume control.

'Enough,' he replied. His guess was that Johnson was anxious to sell. Hard cash wasn't easy to come by, even for the landlords. This youngster is nobody's fool, thought Johnson.

'Are you a Papist?' This could be a delicate question, applied indelicately, and Liam realised that the old man was trying to jockey for position.

'My father was Presbyterian,' replied Liam. This was indeed true, but Liam's mother had been Catholic and she had raised him as such. His faith had died with her, however, and now the only faith he had was his work.

'Are your family Dissenters?' The old fellow was again trying to regain the momentum he had lost but Liam was too clever for him. He knew that some Presbyterians had fought alongside Catholics in the Williamite wars, and were called Dissenters for opposing the English rule.

'No,' said Liam. 'My Da was a blacksmith and had no interest in politics.' As soon as he had said the words, he knew he had made a mistake and lost the advantage. Liam cursed his own stupidity.

'*Politics*? You think wars are fought for *politics*?' Liam had handed control back to the old man. Of course, he knew in his own mind that he was right. Wars were fought for wealth and power and politics. But he also knew that those in power, or those who seek it, wrap their ignoble intentions in noble phrases such as 'Carrying out the will of God' or 'Civlising the masses' or some such hogwash. This was, of course, for the benefit of the commoners and the true believers, so that they would drape themselves in a flag, only to bleed and die on some muddy battlefield, in order that the gentry could cling on to power. Liam retreated and feigned ignorance.

'I'm just a man who works with wood and metal, sir,' he said. 'Such things as war are beyond my comprehension.' The old man sat back in his chair, assured that at last he had the upper hand. Liam was equally sure that he had bested the old man. He smiled to himself and wondered if it was a sin to deceive a Protestant.

Ma Daley was becoming frustrated with the conversation, it was time to get down to business.

'Yer interested in buyin' a piece o' land, are ya not?' she said to Liam.

'I am,' he said, 'but I'll buy the right land for the right price.' Johnson narrowed his eyes. He had played this game on many an occasion and had always come out on top.

'I'm told you're a tradesman,' said Johnson. 'Can I assume you'll be wanting the land to build a shop upon?' The old man resumed his jockeying for position.

'You cannot,' replied Liam. Once again, Johnson felt he'd been thwarted. This game might be harder to win than he had thought.

'Well, what *do* you want it for?' His tone was sharp.

'I want a farm,' said Liam.

'Why? You're no farmer.'

'I want a farm,' Liam repeated. Johnson looked baffled. 'I don't have any experience in farming but I learn quick. I simply want my own farm.' Johnson considered Liam's reply for a moment. This was going to be profitable, he thought. He would sell his farm to this arrogant young upstart for a good penny and when he fell on his face, as he undoubtedly would, Johnson would buy it back for next to nothing and then sell it on again.

Liam sensed he was being underestimated. That was good. Be smart, act dumb. That's what he had been taught.

'When would you like to inspect the land?' enquired the old shark formally. Liam didn't want to appear too hasty so he told Johnson to decide on a day. 'Tomorrow would be convenient for me,' said Johnson, immediately. He's anxious, thought the young man.

'I have other things to attend to tomorrow,' said Liam, 'and anyway, tomorrow is Sunday.' In

inferring that it would be unseemly to do business on the Sabbath, Liam had won round two and the pointy-faced old fox realised he had been beaten yet again by this ignorant young woodsmith.

He promised himself it wouldn't happen again. 'I'm free on Monday morning,' offered Liam.

'No,' snapped the landlord, trying his best to wrest back control of the game. 'I'm busy Monday morning. Make it Monday afternoon, three o'clock.' Liam nodded his assent and asked where he should present himself for the meeting.

'Gortalocca,' answered the old man abruptly. 'I'll meet you in front of Hogan's on Monday at three o'clock sharp. Don't be late, I won't be kept waiting.' Liam considered offering his hand to seal the agreement but Johnson was busy rubbing his hands together like a fly about to dine on a meat pie. Liam smiled to himself. If nothing else, this might be fun, he thought.

Johnson swept up his hat, tapped it onto his head and

without another word, left the kitchen.

Once the front door banged shut, Ma Daley was the first to speak.

'So, Liam Flynn, yer a Protestant', she said. Liam smiled openly for the first time since he had arrived.

'I didn't say that,' he replied.

'Yer Catholic, so.'

'I didn't say that either.' She looked puzzled.

'I wasn't about to give that old bugger anything he could use against me. The Penal Laws forbid a Catholic from owning land. He can think whatever he wants.' She nodded slowly as she began to understand what Liam was up to, and she smiled a knowing smile.

'Ah, yer not as good a businessman as you think y' are, Liam Flynn,' she said. 'Sure, you could've got dat room an' a bath fer tuppence.' His smile widened as he said,

'Ma Daley, if I'd known how helpful you were going to be and how entertaining this afternoon was going to turn out, I'd have gladly paid you double!'

Dan Daley had been observing the proceedings of the last half hour from his seat at the end of the table and he scratched his head.

'What in d' name o' God was all dat about?' he asked. Ma Daley and Liam had forgotten about Dan. They looked over at him, then back at each other and they both laughed heartily.

'Sit yerself down, Liam Flynn,' said Ma, still laughing. 'You'll join d' man o' d' house an' meself fer dinner, an' it's very welcome ya are.'

CHAPTER 4

After they had eaten, Ma set about interrogating Liam, in an attempt to find out all she could about this secretive young man's past. She sensed it made him uneasy but she pressed on regardless, enticing him to drink in the hope it would loosen his tongue. Liam accepted only a single beer to wash down his supper of boiled ham and potatoes. This was the first proper meal he'd had all week and it was delicious. Ma Daley soon grew tired of her questions being met with evasive, tight-lipped answers so she began to clear the table.

'I've work t' do and you need t' get some sleep,' she said. Liam felt he had been dismissed and was glad of it. He was uncomfortable talking about himself.

He snuffed out the candle in his room by pinching it between his finger and thumb. It was just past nine o'clock, the time he usually turned in. He shed his tattered but clean clothes, this time placing them in a neat pile on the floor next to his bed. He stretched himself out gratefully on the bed and thought about the events of the last 24 hours. A faint light from the moon filtered through the tattered net curtains of the little window and, soon, he had drifted into a deep and untroubled slumber.

*

Five miles away, in the little village of Gortalocca, Saturday night's business at Hogan's was brisk. The evening was warm and dry and most of the village's able-bodied men had called in for a tankard of beer or a drop of poteen. Tonight's merriment was marred only by the presence of Sean Reilly and his two henchmen. Sean was 26 years old and his father, Mick, had lived in Gortalocca all his life. He had the largest farm owned by an Irishman in the area. Mick had been a handsome man in his youth, tall with curly chestnut hair and serious but engaging brown eyes, and he had caught the eye of the middle daughter of a prosperous family from County Clare. Mick was ambitious and had quickly married her. Her family was more than happy for the handsome stranger to take her away and showed their gratitude with a generous dowry. Although not hideous, his wife could in no way be described as attractive. Her face was pockmarked and her ginger hair was wispy and thin, showing her pale scalp in places. All this topped a short, oversized body. She carried a carved walking stick with a bone handle and she walked with a profound limp, caused by a bout of polio when she was four. Although their son was endowed with Mick's good looks, Sean had inherited his mother's bitterness, her disagreeable nature and her sense of entitlement.

One of Sean's cohorts was Fergus, a small man who bore an unmistakable resemblance to a rodent, possessing all the same characteristics. His nervous black eyes sat close together and darted from one thing to another. His nose was long and thin and his face disappeared into his neck, with barely the hint of a chin.

He was constantly on the look-out for useful gossip which he would eagerly carry back to Sean. Fergus was, in every way, a rat.

Sean's other sidekick was Seamus, a thick man of average height. He had flat features and half-lidded eyes which always gave him the appearance that he was about to nod off. He was several years Sean's senior and worked for Mick on the Reilly farm. He was a lazy shirker and probably would have been dismissed long ago if it wasn't for his friendship with Sean. When sober, he was a decent enough fellow but, when drunk, he could be as mean as a boar.

The presence of the three had cast a pall over the evening's festivities. Sean was in a particularly foul mood, following the previous evening's abortive encounter, and he was spoiling for a fight. No one wanted to attract his unwelcome attention because it would be three against one. That's the way it always was.

All the bar stools were occupied and so were the tables. The little bar was filled to capacity and men stood around in groups, holding on to their mugs of beer. The usual banter was muted because, with those three thugs in the bar, anything could be construed as a challenge. Michael Hogan was like a man treading on hot coals, trying his best to keep the mood civilised and avoid any confrontation. Roisin weaved her way through the throng, with the deftness of someone who had done the job a thousand times before, refilling mugs where necessary, and did her best to be cheerful. She too was a little nervous about Sean's mood and, every now and again, she cast a furtive glance at him. Each time, he was staring back at her, watching her with ravenous eyes.

When he realised his attempts to provoke a fight with any of the men were to no avail, he turned on her. As

Roisin passed his table, he caught her by the apron and spun her around to face him, grabbing her arm roughly.

'Who da ya t'ink y'are? he spat with a drunken growl. 'Ya t'ink yer better den any o' da rest of us, don't ya!' Roisin's eyes widened with alarm. He had taken her by surprise. Usually things built up to a climax before Sean erupted. This time his frustration was aimed directly at her and, for a moment, she was genuinely afraid. She gathered herself.

'You're drunk, Sean Reilly.'

'I c'n have ya anytime I want! God knows, nobody else'll have ya.' He laughed and tried to pull her down onto his lap. Roisin's face flushed as she tried to wrestle herself free. Michael Hogan's hand reached for the heavy wooden mallet he kept behind the bar to hammer the spigots into the kegs. By God, if Sean Reilly took this any further, Michael would spread his brains across the bar floor and face the consequences. A hush had descended on the crowded room and now everyone was glaring at the three sitting at the table. Roisin was well-liked by the villagers and, if there was going to be a fight this night, it would not be the usual three against one. Fergus pulled Sean towards him and mumbled something. Sean released his grip on Roisin's arm and pushed her roughly away as he staggered to his feet, swaying drunkenly.

'Agh, c'mon lads! Let's get outta dis pig sty!' he growled. He pushed his way through the small crowd of men, his two associates behind him, and the three crashed out through the door, leaving it gaping open behind them.

A sigh of relief rippled through Hogan's and, in no time at all, the mood in the bar lightened. The conversations became animated, Michael began to sing and the men joined in. It seemed as if the fracas had been forgotten ... forgotten, except by Roisin. Sean Reilly's cruel words still rang in her ears. Was it true that no one would have her? Truth told in ale, she thought, it was a popular old adage in the bar. Were Sean's drunken words spoken in truth? Even amongst a room full of revellers, she felt alone. She wished there was someone she could share her thoughts and fears with, but there was no one, so she would keep them hidden deep inside her as she always had. She listened to the singing with no cheer in her heart and she painted the same light-hearted smile on her face she'd worn there a thousand times before.

CHAPTER 5

S unday morning brought with it a cooler wind from the southeast, and a sky that promised rain… steel grey, with clouds that seemed to fly by at the speed of liquid running downhill. The sun was weak and cast no shadows. It was one of those late Irish summer days that arrived, portending Autumn's onset.

Liam took stock of his clothing before he dressed and decided they would look more at home tied to a rag tree than draped around his wiry body. A new start undoubtedly required new garments, so he made a note to visit a tailor at the first opportunity. Right now, he needed to take an inventory of his tools. He hadn't checked them since the thwarted robbery attempt.

When he stepped outside the back door of the inn, he was surprised at the turn in weather. He shivered a little as he walked to his wagon, which he had tucked out of the way in a corner of the back yard. He took his brat from the wagon and draped the cloak over his shoulders. With more than a little trepidation, he opened the chest which contained the instruments of his profession. As he suspected, the tools which he had so carefully stowed away, had been ransacked. The thieves had doubtless been looking for items of immediate value and, finding none, had left Liam's things in disarray.

He repacked his saws and chisels, placing them carefully where they belonged. He gathered together the various bits that he used for drilling, and arranged them alongside the brace, placing his hammers on top where he could get at them easily. There were a few smithing tools, which he didn't bother to check because they had been at the bottom of the trunk and seemed to have been left undisturbed. When he had satisfied himself that everything was as it should be, apart from a bump on his head and some of Ma Daley's embroidery closing the gash, he set off to explore the town.

Nenagh was the largest market town in Northern Tipperary, with an imposing castle at its centre. Liam knew that the castle belonged to the Butler family and he thought that they must surely own most of Tipperary. Wherever he went, it seemed, the Butlers had got there first and laid their claim. They must have powerful connections with the English throne, he thought, because, regardless of who won a war, the Butlers retained a strong presence and power in the county.

The town's well-trodden roads were muddy this day from the morning's light, misty drizzle. The streets were deserted and crumpled scraps of paper, left behind by Saturday's market stall-holders, blew around like butterflies. They were all that remained of the bustling commerce that had transpired here yesterday.

The townsfolk were at their places of worship and no business would be conducted today except, of course, the business of gossip, which never took a holiday. After the Sabbath services, the congregations would gather in front of their respective churches and compare notes on the latest news and stories. Liam frowned, he thought it hypocritical to come out of church and conduct a trade in gossip. The more salacious the tit-bits, the more interest they seemed to excite. Smalltalk of any kind held no interest for him, but then neither did the church services. He hadn't attended Mass or been to Confession since the death of his mother, some 13 years before. He had been inside churches, of course, but only to carry out whatever work he had been contracted to do. To Liam, regardless of how grand the buildings were, they were merely a monument to one man's conceit and the folly of those who allowed themselves to be seduced into building them.

The young fellow wandered aimlessly through the silent streets and noted, with interest, that the wars seemed to have left less destruction in their wake, here in Nenagh, than in most other places he had seen. Perhaps the people of North Tipp. were smart enough not to fight hopeless causes against impossible odds. He pondered on how the Irish aristocracy had always squabbled amongst themselves, and how simple that made it for the English to exploit their dissention, time and time again. He shook his head.

Liam had a sceptical, if not cynical, outlook on life, carved from his own life's experiences. The only person outside his own family who had ever cared about him was dead and, now that he was alone in the world, he would make sure always to put his own interests first. He became lost in thought and barely felt the stones beneath his feet, as he walked barefoot through the muddy streets.

The town had ended abruptly and now the countryside stretched out in front of him, towards the Silvermines, the same mountains that had been his landmark on the voyage from Thurles. The sun broke through the grey clouds momentarily, illuminating the highlands ahead. Dan Daley had told him that the highest point of the Silvermines was Keeper Hill, and his eyes found it without difficulty. Not much of a mountain, he thought. From this aspect, though, he conceded that it did looked beautiful. Dan had also told him that the mining operations going on there had stripped the mountains of forest, leaving slag heaps and desolation. Some things look better from a distance, he reflected, and sometimes become uglier, the closer you get. That was his experience with people too. He rubbed his sore head, turned and set off in another direction.

Even though it was the largest town here in northwest Tipperary, Nenagh was still smaller than Thurles and Liam decided to skirt its perimeter. He passed a family sitting at the side of the road. The man and woman stared vacantly into space and didn't seem to notice Liam. Two children played quietly in the mud and the woman held an unnaturally silent infant to her breast. Their clothes were even more ragged than his own and Liam thought that they looked broken. So it was in Ireland ... broken, wretched families, evicted from land their families had worked for hundreds of years. Liam glanced at the children, their bones jutting out at angles against the tattered clothes that hung on their painfully thin little bodies, and he knew they would not survive, probably not even to the winter. He felt nothing. It was simply a fact of life in this green and muddy country. He thrust his hands deeper into his pockets and walked on past the sorry sight.

He found himself following a high stone wall now and, through a large wrought iron gate, he glimpsed the great house that it surrounded. He imagined how, in a couple of hours, the owners would be back from church and sitting at a grand table, which groaned with food, without a thought for the invisible children starving outside their wall. Perhaps that's how the English lived with it, he speculated, walling themselves into their own private world, to spare themselves the thought of babies without milk or dead children. He could hate them, of course, but what good would that do. He could pray for them, but he didn't pray anymore.

He hurried on past the big house and soon came to a ruined friary. It seemed to him the perfect metaphor for Ireland itself ... once a thriving and vibrant place ... now just the bones of what had been. Ireland was a country of bones now, a cemetery. He spotted what he knew to be the round tower of Nenagh Castle in the distance and turned to walk in the direction of the great Norman edifice, to complete his first visit to Nenagh.

As he approached, he saw the two men-at-arms who stood outside the castle gates. They looked impressive, in their blue uniforms with the gold piping, and their white gloves. Their polished boots shone blackly. Against their left sides, they wore sword hangers with sabres and in their right hands, they held pikes. Liam thought that, although they presented an imposing image, a man with a brace of pistols could easily walk in unhindered.

Just inside the courtyard, a pair of sleepy grooms stood, yawning, holding two chestnut chargers and awaiting the return of the horses' owners, who he assumed were inside the keep.

He had seen enough of Nenagh for now, he decided. It reminded him of Thurles and that was behind him. He made his way back to the inn.

Ma and Dan Daley were back from Mass and Liam walked around to the back of the inn, where Ma was busying herself in the kitchen with the Sunday meal. She heard Liam come in but was intent on chopping what seemed like enough carrots to feed an army, and didn't look up.

'I'd like to pay for another night's lodging,' he announced. This got Ma's attention and she looked up and smiled.

'Grand,' she said, 'dat'll be thruppence-ha'penny, please.'

Liam rummaged in his purse for the coins and smiled as he counted them out into her open hand. 'Didn't you say last night, that I could have had the room for tuppence?'

'I might've, but dat was last night an', if I remember rightly, ya said yu'd have paid double.'

'You're too sharp for a dim-witted carpenter like me, Ma Daley.'

She smiled. 'It's dim like a fox, y'are, Liam Flynn. Join us for dinner, I've some information I think you'll find useful, and maybe I can even prise somethin' about yer life outta ya tonight.'

Only the hint of a smile played now around the corners of Liam's mouth. 'You can try,' he said.

It was late afternoon before Ma Daley's special slow-cooked mutton stew was served up, a hearty concoction made with barley and turnips to thicken the brown gravy. Chopped boiled cabbage, and a loaf of brown bread to sop it up, completed the meal. All three were hungry and tucked in at once. Ma Daley made a noise in Liam's direction, as if she had something to say to him, and he looked at her expectantly, but she put a large spoonful of the stew into her mouth instead. She pinched her eyes shut as the hot gravy burned her mouth, and she rolled the meat around with her tongue, huffing, to try and cool it inside her mouth. Liam returned to his dinner, to wait until the offending contents of Ma's mouth had been swallowed.

'Dere's someone in Gortalocca I'd like ya t' meet,' she said finally. By this time, Liam was busy dissecting a large lump of meat.

'He's a priest,' she continued. Liam looked up and regarded her with disdain.

'Now don't be makin' judgments 'til yu've at least met 'im,' she said. 'In many ways, the two of ye have a lot in common.' Liam kept his sour expression but returned to the business of hacking mutton. 'An' ya might even be able t' get lodgings wit' him,' said Ma. 'Da price is right, sure he might even put ya up fer nutt'n in return fer a little company.' Liam raised his eyes again and scrutinised her expression. Nothing was free, there was always a price to pay. He would say no more on the subject for now. His food was getting cold.

Ma was the first to finish eating and she sat back in her chair, her arms folded under her bosom. She regarded Liam, as he mopped up the last of his gravy with a chunk of bread he had torn off the loaf. She leaned forward, resting her plump forearms on the table and Liam feared that another interrogation was about to begin. He, too, sat back in his chair and this time, with his belly pleasantly full, he decided to be a little more forthcoming.

Before she could ask him anything, he began. 'I'm not very good around people, you see, Ma, I don't know why. Some people find talking about themselves and making friends easy, but not me. I can never imagine why anyone would want to know about someone as ordinary as me, and I hate to talk about myself, so I always have my guard up.' Ma and Dan Daley had both shifted forward a little in their chairs to hear Liam because he spoke quietly and his words were deliberate.

'Do you have any family?' asked Dan, who by now was as curious as his wife to learn more about this mysterious young man.

'I do, sir, or rather I did. My mother and father are both dead and I had an older half-brother, but he went off to fight for the Jacobites in the war and was never heard of again. My father was a smith and I worked in his shop from the time I could operate a bellows until he died, when I was twelve. My mother died two years after him. She got a fever one day and died the next. I wasn't there when it happened. I also had a younger sister but she died from the pox, the same year as my mother. I wasn't there then either.'

Ma Daley knew it was painful for Liam to relate this information. Death wasn't uncommon, of course, but it must have been difficult for a child the age he had been then.

'If your father was a smith, how is it that you became a carpenter?' asked Dan.

'My father built tools for a cabinet-maker in Thurles.'

'Yer father must'a bin quite a craftsman in iron, so,' said Dan, nodding approvingly.

'Yes,' said Liam. 'If someone could describe it, he could make it in metal.'

Ma looked inquiringly at Liam, inviting him to continue.

'When my father died, Mr. Bello asked my mother if he could take me on as an apprentice.'

'Mr. Bello?' she asked. 'What kind o' name is dat?'

'He was Italian,' said Liam. 'He told me that Italy was just like Ireland, with all kinds of feuds and wars between neighboring kingdoms. His kingdom was defeated by another and so he left. He went to France first, then later he got a commission in Ireland. He came to Thurles, and there he stayed.'

'Well, I never heard d' like of it,' said Ma, shaking her head incredulously. 'An Eye-talian in T'urles.'

'I suppose so,' said Liam. 'I never really thought of it as odd, because he was just always there. Anyway, it was lucky for me because he was a good master. He taught me everything there is to know about wood, and he was an artist too. He taught me my letters, said that he wouldn't work with someone who was ignorant, and that I had to learn to read and write.'

'Tell me about yer brother,' said Ma.

'My half-brother,' Liam corrected her. 'His name was Robert, like my father, and he was eleven years older than me. He was my hero before he left to go to war. He knew everything about working with metal. He wasn't a bit like me, a giant of a man with an easy manner about him. He was liked by everyone he met and he made friends easily. Robert believed that the Jacobites would set Ireland free but my father disagreed with him. He told him he would just be trading one master for another, but Robert wouldn't listen to him and there was a fierce argument. In the end, Robert left and my father's final words to him were that he was a fool to fight other people's battles when he, himself, would gain nothing from the outcome. Anyway, we never heard from him again, so he must have died alone, on some battlefield or other.'

Liam paused for a moment. He looked up and saw Ma and Dan Daley's sad faces. He sighed and nodded. 'I think I miss Robert most of all,' he said, 'but, sure my father was right, he was a fool. I will never be anyone's fool.'

The three of them lapsed into silence in the evening gloom of the kitchen. There was no more to be said. Liam felt empty, having related his story to virtual strangers. In all the seven years he had spent with Mr. Bello, he had not given away as much about himself as he had tonight. He thanked Ma for the tasty meal, bid them both 'Goodnight' and climbed the narrow staircase to his room.

He lay on the bed, his hands behind his head, while the shadows darkened around him. His last thought, before he drifted into sleep, was that tomorrow would take him one step closer to his dream.

CHAPTER 6

T his was like any other Sunday in the town of Gortalocca. It had rained a little in the wee hours of the morning and the wind was whipping up now, heralding more to come. Roisin had risen early. She had slept only fitfully, the time creeping by slowly as she lay alone in the dark. She washed her face, put on a fresh apron, and decided that her first job would be to peel potatoes for the boiled supper she would prepare for herself and her father that afternoon. She filled her apron with potatoes from a large sack in the kitchen pantry, and emptied them out onto the rough wooden table. She absent-mindedly tossed a few clods of turf onto the fire, which was still glowing a little from the night before. A few pumps of the bellows that hung at the side of the fireplace, and she decided there was enough light to peel the spuds. Her hands knew the work well and she performed the task deftly. At least the store was closed today, she thought, so there was little chance of any interaction between herself and that pig, Sean Reilly. Roisin wasn't easily provoked but his drunken words and his actions of the previous night had got under her skin like a splinter.

She had just finished peeling the last potato when she thought she heard something outside the door. Wiping her hands on her apron, she went to it, slid back the iron bolt and peered outside. It was cool compared to yesterday, a soft day, with something between a heavy mist and a light rain falling. As she stood for a moment in the open doorway, she felt a chill and shuddered. It wasn't from the cool morning but the kind of chill that comes from foreboding. She wasn't alone.

There in the dark, black against black, stood a small hunched figure. Roisin relaxed as she recognised the shape of Moira and the momentary terror she had felt left her. Moira was an old crone. She had lived in Gortalocca for as long as anyone could remember, a wise woman, well-versed in the use of the various herbs and potions of the 'old ones'. Most of the locals feared her, believing her to be a witch, and her appearance did nothing to allay their apprehension. She was tiny and her back was hunched, making her frame even more compact. Her skin was wizened, her face like an apple which had been dried for months, brown with a mass of wrinkles. The years had taken almost all her hair and the few white wisps that were left were pulled back and covered by an old black woollen shawl. Moira was looking directly at Roisin and the girl was tempted to bless herself as many of the other townsfolk did when they saw the old woman.

Instead she said, 'I have a few potatoes left over from last night, mother, I'll get them for you.' The old woman hobbled over to the door with her blackthorn stick and waited for Roisin to return. 'Where are you about so early, old mother?' called Roisin from inside.

The old woman croaked quietly, 'It's the time o' the moon for me to pick some herbs I need. I wanted to get dem before I go to Mass.' Roisin thought how sad it was that that this old woman, who would attend anyone's sickbed if summoned, was treated as a pariah by most the rest of the time. In truth, Moira didn't mind at all, in fact it suited her. She would much rather be alone than have to listen to the idle gossip and day-to-day trivia of village life. She held her own beliefs and attended Mass, yet still practiced the dark arts of the Druids. She was comfortable with her own mixture of Catholicism and Paganism and, surprisingly, her only friend was old Father Grogan.

Roisin returned with three large, cold, roasted spuds and placed them in a sack which the old woman had slung over her humped back.

'God sees you, my child, and I will tie something on the rag tree to remind Him.'

'You're very welcome, old mother, it's just a few spuds, it's nothing.' said Roisin said kindly.

'Oh, but it is,' said the crone, 'and your wish will come true, my dear. I pray for it.' Roisin watched as the old hag shuffled away towards the holy well and the ancient holly tree which grew beside it. The gnarled old tree was festooned with bits and pieces of cloth where many, before Moira, had made wishes and requests to God, and indeed to the old gods back through the ages. As Roisin closed the door, she shook her head and smiled a thin sad smile ... dreams didn't come true in Gortalocca.

Michael Hogan appeared at the door, yawning. He was dressed in a long woollen nightshirt and, on his head, he wore a nightcap.

'I thought I heard voices,' he said, his voice still full of sleep.

'It was just Moira,' said Roisin. Michael blessed

himself. 'Ah stop, Da, she's just a poor old crathur.'

'Crathur, my arse,' said Michael, now wide awake. 'she's a witch an' a blasphemer.' Roisin rolled her eyes. 'An' I suppose you've given her d' spuds I was goin' to eat fer me breakfast.'

Roisin put her hands on her hips and squared up to her father. 'It's Sunday,' she said, 'and you can't eat until after you've had communion. Now go back to bed, old man, I'll wake you in plenty of time for Mass.'

The little church was just a short distance from Hogan's, no more than a few minutes' walk. It was a small stone building with a roof of thatch. There was neither bell nor steeple and the only thing distinguishing it from the other cottages was a wooden cross over the door. Its tiny size was a sad reminder of the days when the friary at nearby Knigh had been so much grander, with a sturdy slate roof and a beautiful ornate altar. Here, the narrow slits which served as windows had no glass, and the interior was dark, except for what little sun penetrated and the flickering light from the candles which stood on either side of the altar.

The priest was Father Francis Grogan, a large man, from Cashel. He was taller than most, with a big round belly and a thunderous baritone voice which gave an air of gravitas to everything he said. His voice belied what was underneath, however. Father Grogan had a twinkle in his eye and an irreverent sense of humour.

He was getting tired, though, now. He had been a priest for almost 50 years, here in Gortalocca for almost 10 of them. He had been assigned this tiny parish after an altercation with his previous pastor in Cahir, as a result of which he had been 'sentenced' to bring God's word to this little village in North Tipperary. In truth, it suited Francis Grogan. He was glad to be away from the politics of the Church and all the nonsense it brought with it. Here, in Gortalocca, he could finally perform his calling and whatever happened was simply between him and his God.

A small gathering of people stood outside the church door, mostly women and children. The women had their shawls pulled up around their heads to protect them from the penetrating morning mist. The men would arrive later, after Mass had started. They knew what was required of them to fulfill their obligation and they spent not a minute more in the church than they needed to. Roisin and her father arrived and all eyes turned in her direction. Word of the previous night's events at Hogan's had spread and those who didn't know, soon would. Such was the way of an Irish village. Roisin didn't tarry outside. She felt angry and humiliated so she slipped her white crocheted shawl over her head and hurried into the church. She walked half-way down the little church with her father and they sidled into the bench pew they always occupied. They both knelt on the stone floor and bent their heads, Roisin fidgeting with her rosary beads, too agitated to pray.

Old Moira was already there. She always sat at the end of the Hogan's bench because no one else would sit near her. When Roisin felt she had knelt for a respectable length of time, she moved back to sit on the bench and Moira moved nearer to her.

'Remember what I said, child, you have to believe.' Roisin managed a weak smile and moved a little closer to her father, away from the old woman.

Just before nine o'clock, the other women filed into church with their children. The few benches were soon full to capacity and those arriving later would have to stand at the back.

Father Grogan entered ceremonially, followed by his altar boy Jamie, Clancy's oldest child, a boy of eleven years, and Mass began. Father Grogan was not a man to waste his or anyone else's time and he read the Confiteor in Latin as fast as his lips would allow. It didn't really matter, no one understood the words,

'Confiteor Deo omnipotente ….,' on he went and, in no time at all, it was time for him to read the Gospel. Father Grogan paused as the men hurried in and filled the tiny space at the back of the church, some having to cram themselves in around the door so they could say they had 'attended'.

The priest read the Gospel, then delivered the Homily. Most of the congregation half listened … something about temperance, which amused those paying attention since Father Grogan was known to enjoy more than a drop or two of the poteen himself.

When he had finished, he hesitated for a moment. This caught the attention of the whole congregation. Normally, the priest would press right on to the Offertory and then deliver Communion. As he stood for a moment in silence, his face grew stern and everyone knew that 'reading out' was about to be delivered. This was a very serious matter. To be read out from the altar was a humiliating affair, not just for the one being read but for the entire congregation.

Father Grogan's steady gaze rested on Sean Reilly and he began in his deepest baritone voice,

'It has been brought to my attention … that a member of this congregation … behaved in an ungentlemanly and unseemly fashion towards a lady of this parish, last evening. It was told to me … that he laid hands on her in an uninvited and unwelcome manner.' The formality of the priest's tone added weight to his outrage. Sean Reilly didn't wait for any more of the priest's words. His face had become flushed, not with embarrassment, but with fury.

'So what?' he snarled, loud enough for all to hear. 'What commandment says you can't touch a barroom tart?' The entire congregation gasped and turned their eyes from the old priest to Sean. Even Father Grogan was taken aback, this was not the way a reading out should happen. The one being read should assume an expression of penitence and take the humiliation in silence. Instead, Sean Reilly thrust his chin out in defiance, ignoring the rest of the congregation and returning the priest's gaze defiantly.

Undeterred, Father Grogan continued. 'Confess your sins right here and now, Sean Reilly,' he demanded. 'Ask God's forgiveness and that of your neighbours.'

Sean laughed derisively. 'None of ye have time to hear all my sins,' he barked. Now, a low twitter spread through the congregation.

Furious, and in danger of losing control of the situation, the priest boomed, 'Get out of God's house and do not set foot back inside this place of worship until you have seen the error of your ways!'

Sean Reilly stood and turned towards the door. As he pushed his way through the open-mouthed men assembled at the back of the church, he spat venomously over his shoulder, 'I'll go over to the Church of Ireland, first.' and slammed the door behind him.

After a moment of stunned silence, a low buzz of excited whispers began to flutter amongst the worshippers. Until something better came along, this would make a perfect topic for gossip and would soon be the talk of the diocese. Sure, even the bishop might hear about it. Roisin's head had been bowed throughout all this, her eyes fixed on her clasped hands, her face crimson with mortification. For only the second time since her mother had died, and within days of the last, she felt that sting of tears behind her eyes again and was glad she didn't have to speak because she couldn't trust her voice. She asked herself whether, somehow, this was her fault. She would speak with Father Grogan after Mass and, if there was anything to confess, she would do it.

As if he knew her mind, Father Grogan looked at her and, in a voice low enough so only a few could hear, he said, 'Don't worry child, you have done nothing wrong. Some people have a bad seed sown inside their hearts.'

With that, the priest raised his hand, to silence what had now turned to animated chatter. When the church was quiet once again, he addressed the whole congregation.

'One of the sheep from our flock has lost his way and we must ask God's forgiveness for him. Let us pray.'

CHAPTER 7

T he wind had blown Sunday's clouds away and, today, the morning sun shone brightly. Liam knew this was a very important day for him. He was to inspect a piece of land and, if it suited him, he might make a deal with that old landshark, Harold Johnson.

Liam remembered he had to meet Johnson outside somewhere called Hogan's in somewhere called Gortalocca. He had never heard of the village and thought it an odd name, but he had travelled enough to know that many of Ireland's towns and villages had odd names.

He felt the thrill of excitement but reminded himself he would need to control his expression and not seem too enthusiastic, otherwise all his 'courting' of old Johnson would be for nothing.

Today was warmer than yesterday and he was looking forward to the walk of five miles or so. He lifted up the mattress on his bed and tucked his purse well underneath it. It would be unwise to carry money with him so he would leave it here. He had heard stories of men who had thought they would strike a better deal if they had money on them, only to have the seller send out men to waylay the unfortunate buyer on his way to view the land.

Once downstairs, Liam made his way to the kitchen where Ma was busy cooking and Dan was busy watching her. Liam told them what he had done with the purse and she told him to bring it to her for safekeeping. He did so without a second thought. He didn't know exactly why, but he trusted Ma and Dan Daley, even though they were strangers to him. He hoped his judgment of their characters was justified. He asked if he could leave his cart of tools at the back of the house and they assured him they would be safe there until he returned for them.

Ma reminded Liam to be sure and call in to see the priest while he was in Gortalocca. Again, he cast her a doubting look. 'Yu'll be dere already, sure, and I t'ink yu'll be pleasantly surprised at Father Grogan's hospitality.' Liam consented unwillingly. The priest in Thurles had demanded a shilling just to hold a funeral service for his mother. After that, Liam had no use for men of the cloth.

Liam asked directions to Gortalocca.

'I'll go one better, lad,' said Dan. 'I'll draw ya a map.' Liam managed a faint smile, remembering that although he had seen a map before, in a book, the same book had said the world was round. A round world, what kind of goose liver was that. Sure, how would you keep from falling off? Just because someone was daft enough to print it, didn't mean it was true. Liam's world was flat, because that was his experience.

Ma slathered a piece of brown bread with butter and handed it to Liam with a mug of buttermilk to wash it down. Not more buttermilk, he thought, but he drank it down to be polite. She handed him a bag with more bread and butter in it for his lunch and said maybe he could get a proper meal at Hogan's. She'd heard Michael Hogan's daughter was a decent enough cook and usually had a big pot of something hot on the hearth.

'Is dat daughter of Hogan's married yet, Ma?' asked Dan.

'Ah sure, dat girl doesn't even have a twinkle in 'er eye yet, let alone a husband,' she said, 'and her nineteen already.' They both shook their heads pityingly. Nineteen years old and unmarried, thought Liam, she must be a troll. He thanked Ma for the food and Dan for the map and he set off to walk the five miles to what might be his new home, the first home he would have known since his mother died.

The road was still muddy from Sunday's weather and, in Nenagh, it was wide enough for two carriages to pass each other with ease, but it soon narrowed to a one lane dirt track. Liam passed a couple of small, neat farms on his way to the first turn. The fields were mostly of grain, which was turning now from green to golden. He recognised what he knew to be wheat and barley but there was another crop that was new to him. The stalks stood taller than a man and had large pods, with tufts of what looked like golden hair growing from their tops. The fields were large and seemed to go on forever. He thought they must belong to the English, because there were few houses around and only one or two workers, here and there, tending the crops.

After the first left turn towards Gortalocca, Liam crossed a stone bridge and entered a dense forest. The trees formed a tunnel and the sun filtered through them in places, forming dapples on the forest floor. It took a few seconds for his eyes to adjust to the gloom and he heard forest sounds, birds and even the occasional chirrup of what Liam thought must be crickets. The forest was a primeval place, with the bottom branches of its oaks some fifteen feet overhead.

He scanned the undergrowth as he went, snapping his head towards every rustle. After Friday evening's episode, he was not about to be taken by surprise again. Every rabbit on the forest floor, and squirrel in the trees overhead, had his attention. After about half a mile, he heard a noise behind the trees to his right. He picked up a dead branch to use as a weapon. The noise came nearer and Liam's heart thumped like it would burst out of his chest. He raised the branch and, in a flash, a pair of does burst out from the trees and across his path. Before he could gather himself, a huge stag followed close on their heels, stopping only for the blink of an eye to size up Liam's unexpected presence.

Liam relaxed. 'You're on a rich man's hunting preserve,' he said quietly, 'you'd better mind yourself or your head will be on his wall, and the rest of you on his dinner plate.' Startled by his voice, the buck leapt forward into the undergrowth after the does. 'By the way,' Liam shouted after him, laughing, 'tell your wives they scared the liver out of me!' The forest returned to its relative silence once again and, the buck having gone about his business, Liam moved on.

His mood improved after the incident with the deer. It felt good to be sharing the woodland with something so alive and powerful. He even tried to whistle but his mouth was too dry. Now, the only noise unnatural to the forest was the rhythmic sound of his own footsteps.

Soon, he saw bright sunlight ahead of him, at the end of the tree tunnel. He looked at Dan's scribbled map. He must be coming up to Ballyartella. From what he could make out on the map, there should be another, bigger bridge here with a mill nearby. He passed a ruined castle keep, on his right, and wondered if this was Cromwell's handiwork or whether the ravages of time had reduced the castle to ruins. Dan's scrawled drawing proved correct and, satisfied that he was headed in the right direction, Liam crossed the bridge at the mill and looked for the next landmark. After another mile, he saw the ruined church he had been expecting and a little further on, another castle keep up ahead, this time on top of a little rise in a pasture. He looked at his map. This was Knigh Castle. He was on the homeward stretch of his walk, it was a straight shot from here to his destination.

The sun was not yet directly overhead when Liam walked into the village of Gortalocca. The first building he came to had a cross over the door and an old woman was sweeping dust out of its doorway. This must be the church Ma Daley had spoken of. Liam passed a few small whitewashed cottages and, after only a few minutes, he reached Hogan's. Harold Johnson was standing outside talking with another man.

Liam approached and Johnson grinned with delight when he saw him, extending his hand as if he was meeting an old friend. Liam took his limp hand and shook it.

'Mr Flynn,' said Johnson, 'may I introduce Mr. Hogan, the proprietor of Hogan's of Gortalocca.' Michael Hogan held out his hand and Liam took it, his handshake was firm. You can tell a lot about a man by the way he shakes your hand, thought Liam.

Satisfied that the formalities had been dispensed with, the old man was anxious to find out if this wet-behind-the-ears yokel could be duped. Inviting Liam to follow him, he strode away and, after nodding a farewell to Michael Hogan, the young man caught up with him.

They had been walking for only a minute or so when

the old man came to a halt. They were just opposite the village well, on a small boreen which, Johnson informed Liam, led down to the townland of Killadargan. He announced that this was the boundary of the land he was selling and gestured for Liam to follow him across the property which, he assured the carpenter, covered almost ten acres.

As they walked, Liam's eyes took in everything. He noticed a copse of trees and recognised it immediately as a faerie ring. That meant at least two acres of the land would be as good as useless. Only a fool would violate a faerie ring by attempting to farm it. Liam did not consider himself superstitious but some things could not be ignored. Other than that, Liam thought the property would do him nicely but his face gave nothing away.

He got straight to the point. 'How much? he said.

Johnson scratched his chin, shifted his eyes from Liam back to the land, hemmed and hawed for a while and said finally, 'Six pounds.' Liam thanked him for his time and was about to walk away when Johnson said, 'I'd consider taking five.'

Liam shook his head. 'Does it have a goldmine on it or something?' he said and went to turn on his heel again.

'Make me an offer,' said the old man, infuriated that this had not turned into the fleecing he had anticipated.

'Three,' said Liam, 'and no more.'

Johnson raised his eyebrows. 'Why don't you just take a gun and rob me?' he blustered.

'Three pounds, ten shillings,' said Liam, 'take it or leave it.' He didn't wait for an answer and began to walk away.

'Done!' shouted the old man after him, 'and you're no carpenter, Mr. Flynn, you're a highwayman.' Liam turned back and extended his hand to Johnson. They shook on the deal and this time the old man's handshake was firmer.

'When do I receive payment?' he asked.

'I'll get a solicitor to write up the papers,' said Liam. 'When we've both signed, I will hand you the money.'

This was not at all what Harold Johnson had anticipated. He thought Liam would hand over the money there and then and that he would walk away three pounds and ten shillings richer. There was nothing else for him to do, however, but to grudgingly agree and, as he walked away, Liam heard him mumble something about there being no trust in the world these days.

Liam stayed and walked the property several more times. There was a grove of oaks and hawthorn in the southwest corner. This could be the source of material for his work, and perhaps even a house for himself. The remainder of the land was old pasture which nature had begun to claim back.

By this time, Liam was covered in mud. He was tired, his head throbbed and the stitches that Ma Daley had sewn up the gash in forehead with were beginning to itch. He decided it was time to head back to Nenagh and his bed, but he didn't want to turn up at the inn without at least seeking out the priest Ma Daley had asked him to find. He walked from the well, back up the village street towards the church, with his head bent, his eyes fixed on the ground and his mind filled with plans for the future.

'So, you're the carpenter who would be a farmer.' Liam was startled out of his reverie and looked up, wide eyed, at the source of the voice. Standing in his path was a girl. The first thing Liam noticed was that she was almost the same height as him. Her golden yellow hair tumbled over her shoulders and, from under it, a pair of strikingly beautiful grey eyes were watching him. For the first time, Liam was painfully conscious of his appearance. He glanced down at his ragged clothes and his muddy feet. She seemed amused by his obvious embarrassment and looked the filthy apparition up and down. Liam lowered his eyes again.

'Am I so grotesque that you can't even look me in the eye?' she asked mischievously and grinned. She was aware that she was far from ugly. Liam could find no words.

'Do you have a name, raggedy man?' Liam felt himself blush right down to his toes.

'Liam Flynn,' he said and tried to walk on, but she blocked his escape.

'Don't you want to know my name, Liam Flynn?' she teased. Still nothing from Liam. 'Well, I'll tell you anyway. It's Roisin Hogan, my Da and me run the store.' So this was Michael Hogan's daughter. She was no troll, no ogre, no spectre. Liam thought she must be the most beautiful thing he had ever laid eyes on and now, he was so self-conscious, that his toes curled. He wanted to be away out of the village and on the road back to Nenagh, but this girl was bold and she had him like a deer in a poacher's lamp.

'Liam Flynn,' he said again, 'My name is Liam Flynn.'

With that, he pushed past her and heard her laugh as he hurried quickly away. Although he knew she was laughing at him, he didn't care. He thought her laughter sounded like music and he was sorry when it faded off into the distance. You're an eejit, he told himself, a feckin' eejit. You could have eaten supper in Hogan's and then at least had an excuse to look at her.

CHAPTER 8

L iam carried on through the village to the church, still smarting from his run-in with Roisin. There was no doubt that he found her very attractive but he wasn't sure if he liked her. She had offended him, and he was very sensitive if he thought he was being looked down on in any way. He cast his glance down again to consider his appearance, trying to brush the dirt off of himself and straightening out his worn clothing as best he could.

When Liam reached the church, the old woman who had been sweeping earlier was now washing linen in a wooden tub, next to a tiny cottage, which Liam assumed was the rectory. As he approached, she looked up and regarded him with a sour expression. She was old and her pale skin was covered in so many liver spots, lines and bumps that her face reminded Liam of Dan Daley's map. Mary Gleeson had been the sacristan at Gortalocca church since the death of her husband many years before. Her job was to keep the church clean and tidy, wash the robes of the priest and altar boys, set out the items for Mass and generally keep the church running smoothly. She was also Father Grogan's housekeeper, making sure he was fed and keeping his meager possessions in order. Even though her post was a thankless one, she knew that, without her, neither the church nor the priest would function. Mary Gleeson was full of self-importance.

'I wish to see Father Grogan,' Liam told her.

She looked him up and down. 'And who might you be?' she grunted. She slapped another item of laundry onto the wash board and began to scrub it.

'I'm Liam Flynn,' he replied.

'Is dat supposed t' mean somet'ing?' she asked, still scrubbing.

'It means that my name is Liam Flynn.' Liam began to feel the colour rise in his face and this time it wasn't embarrassment. He was becoming irked by the old woman. 'I've come to see Father Grogan.'

'Is 'e expecting ya?'

'No,' he said firmly. This was getting him nowhere and Liam was about to just say, 'Agh, to hell with you and your priest,' when Father Grogan appeared at the door of the tiny rectory, ducking under its low lintel to avoid bumping his head. The smile on his big full face was warm and so was his manner. He came outside.

'Don't torment the lad, Mrs. Gleeson. It's not as if my diary is full.' He laughed a big baritone laugh and Liam began to feel at ease.

'Mrs. Gleeson, if you're not busy, would you pour a flagon of beer for this gentleman and myself.'

Mary Gleeson didn't even look up from her wash. 'Does it look like I have all day t' be runnin' after d' pair of ye?' she said sullenly. 'Pour it yerself.'

The old priest smiled and winked at Liam. 'Come inside, lad. Did I hear your name correctly? Liam Flynn, is it?'

Liam nodded and looked back at Mary Gleeson with

a look of triumph ... but she made sure to have the last word. 'Broom some of dat Tipperary mud off yerself first. I'll not be cleaning up any mess you make.' She jerked her head towards a broom leaning up against the wall at the side of the door.

Liam winced slightly at the rebuke and picked up the broom in an attempt to sweep some of the mud off his clothing. The old priest took it off him and ushered him inside. Liam cracked his head on the low lintel and, as he rubbed his sore forehead.

Grogan laughed again. 'I've done that a thousand times meself,' he said. Inside the tiny cottage, the main room was no bigger than 8 by 10 feet with a small fireplace at one end and a rope bed turned up against the wall. Father Grogan seemed to fill the room with his bulk, his long grey felted Franciscan robe adding to the effect.

He saw Liam scan the room, taking in the sparse furnishings. 'It's not good for a man of the cloth to become too comfortable in this world,' he said, 'especially, when his flock has to provide for him.'

Liam's eyes widened in surprise. Most priests looked upon their position as one of entitlement. Perhaps this one did have something about him, after all. Grogan poured them a large cup of beer each and motioned for Liam to take a seat on one of two wooden chairs at a small table next to the window, the only source of light in the room.

Father Grogan drank first, taking a huge quaff from the clay cup. Liam followed, taking just a sip of the weak beer.

'It's not much but it's the best I can offer you,' said the priest apologetically.

'It's good,' said Liam. It wasn't exactly a lie, his

mouth was dry. He'd had nothing to drink since the buttermilk this morning, and he was parched from all the exercise. Liam reached into his small sack for the piece of buttered bread he had saved for lunch. Father Grogan's eyes followed and he licked his lips. Liam broke the brown bread in half and offered the larger piece to the old man.

'Thank you,' he said, taking it. 'I've never been known to refuse a morsel.' He smiled, scarfed the bread and washed the mouthful down with another gulp of beer. Liam nibbled his to make it last longer.

'What brings you here?' said the priest.

'I came to buy a farm,'

'You're not Catholic, so.' The old man's eyes narrowed slightly. Liam wanted the priest to know the truth so he explained how he'd been equivocal with Harold Johnson.

The priest nodded. 'Truth is in the perception, Liam. A person believes what they choose to believe.' The younger man agreed and the priest continued. 'In these days, a man has to be careful and concealing the truth is not a lie.' Liam was beginning to like this old priest. He didn't see things in black and white like most did, he understood the subtleties. It was easy for the clerical world to interpret these things as simply right or wrong. In real life, the world was countless shades of grey.

'Where are you going to stay, my son?' asked the priest.

Liam was a little deceptive with his reply. 'I was hoping to find a room nearby, so I don't have to make the long walk back and forth to Nenagh every day.'

'Then you shall stay here.' said Father Grogan. 'I would enjoy some company and a bit of intelligent conversation after vespers.'

Liam looked around and said, 'Perhaps I can pay for my keep by doing some repairs around here and in the church.' The old priest beamed with delight and extended his hand in a firmer than firm handshake.

Liam took his hand away and shook it in mock pain. 'Careful, Father,' he said grinning. 'I'll need both paws if I'm to be of any use.'

The priest returned his smile. 'Sorry,' he said, 'I got excited at the prospect of conversing with someone other than Mrs. Gleeson ... and the church could use a few more pews for the women to sit on.'

'Will Catholic arses be comfortable on half-protestant seats, Father?'

'In my experience, arses are non-denominational.' said Grogan with a wink. They both laughed and Father Grogan noticed Liam's tankard was still half full. 'Are you going to drink that?' he asked. Liam shrugged his shoulders. The Franciscan said, 'Waste not, want not,' and with that, he guzzled down what was left in the flagon.

The afternoon had turned to evening now and Liam stood up. 'I must be going, Father. I have to go back to Nenagh to get my tools and I don't relish the thought of walking through those woods in the dark.'

'Nonsense, Liam, you'll spend the night here. I'll get Mrs. Gleeson to set an extra plate for supper and you can have a place on the floor in front of the fire for the night.' Liam exhaled a small sigh of relief. He hadn't been looking forward to the long walk and he wanted to find out more about Gortalocca from the priest. The old man went to the little door and opened the top half of it. He shouted to his housekeeper, who was hanging up the last of her wash,

'We have a guest for supper, Mrs. Gleeson.'

She scowled and mumbled, crankily, 'I t'ought 's much. Will 'e be spendin' d' night as well?'

'He will,' said the curate authoritatively. He was less inclined to mollify the old woman now that he had the prospect of someone new to banter with, '... and for the foreseeable future.' She rolled her eyes to the heavens and thought, saints preserve us, he's taken in another stray.

Mrs. Gleeson set three places at the tiny table and pulled a stool up to it to accommodate the third diner. Liam's mouth watered at the smell of the barley with a hunk of gammon cooked into it for flavour. Mrs. Gleeson set a pile of potatoes, boiled in their jackets, on top of the table, thinking that they would fill any empty spaces left in the assembled bellies. She put on a good spread, he'd give her that. They bowed their heads to say grace but Liam could not keep his mind off the delightful smell of the food. Just as they raised their heads, the door burst open and there stood Roisin, beaming at Father Grogan.

'Here's a loaf of yesterday's bread for you, Father. If I keep it 'til tomorrow, it'll be as hard as a cobble.' She was surprised to see Liam seated at the table but smiled, 'Close your mouth, Liam Flynn, or you'll be catching flies. You probably won't need to open it again tonight anyway, this old man will talk your ear off.'

She laughed as Liam involuntarily put his hand to his ear. Why do I act like such a fool when this girl speaks to me, he asked himself.

'Don't underestimate this young man, Roisin, he's well able to hold his own,' smiled the priest.

Roisin opened her eyes wide in mock disbelief. 'You mean he speaks?' she laughed.

The priest looked from Roisin to Liam and back. 'Ah,

I see you've already made the acquaintance of our new church carpenter, so.' He grinned and she grinned back.

She addressed Liam. 'Well, at least it'll make a change to have someone around here who is not constantly talking about themselves.' Liam looked down. He wasn't used to people speaking about him as if he wasn't present. He felt the colour come to his face again and he cursed it.

'Don't mind her ways, Liam, she's just practicing to be a proper Tipperary wife.' laughed the old priest.

Roisin's smile dropped. It was her turn to blush and she flashed an indignant look at the curate. 'Huh. Fat chance of that,' she scoffed. 'I have to go now.' With that, she whirled around in the doorway and was gone in a flash, closing the door with a bang behind her.

Father Grogan sighed and addressed Liam, 'A word to the wise, my son. Don't get on the wrong side of that one.'

They resumed their supper. Mrs. Gleeson had taken the stale brown bread from Roisin and now she placed a lump of it into each wooden bowl, pouring the barley soup on top of it. By now, she was out of sorts with all the disruption. Not only was the food in danger of getting cold but she was used to being able to monopolise the conversation. She tossed one of the potatoes into Liam's broth and splashed him with the hot soup. Liam knew he was the interloper on what she considered her territory and so he remained stoic. Father Grogan had witnessed the incident and although he didn't say a word, he glared at her.

After supper, when Mrs. Gleeson was gathering the bowls from the table, Liam stood and said, 'I'll wash them.'

His intentions were not taken kindly. 'That's my job,'

she said tartly. He realised he was a usurper for the old man's attention here and that anything he said or did was bound to be wrong so he kept his mouth shut.

The priest stood up from the table. 'It's time for my prayers, Liam,' he said, moving towards the door.

'I'll come with you,' said the younger man.

'To Vespers?' asked Grogan.

'No, no, no,' said Liam, 'just outside.' Liam reached into his pocket and pulled out a small clay pipe, its stem broken off to about 3 inches. When he produced a twist of tobacco, the old man's eyes opened wide.

'Have you enough for two?' he enquired eagerly.

Liam smiled and nodded. 'But what about Vespers?' he asked.

The old man smiled back. 'Agh, sure it'll be six o'clock somewhere when we've finished.'

Liam laughed out loud for the first time in a long time. 'Get yer pipe then, Father, and we'll have a wee smoke together.' Liam thought he had found a friend.

CHAPTER 9

L iam walked around the outside of the little church, making a mental note of some repairs he thought should be attended to. Inside, he inspected the benches which served as pews and thought he could do better on his worst day.

The sun was setting now and the sky had turned a peach color, adorned with a few wispy lavender-coloured clouds. When he had finished, he went back inside the priest's cottage and lit his pipe again, he had allowed it to go out.

Back outside in the lovely evening, he leant against the cottage wall and looked at the sky again. The lavender clouds were now turning to a deep purple. He had never in his life allowed himself the luxury of simply watching the sun go down. He was changing and he felt it. The hardness that he had developed as a coping mechanism was beginning to dissolve and he was allowing it to.

Darkness had fallen when the priest returned from his meditation. He had brought with him the thick tallow candle that Mrs. Gleeson had placed on the altar, and now he lit it and placed on the little table.

'I need light if we're to converse, Liam,' he said, taking his seat. 'I have to be able to see what you're saying as well as hear it, and my eyes aren't as good as they were when I was a young man like you.' He smiled and motioned for Liam to take the other seat. As Liam sat down, he tried to imagine what this comfortable old priest had been like at his own age.

Father Grogan saw Liam's quizzical look and said, 'I'll tell you a bit about myself, and if you want to know anything more, just stop me,' he said. Liam settled back in his chair, this should be a good listen. 'I was born in Cashel in 1636,' the priest began. 'I was raised to be a priest. I went on a pilgrimage to England when I was fourteen and, from there, entered the Franciscan order. Things weren't quite as hostile then as they are nowadays. There were a lot of noble families who quietly practiced their faith. I was happy in monastic life, removed from all worldly concerns. I felt closer to God back then. I was young and never had reason to question God or the Church. My family remained in Cashel ... Mam, Da, my two sisters and older brother, and their families. They milked cows and had a big farm. By the time Cromwell had come and gone, all of them were dead. Kind, generous people who never harmed a living soul and they were all dead. When I got word of it, almost two years later, part of my faith died too. What kind of God would allow that? Was God on the side of the English? And if he was, would that make Him a Protestant? It called into question everything I had ever believed in.'

Liam interrupted him, 'Then you question God too?' he asked.

'No, my son, not any more. I am getting closer to the end of my life and most of it has been taken up by ministering to the poor, trying to give them hope and free them from as much despair as I can. This is my work, just as surely as building with wood is yours. Over the years, I have come to the realisation that my work is to be God's hands here on earth and, when things are darkest and everyone else is asking questions, it's up to me to set an example. Sometimes I'm even more frightened then they are, but I can't indulge myself by wallowing in my fear. There is work to be done and it's God's work. It's up to me and you and people like us, who are stronger than the rest, to do God's work here.'

Liam pondered for a while and said, finally, 'Why?'

'Why what?' asked the old priest.

'Why have you chosen me, of all people, to tell your story to?'

The old priest put his hand across the table and placed it on Liam's to convey his sincerity. Ordinarily, Liam would have pulled his hand away from such contact but, on this occasion, he didn't. 'There are bad times coming, Liam,' said the priest, 'both for the true Church and for Ireland itself. These times will be terrible bad and we're going to need people who are smart enough and resourceful enough to protect what we have here.'

'But I'm just a carpenter,' said Liam, mystified.

The old priest smiled. 'So was Jesus,' he said. 'Perhaps it's always been up to the carpenters of this world.'

The two men talked long into the night, like two conspirators. Liam told Father Grogan the story of his entire life to this point. The priest listened intently, as if it was the best story he had ever heard and, when Liam finished, with his father's parting words to his half-brother, the curate said,

'Liam Flynn, you're nobody's fool and you never will be. Here, you're a stranger, and that provides you with an advantage straight away. You have no family and no history. You can fabricate anything you wish. You will need to use your advantage wisely because what I'm about to tell you could get us both hung and quartered. Listen carefully to me.' Liam swallowed nervously as the priest continued.

'A new set of laws was passed by the English parliament some years ago but, so far, they have only been enforced sporadically. These laws forbid a Catholic to own his own land or hold a political office. In fact, they make practicing the Catholic faith, itself, illegal.' Liam's mouth had gone dry.

'Now that England's laws are beginning to be imposed in Ireland, in a very short time, every Irish Catholic will be working on English holdings in his own country.' Liam's jaw had dropped now and he was staring at the old priest incredulously.

'You, Liam, with your ambiguity could help to save the people in Gortalocca and maybe further afield too.'

'What do you propose, Father?' he asked apprehensively, 'I'll agree to nothing until I know what's expected of me. If I'm going to gamble my head, then I'd like to know what I have to gain and what you think it will involve.'

'Of course, my son,' said the priest. 'This is what I have in mind. You, Liam, for all outward appearances, will become an upstanding member of the Church of Ireland, and the owner of record on all the land hereabouts.'

'Isn't that a sin, Father?' Liam asked doubtfully, 'A mortal sin? I'm not sure which commandment it breaks, but I am sure it sounds like a sin.'

'I'm not sure either, my son,' said Father Grogan, 'but it's my plan and so I will absolve you of any guilt. If there is any wrongdoing, then I am the one who will answer for it.'

'Let's say for a moment that I agreed to this plan,' said Liam. 'What are the drawbacks?'

The old priest looked steadily at Liam. 'You may become the most hated, despised person in Gortalocca. You will be a pariah, a villain to most of the townspeople. We couldn't trust them with this knowledge and it would be best if only you and I knew what was going on.' Liam's head turned involuntarily in the direction of Hogan's and the action wasn't lost on the old man.

'I saw the way you reacted when Roisin came here earlier,' he said. 'She may despise you too.'

Liam dismissed the priest's concern with a wave of his hand. 'I have been on my own for many years, Father, and the opinion of other's doesn't worry me. What does worry me is that my brother was an idealist too. He had a cause too, and look where that got him ... not even a stone to mark him or a priest to say a prayer over him. I think he was a fool, but perhaps that is my father talking.'

The big candle was beginning to splutter. The two men had talked through the night.

'It'll be dawn soon,' said Liam, 'Let me get a couple of hours of sleep. I have to walk into Nenagh tomorrow to get some new clothes and speak with a solicitor to draw up papers for the land purchase.'

'And there you have it,' said Grogan, 'That's what you have to gain, Liam. You can buy your land and not Johnson, nor even the Butlers themselves, can lay claim to it.'

'Let me sleep on it, Father. I'll give you my answer tomorrow.' Liam had already made up his mind. He wasn't an adventurer, but this element of danger appealed to him. Just before he fell asleep, he wondered if perhaps this same feeling of exhilaration is what had motivated his brother, Robert, to go off to war. An excitement he couldn't explain rose inside him and he felt alive for the first time in a very long time.

CHAPTER 10

L iam woke with a start and squinted into a ray of bright sunlight that was shining through the tiny window onto his face. He lifted his head and shaded his eyes with his hand.

Father Grogan sat at the table, stuffing a lump of bread into his mouth. 'It's still early, Liam,' the old priest spoke with his mouth full. 'Did you make a decision?' He swallowed the mouthful of stale bread with an effort.

Liam dropped his head back onto the floor and replied, in a serious voice, 'Let's be rebels, Father.'

The priest smiled, delighted at Liam's decision. 'Excellent!' he said. 'Then we must make plans, my son. You mentioned yesterday that you need a solicitor. I have a name for you. He's a young Anglo-Irish named Wall, Edward Wall. He's new in Nenagh. Both his father and his uncle are barristers in Dublin. He had a bit of a falling out with them over the cause of Irish independence, but they're still fairly close.'

Liam narrowed his eyes. 'You have it all thought out already,' he said. 'Have you been planning this act of treason, so?'

'No, my son, but when you showed up, whether it

was by an act of Providence or by chance, the idea came to me. I prayed about it last night and I think it was God's idea. Now, under no circumstances are you to let this man, Wall, know of our secret. Blood is thicker than water, after all and he has connections. He may prove useful to us, though.'

Liam was sitting at the table too by this time and he picked up one of the last hunks of the stale bread. He began to chew on it, it was as hard as pine bark.

Liam set out on his walk back to Nenagh, but this time he was completely unaware of his surroundings. Several riders and a coach passed him, but he was completely absorbed in his own thoughts.

How could he let himself get involved in a plot that was, at the very least, an act of sedition and perhaps even treason? Up to now, he thought, all I've done is carry out my work and collect my pay. I'm just a carpenter, after all, and that old man is just a village priest and here we are, the two of us, trying to usurp the power of the English crown. What, in God's name, have I got myself into? His mind wandered, too, to the pretty woman in Gortalocca. What was her name? ... Roisin. He said it aloud slowly ... Ro...sheen. What would she think of him now? Agh sure, what did it matter anyway? He was going to make himself an outcast. The land was all that mattered now.

The houses grew closer together, the nearer he got to the market town of Nenagh. The traffic grew busier with carts of wool and produce, wagons of meat with the faint sweet smell of putrifaction, sacks of grain and potatoes and kegs of various sizes and content.

He passed a fancy tailor's shop but decided to move on. In Liam's experience, the shops on the main street were expensive, it was better to try one down a side street. He badly needed a new set of clothes, the ones he wore were ready to disintegrate. He needed shoes too, and a hat of some sort. If he was going to re-invent himself he had better start with his appearance.

He had been on Castle Street, the cobble-paved main thoroughfare through Nenagh town, but now he turned off down a dirt side road. A wooden sign, nailed to the corner building, announced its name, Queen Street. How absurd, he thought, that a dirt road should be named after the queen. But then, every town and village had a King and a Queen Street ... those silly, pretentious English, he snorted.

Liam approached the door of the tailor shop and smelled paint. He touched it, it was dry. He gave it a push but it wouldn't open. He would have to find a different shop to buy his clothes. As he walked away, he heard a shop doorbell ring.

'Feckin' paint,' a voice said, scornfully. Liam turned back and looked at the little man who stood in the now open doorway of the shop.

'Can I help you, sir?' said the little man in an effeminate and affected voice. As Liam turned to face him, the tailor took in his appearance and said, in a much sterner voice,

'Have you got any money or are you wasting my valuable time?' Liam noticed with amusement that the little tailor was putting on an English accent in an effort to give himself an air of importance.

'I have money, my man,' Liam responded, mimicking the man's haughtiness, 'and I hope I'm not wasting my own time.' The little man's expression turned to one of deference. Currency was a rare commodity in these times.

'Come in, so, come right on in.' He ushered Liam through the doorway and into the little shop. The tailor had on a white shirt with an array of pins stuck in the breast and a cloth measuring tape draped around his neck. Pinned through his left sleeve were several needles with various colours of thread. He seemed old to Liam, at least in his mid-forties. His hair was greasy and slicked back, barely disguising a bald spot which was easy for Liam to see because the fellow was so much smaller than himself.

The little man had his arms folded now, and his chin in his hand, sizing Liam up. Liam felt like a pig being exhibited at an auction. 'So what c'n I do fer ya,' he asked. Liam noticed the man's Irish accent had crept back into his voice and the pretensions had all but disappeared.

'I need a new set of clothes,' he replied.

'That's evident,' said the tailor, his haughty air returning. Liam glared at him and the tailor thought he hadn't better risk losing the young man's business.

'It'll take me several days t' make a new set,' he said, his Irish accent returning. 'I'm assuming you need a shirt and trousers, as well as a waistcoat and undergarments.' Liam was growing tired of this already.

'Look, I'm a carpenter and I just need a set of clothing that I can wear to church or to supper, so stop trying to fetch blood from a stone and tell me the best you can do for me.'

Liam's abruptness disarmed the tailor and he thought for a moment. 'I have a used set of clothes that should fill your needs. They're in excellent condition, only worn once ... by a local man at his own funeral. With a little alteration, they should suit your needs nicely.'

'Good,' said Liam. 'When can you have them ready?'

'This afternoon, sir.'

'How much?'

'Twelve shillings.'

'Six.'

'Ten.'

'Eight.'

'Done,' said the tailor, 'and I'll throw in a neck tie.'

The tailor got Liam to try on the used set of clothes and took measurements. While he was busy pinning here and chalking marks there, Liam asked him where in town he could get a bath and a shave and a haircut. The little fellow told him about a barber surgeon just down the street. He said he was the local dentist too so, if Liam wanted a tooth pulled or if he needed a blood-letting, he could get it all done at the same time. Liam thanked the tailor for his recommendation but assured him that a bath, a shave and a haircut would suffice.

The tailor also gave him recommendations on where he could buy himself a pair of shoes and a hat. When he was back in his old clothes, Liam told the little man he would return this afternoon for his clothes and that he would have his money then. The tailor looked crestfallen that he hadn't been paid up front, so Liam relented and gave him an advance of a shilling.

The man's demeanor brightened immediately and he said, 'Thank you, sir, your clothes will be ready for a fitting in a couple of hours.'

Liam headed back along Castle Road. When he came to a shop with red and white stripes spiralling down a pole outside, he knew he had reached the barber's shop. The barber sat inside in his barber chair, sleeping, a fat old man with white hair, pale pink skin and a red nose that looked like it had been fashioned out of putty. Liam stood inside the otherwise empty shop for a few moments, looking at the sharp instruments which were lined up on a little table next to the chair. It looked mediaeval and Liam knew that in truth it was, barber shops had hardly changed over the centuries. Liam coughed loudly and the old fellow snapped awake. He was grouchy. He had been dreaming of days long ago, when he had been young and virile.

'Whaddaya want?'

Liam felt the colour rise in his face. 'You can start with a little respect,' he snapped. 'and, after that, I'll settle for a bath, a shave and a haircut.'

'Tuppence,' grumbled the barber and gestured for Liam to follow him through a back exit where there was a tub of rancid water waiting in a courtyard.

'I'll have some new water in that tub and some soap,' said Liam.

'Thruppence,' replied the grumpy old man. Liam got two pennies from his purse and handed them to the barber, who fingered the coins. 'One more,' he said.

Liam handed him another farthing and lied, 'That's all I've got.'

The old fellow pocketed the coins, emptied and refilled the tub with a siphon and tossed a tiny tablet of soap at Liam, as he mumbled under his breath, 'Here, shove it up yer arse.'

Liam took off his old clothes, shook the dust off them and placed them on a wooden bench next to the tub. He lowered himself slowly into the cold water. It raised gooseflesh on his skin and made him want to pee. I'll hold onto it, he thought, although it would make the water a little warmer. He smiled to himself, lathered up the soap and washed his hair first. He thought he'd better work from the top down. The soap stung his eyes and made him sneeze. He was finished and out of the tub in no time and, with no way to dry himself, stood for a while, letting the water drain off, before dressing himself.

Back in the shop, the barber's mood had not improved and Liam decided it had nothing to do with having been woken, but that it was just his nature. He tried to drag a comb through Liam's shoulder length hair, to no avail, except that it hurt like anything. Next, he tried a brush with stiff hog bristles and managed to get the hairs separated, after a fashion. If a haircut hurt this much, thought Liam, what would it be like for the miserable sod to pull a tooth? He shuddered to think of it. The barber began to hack at Liam's hair with a pair of scissors, remarking that he should have used sheep shears.

When he had finished, he wrung out a towel he had been steeping in a bucket of hot water, simmering on a stove, and wrapped it around Liam's face. Liam thought this must be how a boiled potato felt. He had been both frozen and parboiled in less than ten minutes. From beneath the hot towel, he could hear the barber stropping a razor on a leather belt and he looked forward to having his week's worth of whiskers removed.

Next, he would visit the cobbler's shop, he needed pair of boots that would come up over his ankles, also a hat. He heard the Angelus bell ringing, it must be midday already and he didn't feel a bit hungry. It's peculiar, he thought, that when you have things to do, your stomach is the one thing you neglect.

The cobbler not only had a good pair of refurbished shoes to fit Liam, but also a felt hat with a high crown. Liam was delighted when he had struck a bargain and got them both for two shillings. For less than four pounds, he had transformed himself from tradesman to gentry. Liam walked back to the inn, where his tools and purse were stashed. He would leave his tools for the moment, but he needed his purse to pay the tailor.

The doorbell jangled as Liam walked into the tailor's shop and the little tailor said he had just added the final stitches. Liam shed his old clothes like a skin and put on his new attire. When he was dressed, he put on his new shoes and now he just needed his hat to complete the transformation. He tried wearing the hat in several ways, all of which made him feel a little foolish.

The tailor helped him. 'A hat is the final statement of a gentleman,' he said, moving the hat this way and that on Liam's head, 'his crowning glory. It's the first thing noticed before the shoes and you must always keep those blacked and shining'. This was all new to Liam, but he would have to get used to his new skin if he was to succeed.

The little fellow passed a mirror to Liam, then stood back to admire his own work and take in the whole ensemble. He was pleased with what he saw. He had not transformed a sow's ear into a silk purse but it was as close as he had ever come to it. Liam felt like an eejit, who the devil did he think he was, anyway?

Who? … Liam Flynn, Esquire, that's who.

CHAPTER 11

It was time to visit the solicitor.

Liam asked directions from a well-dressed man on Castle Street and was surprised at how courteous the man was towards him. Earlier today, Liam thought, the man would have avoided him in the street, but now, this gentleman spoke to him as his equal. It must the hat, he mused, 'the final statement of a gentleman', the tailor had said.

He followed the man's directions and soon found the small building he was looking for, near the castle. A cast, bronze sign outside read, 'EDWARD WALL, SOLICITOR'. Liam opened the door and entered a tiny office. There, with his feet up on a desk, was a man whom Liam gauged to be around his own age. The man was startled. He hurriedly dropped his feet to the floor and grappled with a powdered wig, fumbling to get it on his head. He donned it so clumsily that it sat cock-eyed, dangling down over one ear.

'Good day to you, sir,' said the man behind the desk.

Liam nodded. He couldn't take his eyes off the lopsided wig. 'Good day,' he said, at last.

The young man regained his composure. 'I'm

Edward Wall, solicitor. May I be of service to you?' Liam recognised a Dublin accent, under the contrived English one the man was trying to assume, and said, in an equally formal tone,

'You can indeed, sir,' Liam struggled with an accent somewhere between Tipperary and London and decided it was time to stop the circus shenanigans so, in his own Tipp. brogue, he said, 'Me name's Liam Flynn and I'm buying a bit of land.'

Edward Wall regarded Liam for a moment and, when he spoke again, he had dropped the affected English accent for his own Dublin one. 'I know of some land you might be interested in,' he offered.

Liam shook his head. 'I have already seen what I want,' he replied. 'It's in Gortalocca.'

The young barrister wrinkled his brow. 'Gortalocca? I know of no substantial holdings there,' he said, struggling to straighten his wig. He picked up a quill and began to take notes as Liam spoke.

'It's not a large piece of land that I want to purchase,' said Liam. 'It's quite small, in fact, only around ten acres.'

'Ah, just a start, so,' said the solicitor, smiling. 'A foot in the door.'

Liam had never heard that expression before, but he said, 'That's right, a foot in the door.'

'I can certainly draw up your purchase papers for you,' said the solicitor. 'May I ask who the seller is?'

'Harold Johnson,' replied Liam.

The young lawyer forgot himself for a moment and, under his breath, said, 'That wily old fox ...'

Liam smiled.

'And may I also enquire as to what the purchase price is?'

'Three pounds, ten shillings,' replied Liam. The solicitor's eyes opened wide.

'Well now, Mr. Flynn,' he said. 'You must have caught him on a generous day.' Then, under his breath, 'Miracles do occur.'

Liam smiled again. 'How much will you charge me?' he asked.

'Three shillings for the paperwork and another shilling to register the deed at the courthouse, after the sale has been concluded,' he said.

Liam nodded his agreement and placed the four shilling coins in the lawyer's hand. 'Then make it so, if you please,' he said. 'I'll be back tomorrow morning.'

They shook hands and Liam left the office. He walked back towards the tailor's shop. It was only two o'clock and he had accomplished everything he had set out to do that day. His new shoes were killing his feet.

As he entered the tailor's small shop, the little man looked up, questioningly. 'Is everything alright, sir?' he asked. 'Did you forget something?'

Liam gave him the hint of a grin and assured him everything was indeed very well, but that he needed to change into his old clothes before heading back to Gortalocca. The tailor gave him a look of disapproval, but Liam ignored it and asked would he kindly wrap up his new attire for him, to make it easier for him to carry.

The tailor consented but thought: feckin' bog Irish. It's like dressing a pig ... a pig will always be a pig. 'By the way, sir,' he said, 'may I have your name?'

'It's Flynn,' said Liam.

'It has been a pleasure to do business with you, Mr. Flynn,' said the tailor. 'I'm Mr O'Rourke. I wish you a good day and safe home.'

Liam picked up his bundles and tapped the hat onto his head. He thought what a sight he must look dressed in rags with a fine hat on his head. He headed up Castle

Street and was soon out of the town and back on the road to Gortalocca. He allowed himself just the hint of a smile. It tickled him to think that a mere change in attire could garner so much respect, he also felt a little foolish.

'Safe home,' the tailor had wished him.

CHAPTER 12

L iam made the left turn off the main road, and had begun the walk towards the forest preserve, when he heard the unmistakable clip-clop and rattle of a horse, pulling a wagon. As the wagon drew alongside him, Liam saw it was being pulled by an emaciated horse. From the roan hairs around its muzzle, he could tell the horse was old. The wagon had seen better days too. One wheel wobbled and another had a broken spoke. The man driving it was a stout fellow, he looked to be in his late 50's. A scar across the bridge of his nose seemed to pull his nostrils back, giving his face the look of a pig.

Liam tipped his new hat. 'Good day, sir,' he said. 'Would you, by chance, be heading towards Gortalocca?'

'I would indeed,' replied the pig-faced man, 'and, may I add, that's a fine hat you have there.' Liam smiled as the man reined the horse to a halt.

'Have you business in Gortalocca?

'I have, sir,' answered Liam, 'at the rectory.' The driver gestured for Liam to get on board the wagon, so Liam climbed up and sat on the seat next to him. There was the unmistakable smell of hogs and Liam thought, not only does he look like one, he smells like one too. The man introduced himself as Paddy Shevlin and told Liam that he raised swine for the market. Liam extended his hand, Paddy transferred the reins to his left hand and they shook.

The two men made small talk as they headed towards Gortalocca and, even though the speed they were travelling at wasn't much faster than that of a brisk walk, Liam was grateful to give his sore feet a rest. Paddy enjoyed the sound of his own voice and was delighted to have someone to talk to about himself. Liam learned that Paddy was a widower with no children, and that he had lived in Gortalocca for more than twenty years. His family were thatchers but he preferred to raise pigs.

'If times get hard, ya c'n eat a pig. All ya c'n do wit thatch is pick yer teeth, sure.'

Liam had been enjoying Paddy Shevlin's company when, in what seemed like no time at all, they arrived in Gortalocca. Paddy pulled the wagon to a halt outside the rectory and pointed down the road towards Hogan's. He told Liam that he lived just a little way downwind of it, and winked, 'Even a blind man could find my place. Perhaps you'd like t' drop in one day an' we c'n converse again.' Liam smiled, he hadn't been able to get a word in edgeways.

Before he had even covered the short distance to the rectory door, Liam heard the voice of the sacristan, who was tidying up the yard outside. 'Yer back, then?' she sniffed. 'Well don't bother knockin', Father Grogan's waitin' fer ya.' Liam hadn't intended knocking.

The upper half of the door was open and he leaned over it so his head was inside. The priest sat at the little table, 'Come in, boy, and close the door behind you or the whole village will know our business.'

Liam went inside and closed both halves of the door shut behind him. The old priest poured him a flagon of beer and asked, 'Have you eaten anything? How did it go? Did you meet your unwitting co-conspirator?'

Liam looked at him and hesitated for a moment. 'Emmm ... the answers to your questions are – I haven't, it went well and what's a coco-spirator?'

'Sure you must be half-starved, lad. C'mon, have a bite to eat first. I saved you a bit of the gammon from last night's soup.' The priest pushed a bowl towards Liam. A little was right, there wasn't much more than a mouthful. Liam ate it hungrily and washed it down with a good swig of beer.

'If that morsel hasn't satisfied your hunger, you'll have to to go to Hogan's for some dinner tonight. I've been invited to eat with the Clancy's, God help me.' The priest groaned, 'All those children,' he said, 'I like children well enough, you understand .... but I don't think I could eat a whole one.' Father Grogan laughed at his own joke. He had been waiting for an opportunity to tell it. 'Nice hat, by way.'

Liam looked up and realised he hadn't taken the hat off his head. He swept it off with one swift action and both men smiled.

After the curate had left for Clancy's, Liam took a stroll down to Hogan's. He was dreading the prospect of being at the mercy of that sharp-tongued, yellow-haired girl once more but, at the same time, he relished the thought of seeing her again. As he drew closer, the dread grew and the relish diminished. Maybe this wasn't such a good idea. He shook himself out of it. He had made the perilous trip here from Thurles, hadn't he? Why on earth should he feel intimidated by a girl?

Nevertheless, he took a deep breath, as if he were

about to go underwater, before he pushed open the door of Hogan's and walked inside. Not a soul was there. Good. Maybe he would just sneak back to the rectory and listen to his stomach growl. No. He'd wait.

Liam sat down at one of the tables and waited in silence. He only had to wait a few moments before his worst fear and his greatest expectation appeared at the door to the living quarters, and stood with one hand on her hip and an empty tankard in the other.

'Ah, I thought I heard someone,' said Roisin. Liam knew he was going to trip over his tongue if he tried to speak, so he didn't.

'So what have you been up to, raggedy man?' Roisin was enjoying watching the young man squirm and he was all too aware of the pleasure it brought her. 'What have you been about all day?'

Liam mumbled something incoherent. 'What's that? Speak up, Liam.'

If she got pleasure at all out of seeing him squirm, then she must be ecstatic now. Liam looked down at the table and blushed hotly. He spoke louder than normal and slower. 'I bought a new set of clothes.'

Before he could say any more, Roisin had stepped back and was looking him up and down.

'Hmmmm. They look much like your last set. You must like the style. They even have the same crud on them.' Liam wanted to crawl under the table with embarrassment but he also wanted to stay here in this room with the girl.

Roisin couldn't help but enjoy teasing him. God only knows, she got little enough amusement in her tedious life. But she thought perhaps she had been a little cruel, and she relented.

'C'mere. I think you need a beer, Liam,' Her voice

was warmer now. 'Have you eaten yet today?' Liam shook his head. 'Well, you're in luck then. There are two choices … cabbage and bacon, or bacon and cabbage.'

Liam hadn't been listening, he was captivated by her very presence. 'What was the second choice?' he asked. She threw her head back and laughed.

'Never mind,' she said. 'I'll choose for you.' With that she whirled around and left the room. Liam looked after her with a pang of regret. In just a few days' time, she'll despise me, he thought, and he was sorry.

He checked himself. He had to put thoughts like that out of his mind now. He and the old priest were about to engage in a course of action that could get them both hanged. But I'm no idealist, he reminded himself, shaking his head. All I wanted was a little piece of land and a new start. Now, here I am about to risk my life for strangers who will probably hate me for it.

I need to talk to the priest, he thought, and try to get myself out of this. What was I thinking? Why did I say I'd go along with it? He was about to get up from the table when Roisin brought out a huge bowl of potatoes boiled in their skins, and a wooden plate loaded with cabbage and a hefty piece of gammon The wonderful smell of the food brought Liam back and he forgot his thoughts completely. He was ravenous.

Roisin watched him eating for a moment, then said,

'I saw the light on in the rectory all last night and into the early morning. You and Father Grogan must have had a lot to say to each other.' Liam stopped eating abruptly and looked up at her.

'Did my name come up, at all?' she flirted. Liam looked puzzled. 'Oh, never mind,' she said, exasperated. 'Eat your food before it gets cold and, if you want another beer, just shout.'

With that, Roisin left the room and Liam was alone again. He ate in silent thought.

Roisin was engrossed in thought too. She had looked out from the door of Hogan's several times last night and had seen the faint glow of a candle coming from inside the rectory. What could the carpenter and the priest possibly have to talk about all night, she wondered. That Liam Flynn doesn't seem to have much to say for himself and the priest is normally in bed long before the door of Hogan's is locked. Her curiosity was aroused and so were her suspicions. A hundred questions flooded her mind, with a thousand possible answers to them. Perhaps the raggedy man isn't what he appears to be, she thought. Perhaps the guise of a simple carpenter is some kind of deceit, and his business here in Gortalocca is something entirely different ... perhaps even sinister.

Roisin Hogan, she scolded herself, you have no time for such girlish fancies. She tucked a stray curl of blonde hair back behind her ear and began vigorously scrubbing a cooking pot.

CHAPTER 13

W hen he had finished eating, Liam waited. He needed to pay for the food and ale but, more importantly, he wanted to see Roisin again.

Michael Hogan appeared from the back room and greeted Liam. When he asked if everything had been to Liam's satisfaction and Liam had nodded the affirmative, Michael asked him for a penny. Liam was disappointed, but he had to get back to the rectory, so he walked outside and lit his pipe.

He stood and puffed at the pipe for a few minutes, debating whether he should go back inside on the off chance that Roisin had returned to the bar. He noticed three men walking down the lane towards him ... a large young man, a little mousey-looking one and a thick man of average height. They were engaged in animated conversation, laughing and carousing.

As they drew nearer, Liam recognised them as the blaggards who had robbed him on Friday evening. A wave of anger swept over him. When the three men reached Hogan's, they walked right past Liam and into the bar, paying him no heed at all. Liam guessed they had been too drunk that night to remember what he looked like. He was unlikely to forget them in a hurry and his head began to throb again, as his rage heightened. He would even the score with these lowlife, but not with all three at once, that would be suicide. He began to walk back to the rectory.

Father Grogan returned a few minutes after Liam and closed the upper half of the door. Before Liam could speak, the big old priest began.

'I haven't given you any details about my plan yet but, now that I'm sure you can be trusted, I will.'

Liam stammered, 'Ah Father, I ... I wanted to talk to you about that.'

'You're afraid, I can see that,' said Father Grogan, 'and you've every right to be. Let me ask you something, Liam. Do you know the difference between courage and bravery?'

Liam didn't answer but just shook his head, bewildered with all the intrigue.

'Courage comes from pure blind faith, Liam, there are no questions. Whatever your cause, you believe that right will prevail. Bravery, on the other hand, is when you are scared half-blind, and you know that the possibility of failure is real, and that you will pay the consequences. There is more grace in being brave than in being courageous, because you face your fears to overcome your doubts. Do you understand, my son?'

Liam still looked uneasy, 'I just know that all this is very new and confusing for me, not to mention terrifying,' he said. 'I'm not sure if I can even pull off this farce, let alone keep it up for very long.'

The old man smiled sympathetically, 'I'm an old man but I certainly don't want to die and you're only a young man, being asked to risk your life for people you don't even know. That's asking a huge amount from you, I know that, but I need your decision, Liam. Time is closing in on us, more than most people know.'

Liam returned the old priest's direct gaze for a moment. He was still confused, and he had better get it clear in his head if the plan was to succeed 'Tell me exactly what's expected of me, Father,' he said, 'I'll do my best.'

Father Grogan retold the story of how he had spent his youth in England and how the same thing that had already happened there, was about to happen in Ireland too. 'The crown will confiscate Catholic held land and sell it to her loyal subjects,' he said. 'It's a political and economic move, wrapped in the guise of religion.' He told Liam how some prominent families in England still secretly practiced their faith, but that their numbers had dwindled. He said that, by law, the lands owned by Irish Catholics here in Ireland already belonged to the crown, even though the small farmers didn't know it yet. Now, the crown wanted the money from all this land and property, and so it needed to get them onto the tax rolls.

The old priest explained that Liam's role in the plan was to purchase the land from Harold Johnson and approach him about becoming a member of the Church of Ireland. Johnson was a deacon in the church and had even built his own church on Johnson property, just west of Gortalocca. That part Liam understood. Maybe it would be wiser for him to do this one step at a time, without too many details in his head to confuse him.

'Tomorrow morning, Liam, you will go to the solicitor's office and pick up your papers. You will approach him with the prospect of buying more land directly from the crown.'

Liam interrupted, 'But I haven't got enough money

to buy all the farms,' he protested, 'I've already spent half my savings just buying that one piece of Johnson's land.'

'No, you don't understand. Like I said, the English government wants the land on their tax rolls, so that they can demand taxes from those who will be renting their own land. You'll be able to buy it for just pennies an acre.'

'But I'm after paying four pounds for just ten acres,' Liam protested.

'But you bought it from a middleman, Liam. Johnson is the middleman. He made the profit. Now do you see?'

It was as if a candle had been lit inside Liam's mind. 'So I buy the land from Johnson and become a member of his church,' he said. 'That puts me in his good graces and that, in turn, allows me 'a foot in the door. I understand, Father.'

The old priest smiled and poured them a flagon of beer each. The two men again talked late into the night, going over the plan again and again until Liam truly believed he could actually pull off the sham.

When the priest had satisfied himself that Liam fully comprehended the plan, that he was aware of his own role in it, and conscious of the potential consequences it brought with it, he moved over to Liam and placed his hand on his head.

'Let me give you absolution, my son, because you will be living a lie from now on.' The old priest began to speak in Latin, 'Absolvito…..' Liam bowed his head.

CHAPTER 14

Liam's logic was simple and so he needed to put everything in a context that he understood. He was, after all, just a carpenter. In his world, the first thing would be to draw the plans. That had been done. The next job would be to find the trees needed. In this case, that meant finding the right people and that was done too. Now, the trees must be turned into usable wood. He smiled to himself, that's exactly what the canny old cleric had already done to him. If all went well, he could perhaps save the village of Gortalocca. If not, at least his hanging would provide entertainment for the people of Nenagh, and his head would provide food for the crows when it was mounted over the castle gate. He shuddered at the thought of rooks pecking at his lifeless eyes.

Liam dressed in his old clothes because he didn't want his new ones soiled. He hoisted the pack containing the shoes and waistcoat onto his shoulders, ready to head back to Nenagh. He had nowhere to put the new hat so he put it back on his head. Liam knew exactly what he had to do.

A flock of sheep, driven by a young lad, blocked the

road in front of the rectory. As Liam waited for them to pass, a man came over to him.

'Ya must be Liam Flynn, d' carpenter,' the man said, and grinned. He was only in his mid-thirties but his grin was toothless. 'I'm Ben Clancy,' he said. 'I raise sheep here in Gortalocca … an' children.' Clancy chuckled at his own joke.

'Father Grogan was at me house fer dinner last night and told us about ya. And Shevlin was talkin' about ya dis mornin', too, but he knew nutt'n, sure' Liam gave the man a slight smile and, encouraged by it, Clancy gestured towards the boy driving the sheep.

'Dat's me eldest, Jamie. He's an eejit. He'll learn nutt'n about farming and knows precious little about anyt'ing else."

Liam found himself staring at Clancy's toothless gums as he talked. Clancy noticed and covered his mouth with his hand, self-consciously. 'Yu'll be wonderin' where me teeth went,' he said. 'Well, I'll tell ya. A few years back dere, a couple o' me lambs went missin'. I confronted d' man I knew was t' blame … dat blaggard, Sean Reilly, and his two toadies. For me trouble, he swiped me round d' head wit dat auld stick he always carries an' didn't he knock me front teeth out.'

Liam's hand went involuntarily to his forehead where he'd been clouted on Friday night and his action wasn't lost on Clancy.

'Looks like ya had a bit of a run-in wit' dem sods yerself, lad. Am I right?'

'A tall, good-looking one, a stout one and a ratty little bastard?' asked Liam, thinking back to his encounter with them last evening outside Hogan's.

'Da very same,' replied Clancy, 'Watch yer arse wit' dose t'ree, lad.'

'I will indeed,' said Liam, 'and I thank you for the information.'

'G'd luck,' said Clancy. He touched the brim of his cap and went after the flock.

Liam felt the wave of anger return. Sean Reilly, he thought. If I catch him alone and I have me hammer, I'll pound him like a nail and leave his mammy keening over his grave.

Liam waited until the sheep were at last driven through an open gate by a pair of collies, watching how expertly the dogs worked together and, for a moment or two, he forgot about the task he had to perform. Clancy looked back and gave a wave of his hand. Liam returned it and began his walk into Nenagh. The landmarks came more quickly today and the walk seemed shorter somehow. Liam pondered on how the same journey on the same road could sometimes seem shorter, sometimes longer. Often, he thought, he would get somewhere and couldn't even remember how he had covered the distance. This was one of those mornings.

Liam made his way straight to the tailor's shop to change his clothes. The little man seemed genuinely pleased to see him.

'Da top o' d' marnin' to ya, Mr. Flynn,' he said.

'And the rest o' the day to yerself, sir,' replied Liam, grinning.

'Dat's a grand fine hat you have on your head there,' said the tailor. Liam rolled his eyes upward as if to see the hat on his own head and doffed it formally.

'You getting the hang of it, Mr. Flynn. Clothes decide the man. Talkin' about clothes, fer tuppence, I've a serviceable shirt an' a pair o' trousers dat should fit ya. Den we c'n take dose rags ya have on and toss dem on da fire.

Liam looked down at his clothes and, as painful as it was to part with a penny, he said, 'Let me see them, so. If they'll do me, I'll give you a penny farthing.'

The little tailor went through to the back of the shop and brought out a linen shirt, well mended and a pair of heavy twill trousers. 'Tuppence,' he said, 'an' not a farthing less.'

Liam agreed without any further attempts at bargaining ... he may have to make use of the little fellow yet. Remember, he told himself, keep your foot in the door.

Liam tried on the new garments and had to admit, they were a vast improvement. He took them off again and dressed himself in the formal clothes he had bought the previous day. He played back in his mind everything the priest had told him.

'Most importantly, look people straight in the eye,' Grogan had said. 'A gentleman never averts his gaze.'

Foot in the door, thought Liam, clothes decide the man, look people straight in the eye. What else? Oh yes, never laugh at your own jokes. He had so much to remember but, if he was to transform himself from a humble tradesman to a gentleman and pull off this charade, he was going to have to give it a try.

When he was dressed, the tailor held up a mirror and Liam inspected himself. The little man smiled and nodded with approval, until he came to the necktie.

'Liam,' he said. 'You don't mind if I call you Liam, do you?'

'No, sir.'

'That's another thing, lad. Stop calling subordinates Sir. I don't know what you're up to and I don't want to know but, whatever it is, you're going to have to learn to tie a proper cravat.' The tailor shook his head and re-tied the necktie, before seeing Liam out of the door.

Liam made his way to the solicitor's office and, as he did so, he wondered just how bad a conspirator he was. In a matter of minutes, the tailor had worked out that something was not as it seemed. If a tailor could work it out, what of the lawyer and Harold Johnson. Liam was beginning to doubt himself.

Edward Wall had been awaiting Liam's arrival. He was sitting behind his desk with his wig on straight and his feet on the floor. He had the papers waiting.

'Ah, here you are, Mr. Flynn,' he said. 'These just need your signature and that of Mr. Johnson and then it will take but a few hours to get them registered by the clerk, in the courthouse.' Liam decided the time was right to entice this fellow into a trap. The prospect of financial gain would be the bait. Liam began,

'It is my understanding that Catholics cannot own land in Ireland,' he said. 'Am I right?'

The lawyer narrowed his eyes and leaned forward. 'That is correct, sir.'

'Then the land around Gortalocca belongs to the crown,' Liam said, more as a statement than a question.

'That is so, indeed,' he replied, 'except for the holdings of Mr. Johnson himself and those farms owned by the Butlers.' Liam stood silently for a moment, giving time for his comments to sink in to the solicitor. Liam could almost hear the sound of cogs clunking into place inside the lawyer's mind.

'Sit down, Mr. Flynn,' he said. 'I think we may have some business to discuss.' The lawyer went to the door, opened it and looked in both directions, then closed and locked it. Liam felt as if he had just landed the biggest fish of his life. Edward Wall took his seat again. 'What kind of arrangement do you have in mind?' he asked.

Liam felt he had said enough for now. He told the solicitor he needed to work out a few more details and, if he decided his proposal was viable, he would be back tomorrow. The young lawyer opened his appointment book and pretended to check if he had any spare time the next day. Liam could see that the pages were empty.

Edward Wall was thinking too. This could be his chance to show his successful Dublin father that he was not a buffoon, nor was he the eejit that his parent assumed him to be. From the time he had been a lowly clerk in his father's offices, he had been able to do nothing right. His father found fault with everything Edward did until finally, after having had enough of it, he struck out on his own in Nenagh. Even that, his father thought, was preposterous. Why in God's name would someone leave a thriving family business in Dublin to go and practice in some provincial market town in North Tipperary?

Liam stood and forced himself to look straight into the solicitor's eyes. 'Until tomorrow, then. I shall call late morning. I bid you good day, Mr. Wall.' He extended his hand to the lawyer who almost shook it off his arm. Edward Wall had decided that he was going to hitch his wagon to this horse and the sky was the limit.

As Liam stepped back out onto the street and closed the door behind him, he thought he heard a muffled 'Hooray' come from inside. He felt a slight pang of conscience. It was going to get a lot dirtier before this was over. As he headed back to the tailor's shop to get changed out of his formal clothes, the Angelus bell heralded noon. After this, he would go and get the tools he had left at Ma Daley's inn and hike back to Gortalocca.

*

Roisin had woken that morning in the foulest of moods. That accursed Sean Reilly had spent the previous evening in the bar with his two cohorts. At least he didn't touch her but he had ordered her around as if she was his personal maid. He had even implicated that there was some sort of 'understanding' between the two of them.

Roisin had grown up in Gortalocca and had watched Sean as he grew from boy to man. He had been a spoiled brat of a child and had grown up to be the irresponsible, violent man that everyone expected him to be. For Sean Reilly to assume anything concerning Roisin was just another example of his conceit. While he was undoubtedly physically attractive, tall and strong and handsome, his shortcomings outweighed any physical attraction she might have otherwise felt or any 'understanding', let alone marriage. He would doubtless be the kind of husband who would beat his wife if dinner was late or if there was a dirty spot on the floor. Roisin would far rather be a spinster, any day, than marry a man such as Sean Reilly.

Michael Hogan joined Roisin and immediately detected her mood. He would try to placate his daughter because, if Roisin wasn't happy today, then she would make sure he would not enjoy the day either.

'Things could be worse, Macushla,' he offered.

'How?' Roisin had expected a weak answer but it was thinner than she had even imagined.

'Weeelll,' he drew out his response as long as he could to give himself time to think how things could be worse. 'He could be poor ... or ugly. Sure he could even be a Protestant like Flynn, the new fellow in town.'

Roisin turned and faced her father, putting her hands on her hips. Michael winced because he knew she was going to fire a broadside and all he could do was wait. 'You mean Liam?' she accused. 'Well, he had enough money to buy Johnson's land, didn't he? And he can't be a Protestant because he and Father Grogan are tight, and as far as his looks go, well ...' It was Roisin's turn to stall for time and it deepened her mood further 'Well, he's quiet, and he's polite!'

Michael decided he had better find something to do elsewhere because he was afraid Roisin hadn't finished picking his bones yet. 'I have to check the weight of the ale firkins to see if I need to get some more,' he said, heading off behind the bar.

'You do that!' she snarled after him.

Roisin swept the hot coals off the top of a big covered iron pot that had been resting in the fireplace. She swung the crane out from over the fire with a hook that stood next to it and used the same hook to remove the lid. In the pot were four large round loaves of soda bread, the tops of which were a rich golden brown and speckled with flour. The aroma of fresh bread reached across the room to where Michael was acting busy at back of the bar. He opened his mouth to say something, then closed it when he saw his daughter's expression. Roisin took out three of the loaves, placed them on the table and covered them with a damp cloth to prevent the crusts from getting too hard. She wrapped the remaining loaf in another cloth and, without a word, walked out the door.

Roisin needed someone to talk to other than her father. She had already decided who it would be and set off down the lane, away from the church. Father Grogan hadn't been a possibility because he was her confessor and, anyway, it was female company she needed now. She had thought of Clancy's wife but had decided against it. She was little more than a brood mare and just as empty-headed. Anyway, with all those children running around, she scarcely had time to draw breath, let alone chat. Roisin had decided she would go and speak with Moira. Although most considered the old crone to be a witch, Roisin respected her non-judgmental attitude and her wise words. This wouldn't be the first time Roisin had visited Moira but it had been a long time since she had done so.

She walked the mile or so south from Hogan's and turned off the main road into a patch of woods. The path followed a dark tree tunnel for a while, the floor of which was packed as hard as paving stones from centuries of footsteps. The trees seemed to embrace her. It felt cool out of the sun and she pulled her shawl tighter around her shoulders. At the end of the path stood a tiny mud cottage. Its thatch was covered in plants and foliage and it seemed to be simply part of the forest.

Roisin hadn't even reached the closed door of the little cabin when she heard a frail voice from within.

'Come on in, child,' came Moira's voice. 'It has been a long time since you came to see me.' Roisin pushed open the tiny door and ducked inside. Moira was sitting on a chair beside a tiny table and had herself covered with a shabby woollen blanket.

'How did you …?'

'My eyes might be failing me but my ears have made up for it,' she smiled a toothless smile and added, 'My nose works good too. Is that loaf you're carrying for me?' Roisin put the bread down on the little table and, as her eyes grew used to the darkness of the tiny cabin, she could see herbs of every kind hanging in bundles from the rafters, drying. 'No one visits me unless there's a reason, child. What can I do to help you?'

'I wish I had brought you some meat to have with the bread,' said Roisin.

The old crone shook her head. 'No, dear. I don't eat creatures of any kind.'

Roisin was puzzled. 'You mean you don't eat meat?' she said incredulously.

'We're all God's creatures,' said the old woman, 'and I wouldn't think of eating you now, would I?' Roisin thought this kind of talk had to be blasphemy of some kind and the hag sensed it. 'Father Grogan understands, and if he understands then, certainly, God must do too.' Roisin shrugged her shoulders. This was all beyond her comprehension. 'You wanted to talk to me about something, child.'

Roisin always felt as if this old woman knew what was in her head before she even said it. Did she really have the wisdom of the old ones?

Moira answered the unspoken question. 'I have a little of the wisdom, yes, but I'm getting old, very old and soon that knowledge will be lost, until either someone finds it or God creates another heaven and earth. Now tell me what's troubling you, my dear.'

Roisin couldn't help but be a little fearful and in awe of this tiny ancient woman, yet she sat with her in the gloom of the tiny cabin, and she poured out all her deepest and innermost hopes and fears.

CHAPTER 15

'I want you to write a letter to Harold Johnson, Liam.' said Father Grogan, 'It must be formal and well-written. I can compose it, but my handwriting isn't any good these days. How's yours? You can write, can't you?'

'O'course,' said Liam, indignantly, 'I can read and I can write, but my writing looks like chicken scratchings.' The priest thought for a moment, then his eyes brightened.

'I think I have the solution,' he said. 'After all, it's only a letter and it in no way implicates either one of us in any sort of scheme.'

Liam waited. Formal letter writing seemed a trivial point, he thought. Surely, he could just walk to Johnson's house and present him with the papers and with his payment for the land.

'Go and see Roisin.' Father Grogan gave Liam a wry grin. 'That shouldn't be too difficult for you. Tell her I need her to write something for me. She has a beautiful hand, and she's written letters for me before, so being asked won't arouse her suspicions. Liam was lost in thought … she has a beautiful hand indeed, and beautiful eyes and a beau…… The priest's voice interrupted his trail of thought, 'Now, Liam, go and ask her right now. The sooner, the better.'

Liam walked the short distance to Hogan's, rehearsing what he would say, and he realised he was talking out loud. He had spoken to women before, of course, but always about whatever work he was doing for the household or about whatever business he was conducting and there had been no more to it than that. This was different. How will I word it, he wondered. He realised that, however well he played it over in his mind, Roisin would somehow unhorse him.

When he entered Hogan's, she had her back to the door, bending over a cooking pot. She's busy, he thought, maybe he'd come back later.

'I'll be with you in a second,' she said, without looking round. She stood up and turned to face Liam. Her hair was tied back but a few errant strands of her golden hair had fallen forward over her face. Liam felt his knees go weak and his guts turn to jelly. She smiled. 'Ah, it's you Liam. What can I do for you?' She brushed the stray hair off her face with the back of her hand and took a better look at the young man. 'I see you've shed your rags and some of that Tipperary dirt. You're looking grand, sure.'

Liam looked at her beautiful grey eyes and completely forgot the speech he had been rehearsing. 'I….emmm… that is to say, Father Grogan says would you write something for him?'

'Can't you write?'

Liam hauled himself up to his full height and thrust out his chin. 'I can write … just not very well.'

'Oh, you're a man of letters, so?' Roisin grinned. This wasn't going at all the way Liam had planned.

'Tell him I'll be there in five minutes,' Roisin turned back to her cooking pot and Liam left Hogan's without a word. He heard her laugh as he closed the door. He didn't care. He loved the sound of her laughter and it didn't matter that it was him she was laughing at. Outside, he put his pipe in his mouth and thought about going back in to get a light for it from the fire. Maybe if he waited and smoked for a while, he could walk with her to the rectory. But he didn't have the nerve to go back in, so he stood outside dumbly and re-played the scene over in his mind, only this time his conversation had been sparkling and witty and Roisin had been dazzled by his charm.

The door opened abruptly, crashing in on Liam's perfect scenario. Roisin looked up at him, surprised that he was still there. She had wrapped a woollen shawl around her and Liam noticed it was the same grey-green as her eyes. As had become usual, Roisin spoke first,

'Ah, a gentleman to escort the lady.' She smiled easily at Liam, examining him at close quarters for the first time. His eyes weren't blue like she had thought, at least not the grey-blue that most people have. They were *blue*! She noticed his hair was cut and washed and that it was light brown with just a hint of red. His face was chiseled, with angles everywhere except for his nose which was just a little on the pug side. He wasn't bad looking at all really, she thought. Not her 'type' of course but not too bad. Liam returned her smile with a rare one of his own.

'You ought to smile more often, Liam Flynn,' she said. 'It suits you.'

'I smile when I have reason to.'

'And what reason do you have now?' Roisin found herself flirting.

Liam panicked. 'Nothin',' he said. He blushed and looked down at the ground.

Mortified at his own pathetic attempts at any kind of conversation with Roisin, Liam set off for the rectory and she immediately fell almost into his stride alongside him. He wasn't at all surprised that he had made a complete fool of himself with her yet again. And after all, what could he expect this beautiful young woman to see in an unsophisticated bumpkin like him? But it didn't matter. For these few minutes at least, they were walking alone together, side by side, and that was enough for him. He was to remember it for the rest of his life.

Liam's hand accidentally brushed against Roisin's. 'Sorry,' he said. He was blushing again.

Roisin looked at Liam and felt something for this ordinary fellow. She couldn't explain it … a warmth, perhaps. She smiled. 'It's alright.' He could still feel the touch of her hand.

Liam opened the door of the rectory and stood back, allowing Roisin to enter first. No one had done that for her before and she was taken aback by his manners. She responded with a slight bow.

'Why thank you, kind sir,' she said. Liam cursed the flush that rose again to his face.

Father Grogan had set up the little table as a desk with paper, a quill and a pot of ink, as well as a blotter.

'Ah Rosin, my dear. Thank you for coming. I have a little task I would like you to do.'

'Of course, Father.'

'I need you to write a letter on behalf of this gentleman.' He nodded towards Liam and Roisin turned her attention to him too. She gave Liam a puzzled look, then turned back to the old cleric who ushered her into the chair in front of the writing implements. She sat down and looked at Liam again, as the priest handed her the quill. She dipped it in the ink.

'I need you to write a letter to Mr. Harold Johnson for the final transaction of a land purchase,' said the old fellow. 'I'll dictate it and you'll write it.' Roisin dabbed the quill on the blotter and Father Grogan began to dictate.

"Dear Sir, I request your presence at a mutually agreeable place, to complete the transaction for the land which I inspected on Monday. I wish the transaction to be completed at your earliest possible convenience and I anticipate your swift reply. Sincerely, Liam Flynn."

Roisin wrote deftly and, when the letter was finished, Father Grogan read it over. He smiled with satisfaction and winked at Liam.

'It has begun,' he said.

Roisin walked back slowly to Hogan's with her head spinning. What was going on? Just who was this new fellow? What had he and the priest concocted? This young man had the manners of a gentleman. Was he just disguised as a simple carpenter? Nonsense, girl, she scolded herself. This is Gortalocca. No intrigue ever happens here in this tiny village, or indeed anything remotely interesting. There must be a simple explanation, she thought. But her mind was racing and she was almost bursting with curiosity.

'I have one more errand for you, Liam,' said Father Grogan. 'Run over to Clancy's house and tell him I need Jamie over here as soon as possible.' Liam remembered Ben Clancy from his earlier encounter with him and did as he was instructed.

When Liam got to Clancy's, he found a young boy of around eleven years watching some of his younger brothers and sisters. He assumed this must be Jamie and he transmitted the old priest's instructions to him. Jamie was more than happy to be relieved of his duty and burst out of the house, running in the direction of the rectory. Liam followed at a slower pace.

The old priest handed the letter to the boy and told him to deliver it to the Johnson house and that he was to wait for a reply. He said if he was quick about it, Liam would give him a farthing. The boy's face lit up with delight and he immediately bolted out the door and ran the two miles to the 'big house'. In an hour he was back with a reply. It stated, tersely,

"Tomorrow morning. Nine o'clock at Hogan's."

CHAPTER 16

Liam woke early the next morning although, surprisingly, he had slept well. He walked around to the back of the church and filled a bucket of water from the large barrel that was kept topped up from the holy well. The priest had given him his own bit of soap and he cleaned himself as best he could. He lathered up his face and shaved. The water was cold and the razor stung, but he wanted to present as good an appearance as possible. He ran his hand through his hair repeatedly, trying to beat it into submission and make it lie down. It was a waste of time.

When Liam returned to the rectory, the old priest was sitting at the table, his face serious. 'This is your last chance to change your mind and get yourself out of this, my son,' he said.

'Too late, I'm going ahead with it.'

The priest smiled and clapped his hands together. 'Then get your party clothes on. I only wish I could be there to witness the meeting myself.'

Liam winked at him. 'Don't worry, Father, I'll tell you everything.'

'You'd better,' said the priest and returned the wink.

Liam unwrapped his formal clothes and laid them on Grogan's bed. He put on his undergarments and then the shirt. He pulled the trousers on, making sure his shirt tails were tucked in tightly and, after four attempts, he finally managed to knot the necktie the way the tailor had shown him. He put on his boots, those murderous boots that pinched his toes together and hurt like hell. Finally, he buttoned his waistcoat and he was almost ready. The old priest gave a low whistle and Liam blushed.

'Well, you would have me fooled,' said the priest. 'Now put the hat on.' Liam put it on and the old man tilted it a little for him.

'That's better,' he laughed 'just a little jaunty. Wait here until you see Johnson's coach arrive. You don't want to appear too eager. Now take off the hat and don't sit down, you'll wrinkle the trousers.'

While Liam was waiting, he counted out the exact amount of money and put it in a leather purse which Father Grogan had loaned him for the occasion. Three pounds and five shillings, he counted it several more times. The priest had been sitting at the window, watching for Johnson's arrival.

'It's time, Liam, he's here. Go and put on the performance of your life.'

Liam put the hat on and set off for Hogan's. In his hand he held the leather purse and the papers the solicitor had given him. He had almost forgotten about Edward Wall. No doubt he's sitting on tacks waiting for me to turn up, he thought. Tomorrow would be soon enough. He needed to discuss that part of the plan with the priest first.

Harold Johnson was sitting in his carriage waiting, when the gentleman approached. He hadn't wanted to appear too anxious either. As Liam got nearer, Johnson's mouth dropped open involuntarily as he recognised him. He stepped down from the carriage and Liam ignored his stupefied expression.

'Good day, sir,' said Liam. 'We have some business to conduct.' Johnson was still agape when they walked into Hogan's. His brain was racing. He's better dressed than I am, he thought. He's no carpenter. Was it a sham?

Roisin and her father nodded their greetings to Johnson. They only saw the attire of the other man and assumed he was either a friend of Johnson's or some wayfaring gentleman who had stopped by their humble establishment for refreshment.

Roisin recognised Liam as soon as he spoke. 'May we occupy one of your tables,' he had addressed Michael Hogan. 'We have business to attend to.'

Michael was speechless and just motioned to an empty table. Liam placed his hat and the papers on the table.

Now, he addressed Johnson. 'When I have your signature, sir, I shall give you your money and, if you are agreeable, perhaps we can partake of a beer to consummate the deal.' Liam was pleased with this little speech and hoped that Roisin had heard him speak eloquently. He thought perhaps he could have been an actor, and been rich and famous in Dublin.

Harold Johnson felt foolish and thought he had completely underestimated the young man. Occasionally the younger son of a lower level aristocratic family was sent to become a tradesman. It wasn't common practice but it did happen. He imagined this must be the case here.

'If I had realised you were a gentleman, Mr. Flynn, I would have sent my carriage for you and we could have done this in my library. I heard you are staying with that Papist in his hovel up the lane. What could a gentleman such as yourself possibly have in common with an old Papist?'

'It is true, sir,' said Liam. 'I am indeed staying with Father Grogan in the rectory. And you might be surprised at the conversations we have.' He was incensed at Johnson's insult to his benefactor and felt his ears burning, a sure sign of his annoyance, but he gathered himself.

'I'm sure you would be much more comfortable in one of my bedrooms at Johnson House.' said the old fellow.

Liam had no doubt he would be. 'Thank you, but I have promised Father Grogan that I will do a job for him and I will see it through,' he replied, 'but I appreciate your consideration.'

'If you take my advice, Mr. Flynn, you won't waste your time with work for that church. That property will be confiscated by the crown sooner than later.' Liam winced. He had thought that perhaps the priest had been exaggerating the gravity of the Penal Laws.

'My thanks again for your concern, Mr. Johnson. Perhaps we can talk when you have more time.' This was Liam's way of dismissing the old gentleman.

Johnson stood, shook hands with Liam and said, 'Yes, of course. I am a busy man but I would enjoy your company one evening up at Johnson House for supper in more congenial surroundings.'

Liam thought the old codger was full of shite but smiled politely. 'Yes,' he agreed. 'And perhaps we can discuss you having a new member in the Church of Ireland.'

Pleased with this prospect, the old fellow bid Liam

'Good day' and left Hogan's. Liam heard his carriage turn and head back in the direction of Johnson House.

He remained at the table, he felt he needed something stronger than weak beer to steady his nerves. Roisin brought him a small cup and a saltware jug of whiskey. Instead of just setting it down in front of Liam, she sat opposite him in the recently vacated seat. Michael Hogan stood behind the bar, watching. Roisin leaned forward to within inches of Liam's face, so close he could feel her breath as she spoke quietly.

'What has begun, Liam' she asked.

Liam looked over towards her father, then back at Roisin. He laughed nervously. 'What are you talking about, woman?'

Roisin shot a glare at her father and, reluctantly, he left the room to the two young people. 'Yesterday afternoon,' she said, 'when I had finished writing the letter, Father Grogan said that it had begun. What has begun, Liam?' He looked into her grey eyes and furrowed his brow. She was beautiful. For a moment, he didn't know how to answer her, so he gulped down the whiskey. It burned his throat so that he couldn't speak, even if he wanted to. Roisin refilled his cup from the jug without taking her eyes off his.

Liam had reverted back to the simple carpenter and looked down at the table. 'It's dangerous,' he mumbled.

Roisin was exasperated. She had a hundred questions but, if she wasn't careful, she would get no answers. Liam drank just a sip of the poteen this time. Part of him wanted to run away and another part of him wanted to stay with this lovely girl.

Roisin started off slowly. 'Are you a Protestant?'

He shook his head. 'I never said that.'

'You're Catholic, so.'

'I never said that either.' It was a re-enactment of the exchange he'd had with Ma Daley a few days earlier, but this time wouldn't be quite as easy.

He felt the liquor begin to loosen his composure. What was the point of being a hero if no one knew about it, he thought. Roisin sensed his guard was dropping and she picked up the jug to pour him more poteen, but he gulped down what was left in his cup and stood up.

'You know I'll find out sooner or later, Liam,' she told him.

'Not from me,' He smiled and headed towards the door. Outside in the sun, his head whirled a little as he walked back to the rectory. His new boots pinched his toes together and hurt like hell.

CHAPTER 17

Father Grogan had been waiting anxiously for Liam's return. 'Well, how was the performance?' he asked, excitedly.

'Let me at least get these infernal boots off.' Liam sat down, pulled off his shoes and rubbed his sore feet. The poteen had taken full effect now and he closed his eyes for a moment. 'Wait 'til I get out of this disguise.'

The priest didn't want to wait. 'At least say something,' he said.

Liam looked at him with a very serious expression. 'Something,' he said, smiling at himself.

'Now then, enough of your shenanigans, you young pup,' the priest said jovially. 'Did Johnson buy into the act or not?'

'Oh, he did indeed,' said Liam. 'He even invited me to come and stay at the big house with him. He doesn't think a gentleman like me should be staying here with an auld Papist.' Liam laughed out loud. It wasn't very funny but the whiskey had made it funnier.

The curate rubbed his hands together, delighted with the result. Then his face took on a look of concern. 'But you won't go, will you? You'll stay here.'

Liam laughed again, 'Hmmmm, let me think. I can either sleep on the floor here, and eat simple food, or I can sleep up at the big house, in a feather bed, and have a servant bring my meals to me. Hmmmm, it's a difficult decision, to be sure.' Even the priest managed a smile at the comparison.

'Oh, I suppose I'll stay put,' said Liam. 'At least there's never a dull moment.' He took off his formal clothes, folded them and put them neatly away, for the time being. He put on his work clothes. I need to build something, he thought.

Liam decided he would start building the church pews he had promised Father Grogan. He had noticed a small copse of trees growing on the land at the back of the church, and now he walked around it to make sure it wasn't part of a faery ring. It wouldn't do to upset any supernatural beings, especially now.

He found an oak that looked like it had been recently struck by lightning. It wasn't too dry yet to cut and split, nor too wet to work, not perfect but it would do. Pine would be easier to work, but oak would last longer. He went back to his tool box and got out his felling axe. The tree was about two and a half feet in diameter and would take a while to cut. Liam swung the axe and felt the sharp blade bite into the hard wood. A change in angle and, on the second blow, a neat wedge-shaped chip flew out. He enlarged the cut and, in less than half an hour, he was ready to cut from the other side. It felt good to stretch his muscles and even better to be doing something he loved to do.

After Liam had been chopping for about an hour, the

tree began to creak, as the cuts made it unstable. A few more swings of the axe and the creaks became louder and more frequent. The tree fell slowly at first, then picked up speed as it dropped to the ground. As he looked down at it, Liam couldn't help but feel a little sad. This monarch had stood proudly for two hundred years or more, and now it lay uselessly prone on the ground. Liam blessed himself and he didn't know why. Perhaps it was the effects of the drink making him sentimental. After all, a farmer doesn't feel sad when he harvests wheat, or when he kills a pig. Surely this was the same thing. But he had a great respect for trees and he looked down at the fallen giant.

'You'll not be forgotten,' he said out loud. 'I will make you into a thing of beauty that will outlast any memory of me or of my kind.'

The ancient tree had already begun to split as it had fallen, and Liam knew this would make it easier to rend, when it came time to riving the trunk, and making it into boards, with wooden wedges. Now, he set about trimming the branches off. It took the rest of the afternoon. He had one more task to perform tomorrow and that was to see the solicitor. After that, he could shed the pretenses and go back to being a carpenter, at least for a while.

Liam returned to the rectory, sweating and tired from the afternoon's work. The sun was already getting low and a rumble in his belly reminded him that he had eaten nothing all day. The old priest was at prayers and Liam was too hungry to wait for him to return, so he washed himself in the bucket at the back of the rectory, and brushed the wood chips off his clothing. He would visit Hogan's for a bite to eat.

He looked at his hands, they were rough and

calloused. If either Johnson or the lawyer had been observant, they would have noticed that these were not the hands of a gentleman. He opened and closed his fingers and thought how good it was to be back working, and not have to tread so lightly. He would be glad when all this was finished and he could be himself again. In the meantime, he had to be careful. One miscalculation and he could be as dead as that oak, perhaps quartered too, just as he intended to do with the tree. He shuddered at the thought and tried to block it from his mind. Perhaps seeing the beautiful Hogan girl would give him something more pleasant to think about.

Liam trudged over to Hogan's. Paddy Shevlin was at the bar and had already downed two or three beers. He was in his chips because he had sold two pigs today in Nenagh. Liam was glad to be in the dark coolness of the pub.

Paddy ushered him over. 'C'mere, let me buy ya a beer,' he offered cheerfully. 'or if what auld Hogan here says is right, maybe it's you who should be buyin' me one.' Liam looked up and saw that Michael was embarrassed. Paddy was grinning because he had just heard the best gossip since Sean Reilly had been read out in Mass on Sunday. Liam knew well how the gossip mill worked. A little information was passed on and, by the time it was retold several times, it had become a full length book. Liam was embarrassed too and he hadn't even sat down yet.

'Thanks, Paddy, but my belly thinks my throat's been cut. After I've had something to eat, maybe I can buy you a beer then.'

Paddy was delighted at the prospect that someone else might be paying for his beer. 'Can I have one on account, da ya t'ink? On account o'me t'urst is chokin' me.' Shevlin roared with laughter at his own joke and Liam laughed too. He didn't know if he was laughing with Paddy or at him, but it didn't matter.

Roisin had been in the living quarters but she'd heard Paddy and Liam's voices and came through to the bar.

'Paddy Shevlin,' she threatened, picking up a large jug from the counter. 'If you tell that old chestnut of a joke one more time, I might have to brain ya with this jug!'

'It was a new one for me,' said Liam, still smiling at the pig farmer.

'Agh sure, if he's told it once, he's told it a thousand times,' she replied.

'On account it's true,' laughed Shevlin, delighted at the success of his earlier joke. Roisin held the jug up higher.

'Shut'cher gob, Paddy Shevlin, or I swear…'

Just then, Clancy came in and Paddy Shevlin was grateful for the interruption. Clancy looked despondent.

'What's eat'n ya, Ben?' asked Shevlin, concerned. Clancy shook his head.

'Agh, sure I have too many sheep t' winter over on me land,' he said. 'I'm goin' t' have t' sell some and d' price of mutton is fierce bad. Come spring, I can shear d' sheep an' sell some lambs but I don't know if I c'n make enough t' feed me brood 'til den.'

Liam had begun to dig in to a pile of bacon and potatoes that Roisin had placed in front of him. His mouth was full and he struggled to swallow it. He couldn't wait to get his words out so he managed to speak around the food in his full mouth without spitting too much of it out,

'Why don't you use my land?' he spluttered.

Clancy looked with disbelief at the man who sat at

118

the table in the gloom of the bar. 'Sure, I don't even know ya,' he said. 'Do ya mean fer nutt'n?'

Liam swallowed the rest of his food so he could speak clearer. 'You get nothing for nothing in this world, Mr. Clancy,' replied Liam with a smile.

Clancy's face fell. 'I've no money t' give ya. I might have a little around Christmas, you know, when folks like t' buy a piece o' mutton fer d' Holiday dinner, but ...'

'Did I ask you for money?' said Liam, still smiling. 'You can keep your Christmas money for your children. All I'll ask from you in return is a favour.' Clancy looked wary. 'I need to build myself somewhere to live,' continued Liam. 'just a small cottage, about twelve by sixteen foot with a door facing east and a back door and window on the west side.'

There was silence for a moment. Shevlin was no longer the centre of attention and his nose was out of joint so he chimed in,

'Sure, dat's no problem to d' likes of us, is it Clancy? We can use me horse and wagon to haul d' stones, and me family were t'atchers, so I know d' craft and I still have me tools.'

And so it was settled.

This is how things should be done, thought Liam. No solicitors, no play-acting or dressing up in costume. Just a spoken, but solid, agreement between honest working men.

CHAPTER 18

The next morning was cold and blustery, with more than a suspicion of rain. The wind had veered to the northwest and that meant the weather would come all the way to Tipperary from the North Atlantic. Even though it was still only August, albeit late in the month, the summer was dying and a chill wind blew in from the ocean.

Liam would go into Nenagh today. He had told the solicitor he would return and his word was his bond. Again, he would make the journey in his work clothes and change in the tailor's shop. He set out early in an attempt to try and beat the coming rain. He had got as far as Knigh Cross when he heard the sound of a horse's hooves on the gravel and dirt road. He turned and, once again, Shevlin was coming towards him in his wagon. In the back, two fat pigs were hog-tied, their four feet bound together. They squealed in unison as if aware of what fate was about to befall them.

'Mornin', Liam, can I int'rest ya in a lift ta Nenagh?' Liam hopped on board before the horse could stop.

After a brief silence, Paddy began to speak, bluntly and to the point. 'So how did ya come by yer fortune, lad?'

Liam was amused by the candour of the fat man. He was sure that, after the events of yesterday, the rumour mills of Gortalocca would have been churning out a myriad of speculative flights of fancy. This, at least, was an opportunity to put the record straight.

'I came by it honestly, Paddy, and by no small stroke of luck,' he replied, as frank with his answer as Shevlin had been with his question. 'I worked for years for a master who had no living family. He was Italian ... an artist in wood.'

Shevlin interrupted him 'And what might an Eye-talian be doin' here in Ireland?'

'Ah, that's a whole other story, Paddy, and nothing to do with this one. Let me finish. He was a frugal man, not inclined to drink except for the occasional bottle of wine, and not disposed to spend his money on material things. He was no friend of the Church, nor any other church for that matter. He believed in wood and he believed in his craft.'

Paddy interrupted again, 'Like I believe in me pigs.' Liam scowled at him and Paddy shut up.

'A few months back, he died and I was at a loss as to where my future lay. A solicitor came around to find me and brought a note from my master. The note told me to follow my dream and buy my piece of land. He had left me all his worldly possessions and almost eight pounds. I had already saved another pound myself.'

Shevlin made a low whistle, 'Yer a rich man, so,' he said. Liam shrugged his shoulders. By this time, they were just coming into Nenagh and Liam thanked Paddy for the ride and asked him to let him off.

'But I wanted t' hear d' story of how dat Eye-talian got toTipperary,' squealed Paddy, joining in with his hogs. Liam smiled and told him that would have to wait for another day.

It had begun to rain in earnest as Liam opened the door to the tailor's. He didn't relish the idea of getting his good clothes wet.

The little man was happy to see him. 'Howaya, Liam. Isn't it lovely weather for ducks? I have something grand to show you, today.' The little fellow spoke with such enthusiasm and rubbed his hands together with such glee that Liam's curiosity was aroused. But he wasn't going to buy any more clothing today, at any cost. The tailor brought out what looked like a walking stick covered in some sort of cloth.

'What is it?'

'It's called a portable roof. It's the absolute latest thing in London!' The tailor could barely restrain his excitement.

'What's it for?'

'To keep the rain off, o'course!' With that, he reached under the cloth, pushed something and the whole thing opened out into a square, tent-like shape. 'You hold it over your head and it keeps you dry. See?'

'That's ridiculous,' scoffed Liam, 'Now, wouldn't I look like a right horse's arse walking around under that thing.' He peered closely, he loved any kind of contraption. 'Give it here, I want to see how it works.' Liam examined it and saw that it had a little catch at the bottom and the top of the stick, and strips of whalebone to hold the cloth tight. Ingenious, he thought, as he opened and closed it a few times. Perhaps he should give this new curiosity a try. It would be better than getting wet, at least.

'Let me try it out,' he said, 'and maybe I'll purchase one.'

'The absolute latest thing in London,' repeated the tailor, thrilled at his success. 'Invented in China.'

'It must rain fierce in China,' replied Liam, 'if they had to invent a portable roof.'

He changed into his dress clothes and the little man handed him the stick as he walked out the door. Out on the rainy street, Liam opened it and, to his surprise, it worked quite well. The market was crowded. Everyone gave him a wide berth and pointed at him. Liam felt like a celebrity.

He arrived at the solicitor's office and didn't think to close the device until after he was inside, struggling to get it through the doorway. Edward Wall looked at it with alarm.

'It's the absolute latest thing in London,' Liam told him. 'Invented in China.' The young solicitor didn't want Liam to think him ignorant of London's latest fashions or to convey any lack of sophistication so he acted as though he was quite familiar with the peculiar stick, although he could barely take his eyes off the contraption.

Liam had already set the trap for Edward Wall and now he was going to spring it. The solicitor shifted forward in his seat as Liam stated his business.

'I want you to find out if the crown owns all the land in the township of Gortalocca, apart from the piece Johnson just sold to me.' The solicitor nodded that he understood. 'I want to know what price they want per acre to get it on their tax roles.'

A smile broke out on the barristers face. 'And then you evict the farmers, is that it?'

'No.' Liam shook his head. 'No. Landlords don't get

anywhere near as much productivity out of their land as they should, because a hired man is only going to do enough work to keep him from getting sacked. Now, if a man has a financial interest in his work, he will be much more productive.'

'Go on,' the lawyer was interested.

'If a man can make a living for himself and his family, he'll be happy, and a happy worker is the one who will put in the extra hours and the extra effort to make the land more productive.' Liam let the lawyer consider what he had said.

'It sounds revolutionary,' he said, finally.

'No,' smiled Liam. 'It sounds like profitability.'

'Do you need a partner?' blurted the solicitor.

'It's an experiment,' lied Liam. 'Before I take on a partner, I want to be certain that he's not risking anything.' In the meantime, Liam thought, I'm risking my neck.

'I fully understand, Mr. Flynn, and I thank you for your candour.' Liam stood and, as he was about to leave, the lawyer asked, 'It may take me a few weeks to get the information you need. Where can I send it to?'

'Send it to me personally, by care of Hogan's in Gortalocca.' Liam bid the man 'Good day,' and, once outside, opened the portable roof to protect his clothes from what had now turned into a downpour. He made his way back to the tailor's shop and changed back into his ordinary clothes before heading home.

Paddy was just coming out of a bar on Castle Street and shouted a greeting. They both boarded Paddy's cart and started back to Gortalocca, with Paddy opening the conversation.

'Didn't I see a gen'leman walkin' down Castle Street today, carryin' a tent over 'is head. Well, you never saw anyt'ing like it. Sure he looked like a horse's arse.'

Liam laughed out loud. 'He must have been English,' he replied.

CHAPTER 19

I t was early afternoon when Liam arrived back at the rectory and he was surprised to find Roisin there. She was sitting at the little table with the priest and her face broke into a smile when she saw him. His heart skipped a beat.

'How did your meeting with the solicitor go?' asked Father Grogan.

Liam was hesitant to answer in front of the girl and just said, 'It went well.' He unpacked his dress clothes. The trousers were wet, especially around the bottoms.

'You can't put those away wet, Liam,' said Roisin. 'Give them to me and I'll iron them dry.' The old priest advised Liam to do as Roisin said because Mrs. Gleeson, the sacristan, would likely scorch them if the job was left to her. Liam handed the trousers to Roisin.

'And the shirt and waistcoat, Liam,' she said authoritatively, holding her hand out. Liam looked at the priest, then back to Roisin and meekly handed the rest of his clothes to her.

'Well, gentlemen,' she stood up. 'I'll leave you two

alone with your conspiracy. I have a leg of lamb I'm roasting today. I'll save some of it and bring it over for you both this evening.' With that, she left and closed the open door behind her.

Liam smelled the odour of poteen on the priest's breath. 'What does she know?' he demanded. 'What did you tell her, old man? You'll get us both hanged and her in the workhouse.'

Father Grogan put up his hand to quieten Liam. 'Calm yourself, my son. She came over a couple of hours ago to confess her sins and, while she was here, she asked about your background. You're quite a curiosity around here, you know.'

The priest's answer had not satisfied Liam. 'So is it your usual habit to hear confession, drink whiskey, and make a confession in return?'

'Ease yourself, Liam, ease yourself. Roisin is nobody's fool. She already knew there was something going on, call it woman's intuition or something of that nature. I only explained to her that what her eyes and ears were telling her, wasn't what it seemed, and that she would have to trust our judgment.' Liam was still anxious. It was one thing for him and the priest to risk their necks, but an entirely different affair to involve someone else, especially Roisin.

Liam couldn't shake off his annoyance. He knew that strong drink could loosen the tongue and that was the second time Roisin had mentioned the word 'conspiracy.' He decided work was the only thing that would calm him and so he went outside in the cold rain, taking deep breaths of the chilled air. He went to his chest of tools and removed a wooden maul and a saw. He would cut the branches off the old oak and leave himself with the bare trunk, use the heavy wooden maul to pound wedges in, and split the mighty trunk into boards which he could move by himself. He hoped the exercise would soothe his anger. He pounded the first wedge into the split at the base of the trunk. There was a tearing sound as the split travelled up the body of the old tree. He placed a second wedge into the new end of the crack and repeated the process. In an hour, the trunk was opened like a book, each semi-circular half laying side-by-side. He fetched his felling axe and finished cutting the hinge and the two halves fell free of one another. All his anger was now directed towards the task at hand. I can still get out of this and just look after myself, he thought, then dismissed it. He had given his word. He would have to play this scheme out until its conclusion. He thought about old Shevlin and Clancy and the others and how tragic it would be for them to be thrown off the land that they and their families had worked for generations, and his anger now turned towards those who had made these unjust laws.

Liam worked on, repeating the splitting process and, by the time the sky had taken on a peachy colour in the west, he had three boards, about 20 feet long, 2 feet wide and about 3 inches thick. The almost green wood was still too heavy to move on his own but if he cut the boards in half, he might be able to drag them. He carried his tools back to the church, where he had left the toolbox. He wasn't angry any more, he was hungry.

The old priest sat waiting for Liam in the rectory. Liam regretted accusing him earlier and tried to apologise. The old priest stopped him and said that he understood and that it was he who should apologise to Liam. He admitted that he had indeed drunk too much whiskey and that he didn't really didn't remember how much he had told Roisin.

Liam's uneasiness returned. 'I'll have to find out, so, from Roisin herself,' he said. The priest lowered his head in shame and Liam shook his in disgust. He decided that any words he spoke now would be bitter ones and so he had better hold his tongue.

Roisin returned to the rectory just after Vespers, as she had promised. She smiled at Liam and placed a sack on the table and told the two men it contained the lamb and some roast potatoes too. Father Grogan thanked her. Liam had still not spoken to the priest and Roisin sensed the tension between them. She looked from one to the other.

'Leave the food alone until I get back,' Liam said coldly to the old fellow, then spoke to Roisin in a similar tone. 'We need to talk, away from this magpie.' He cast a withering glance at the priest and opened the rectory door, allowing Roisin to exit first. He followed her into the churchyard and, when they had walked out of earshot of the cottage, he asked tersely, 'What did he tell you?'

Roisin told Liam what had transpired earlier. She tried to mitigate the priest's involvement and blamed herself for plying the old man with the poteen. Liam was furious. Grogan had told her everything and now Roisin was as deeply involved and they were.

'You must give me your oath,' he told Roisin, 'You must swear to Almighty God that, no matter what happens, you won't tell anyone what you know, not even your father.' Roisin looked at him. He was looking directly into her eyes and, this time, he didn't look down or away but held her gaze, waiting for her response. She took his hand in hers to let him know she understood and she swore her secrecy.

'Now, tell me about these new laws, Liam.' she said.

'They're not new,' explained Liam. 'They have been

around for some time, but they're only now starting to be enforced.'

'And is it true that no one owns their land anymore?' He nodded and her eyes moistened. 'What are we going to do, Liam?'

He felt something stir inside his chest. This strong young woman was now just a little girl and he wanted to protect her. 'There's nothing you can do,' he said. 'It's up to me now and I may have to trade my immortal soul for a bit of land.' Roisin felt a wave of sympathy for the young carpenter who carried the burden of saving her village on his shoulders. Liam felt only the warmth of his hand in hers.

'What do you intend to do?'

Liam smiled inscrutably and there was no humour in it. 'Whatever I have to do, Roisin.' he said. 'Lie, cheat, anything it takes to keep the land.'

Only when they had returned to the door of the cottage did Roisin loosen her grip on Liam's hand. The priest sat staring hungrily at the sack of food.

Liam feigned a smile. 'Let's eat,' he said. The priest said grace hurriedly over the food. He was as hungry as Liam, but that's not all.

'You didn't happen to bring a drop of refreshment, my dear?' he asked.

Liam scowled at him once again. 'I think you've had enough *refreshment*for one day,' he reproached Grogan … saying to himself …and done enough blathering to last you a month.

'No more strong drink for the old man,' he told Roisin. 'He's a little too honest for my own good.'

Father Grogan stopped eating and looked at Liam, 'I have known more than my share of fasting and abstinence in my life, Liam, and I will do it again.' Liam smiled a genuine smile at the priest and thought that perhaps this was a lesson for them both. Stay away from liquor.

Roisin said she was needed in the bar and that she hoped they would enjoy their meal. She bade 'Goodnight' to the priest and shot a smile at Liam. He thought he saw her wink, but wasn't sure. They ate their meal in silence and Father Grogan assumed the young man was still angry with him, but Liam was thinking about Roisin.

At last Liam broke the silence. 'Don't you want to know what happened at the solicitor's today?'

'Oh, yes indeed. So tell me, is he in on the deal?'

'No. He suggested I evict the farmers.'

The priest swallowed a mouthful of lamb, 'That won't do at all.'

'He's one of them. But I think I talked myself out of it and gave him a reasonable explanation. We can use his own greed and arrogance against him.' Liam reminded himself that, although it had been easy to fool the gentry so far, he had better be careful not to get too arrogant himself.

'How will you deal with Johnson?' asked the priest.

'I will attend services in his chapel every Sunday and, to all intents and purposes, become an upstanding member of the Church of Ireland.'

The priest blessed himself. 'Don't get yourself too lost in this fiction, my son.'

Liam smiled a crocodile smile, 'You don't have to worry about me, . I'm the least lost sheep in your flock.'

CHAPTER 20

I t was Saturday and Liam thought it was about time he took a look at his land, to decide on the best place to build his cottage. He wanted it both near to the road and close to the holy well, so that he would have a water source nearby. He walked a little way down the street until he was in sight of Hogan's on the other side of the lane. This was an ideal spot for him to live, he decided.

He had brought with him four wooden stakes, each about three feet long, and a ball of twine. He pounded a stake into the ground with a two pound maul. This would be the southeast corner of the cottage. He stepped off five paces and hammered in another stake. This would be the northeast corner. The front of the cottage would be about four paces from the edge of the road. He walked off 4 paces west, placed a stake in the ground and measured off five more steps. This was to be the perimeter of the little cottage that he would call home. Sixteen feet by twelve, with space enough for a bed and table with two chairs, and compact enough for a man to heat comfortably. The fireplace would go on the north wall. Liam closed his eyes and conjured up the image of a whitewashed thatched cottage with two doors. The doors would each be made up of two half-doors, so that the top half could be left open for ventilation if the weather was warm. In his daydream, a certain blonde-haired girl was standing in the open doorway, smiling her smile, and welcoming him back from his work. He snapped himself out of his reverie just as Ben Clancy walked up to him with his eldest son, Jamie, in tow. Clancy greeted Liam cordially and asked if he was thinking of starting to build.

'I have a basic idea,' Liam told him, 'but I have to get a 'story stick' to check the plan for square.' His jargon was wasted on Ben Clancy but Liam noticed that Jamie was hanging on his every word.

'I'll leave this lazy dreamer with ya, so, and when it comes time to put up da walls, give me a shout.'

Jamie seemed relieved when his father left. 'I don't think you're lazy, boyo,' Liam said, 'or dim either.'

Jamie looked at him shyly. 'I can t'ink,' he said quietly, 'and I t'ink dat I don't want to spend me life raisin' sheep.'

Liam softened his demeanor and said, as a father would to his son, 'How *do* want to make your living, so?'

The boy beamed now and replied enthusiastically, 'I want to be a carpenter, Mr. Flynn, just like you.'

Liam smiled broadly in spite of himself. 'Why?'

'Because then I can take a lump of wood and turn it into something beautiful and useful.' It was the right answer. Liam put his hand on the boy's head and ruffled his hair, just as an Italian carpenter had once done to him. Liam told Jamie that the task here was done for now. The boy looked disappointed and turned to leave.

'Hold your horses, boy! Where do you think you're going?' The boy stopped and looked at Liam questioningly. 'Aren't you after saying you want to be a carpenter?' The boy nodded eagerly. 'Well let's go and do some carpentry, so.' Jamie tried, in vain, to fall into

Liam's stride as they walked back to the rectory, gushing with exuberance and asking an endless array of questions. 'Whisht, boyo,' said Liam good-naturedly. 'You'll get your answers as we work.' The carpenter's head whirled, as much with the boy's questions as with all that had happened in one single week. Now, it looked like he even had himself an apprentice.

When they got back to the felled oak, the boy was about to resume his tirade of questions when Liam held up his hand. 'I will do the talking, Jamie, you will do the listening.' The boy fell silent. 'First, I have to make sure I have enough wood for the job. You go and get me my mallet, the wedges and the felling axe.' The boy looked at him dumbly. Of course, thought Liam, the kid doesn't have a clue what I'm talking about. 'C'mon,' he said, 'Let's go and get the tools we need.' The boy raced off ahead of him like one of his father's lambs, turning back to make sure Liam was catching up. He wondered if the youngster would be as enthusiastic after a day of carpentry. Liam picked out the tools he needed and handed them to Jamie; he told the boy he would show him how they worked. Jamie grinned and examined the simple tools with awe.

They needed to rive one more plank from the oak. Liam repeated what he had done the day before, only this time, the child's energy had rubbed off on him and he did it in about a half an hour. Four rough planks lay on the ground. They were inspecting their labour when Roisin walked up.

'Slackers!' she joked, 'Maybe I should take this bread and cheese to the old priest. He'll know what to do with it.' She handed the sack to Jamie. He opened it and was about to dig in when she interrupted,

'Emmmm ... isn't it customary for the master to eat

his fill first and leave the crumbs to the apprentice?'

Liam joined in the feigned reprimand. 'That's right,' he said. 'Crumbs only, for the apprentice.' The boy looked disheartened and Liam ruffled his hair again. 'There's enough there for two, no bother,' he said, 'or perhaps even three?' He looked at Roisin.

'Thanks, but I have to be getting back to the store to lay on some victuals for the customers. There might even be some left over for a pair of working men later.' She smiled at Jamie, who was looking adoringly at her, and then at Liam. This time, her wink was unmistakable.

As soon as Roisin had left, the young man and the boy dived into the bread and cheese. Liam ate sparingly but Jamie ate as if he had a tapeworm.

'It's time to get back to work, lad,' announced Liam, when the apprentice's last crumbs had indeed gone. The boy would like to have taken a nap, but he was going to do as he was told. Liam explained that the planks had to be made into boards, about as long as a man is tall.

Jamie asked in a sincere voice, 'A tall man or a short man?' Liam laughed. He measured the length and showed Jamie how to saw one, then measured the next and told the boy to do it himself. It was painful to just stand and watch, but the boy would only learn by doing it alone. The process went on until all the boards were cut. They were heavy because the wood was still a little green and the water content added weight. Liam got on one end and Jamie the other, and, one by one, they walked the planks to the church and stacked them inside, out of the weather.

'Well, I think we've done a good day's labour,' said Liam, 'We'll both sleep soundly tonight.'

'What about supper?' enquired the boy, his eyes wide with expectation.

Liam had completely forgotten the invitation that Roisin had offered. 'Ah yes, my boyo. Let's get washed up and get some food in our bellies.'

They walked to Hogan's together, the boy and the man. Before they even got to the door, they could hear the clamour of men talking loudly. Liam opened the door and ushered Jamie inside. He followed and there, sitting at a table, was Sean Reilly with his cohorts, Fergus and Seamus. The trio grew momentarily silent, then Sean spoke up,

'Will ya look, lads.' He pointed at Jamie, 'Da carpenter brought a sheep in wit' 'im. No sheep allowed.' The three of them laughed raucously. Jamie was terrified of Sean Reilly and he hid behind Liam.

'The boy did a man's work today,' said Liam, sharply, 'so he goes where I go.'

Sean stopped laughing and glared at Liam, 'I've seen ya before,' he said, suspiciously. 'Where do I know ya from?' The atmosphere in the bar changed and the three shifted forward in their seats. Liam reached out and took a clay pitcher from the bar. If there was going to be trouble he'd make sure that Sean would be the first one to hit the ground. The move wasn't wasted on Sean and he was not about to have his Saturday evening ruined by a clay pot to his face. He turned back to the table, relaxed in his chair and went about conversing with his gang. Liam sat at the bar with Jamie, but he sat where he could keep an eye on the blaggards and he kept the pitcher handy.

Roisin brought Liam and Jamie a plate of bacon and potatoes each, and they ate in silence. Liam offered a farthing to her for the meal but she waved him off and said, 'Ah, sure you're my guests this time.'

Sean overheard and he growled venomously at

Roisin, 'Yer guests, is it? I'm d' best customer in dis shit-hole and I've never been yer guest!' Roisin hadn't expected the verbal assault and she looked at Sean in surprise. Liam grabbed the handle of the jug again, and turned to face the three.

'It may be time for you to leave,' Roisin said quietly to Sean.

He got up, followed by his two lackeys, but before he left, he held Liam's gaze for an uncomfortably long time. 'Dis ain't over,' he said, 'not by a long chalk.'

When they had gone, Roisin asked, 'Why did Sean say he thought he knew you from somewhere?'

Liam's fingers went to the stitches in his forehead and he looked down at Jamie. 'It's time you got yourself back home, lad. I'll see you bright and early tomorrow morning.'

'Tomorra's Sunday, sure.'

'So it is. Well then, get yourself some rest and I'll see you the day after.' Jamie left the bar feeling delighted with himself. He had enjoyed working all day with the wood, he had eaten his fill and he had some grand gossip to tell his Mam and Da. His master had stood up to Sean and his gang and had run them out of the bar.

Three of the local famers filtered into the pub after the bully boys had departed. There was Conor McCormack, who had a little farm just west of Hogan's, where he lived with his wife and three children. He sometimes did work for Johnson when he needed day labour. He was average in height and build and in his mid-thirties, devout in his beliefs but he cursed like a trooper. Then there was Mick Sheridan, a big thick man. He looked every bit as strong as one of his horses and was as introverted as a man could be. He knew everything a man could know about horses and was in charge of Johnson's stables. The third was Paul Gleeson, a quiet fellow who never gave a hint as to what he was thinking, and always seemed to be wrapped in thought. His family had lived and farmed hereabouts for as long as history. He made the local distilled spirits. The three had been waiting for the gangsters to leave the bar. They had all heard about Liam already but now they had a chance to meet him. Roisin made the introductions.

'Mac, you'll mind yer manners and curb that tongue o' yours,' she said, turning a serious face on McCormack.

'Not a bother,' he replied, 'I'll be as quiet as a feckin' mouse and as good as a feckin' saint.' Roisin laughed, as did everyone else, except Liam who was beginning to retreat back inside his shell with the attention of so many strangers. Clancy and Shevlin came in next and Liam felt a little more comfortable to see some familiar faces.

Clancy spoke to Liam, approvingly. 'Our Jamie told us ya chased Sean and 'is goons out o' dis place.' All eyes were on Liam now. He looked down and stayed silent. He could feel that flush coming to his face again.

Shevlin joined in, 'C'mon, Liam, give us d' story.'

Liam looked up, 'I didn't chase anyone anywhere, sure. It was Roisin who did it.'

Roisin stood up straight, folded her arms and scanned the small gathering of men. 'I did indeed,' she said, struggling to keep a straight face, 'and I'll be chasing out anyone else who steps out of line, make no mistake.'

McCormack piped up, 'It's d' truth, sure, she's t'rown me out on me ear on several feckin' occasions!'

'Yes, and I'm thinkin' about it right now, Conor McCormack.'

'I'll hold d' door fer ya,' said Gleeson and everyone laughed, even Liam.

'Ah c'mon, Liam,' implored Roisin. 'Give us a story.

Tell us how you came to get that embroidery in your forehead.'

'Yeah,' said Paddy Shevlin, 'I noticed dat too.'

Clancy jumped in, 'Noticed, me arse. Yer so busy runnin' off yer mouth 'bout dem pigs o'yours, ya wouldn't notice if a horse an' trap ran over ya.'

'Pigs is d' smartest animals in d' world,' said Shevlin indignantly.

'We're not talking about pigs or sheep or even the weather tonight,' said Roisin. 'Liam's going to regale us with how he got those stiches. Isn't, that right Liam.' There came that wink again.

Liam told the story of what had happened on the road to Nenagh a week before. The locals interrupted him from time to time with stories of their own, and they embellished Liam's tale too.

So it was in Gortalocca. The unvarnished truth never got in the way of a good story. Liam wondered at how getting conked on the head could so quickly become such a heroic tale.

'D' fox outsmarted d' wolves,' exclaimed Paddy Shevlin with delight, and pounded Liam on the back.

'Yer a lucky one.' said Mick Sheridan. The bar went silent because Mick hardly ever spoke and so, when he did, it was an occasion. 'Remember last year when dey found dat travellin' salesman's body near Knigh Cross.' Everyone nodded in agreement.

Paddy took up the story and ran with it. 'Bejayzus, wasn't he only after stoppin' in here fer a beer just d' night before. A nice enough fella, sure. Da very nex' mornin', dey found 'is body in a hedgerow wit 'is head all bashed in.' There was more nodding and everyone agreed it was a terrible thing, even if he was a stranger. Liam was beginning to think they were right and that he had indeed been lucky to get away with his life. It was a good thing he had a thick skull. He was also beginning to think that maybe this Reilly fellow wasn't just a thief and a bandit but a murdering one to boot.

His thoughts were interrupted by Clancy. 'Watch yer arse, Liam. Sooner 'r later dat sod, Sean'll be tryin' ya on fer size an' ya can be sure dat he'll have dem two nose-pickers wit him.' Liam looked at Clancy with his front teeth knocked out and supposed that he should knew what he was talking about.

Michael Hogan had been absent most of the evening, most assumed he was taking a nap before he retired for the evening. He came into the bar from the back.

'Dis place needs a little music,' he said, 'an' I just recently heard a new song.' Everyone turned to the landlord and waited, eagerly, for him to start. This was how evenings in Hogan's usually ended. 'D' name o' d' song is Whiskey in D' Jar.'

Paddy smiled approvingly, 'Sounds like a good one t' me,' he said. Everyone nodded in agreement and listened to Michael's rendition, waiting for the chorus so they could join in.

Liam drained the last of the beer from his tankard, stood up and bid everyone a 'Good evening'. Paddy thanked him for the story, as did the others, and Liam left them singing in the bar. He walked back to the rectory, keenly aware of his surroundings. Clancy's words of warning had not been wasted on him. He would carry a weapon of some sort with him at all times from now on.

CHAPTER 21

F ather Grogan was up and out of bed early. He was getting ready for Sunday Mass and was sitting at the table with a candle, writing a homily. It was his practice to write his sermon at the last minute and keep it short and sweet. He knew his congregation didn't have time for long drawn-out sermons because, even though it was Sunday and, supposedly, a day of rest, the farmers could not afford to take a day off and farm wives never rested. He looked down at Liam who was snoring in front of the now barely glowing turf fire and wished he too could sleep a little longer. He thought back to when he was Liam's age, when he was full of the Holy Spirit and would save men's souls. That was many years and many disappointments ago and now he was about to commit treason, maybe even go to hell, in order to keep his little congregation intact. Was it hubris and pride or was it simply the final sacrifice he could make before he died? He felt his age. His eyes were failing and his bones ached.

Liam roused himself. He sat up and stretched, yawning mightily. The priest asked if he would be at Mass and Liam gave an empty, mirthless laugh. He said that if he was to be a good Protestant and a member of the Church of Ireland, it was hardly the thing to be seen in a Papist church. The priest said he'd say a prayer for his soul and Liam agreed that it might be a good idea. He reminded the old man that, one day soon, the sheriff would come and close down the church and that he himself might even be arrested. Grogan nodded, solemnly. He was well aware that he too had become an outlaw.

Liam decided that Sabbath or not, he had work to do. He would make some shovel handles and then, perhaps tomorrow, get some shovel heads from the smith who had a shop next to the corn mill in Ballyartella. He would need a couple of them to dig out a trench for the foundation stones of his house. He also wanted to rough out a spoke for Shevlin's wagon. If Paddy was going to help him haul stones to build the walls of his cottage, he had better fix his wheels for him first. He pondered on how to replace the spoke without having to rebuild the entire wheel. Wheelwrights could be expensive.

He was making his way back to the felled oak when Jamie appeared at his side. 'Where do you think you're going, boyo?' said Liam.

'I'm your apprentice. I go where you go.'

'Not today. Or at least not yet. Get yourself off to Mass first. Today, you're God's apprentice. Get away with you.'

Jamie was crestfallen and began to walk away slowly. Then he turned and said, gleefully, 'I'll say a prayer for you, so. That way I'm still helping.'

'You do that, my man. It'll be a big help.' Jamie ran back to the church beaming. The master was after calling him a man.

Liam had stripped so many branches off the old tree that it wasn't hard to find the ones he needed to fulfill both his criteria, straight grained and true. He sighted along each and chose the ones he wanted. It entered his head that he needed a walking stick too, or some other instrument of mayhem, on the off-chance that he had another run-in with that Reilly fellow. He gave it thought. Holly, the hardest wood he knew, as hard as bone, that would do the job nicely and he knew where he might find it. He passed the church, now filled to capacity with worshippers, and went down to the holy well. He hoped one of the branches might have fallen from the rag tree there.

Liam was not the first at the holy well. A small bent figure was there and, as he approached, he saw it was an old woman, an ancient woman. She was collecting water in an old leather pail. She addressed him in a frail, croaky voice.

'Ah, you're here,' she said, 'I've been waiting.' Liam thought she must have him confused with someone else. 'I didn't know it was you I was waiting for,' she explained, 'but I was on my way to Mass, and something told me it was more important to wait here.'

Liam thought the old woman must be a little soft in the head. 'Can I help you carry your load?' he asked kindly. She smiled a gummy grin and Liam thought how even her wrinkles had wrinkles. Her hair was thin and wispy and she had a dark shawl pulled around her.

'My name is Moira,' she said, 'and you're Liam. Most people hereabouts fear me. They think I'm a witch or some such thing, except when someone is ill, of course, then they call for me.'

Liam fought the temptation to bless himself. He remembered a story he had heard in Thurles about a man who practiced the old ways with herbs and potions. He had cured a man whom the physicians had said was dying and, for his troubles, had been rewarded by being burned at the stake for practicing the dark arts. One of the physicians who had attended the man was an elder in the church and had seen to it.

'Walk with me, young man.' Liam took the bucket from her hand and, without a second thought, he followed her. 'You're not afraid,' she said, 'that's good. I have no evil intentions towards any of God's creatures.'

Liam smiled and switched the bucket to his other hand so he could walk closer to her. 'Healing is a dangerous game, mother.'

She cackled. 'The game you are playing is a much more dangerous one, my dear.'

Liam stopped, he was dumbfounded, 'How ...? I mean what are you talking about?'

She cackled again. 'I see things as they are,' she said. 'The evidence is there for everyone else to see too but they are blinded by what they think they see.' Liam watched the old woman's face intently. 'Roisin told me some of it, and the old priest didn't tell me some of it, and I put it all together and, judging by your reaction, I'm right.'

Liam didn't know exactly what she knew or what she didn't know, but he said, 'You won't say anything, will you?'

'I know many people's secrets and they are all safe with me. People tell me things. Sure, I'm just mad old Moira, after all.'

The youthful man and the bent old woman made an unlikely pair as they walked in silence down the lane. After a while, they reached a little dirt path that led into the forest. The path became narrower as it reached further into the woods but Liam noticed wagon tracks. They weren't wide enough for a horse drawn vehicle but wide enough for a cart pulled by a man or a donkey. Old

Moira's eyes were growing dim and she saw through his.

'Gleeson buys the beer from me and distills it into poteen,' she said. 'He comes every two weeks to empty out my barrel. He gets a few pottles of good whiskey from it and a firkin of the bad shite. That's what the tracks you can see are. He walks his cart down this path.' Liam was astonished at how sharp this half-blind old woman was. She seemed completely in tune with her surroundings.

Moira's house was so much part of the woodland that Liam almost walked past it. The forest seemed to grow around it and through it. She opened the door and went inside without bending. Liam ducked in. The tiny house was strewn with all kinds of bottles and vials, mostly made of wood, although a few were clay, and there were cloth sacks of every size hanging from pegs on the walls.

Moira pointed to a chair and motioned for Liam to take a seat. She took a pottle, a clay jug that held about two quarts, and poured a generous amount of its contents into a clay cup. She handed it to Liam and filled another larger cup to the brim for herself. 'This is the good stuff,' she said 'Drink.' Liam took a sip. It was like liquid fire. It burned his throat and brought tears to his eyes. Moira took a big quaff of her own. 'Ahhhh,' she smacked her lips. 'It'll take da chill off our bones, lad.' Liam thought it a little early for the strong stuff.

'It's never too early for an Irishman,' she said. 'even one who plays games with the English.' Liam's face flushed and it wasn't from the poteen. This old woman knew too much and it un-nerved him.

'You'll be taking a bit back to Father now, won't you,' she said and grinned her toothless smile.

'He's abstaining,' Liam said sternly.

She gave out a cackle. 'Oh, yes indeed,' she chortled.

'It doesn't take much of the hard stuff to loosen someone's tongue.'

Liam stayed and talked with Moira for an hour or so and she shared her philosophy with him. It seemed to him a blend of the old ways and those of the Catholic Church. He told her he believed that much of the old wisdom had been lost, because of the dogmatic narrow-mindedness of the so-called Christians. She laughed and agreed, but warned him that he had better keep his blasphemy to himself or else he'd end up at odds with the old priest.

The old woman stood up and walked shakily towards the door. 'I have enjoyed your visit, Liam, and you are welcome back any time you feel like visiting a foolish old lady.'

Liam smiled at her. 'Foolish is the last word I would use to describe you, Moira.'

'Goodbye then, my son. And if you think I can be of help to you any time, just come and ask me.'

On his way back to the rectory, Liam stopped again at the rag tree. There, at the base, amidst the litter of twigs and remnants of cloth that had accumulated over the ages, was a broken branch from the holly tree. It was about three feet long and around two inches in diameter, with a burl at the end about five inches across. Liam hefted it and swung it. It would make an excellent cudgel, disguised as a walking stick. He imagined himself cracking Sean Reilly and his stooges across the shins with it … maybe even cracking a skull or two if needs be. Yes, this would be grand.

CHAPTER 22

L iam shaped the shovel handles from the felled oak and roughed out the spoke for Paddy's wagon, but he would need some measurements for that. He had already worked out exactly how he would fix the wheel, without having to rebuild the entire thing. He made his way over to Paddy Shevlin's cottage. Paddy greeted Liam heartily and replayed the entertainment from the night before. Liam didn't want to be reminded. The hangover he had awakened with that morning was reminder enough. He told Paddy he had come to fix the wheel on his wagon for him. Paddy didn't feel like doing any work that day but, grudgingly, he gave in because the younger man was unrelenting.

Paddy fetched a rusty wrench that would fit the nut on the wagon axle, still trying to dissuade Liam. 'Don't be botherin' yerself, it'll be grand. Sure, it's bin broke fer months.' Liam ignored him and steadfastly kept working until, finally, the nut broke loose and the wheel came off. Liam pushed the wheel down the road to the churchyard and hoisted it up onto the back of his cart. He wondered how in the name of the saints the wheel hadn't come apart long ago. He wiggled the two halves of the spoke loose, first the part with the tenon that fit into the mortice in the rim. With a little persuasion from his mallet, the axle end worked loose. He held the two pieces of the broken axle together and shaped a duplicate in fairly short order. He cut the new spoke in half with a fork in the axle half and a matching v-shape in the other, so that they fitted together perfectly. It felt good to be doing the work he loved. He coaxed the axle end into the hub and then the rim end. The v-shape splice worked, it was a dry fit. He separated the two and applied a generous amount of pitch to the splice, then whipped a piece of cord around the joint, tarring it with the pitch.

With the wheel repaired, he moved on to the shovel handles. He made quick work with the spokeshave and soon he had two smooth staves on which to mount the shovel heads.

Liam decided he had done enough work for now and that he would take a walk, to explore his new home. First, he would take the wheel back to Shevlin. As soon as he arrived, Paddy began in a serious low tone.

'I heard a rumour dat some folks' land 's bin confiscated, east o' Nenagh. Da families have bin turned out, and d'eir houses wrecked, to keep 'em from movin' back in.' Liam sought to take the conversation in another direction and asked Paddy to get some grease for the axle. Paddy returned with a bucket of pig fat.

'That'll be grand Paddy,' said Liam. He thought Shevlin looked older, the worry lines etched deeper into his face. 'Just put your weight on that lever and raise the wagon so I can get this wheel on.' Paddy did as Liam directed and the wagon lifted. Liam put the wheel on and put a few turns of the lug nut onto the axle, then tightened it on with the wrench. He was tempted to allay the man's fears by telling him about the plan, but instead he said, 'Don't you worry yourself, Paddy. Nobody's going to kick anyone out.'

Paddy thought the young man's optimism didn't make sense. 'But it's happenin' all over Ireland, sure,' he said. 'What's t' keep it from happenin' here?'

The wheel was finished and Liam tried to change the subject. 'There y'are Paddy. Now we can use your horse and wagon to gather stones to build me house.' Paddy didn't welcome the distraction.

'I'm old, lad, and I don't have any family to take care o' me. If the bastards evict me, I'll die.'

'You won't die, Paddy, at least not for a good while. You'll just have to take my word for it.'

'What about poor Clancy, too? He has a whole litter o' kids and he's a young man yet. What will become o' him?'

'They'll be grand too. Just trust me on this, Paddy.' Liam turned to walk away and Paddy called out to him.

'Wait. What do I owe ya fer d' wheel? Liam just smiled and raised his hand.

It had been going on in the east of Ireland and now the confiscations and evictions were happening here in North Tipperary too. Soon, there would be no land anywhere in the country that was owned by Irish Catholics. Liam pondered whether the Hand of God had something to do with his arrival here, although, in his experience, if God did indeed have a hand, then He only seemed to give the Irish the back of it. Liam's cynicism returned like a tidal wave. If there is a merciful God, how can He watch the misery and the suffering of poor people who are simply trying to wrest a living from a little piece of land? How can He watch as the rich and powerful become wealthier and more avaricious at the expense of those who have nothing?

Agh, I need to take a walk and clear my mind, he thought. He made his way towards Knigh Cross and he hadn't got far when Jamie appeared alongside him, like a silent shadow. Liam looked down at him, the youngster wore a troubled, tortured expression.

'Why the long face, boyo?' The lad's eyes had welled up and Liam thought he was going to cry. 'Buck up, Jamie. What is it? Is the family alright?' The child's tears began to flow then, and Liam felt his heart soften.

The boy's voice cracked as he told Liam about what he'd heard before Mass. 'Dey say we'll all be homeless and me Da will lose our sheep. Him and me Mam were already worried about d' Winter an' now, dey t'ink d' English are goin' t' take our land.' He hid his face in his hands.

'Don't worry, lad, everything will be grand,' said Liam gently.

Jamie wiped his running nose on his sleeve. 'That's what Father Grogan said in his sermon, but I don't know. Maybe God's punishing us for something we did. Father said we had to say a prayer for you, too. I suppose it must be because you missed Mass.'

Liam chuckled and tousled the boy's hair. 'No, boyo. I think he had another reason in mind.'

They walked together in silence the mile or so down to Knigh Cross. As they passed Knigh Castle's ruins, the boy told Liam that he'd heard it was built by some famous knight called Norman. Liam smiled.

The boy stopped and blessed himself, then pointed to a spot on the hedgerow alongside the road. 'Dat's where dey found d' travellin' man's body last year. I seen him. I seen dead people before but I never seen nutt'n like dat before. He was all twisted up, like, curled into a ball, an' 'is head was bashed in and dere was blood all over d' place.'

Liam looked around him in a moment of alarm. He had forgotten his holly stick and, if Sean and the duo appeared now, both he and the boy could end up in the bushes like the salesman. There was no-one in sight. Liam put his hand on the boy's shoulder. 'We've walked far enough, lad. Let's get back to Gortalocca.'

When they arrived back in the village, Liam sent Jamie home, reminding him that there was nothing to worry about. Then he set about turning the stick from the rag tree into a weapon. He narrowed down the handle, until it was just a little too small to get a firm grip, then he smoothed off the burl on the end of it, until it was about 3 inches in diameter. Next, he wrapped twine around the handle until it fit his hand. He swung it a few times. It looked innocent enough but, when used in the right hands, it would make a lethal weapon. Liam would make sure he carried it everywhere he went from now on.

He carried the stick with him into the rectory, where he found Father Grogan waiting for him.

'Things are happening fast, Liam, too fast for my liking. I might know more this afternoon when old Moira comes for our usual chat. She might have some news.' Liam told the priest about his own encounter with her that morning.

The priest smiled and shook his head, 'I swear that old woman has a gift for showing up at the right time. Sometimes, even I suspect she's a witch.'

'She's no witch,' said Liam, surprised at his defense of the old crone. The priest shrugged his shoulders.

As if on cue, they heard someone outside, shuffling towards the door in the gravel. Liam opened the door before the old lady could knock. She wasted no time.

'You have to get out of here, priest,' she rasped, breathlessly. 'Get what you need out of the church and come to my house. Don't tell a soul where you're going.' The priest looked at her, perplexed. 'They're coming to arrest you in the morning,' she told him. 'If they find you, they'll cut your thumbs off, so that you can't hold the Eucharist over your head during consecration. They might even torture you to recant your beliefs, and hang you for a heretic.'

The old priest was visibly shaken, 'But what about my congregation?' he asked, 'I can't just abandon them.'

Liam spoke now, 'When we find a safe place for you to hold Mass, we'll let them know.'

'I know a safe place,' said Moira, 'Now get your things together.' The old priest hurriedly packed his own few belongings into a sack. Then he went into the church to retrieve the chalice and a small altar stone, which held what were supposed to be the relics of some obscure saint.

CHAPTER 23

B y the time Liam woke, Monday morning had blown in, cold and raining. It was quiet in the rectory, the old priest having slipped away with Moira long after dark, so that no one would see them. At least I won't need to build the pews now, Liam thought.

He had to visit the blacksmith to get a couple of shovel heads so he washed himself and decided to get the errand done early. He threw a piece of canvas over himself to try and keep off some of the rain. He smiled when he thought of the portable roof contraption that he had used in Nenagh. Was that really only a short time ago? So much seemed to have happened since then.

He walked down to Knigh Cross, making a turn at the crossroads. He had walked for about half an hour when he saw the mill. He knew the smithy was right alongside it, on the Nenagh River. The mill wheel was turning. The first of the year's grain was being made into meal and would later be ground again to make flour. As he approached the mill, he could hear the familiar sound of bellows and the rhythmic clank of metal on metal from next door as the smith fabricated something out of iron.

Liam stood at the open door and saw that the blacksmith was making horseshoes, putting them into a small keg as he finished each one. Liam inhaled the familiar smell and it took him back in time to his Da's shop. He thought about Robert, his older brother, and he grew sad. Poor Robert, his bones in some unmarked grave in some unknown field.

'I'm busy.' The blacksmith had stopped his work and was staring at him.

'I need a couple of shovel heads making,'

'If ya want 'em in a hurry, make 'em yerself.' The smith went back to his work. Liam hadn't heard the sarcasm in the man's voice and he began to look around the smithy for some metal stock and a hammer.

'Whoa! What do ya t'ink yer doin'?' said the smith. Liam told the man his father had been a smith and that he himself had spent years watching, and later helping with the work. The fellow eyed him with scepticism, 'Lemme see yer work, den.' Liam proceeded to heat the iron in the forge, working the bellows until the metal had become bright yellow white. He grabbed the metal with a pair of tongs and began to work the metal thinner and into a rough shovel shape. He was hesitant at first. It had been many years since he had worked in iron, but it was satisfying to watch the metal changing shape with each blow. The metal was cooling and so he returned it to the forge. It was thinner now and heated back up more rapidly. Once again, he grabbed the work with tongs and returned it to the anvil, working what was to be a shovel. The process was repeated several more times and he switched from the heavy hammer to a lighter one, beginning a rhythmic, two taps on the anvil and one on the work.

The smith was impressed, 'Yer no stranger t' d' forge,'

he said, approvingly. 'A bit slow, mind, but ya know summt'n about d' iron, alright.'

'Ah, I've spent more than a few hours of me life making sparks,' Liam told him. The smith introduced himself and asked Liam about how he came to know the trade. Liam explained his background and the smith seemed satisfied. Matt O' Brien was not the stereotypical blacksmith. He wasn't big or burly, but he had the forearms of a man who had spent many hours at the anvil.

His demeanor towards Liam had changed now and he said, affably, 'Well, if ya ever get fed up o' workin' wood, I could always use a bit o' help around here. Ya could make dese horseshoes fer d' farrier, fer a start. It helps pay t' feed me kids but it's idiots work.' He handed Liam a leather apron to keep his clothes from burning, 'You go on wit' what yer doin' an'....,' he hesitated for a moment. 'No, I've a better idea. I'll finish d' shovels an' you can pound out some o' dese horseshoes. I'm goin' daft wit' doin' d' same auld thing all day.' That was alright with Liam and so he and O'Brien switched jobs. Making horseshoes was something entirely familiar to the carpenter. Whenever his father had been working on something more complicated, he had often put his young son to work, fabricating the iron that would grace a horse's hooves. It was a simple and uncomplicated process. The shovels were both finished in about 15 minutes but O'Brien was reluctant to see Liam leave.

'D'ese farmers haven't a clue what I do here,' he complained. 'Dey come in wit a broke plough, or dey wanna crane fer d' fireplace, an' den dey complain about d' prices!' Liam nodded. He understood. Everyone thought their time was more valuable than anyone else's. Liam felt a kinship with the smith. It was more than an appreciation of the other's craft, for Liam, it was a journey back to his father's shop and memories of the family that he missed.

The blacksmith's wife arrived with a sack of bread and cheese for her husband's midday meal. She had flaming red hair and the remains of what must once have been a beautiful figure. Liam thought that these two must have made a striking pair when they were young ... he, dark and handsome with blue eyes and she, with her flashing red hair and her green eyes. They weren't old, but they had aged beyond their years with hard work. In spite of that, they still presented a handsome couple. The smith gave his wife a kiss on the cheek and watched her leave.

'I don't know what I'd do wid'out her,' he said wistfully, almost to himself. He saw Liam smiling at him and became embarrassed. He cleared his throat. 'I'll only charge ya fer d' iron, Mr. Flynn. I've enjoyed d' visit an' ya c'n come back anytime, if yer not too occupied.' Liam handed the man tuppence for the iron and said he too had enjoyed sharing the company of a fellow yeoman. They shook hands and Liam felt the strength of the man's grip. 'If I hear o' any carpentry work, I'll get in touch wit ya in Gortalocca and, if ya hear of any smithin' t' be done, sure you know where to find me.' They bade each other good day and Liam headed back towards Gortalocca.

He had barely reached Knigh Cross when he saw three familiar figures heading his way. It was Sean Reilly with Seamus and Fergus. There was no way to avoid them and Liam was alone. His hands were full, a shovel head in each fist. Sean approached and the other two fanned out, exactly as they had done a fortnight before. This was bad. It was still early in the day and Liam knew they would be stone cold sober. It was easier to fight someone in their cups, because their reactions were slower and less calculated. Liam remembered the story about the travelling salesman.

Sean greeted Liam cordially and, for a brief instant, the carpenter thought this could be no more ominous than neighbouring villagers passing each other on the road. But the instant passed, he knew better. This would be a confrontation and, in a curious way, Liam welcomed it. However, this wasn't how he had hoped to even the score. Once again, it would be three against one.

Liam was no hero. He wasn't one of the courageous, daring champions from the old Irish legends. Indeed, he wished he was anywhere but here. But here he was, and things were about to come to boiling point. There was no escape and nowhere to run so he would just have to bluff it out or fight it out. He knew his chance of success was slight but he also knew that, tomorrow, all four of them would know they had been in a fight.

Sean switched the blackthorn stick he carried into his left hand. Liam knew his biggest danger was getting hit with that, it could be fatal for him. Sean wasn't thinking about his stick but about how satisfying it would be to knock the teeth out of this pipsqueak's head with his right fist. He could always crack his skull with the shillelagh afterwards. Sean was close now ... too close maybe, thought Liam, for the stick to be effective. He knew he was going to take a beating, hand to hand. Sean was wearing an evil grin and the weasel, Fergus, was goading him on.

Fergus was the first of the three to recognise the victim from the night they had stolen Liam's wagon, less than two weeks before. 'Hey! He's d' one what stole our cart!' he cried. A flash of recognition crossed Sean's face and his smile disappeared, his handsome face now contorted with hatred.

'Dis time, I'll kill ya,' he snarled. He closed his big right hand into a fist and let fly a mighty swing at Liam's face. Liam held his left hand up in front of his face to take some of the force from the punch. There was an almighty clang as Sean's fist slammed into the metal of the shovel head. He screamed in pain and doubled over, dropping the stick to grab his right hand with his left. Liam still had the metal shovel head in his left hand in front of him and hadn't seen any of it. Now, he heard movement behind him and swung his right hand blindly back. This time, the clang of metal on flesh made a more muffled sound. Liam turned and saw that he had hit Seamus square in the face and knocked him off his feet. He was holding his nose and blood had begun to flow from between his fingers. When rat-faced Fergus realised that this might come down to a one-on-one fight, he decided he wanted no part of it and tried to flee, tripping himself and falling flat on his face. As he tried to scramble up, Liam slammed the metal onto his head and Fergus fell back, this time lying motionless. The fight was over, and Liam hadn't even soiled his hands.

He left the three reprobates on the road, with Sean screaming that it hadn't been a fair fight, that his hand was surely broken and that he would kill Liam. Liam turned back. Only seconds before, Liam would have been happy just to take a beating. Now, either by chance or by an act of God, he was the victor. Sean was on his knees cradling his right hand, and he panicked when he saw Liam return. He reached out and tried to grab his stick but Liam stepped on it, knocking it from his grasp. There was a look of terror on Sean's face now. Now, he was faced with the same fear that he was happy to instill into others. Liam held the iron over his head as if wielding an axe and Sean began to sob. The carpenter looked down on him with disgust.

'I could kill you now, you piece of shite.'

The big man covered his eyes. He knew the day of retribution had come and that, with a single swing, his head would be crushed. He began to recite the Act of Contrition.

Liam slowly lowered his arm and looked at Sean's cowering body with loathing and revulsion. Then he turned and walked away. Sean Reilly had lost face in front of his gang. Liam's victory was complete.

CHAPTER 24

W hen Liam returned to the rectory, the rush of adrenalin still coursed through his veins. He knew he had to do some work, in an effort to try and calm himself. He set about putting handles on his shovels. It worked and, in no time, he had all but put the fracas out of his mind. He was getting hungry now, and he pondered on whether he should go over to Hogan's to eat his one meal of the day. The prospect of seeing Roisin's face, and hearing her voice, pleased him and he decided that's what he would do.

At the back of the church, Liam emptied the bucket of water and refilled it from the water barrel. He stripped to the waist and washed himself. When he put his shirt back on, he noticed it still smelled of the fire from the blacksmith's forge. The smell comforted him and, once again, it took his mind back to his youth. He saw his mother's face and his father's and those of his older brother and younger sister. It saddened him that, although he could remember their faces, he couldn't remember how their voices sounded. They're all dead now anyway, he thought, what does it matter? He thought that perhaps, if he was lucky, one day he would be a memory for someone. What would that matter, either? He would be dead too.

The carpenter made his way over to Hogan's and he was surprised at the spring in his step. Perhaps it was having settled the score with Reilly. He was pleased with himself and strode into the bar confidently, with his head held high. It was empty, apart from Roisin, and any confidence he'd had, evaporated at the sight of her.

'Sorry, Liam. I haven't prepared anything to eat tonight,' she told him. 'I have some bread and cheese, if that's any good to you.'

Liam looked down at his feet. 'Thank you, m'am, that'll be grand.' He sat himself down at a table and the girl brought a flagon and filled it. She returned a few minutes later with a half a loaf of brown bread and some hard yellow cheese. Having set them on the table, she went back through to the living quarters, leaving him alone in the bar. Liam was disappointed that she hadn't asked him what he'd been about, then realised that he hadn't asked her either. As if on cue, she reappeared in the doorway, drying her hands on her apron.

'So tell me, Liam, what have you been up to day?

He looked up from his food and hurriedly swallowed what he'd just stuffed into his mouth. 'I went to the blacksmith and got a couple of shovels. He's a grand fellow, that one.'

Roisin laughed, 'A gruff fellow is what Matt O'Brien is. You're the first I've ever heard call him a grand one.' Although he had wished her there, he now felt uncomfortable at the prospect of having to converse with this beautiful creature. Interaction with folk of any kind had never come easily to Liam. Having had to act the gentleman had been a strain on him, and now he was happy to go back and hide inside his introverted self. He cut some more bread and cheese and wondered whether he should tell Roisin about the incident with Sean. He didn't have to because, just then, Shevlin and Clancy came barging into Hogan's, breathlessly gushing about how Sean and his blokes had finally got their comeuppence from, none other than, the new fellow in town. Roisin looked at Liam questioningly.

'Agh sure, it was nothing,' he said, embarrassed.

'Nutt'n, the fella says,' cried Paddy. 'Isn't Sean Reilly at Moira's this very minute gettin' his hand put back together. Seamus' eyes are swelled shut and, sure, Fergus is walkin' around holdin' his head on wit his hand like he's afraid it'll come off. It must have bin a homeric fight altogether, and you widdout a single mark on ya!'

'It was all over in seconds,' Liam insisted, his face flushing. He had noticed Roisin looking at him with different eyes and he didn't want credit for something that seemed so insignificant to him.

Clancy, who hadn't spoken up to this point, just put his hand on Liam's shoulder, 'Thank you, lad,' he said quietly.

It was too much fuss for Liam, 'All I did was defend myself,' he said. 'It was no more than that.'

Shevlin took it up again, 'On the defensive, were you?' he exclaimed, 'Well, it's a good t'ing fer dem fellas dat you didn't take d' offensive, so. You'd o' killed 'em, sure!' Shevlin roared with laughter. Liam had thought he might enjoy people knowing about the incident but this was turning out to be an uncomfortable experience for him. He shook his head.

Without even having a beer, Shevlin turned on his heels, 'I hafta go tell yer man, Gleeson, and d'udders.'

Shevlin's Tipperary accent thickened the more excited he got and, now, he had the best gossip ever to impart.

Clancy took over where Shevlin had left off. He clapped Liam on the back. 'Boyo, I didn't t'ink I would ever find sumt'n t' smile about again after hearin' about d' evictions yesterday but, by God, hearin' ya trimmed Reilly is almost as good news as d' udder is bad.'

'Stop making such a fuss about it, Clancy,' said Liam, 'It was all just an accident, really. And stop worrying about those evictions. They happened on the other side of Nenagh, not here in Gortalocca.'

'If ya say so, sir,' grinned Clancy.

Liam smiled back, 'I say so,' he said and winked. Clancy left now too. He felt better about things. There was something about this young fellow that made him think everything might work out alright after all.

Now Roisin was alone in the bar with Liam. 'You know this fight with Sean will grow into an epic battle, once the rumour mill has started grinding,' she warned Liam, amused at his embarrassed modesty, 'and the battle will become legendary, like Cu Chuillan's back in the auld times.'

Liam's face flushed. He needed to change the subject. 'The priest's gone,' he said.

'He isn't far. I spoke to Moira this morning,' Roisin told him and his face relaxed. 'I saw her at the rag tree,' she continued. 'I asked who was she was praying for and she handed me a rag and said it was for you. She had me clambering up to tie it onto one of the highest branches … said she wanted to make sure God could see it,' Roisin laughed. Liam wondered if Moira was praying for him because of what he was trying to do for the village or whether she foreseen the incident with the gang of thugs.

'Old Moira has no time for Sean,' Roisin told him,

'he's tormented her since he was a boy. But she never turns down anyone who asks for her help.' Liam nodded. Now he was wondering if the old woman had a direct conduit to the Almighty because, the more he thought about it, the more he realised that winning the fight against such insurmountable odds was almost impossible, yet he had walked away without a scratch. What Roisin hadn't told Liam was that she herself had hung a rag on the tree for him too.

Liam got up to leave and Roisin said, 'You smell like a fireplace.' She laughed when Liam involuntarily raised his arm to his nose to smell his shirt. He blushed and she laughed louder.

When Liam got back to the rectory, there was a notice nailed to the door. It announced that the Church and all church lands had been seized by the crown, and that the priest must report to the magistrate's office in Nenagh forthwith. If he didn't report within 24 hours, then a warrant for his arrest would be issued and treason would be the charge. Liam read it twice before tearing it off the door. He went inside and considered his next move. Without the priest to discuss things with, his confidence had waned.

A hundred things ran through his mind. Should he go back to the lawyer? No, that would be premature. First he had to establish his credentials as an upstanding member of the Church of Ireland. He needed to contact Harold Johnson. He had to take up the masquerade once more. He thought hard. This needed to be done formally. Although it was fine to just drop in on your neighbouring Irish villagers, with these English upper crust types, a person had to communicate his intentions, then await a reply. He remembered that Roisin still had his clothes since she had taken them to iron them dry. That's what he'd do. He'd ask Roisin to write him another note and get young Jamie Clancy to deliver it, as before. This was going to require delicate wording and he wished the priest was here.

Liam ran down the road to Hogan's. In the short time since he'd left there, the place had filled to capacity, and some of the men were even milling around outside. Liam became apprehensive as he approached. Had something befallen Michael Hogan, or worse, Roisin?

Someone yelled, 'Here he is!' and, when he tried to enter the bar, the small crowd parted like the Red Sea to let him through. A cheer went up and he realised it was directed at him. He was both bewildered and dismayed. At first, he thought surely someone had let the cat out of the bag, and that now everyone knew about the plan to save the village. Very soon, he realised that the commotion was all to do with the encounter he'd had earlier with Sean and his cronies. Word, it seemed, had spread like a fire on a thatched roof, and people had come from all around to hear the details, according to Shevlin, related by the man himself. As Roisin had predicted, the tale had grown such that it now bore very little resemblance to the truth.

Michael Hogan was delighted, he couldn't remember ever having had so many paying customers in the place. Roisin rushed here and there, filling and refilling tankards of beer and pouring the occasional cup of poteen. Her hair, usually pulled back tightly from her face, was escaping its incarceration and, with her hands already busy, she was having to flip back the escaped tendrils with a toss of her head. Liam caught her eye and she flashed him a smile and went about her business. He needed to speak to her about the letter but it wouldn't be tonight.

Several people offered to buy him a beer, a rare occurrence indeed, but he declined. He needed his wits about him. Shevlin sat at the bar, holding audience, and telling the tale over and over of how Liam Flynn had triumphed over Sean Reilly and his rabble, embroidering it more with each telling. On several occasions, Liam tried to dispute it but was shouted down as being too modest. Eventually, he gave up and turned to work his way back to the door. Again a swath was cut through the assembled crowd for him. He thought this must be how a sheepdog felt, walking through a flock. He wanted some air and he wanted a smoke but he would go back to the peaceful confines of the rectory to do it.

CHAPTER 25

I t had been a hectic night in the bar, the busiest Roisin had ever known, and she hated getting up to a mess in the morning. Normally, she would have stayed up long after her father, to clean things up, but Michael Hogan had been loath to close his bar while business was so brisk. He had finally shut up shop when the last firkin of beer had been drained and the last drop of poteen drunk. Now, the bar was in a proper mess and it would take her some time to return it to any semblance of order. Roisin remembered that Liam had stopped by for a while and that he looked as if he wanted to talk to her. She wanted to find out what was troubling him but, first, she needed to get her work done here.

She washed her hair, it smelled of stale beer and tobacco smoke. She stood outside and brushed it as the wind blew it dry, then pulled it back and tied it with a piece of string. She gathered all the flagons and cups from the bar and brought them out to the wash tub at the back. Then she walked across the dusty street to the holy well and fetched a bucket of water. Usually one bucket was enough but, this morning, she was going to need at least two.

Back in the bar, Roisin's mood soured as she saw her father sitting at one of the tables, counting the previous day's receipts over and over and smoking his pipe. As she passed his chair, she clouted his head.

'Get off your lazy arse and help me fetch some water. It doesn't matter how many times you tally it up, the sum will stay the same!'

Michael Hogan snapped out of his euphoria. 'Sorry, m'um. Yes, m'um.' He knew by her tone that any other response would have been the wrong one and the last thing he wanted, this morning, was to have Roisin chewing on his ankle. He sought to mollify her by mentioning the young carpenter he knew she was sweet on.

'Well now, that new fellow, Liam Flynn, is certainly a boon for business,' he said, as he took the water bucket from her. Oh yes, she thought, Liam. He wanted to talk about something last night and I didn't have the time. She told her father she would be back soon and that he could start washing the dishes. He had wanted to count his receipts one more time but he did as he was instructed, lest he incur his daughter's wrath.

Liam sat at the little table in the rectory, lost in thought. He had the paper and pen and ink in front of him and was contemplating writing the note to Johnson himself. Roisin came in without knocking.

'Did you want to speak to me about something?'

'I need another message written to Johnson.'

'You were quite the hero last night,' she smiled.

'Pishogue!' he retorted sourly.

'Oh, and a good morning to you too!' she said, sarcastically.

'I'm sorry, Roisin,' he relented, 'but once this letter is written, there will be no escape for me. I will be the most despised person in Gortalocca, more so than ever Sean Reilly was.'

A wave of sympathy for the man washed over Roisin. 'Yes, that may be true but some of us will know the truth.' It was small consolation for Liam. He had come to like the men who wrested a meager living off the land for themselves and their families. He knew that he himself could exist quite easily just by using his wits and the skill in his hands, but that all these people had was the land they lived on. If they suspected any threat to their livelihoods, then the source of that threat would be despised.

'Well, let's get it done, so, before our hero loses his nerve.' The sting of her words bolstered Liam's resolve. He didn't want to disappoint the old priest and, especially, he didn't want to disappoint the beautiful flaxen-haired woman who now sat beside him.

The note was written. It wasn't as eloquent as it would have been with Father Grogan's input, but it was to the point, requesting a meeting with Harold Johnson "of a personal nature". Liam read it over and over and finally handed it back to Roisin.

'Good,' he said, 'it's done, then. We'll give it to Jamie and have him deliver it to Johnson and we'll wait for his reply.'

Roisin dropped the letter off at Clancy's on her way back to Hogan's. The boy was helping his father drive half their flock over onto Liam's land to winter them. The sheep were recalcitrant. They were accustomed to being in a single flock, and separating them was proving problematic. When it was finally done, the boy dutifully ran the two miles to Johnson's and waited for a reply.

When the reply came, Jamie delivered it to Hogan's ... after all, it was Roisin who had handed the note to his mother. Roisin was surprised at how quickly Johnson had replied. She was also pleased to have another excuse to go and see Liam again.

She had done her cleaning and just placed the potatoes in the boiling water for tonight's supper when Jamie delivered the letter. She was tempted to open it immediately, but she suppressed her curiosity. She could wait a few more minutes. She placed the note in the pocket of her apron and made her way over to the rectory.

Shevlin was sitting at the table with Liam, who was drawing a plan for the cottage he planned to build. Paddy was captivated. In his experience, cottages were built by the seat of your trousers but this young man was drawing a precise plan. Roisin was disappointed that someone else was there and she kept the note in her pocket. Liam wasn't expecting the reply so quickly and he wondered what the girl wanted. She affected curiosity about the imaginary cottage that was being built on paper and, when Paddy had finally seen enough, and had stood up to go, Roisin took his seat and continued to feign interest in Liam's plans by asking him questions about the proposed building. Paddy excused himself, saying he had to tend the pigs and added that tomorrow he and Liam would go and collect stones to build the wall.

As soon as Shevlin had left, Roisin closed the upper half of the door and pulled out the note. She waved it over her head like a knight with a sword and Liam was amused by the woman's girlish delight. He thought she must have read the reply already and, when she said she hadn't, he said, 'Well don't count your eggs while they're still inside the chicken, so. We don't know what it says yet. Open it and let's find out.' Roisin opened the letter and read silently to herself. Liam squirmed in his chair, trying to read her expression but it betrayed nothing.

'You have the divil's own luck, Liam Flynn. Sure, he's only inviting you to attend Sunday services with himself and his wife at Johnstown!' She looked triumphant, 'You are to attend with the gentry, Liam!'

Liam frowned, 'I won't know what to do at a protestant Mass,' he said.

Roisin grinned. 'You do the same as if you were at a Catholic one. You try and stay awake and you paint a pious expression on your face.' Liam thought he could probably manage that if that's all there was to it. Just then, the door burst open and Jamie stood in the doorway, his eyes wide and a look of thrilled excitement on his face.

Liam gave the boy a serious look and said, 'In future, boy, you knock first.'

The boy's face dropped and his expression became one of self-reproach. 'Sorry,' he said. 'Me Mam an' Da say dat too, when dey want t' be in d' house on d'eir own together.' Roisin blushed at the lad's unwitting inference.

The grin of excitement returned to Jamie's face, 'Aren't dose t'ree bad men after walking into Hogan's,' he gushed, 'and ya should see 'em! Sean Reilly has his hand and arm bound up in clay and stick t' hold it straight, Seamus' face looks like a melon wit his eyes swelled shut an' his nose stuffed wit wool, and Fergus has a bandage around his head dat goes all the way under his chin!' The boy looked as proud as if he had done the damage himself. Roisin hastily excused herself, saying she had to return to the bar in case there was any disturbance. Liam considered going with her but she had guessed his thoughts.

'No, Liam. If you show up, there will be trouble. Come over for supper, I'll make sure that they're gone by then.' Roisin left but Liam still wasn't happy about it. He decided that, if he wasn't to go to Hogans, he would talk a walk over to where his cottage would be built instead. Hogan's was within view of there and he would be able to see when the villains departed. He took Jamie with him. The carpenter carried a shovel and handed one to the boy. They could start excavating for the lowest level of stones which would make up the foundation. The string had been stretched and the corners squared, it was time to do some digging.

They got to the site and wasted no time. Liam kept one eye on the bar across the road as the two of them began to dig a trench about two feet wide and a little over a foot deep. By throwing the dirt into where, one day, the floor would be, they could raise the grade, so the house wouldn't be damp. Even with the rocky soil, the work progressed quickly. The boy, when motivated, worked steadily and didn't shirk or stop to talk. Within two hours, they had both the east wall trench and the west wall done. Liam sighted down the string and was satisfied. The sun was getting low now and it was time to send Jamie home for dinner. It was time, too, for Liam to wash some of the Tipperary soil off himself.

CHAPTER 26

Liam hadn't forgotten Roisin's invitation to supper, and he was hungry enough now to risk running into the three bullies, hungry enough, even, to withstand her wrath. He grabbed his holly stick, now polished as white as bone, and every few steps, he tapped it on the ground. He had watched the gentlemen in Thurles do it and he imitated the rhythm ... two steps, tap, two steps, tap. On his way to Hogan's, he saw Sean Reilly and his associates leave the bar. Sean saw him too and, for an instant, their eyes locked. Then, the big man pushed Fergus out of his way and turned in the opposite direction. He had no intention of tangling with the carpenter yet, not while he had one hand incapacitated.

Michael Hogan welcomed Liam like a long lost relative. He was still overjoyed at the amount he had made from last night's celebrations and had even been in a jovial mood with Sean Reilly because, without his misfortune, there would have been no reason for the profitable revelry. Indeed, it had been a welcome distraction from the threat of eviction that was now hanging over the community. Michael hoped there would be some stragglers coming in today to hear the gossip which, by now, had reached all the way to Nenagh.

Hogan regarded Liam and it occurred to him that any folk, coming to see this giant of a man, might be disappointed to see he was just as ordinary as they were. No matter, he thought, as long as they brought a thirst and a few pennies with them. The two men sat at a table and Roisin placed three plates of bacon and cabbage down and took a seat herself. Her father wanted to hear the whole story directly from Liam. Liam sighed and related the previous day's episode. Michael was disappointed. He was expecting a story more along the lines of the one Shevlin had concocted and which had, by now, spread like wildfire through the townland.

'Yu'll have t' do better dan dat, me boy. Can't ya at least make d' story longer?' He considered it might be better for business if Liam stayed away. Without the hero himself to play down the magnitude of yesterday's 'bloodbath', he could make hay on the local legend, at least until it was surpassed by juicier gossip.

Roisin had had quite enough of her father. She scolded him, 'Will you leave the man to his bacon!' In an effort to get off the subject, and because she was genuinely interested, she asked Liam questions about the cottage he was preparing to build. This was a subject he was passionate about and comfortable to discuss. He answered her questions enthusiastically. She wanted to know the dimensions of the inside, and about the fireplace, and how he would build the furniture ... the domestic things that concerned a woman. Roisin had very clear ideas of the home that she herself would want one day and had wondered if Liam's ideas were in any way similar. She was surprised at the direction her thoughts had taken because, although Liam was a nice enough fellow, and clearly a brave one, he was hardly the kind of man she pictured herself taking up with.

Liam, meanwhile, was wishing the job had already begun. It was his nature to be single minded and he would get that house built, and built right, as quickly as possible. Even though he had only drawn the plans that afternoon, as he spoke, he was already making changes and refinements to them in his mind and, sometimes, it was better to speak your ideas out loud, in order to give them more clarity. Indeed, it wasn't unusual for Liam to talk out loud to himself when he was working.

The following morning, as soon as it was light enough to see, Liam was at the work site. He needed to finish the foundation trench. He began digging furiously at first but reminded himself that he should slow down the pace or he would run out of energy before the job was done. Jamie showed up soon after, and immediately picked up the other shovel. Without a word, he began to dig on the side of the other wall. Liam was pleased and thought that, if they didn't come up against any large stones, they could complete the task between them in an hour or so.

Paddy Shevlin showed up just as they had most of the work done, with the sorry-looking horse hitched to his wagon. 'Will we get d' shtones, so?' he said eagerly. He was ready for Liam's questioning look. 'I have somet'n around a hundred feet of auld shtone wall out at the back of me land. It serves no purpose t' me, 'cause I keep me pigs close, near me house. We can take d' shtones and bring dem here.'

For several hours, they went back and forth, ferrying the stones. They sorted them out as they unloaded them onto the ground and had two piles … one pile of larger rocks, which would be used for the lower courses, and a pile of smaller ones which would be easier to lift onto the higher parts of the house wall. Liam realised he would have to build a foundation for the fireplace, because that and the chimney would be the heaviest part of the house and would need support. He traced an outline in the dirt inside the perimeter, and dug it to a depth of about a foot and a half.

'Tomorra, we'll fetch some lime so we can mix it wit sand an' water to hold d' shtones togedder,' said Paddy. Liam appreciated that Shevlin had clearly done this many times before, and so he deferred to the old man's expertise in cottage building. The day was finished for old Shevlin. He put his hands on the small of his back and stretched, "Deese auld bones don't work like dey used t'. I could use a beer, maybe even a drop o' d' good shtuff. Liam smiled, he had taken the hint.

'I could use a drop, meself, sure, Paddy,' he said and they made their way to Hogan's for a draught and a dram.

The two men sat at the bar and Liam took his pipe out of his pocket. Paddy regarded it longingly as the young man packed a pinch of tobacco he'd taken from the twist. Liam asked if he'd like a smoke. Paddy gratefully accepted the twist of the leaf and and took a clay pipe from a cup on the bar. The stem was long and he broke a little off the end and packed the bowl with tobacco. Liam went over to the fire and lit his pipe with a piece of straw, then offered the light to Shevlin. The old fellow drew in the smoke deeply and immediately began to cough. Roisin laughed and the sound of her laughter made Liam grin.

'I'm outta practice,' said Shevlin, apologetically.

'Ah, I don't know about that, Paddy,' laughed Roisin. 'It sounds like you're good at the coughing to me.'

Paddy ignored her remark, 'I heard dat d' Frenchies an' d' English shtuff tobacco up d'eir noses. Would ya believe it?'

Liam looked at him incredulously, 'How do you know that, Paddy?'

'Mick Sheridan tol' me. He said he's seen auld Johnson do it a couple o'times. I told him they can shtuff it up their arses fer all I care.'

Liam was still puzzling over why someone would want to put tobacco up their nose when Paddy came up with another gem of wisdom.

'An' sure, ya know it's grown by red savages in d' New World, dontcha?' Liam shook his head and looked at his tobacco twist. He imagined it being handled by pagan red men and put it back in his pocket, wiping his hands off on his trousers. With the thought still in his mind, Liam handed Roisin a penny for the drinks and made his excuses, saying he still had a couple of jobs to attend to. Roisin handed him half a soda bread loaf and a boiled potato.

'If you keep forgetting to eat, Liam Flynn, you'll be thin enough to crawl through a knothole in no time at all.' He gave her a wide smile, nodded his thanks and headed out the door. Roisin couldn't help thinking that maybe he wasn't so bad looking after all … at least not when he smiled.

Liam needed to make some rough frames for the window and door openings in the cottage. Work was progressing faster than he had imagined and, if they were to start laying stones tomorrow, he had better get the preliminary work finished first. Sawing the wood would be time consuming so, since the oak had a straight grain, he would split it into billets. He stood the board up on end and, with a wooden mallet and a froe, he broke it up into thinner pieces. He laid them out on the ground and calculated how much he would need. He cut the pieces to the required length and hammered them together with nails that he kept in a cloth sack.

The work took several hours and he was tired and his muscles were getting sore. He took a few bites from the loaf of bread and decided that he needed sleep more than he needed sustenance.

CHAPTER 27

L iam slept soundly and, when he awoke, every muscle in his body was stiff and sore. He stretched gingerly and finally got all his limbs moving. He didn't expect to see Shevlin early because the old man had done almost as much work yesterday as he had himself. He was wrong, Paddy showed up a few minutes later, bright and chipper.

'C'mon, boyo,' he said. 'We have an errand t' run.' Liam climbed up onto the wagon carefully. The muscles in his thighs felt like knots. 'Yer getting' auld, boyo,' laughed Shevlin. Liam agreed. 'You owe yer man, Hogan, a penny,' added Paddy. Liam looked confused. He was sure he remembered paying Roisin. 'I stayed in d'bar fer anudder couple o' hours an' I tol' Hogan you were buyin'.'

The cheeky old bastard, thought Liam, but he forced a smile and asked Paddy where they were to get the lime. 'The smith has it in d'back of his forge. Only d'divil himself knows more about fire dan a smith does.'

Liam knew that to make lime, limestone was gathered

and a huge hardwood fire would be set over it. The fire would be kept lit for days until the stones were reduced to a crumbly, ash-like condition. Water would then be poured onto the lime to slake it and get the heat out and then, when it had cooled, it could be ground back into a powdery state. If it was mixed with sand in the right proportions and with the right amount of water, it would last for centuries. Castles were built this way as well as lowly stone cottages.

The smith was visibly pleased to see the carpenter. Liam inhaled the smell of the forge and became nostalgic once again for his youth, wishing his life was as simple now as it had been then. A deal was struck for the lime. It cost almost 3 shillings which Liam thought was expensive but knew was necessary for the work and he remembered the labour that went in to making the cement ... several sleepless nights, tending the fire and inhaling the noxious oak fumes.

The smith called Liam aside, 'I have a job, buildin' a pair o' gates fer d' Butlers. It doesn't have t' be done immediately, an' I know ya have a house t' build, but perhaps we can strike a deal.' Liam liked the sound of this. 'I have a stack o' pine dat I cut t'ree years ago an' it's been curin'. Go an' inspect it, it's in d' little barn at d' back of me house. If it's t' yer likin', I'll give ya d' pine fer a week's work here in d' forge.' Liam said he would go and take a look but he wasn't expecting the wood to be any good because, after all, what did a smith know about wood except how to burn it?

The wood was spectacular ... old growth pine, straight grained ... and it had been stacked carefully, not warped or cupped, and with very few checks or cracks. The carpenter scrutinised the wood pile and imagined the furniture that he could make from it. He returned to the forge and shook the smith's hand, one yeoman to another.

Paddy and Liam returned to Gortalocca with the load of lime in the back of the wagon. Liam asked if Paddy thought it would be enough. Paddy said he thought it would, but that if they needed any more, the smith would supply it for free. Liam was mystified. Paddy smiled and explained that he had told the smith the story of Sean Reilly and his ruffians and their encounter with the scrawny carpenter. The smith had been delighted because, a long time ago, Sean, in a drunken state, had made an advance on his wife. The smith said he had harboured a bee up his arse for the man ever since.

It was time to build a house. Paddy would be the foreman. First, a course of large stones had to be placed in the trench. Paddy showed young Jamie how to mix the cement ... six shovels of sand and one shovel of lime and turn the mixture dry, until the ingredients were mixed. Jamie thought it was like the way his mother mixed the soda and flour to make soda bread. Then, water was added. Too dry and it wouldn't stick to the stones, too wet and it would be weak and would crack when it dried. Liam watched too. He had seen it done before but hadn't known why the amount of water needed to be right. Paddy supervised Jamie on the mix and, when it came to selecting stones, he showed Liam which ones to use.

'Always stagger d' joints between courses, dat way d' house'll last fer hundreds o' years,' he explained. Liam buttered the first layer of stones with the mortar and carefully seated the second. Work progressed quickly, much quicker than Liam had imagined and, when several other of the farmers showed up, it went faster still. Clancy, Gleeson, with his two sons, and two others who

Liam knew by sight ... Ger O'Leary and Conor McCormack ... all pitched in, and the walls rose to the height of the window sills.

The entire structure had reached waist height and it was time to stop work for the day. Liam stepped back with the others to inspect the day's labour. At this rate, he thought, the walls would be completed in two more days. Paddy put his hand on Liam's shoulder.

'By next week, we'll be ready t' put d' ridge beam up on d' roof, an' den you c'n put in d' rafters. I'll teach ya how t' thatch after dat, boyo.' The younger man grinned his appreciation and told everyone that he would buy the first round of beer. They all marched over to Hogan's, talking incessantly about all the other houses they had built. Michael Hogan had just taken a delivery of three more firkins of beer and was tapping the first when the men walked in.

'Start pouring,' called Paddy, 'Liam's paying!' Liam looked at Michael and imitated Shevlin,

'Da first round only, mind. Dis fella's t'urst is deeper den me purse.' Everyone laughed and Liam handed the landlord tuppence ... one for Paddy's session last night and one for today's round of beers.

Friday was a soft day, overcast and misty. Liam wasn't sure if any work could be done, but he went down anyway to where his house had begun to rise from the ground. He walked inside and looked around. It was bigger than he had imagined. Even though most people slept on a mat or a pile of straw on the floor, he had decided he wanted a bed like the old priest had in the rectory. It was unusual, some might say a luxury even, but the idea of sleeping away from the damp floor appealed to him. He would have a small table in front of the fireplace and perhaps two, maybe even three chairs.

The window and door frames were already in place, which made it easier to imagine how the room would look. Right now, the sky was the only thing above him but he pictured how snug it would be, once the thatch covered the roof. He was pleased with the progress and he smiled to himself, despite the fact that his back muscles still ached from the previous day's work.

Five minutes later, Paddy Shevlin arrived.

'It'll be a fine house, Liam,' he nodded. 'We can get most of d' walls in today, if everyone shows up.' Paddy had a big wooden bowl of oat porridge and was shovelling it into his mouth with a wooden spoon. 'Ya have a job t'do before we c'n work on d'fireplace. You need a piece o' wood, about six feet long an' about a foot wide and deep, t' put over da firebox t' support d'chimney. So get yerself out o' here an' see to it. If da udders show up I'll set dem t' work.' Liam nodded his assent and went off to cut a piece of oak. As he walked away, he was overcome by a sense of gratitude. He turned and thanked Paddy. Paddy just waved him off with his usual 'Not a bother.'.

Liam return to the oak tree. One of the lower branches that he had trimmed was over a foot in diameter and had a straight trunk about 10 feet long. It would be easier to use a hewing axe to square it up than to split a piece from the remaining half of the main trunk. Liam cut notches at one foot intervals into the branch and then, one chip at a time, he worked his way down the side. He flipped it onto its now flat side and repeated the process. He worked all four sides until he had a beam that came close to Paddy's dimensions. He cut it as long as a man is tall and began to drag it. Paddy arrived with a length of rope and his weary-looking horse.

'God man, Paddy,' said Liam. 'Are you here to help me?'

'I'm not,' replied Shelvin, 'but me harse is.' Quickly and expertly, Paddy tied the beam with a timber hitch and the horse began to pull it.

'We could have lifted it ourselves, sure,' said Liam.

'Are ya daft?' replied Paddy. He told Liam they would need another piece of wood next week, like this one but about seventeen or eighteen feet long, for the ridge beam. Liam knew there was still plenty of the old oak left on the floor of the forest.

By the time the two men returned to the construction site, the walls had reached the top of the window frames. It seemed the cottage was growing like a mushroom. One day there was just grass and the next day, a faerie ring, as if by magic. What would have taken Liam three weeks by himself, was done in three days. Paddy showed the young man how the fireplace was integral in the gable end so they would be as one. This would keep the chimney from falling or tilting, over the years. Long stones were placed on the gable wall, extending into the house, and the chimney would be built around them, tying the chimney to the wall. In short work, the men had hoisted the hewn oak mantel over the firebox and Paddy oversaw that it was properly levelled. He had them do it three more times before it met with his approval.

'Yer a tough boss, Paddy Shevlin,' said Clancy. 'Are ya sure ya ain't part-Inglish?'

Paddy scowled, 'Yer arse is part-Inglish.'

'Dat's true,' replied Clancy, 'but me bollocks is all Irish.' Everyone laughed and stood to listen. There was a whiff of banter in the air and no one was better at it than Clancy and Shevlin. The banter died at the sound of a horse trotting down the road. It was Mick Sheridan, astride a magnificent blood chestnut hunter. All eyes focused on the horse and rider.

'Sure Johnson'll have yer hide if he sees ya on dat harse,' said Paddy. Mick worked for Johnson, overseeing his stables. He preferred horses to people.

'He needs da work,' said Mick. He looked at Shevlin, 'He's getting' as fat as you, Paddy Shevlin. He come up lame a few weeks ago an' he's bin at my place ever since.'

Clancy hadn't finished with Paddy. 'Maybe ya should take Paddy home wit ya,' he said. 'Ya could ride some o' dat fat off him too.' Mick gave just the hint of a smile and waited for Shevlin's retort. Paddy Shevlin usually got the last word in.

'Agh, go ride yer wife,' he told Clancy.

Clancy was desparate to have the final word for once, even if was at his own expense. 'I would, sure, but every time I do, I end up wit anudder mouth t' feed.'

Shevlin was unrelenting, 'Oh, so ya've finally worked dat one out, have ya?'

Liam walked over to the beautiful horse and, when he tried to stroke its neck, the horse shied away. 'Approach 'im slow," said Mick. "He gets nervous when he t'inks yer goin' t' touch 'is face.' Liam slowly took his hand away. He smelled the scent of horse, not the stinking smell of an unwashed one, but the musky smell of well-groomed horse. He put his face against the horse's neck and inhaled.

'Dey smell good, don't dey?' Sheridan said quietly to the young man. Liam nodded. 'Come down t' my place some day an' I'll show you around,' said the big man.

'When?' asked Liam, with more than a little enthusiasm.

'Just one day. When yer not too busy,' said Mick, and gave Liam a nod. Mick wheeled the horse round expertly and began a long trot back towards his farm. When he was sure all eyes were on him, he spurred the horse into a canter and then a gallop. Everyone, including Paddy, watched, in awe, of the man's prowess.

CHAPTER 28

I t had rained hard throughout Friday night and the rain continued into Saturday morning. There would be no construction work done today. Back at the rectory, Liam had put some ground oats in a pot of water before he went to bed and now he poured off the excess water into a bowl. The water would quench his thirst later in the day. He set a turf fire and, although the turf was a little damp, he used more kindling than usual and got it to light without too much trouble. The smell of the smoke from the turf fire was comforting and the flames, dancing and lapping around the turf sods, made even a hovel like this seem cosy. As the chimney warmed, the fire began to draw more efficiently and the aroma of the smoke became less intoxicating.

Liam sat staring into the flames and thought back to the days he had spent with his father at the forge and those spent at home, listening to his mother talking about her old life on the farm and telling him stories. He recalled a particular story that she often delighted in telling him ... that of her own encounter with a foul-tempered leprechaun, when she was a child in Cork. Liam fervently believed all the tales his mother told him... those of faerie forts and other worlds and of creatures from myth and legend, many of whom were malevolent, like the banshee, the pooka and the changeling. He knew now that none could equal the evil of man's inhumanity to his fellow beings.

It was already past nine o'clock and Liam hadn't yet left the fireside. He roused himself, took another glance at the miserable weather outside and spooned a wad of the sticky oat porridge into a wooden bowl. He tasted it. It was a little nutty but, otherwise, quite bland. He wished he had a little honey to sweeten it or, at least, some milk to give it flavour. Not a bother. He would eat it anyway because he was hungry. He finished the oats and then licked the bowl clean. He left the iron pot hanging on the fireplace crane but pulled it off the fire. The porridge would be little less gritty this afternoon. It occurred to him that, if the priest had been here, he would have eaten every bit out of the pot. Liam had heard no word about Father Grogan and assumed he was lying low. If anyone knew of a good hiding place, he was sure it was Moira. He decided to pay Moira a visit and perhaps carry on to see Mick Sheridan. They didn't live a great distance from each other and he would like to see Mick's horses.

The rain had not stopped but, for now at least, it had stopped lashing down and was drizzling steadily. Liam grabbed his brat, a square, heavily-felted cloth cape, from a wooden peg by the door and threw it over his head and shoulders. There was no sign of anyone out on the road and no tracks in the mud. Liam was just beginning to think he was the only person in the village today when he noticed smoke rising from Hogan's chimney. He imagined that Roisin was busy preparing something for dinner in the bar. He hadn't visited Hogan's last night but he was sure that it must have been busy. Friday and

Saturday evenings were always busy in Hogan's. Liam walked up the road toward Johnstown. The rain had returned in earnest now, his brat had stopped shedding the water and he was wet.

Within around fifteen minutes, he had reached the boreen that led into the forest and down to the little cottage which old Moira called home. His woodland walk seemed longer this time, and not as pleasant as it had been when he had walked it with Moira. This time, the tree tunnel was dark and the rain fell in big drops from the overhead trees. The leaves on the ground were undisturbed, so Liam knew that the old crone had not been about yet today. He was just beginning to think he had missed Moira's mud cabin, when he spotted it through the trees, a thin coil of smoke emerging from the flue above it. As he approached the tiny door, he heard the low murmur of voices inside and they fell silent as he approached. Liam knocked and was ushered inside by Roisin, who seemed as surprised to see him as he was to see her.

'Did anyone see you turn off the main road?' she asked, peering out of the door before she closed it behind him.

'I haven't seen a soul today,' he replied. Relief spread across Roisin's face.

'What brings you here this fine morning?' said Moira, with a hint of sarcasm in her voice.

'I just wanted to make sure Father Grogan was alright,' he replied.

The familiar baritone voice came from out of the gloom of a dark corner. 'I have missed our conversations, Liam,' said the priest. 'Are there any new developments?' He had been hiding when Sean Reilly arrived at Moira's cabin earlier in the week, asking for her help with his injured hand, and he knew all about the altercation.

'Not at all, Father,' said Liam. 'Nothing new.'

The old priest laughed loudly. 'You are too modest, Liam Flynn. I might be out here in the woods, but there's not much goes on in Gortalocca that I don't know about, thanks to my eyes and ears.' He nodded, smiling, towards Roisin, who had been silent to this point.

Moira quietly croaked, 'I doubt that young man's hand will ever be the same again. There are several bones broken.' Liam felt a pang of remorse. A one-handed farmer was as good as crippled. The old crone interrupted his thoughts. 'If I really was a witch, I would have turned that scoundrel into a natterjack long ago, along with his two cohorts.'

'Now Moira, you know you would not,' chided the priest, 'If you were a witch, you would be a white witch, doing only good works.'

'I would have made an exception,' she replied tartly.

Liam did not wish to have to relate the story yet again so he led the conversation away. 'Where will Mass be tomorrow?' he asked.

'It has to be discrete,' said the old man, 'There's a place further into the forest, just north of here, called Lodge. Back in the days of the Boru, it was a hunting lodge, a stone building where the nobles stayed during hunts. It's nothing but ruins now, but it does have a stone that can serve as an altar. The approach is difficult and can't be made on horseback. Men at arms will make enough noise so that, if the authorities show up, the people can scatter into the woods.' In the short silence that descended over the gloomy cabin, the old priest became pensive. He knew that the Catholic Church must do what it had done during the Roman persecution. If it was to survive, it must go underground.

Roisin had been strangely sombre. She had been studying everyone's expression and trying to make sense, not only of the words, but also of the meaning of what was being said. She understood the consequences of everything that was unfolding before her eyes and she was afraid.

'Well, tomorrow I shall be a fine upstanding member of the Church of Ireland,' Liam announced, with false bravado. He was just as fearful as the girl was but thought that if he at least sounded confident, he could instill some sense of hope into a hopeless situation. The little tailor had told him that appearances were everything. Liam flashed a weak smile at Roisin and she returned it. Then he left for Mick Sheridan's.

CHAPTER 29

M ick Sheridan lived less than half a mile from Johnstown, just a short distance along the main road from the boreen that led to Moira's cabin. When Liam arrived, Mick was working the big chestnut horse on a longe line. He was studying the horse's gait and glanced at Liam only long enough to nod his greeting.

After a few minutes, he announced, 'He's not right yet.' To Liam, the horse looked to be moving perfectly. 'He's just a little off on his right rear,' said Sheridan, anxiously. 'You can't really see it in a long trot or a canter but, when he makes a transition into a gallop, you can see him short step on that right rear.' The subject of horses was a mystery to Liam. It was as if Mick was talking in a different language and, although he would normally have just nodded knowingly, pretending to understand, he thought this was perhaps something he should learn about. The upper class gentry spent much of their time talking about horses and hunting dogs and, if he was going to converse with them with any credibility, he had better at least have a few phrases to impress them with.

'O'course, auld Johnson couldn't ride a stick horse,' said the big man, scornfully. 'I told him two weeks ago dat d' horse was a bit off but, o'course, he knew best ... insisted dat dis was d' beast he wanted t' use. The horse had a small felon on d' sole of his hoof an', if I cudda drained it, den he would've bin grand. Instead, d' thick-headed old bastard rode d' poor horse until it was dead lame, den, as usual, it was down t' me t' put d' damage right.' Mick still hadn't looked at Liam, he was examining the offending hoof now.

Finally, he straightened up and turned his attention to the carpenter. 'Can you ride?' he asked.

'I don't know,' replied Liam, innocently. 'I've never tried.'

Mick laughed. 'In udder words, ya can't. Anyone c'n sit on a horse's back but ridin' one is a different matter, altogether.' Liam had always thought there was nothing to it, that you just got on a horse and away you went. He had a feeling this would be an education.

Mick turned back to the horse. He moved his hand slowly from its cheek to the front of its head 'Dis is his face,' he said. 'Be very careful when ya do dis and don't do it quickly. A horse has a blind spot between 'is eyes an', if ya move too quickly, yu'll frighten him.' Mick moved his hand further up the horse's head, 'Dis is d' poll,' he said. 'Dis is where d' crownpiece of d' bridle passes over. It's very sensitive to pressure.' He tousled the horse's forelock affectionately. 'Dis is 'is crest,' he said, pinching the fleshy part under the mane, at the back of the horse's neck. Liam wished he had a piece of paper to write to write the words down. Mick went on to identify just about every part of the horse and Liam's head swam.

When he had finished, Mick laughed at Liam's bewildered expression. 'C'mon,' he said. 'Help me put Rohan up an' rub 'im down.' The young man followed him, as he led the horse to a small stable at the back of his house. Mick took the longe line off the horse and tied him, with rope, to an iron ring mounted on the wall of the stall. He wiped the sweat and rain off the horse with a handful of hay and began to brush him. Liam watched silently as he brushed every inch of the horse. The creature seemed to enjoy it. Mick threw cracked oats into a bucket and the beast plunged its head in, scarfing the grain with its rubbery lips, not raising its head until the last speck had gone from the bucket.

'Wanna sit on a horse?' Mick smiled at Liam. The young man's eyes opened wide. 'I'll take that as a yes.' Sheridan grinned. 'People either got it or they ain't. It's like dancing, sure, except yer partner weighs a fair bit more.'

Mick gestured for Liam to follow him into the next stall, where an Irish Hobby was drowsing. It was a grey horse with a grass belly, from lack of work.

'Dis is Aoife,' he said. 'I call 'er Eve. She was d' first mare born here, 'bout twelve years back. She's dead broke an' a grand horse t' ride.' He led her out of her stall, handed the lead line to Liam to hold, and gave her a quick brushing. Then he placed the saddle and the pad on the animal and cinched it tightly. Next he put on the bridle and bit, then led the horse out into a big pen, about sixty feet in diameter.

Mick looked down at Liam's shoes 'Ya can't ride a horse wit' dem auld brogues on yer feet,' he scoffed. 'Go an' put d' leggin's on. At least den you'll look like ya know what yur doin'.'

The carpenter looked sheepish.

'Da leather t'ings,' said Mick. 'Dey're hangin' in d' room where I got d' saddle from. Lace dem up yer legs, an' get yerself back here.' Liam returned to the tack room to search for something that looked like it would go around his legs. He sensed that Mick was losing patience with his ignorance, and that he would rather be left alone with his animals. He found the leather leggings hanging just inside the door and put them on quickly, tightening the laces as he walked back, stopping awkwardly every few steps to try and work the strings tighter.

Mick shook his head. 'C'mere. Put yer left foot in dat iron t'ing dere. It's called a stirrup. Now, take d' reins, a little piece o' d' horse's mane an' d' front o' d' saddle wit' yer left hand an' haul yer arse up.' Liam did as he was told and found himself on top of the animal, giddy from the unexpected distance between him and the ground.

'Feels good, don't it?' said Mick rhetorically, 'an' d' best is yet t' come.' Liam wasn't sure whether it felt good or not.

The horse had remained still, to this point. Mick attached a longe line to the bit in the horse's mouth, and walked her back to the centre of the round pen. 'Sit up straight, boyo, get yer chin up, like ya own d' world, an' we'll get started wit' a lesson.'

There were so many things to remember all at once. 'Put yer heels down,' barked Mick. 'Keep yer head up an' don't look at d' ground. Stay outta d' harse's face.' This was going to prove harder than it looked. Liam was now walking the horse around the arena

'Cluck yer tongue at her an' press yer thighs against 'er sides.'

He did as Mick instructed. The horse began to trot and Liam felt the thrill that only a horseman knows. 'Squeeze a bit tighter,' said Mick. The animal extended her trot and the ground seemed to rush by. 'Don't ferget, head up, back straight, heels down. Stop bouncing on yer arse, man! Stand up in d' stirrups an' push yerself up an' down. Rise an' fall wit' d' leg on d' wall. Follow her inside foreleg.'

The instructions kept coming and the young man had begun to get discouraged. Perhaps this wasn't such a good idea, after all. He kept trying and getting it wrong, Mick kept barking his instructions and, slowly, slowly, it began to feel comfortable.

At last, Mick cried triumphantly, 'Ya have it, lad! Now stop 'er an' try it again.' Liam pulled gently on the reins. The horse came to an abrupt halt and he almost shot over the horse's head. Mick laughed. 'Sit back when ya come to a stop,' he said, 'or you'll go right past d' horse.'

Liam began again and, gradually, Mick's orders became less frequent. It seemed to be getting a little easier ... head up, heels down, back straight.

'Alright,' said Mick, finally. 'Last lesson fer t'day.' He made a kissing sound and the horse suddenly leapt into a canter. Liam's heart leapt too. He was sure he would fall off and be trampled to death. There was a look of terror on his face and Mick was laughing so hard that tears ran down his cheeks.

'Dat's it,' he laughed. 'Keep it up, boyo! Yer a natural, sure. A natural born eejit!' Mick was enjoying this now.

Liam gathered himself. He wasn't going to give up until he could do this with a smile on his face. He had to admit, it did feel good. He had never moved so fast in his life. He soon got used to the speed and it became more exhilarating than it was terrifying.

The lesson finally came to an end and Liam drew the horse to a halt. Mick dried his eyes.

'When can we do it again,' asked Liam, flushed with excitement.

'Tomorrow,' said the horseman. 'Come after church. I think yu've bin stung by d' bee.'

CHAPTER 30

Northwest of Gortalocca, in the dark gloom of the forest, stood the small ruin of what had once been a hunting lodge, used by the local nobility back in the days of the Normans. Only a few intrepid souls ever ventured here now, and the path leading to it was little more than a game trail, the earth hard from centuries of deer and wild boar trampling the undergrowth. The permanent twilight of the forest was forebidding, particularly to those folk whose imaginations were subject to flights of fancy. To them, ghosts and malevolent spirits dwelled here side-by-side here with other supernatural creatures, all bent on causing terror and mayhem to the unfortunate passer-by. The place was called Lodge and this was where Mass would be held today.

Only one wall of the building was still intact, the other three having succumbed to the weight of time and neglect. The ground was strewn with the stones that had once helped to support the ramparts. An area of about forty feet by thirty represented what was once the interior. Then, the walls had echoed with the revelry of men at arms and nobility. Now, it was to be a refuge for the faithful, a place for them to hear Mass and practice their faith. At the base of the only wall was a stone. It was about a yard wide and stood little more than two feet high but it was to serve as the altar.

Next to the ersatz altar, growing out of what was once the floor, stood an old yew tree. A seed had landed on the ground here, many hundreds of years before, perhaps dropped by a bird or an errant gust of wind. Now, the boughs of the old tree would serve as the only shelter for this place of worship.

Father Grogan and old Moira had inspected various locations, finally deciding on Lodge because of its remoteness, and because riders would have to dismount and approach on foot. They had decided that Lodge would suit the needs of the congregation.

Contrary to his usual custom, Father Grogan had written a sermon in advance. He would talk about the early Christians, and how they had endured hardship and persecution to practice their faith. He would remind his congregation that Christ had delivered his sermons in the open air, as he, himself, was doing today. He would preach that they had come full circle to rediscover the roots of their faith, the roots which had given birth to the Church. His message would be simple. He would ask them not to think of these troubled times as hopeless, but merely as God's way of testing the sincerity of their faith. The old priest had written the sermon in the confines of Moira's cottage, with all the zeal of a missionary. Now, as he reread his own words before Mass, they seemed trite somehow, and his conviction for what he had written had waned.

The weather had turned sour and the priest was expecting a poor attendance. He doubted that many would know the location or that they would simply be afraid to attend. In his heart, too, he suspected that the hardship of tramping through the woods in the rain might prove a greater test than their fear of being caught.

He waited an extra fifteen minutes before he began, in the hope that a few more stragglers would arrive. So far, only about a dozen people had shown up. Roisin and her father were there, as well as old Moira and Clancy with his wife and all their children. O'Brien, the smith, and his wife were there too, as was Paddy Shevlin. It was a disappointing turnout, but not an unexpected one. Father Grogan feared that this business could signal the death of the Catholic Church in Ireland. He put the distressing thought out of his mind and he said Mass, as he had done for the last fifty years.

When it came time for the sermon, he crumpled up the now wet piece of paper he had written his words on, and let it fall to the ground. He said, simply,

'Martyrs come in all shapes and sizes … and they don't always sacrifice their lives. They often make more subtle, but equally important, sacrifices. Saviours, too, come in many unlikely forms. Indeed, the Redeemer himself was the son of a humble carpenter.'

He asked for a moment of prayer for the souls of those present and for those who couldn't be there. Roisin knew he was thinking of Liam.

*

Liam had been awake long before it got light on that dreary Sunday morning. The muscles in his legs were sore from riding Mick's horse the day before. He was glad that he would have to walk the two miles to St. Mary's Church of Ireland, the exercise might loosen things up a little. It would not present a good image to the gentry if he hobbled in stiff-legged. He roused himself and got up gingerly. His legs felt like sticks. He hobbled out to the back of the rectory, to the bucket which served as a bath, and he washed himself. Now that the priest was gone, there was no need for modesty, so he had slept naked in front of the fire. He tied his hair back now with a piece of string and began to shave. The rain was cold.

Liam didn't want to arrive at the church too early. He might have to converse with those of the upper class and feared making a blunder and wrecking everything. He dressed himself, but decided not to put on the stockings and shoes until he had almost reached his destination. The cursed shoes pinched his feet so he would walk barefoot, then put them on when he got within a discrete proximity to the church. A hundred things went through his mind. It had been a while since he'd had to put on his gentleman act and he could feel the pressure mounting.

He was ready to go and he stooped to looked out of the little window. The weather had not improved so he took his woollen brat, which hung from a peg by the door, and threw it over his shoulders. It would be some protection, at least, from the rain. He smiled as he remembered the contraption the tailor had lent him in Nenagh. He wondered how the respectable gentry at the Protestant church would have greeted the sight of him with the portable roof over his head. He imagined that, like everyone else, they probably would have wondered who the horse's arse was. He grabbed the holly walking stick and tucked it under his arm. The prospects of another encounter with Sean and his thugs was slim but perhaps now, with the evictions taking place, there might well be other desperados on the road.

His apprehension about what could go wrong at the church had begun to get the better of him and, as he walked the road, he tried to remember all the instructions he had been given. Keep your head up, don't slouch and, most importantly, look people straight in the eyes when you speak to them.

While Liam was rehearsing his introductions, his attention was caught by a slight figure walking towards him in the distance. The form was too erect to be Moira and, besides, the old woman was probably attending Mass, wherever it was being held. Whoever it was wore a woolen brat, so it could be either gender, and appeared to be wearing a hat of some sort. As the figure grew closer, Liam recognised it to be Fergus. He decided that, rather than ignore the little weasel, he would have some fun with him. After all, it wasn't a sin to enjoy a diversion on the Sabbath. Fergus hadn't recognised Liam, dressed in all his finery, until it was too late to dodge him. He veered to the left of the road and the carpenter followed suit. Then he veered to the right and Liam mirrored his move. Finally, they were face to face, and Liam slipped the walking stick out from underneath his cloak.

Fergus was the first to speak. 'Beggin' yer pardon, sir, but I don't want any trouble wit ya. Liam just looked down at the cowardly little stoat, tapped the head of the walking stick against his leg and enjoyed watching him squirm.

'I was jus' going to d'auld witch's house t' see if she had anyt'ing fer a headache,' whined Fergus, his eyes shifting one way and another, looking for an escape route.

'Where's the boss?' asked Liam.

'He's at home. You crippled his hand.'

'When you see him, tell him I'll cripple the other one and then he won't even be able to wipe his own arse. Where's the other one?'

Fergus just wanted to get away before Liam lost his temper. 'He's home. His eyes is swelled shut an' 'is nose is broke.'

Liam was surprised at the perverted satisfaction he was getting from watching the man's discomfort and he wondered if this was why bullies tormented their victims. He didn't like the feeling, it wasn't his way, so he eased up on Fergus. 'Well ... I'm sorry it had to come to that, Fergus, but I had to protect myself. I hope I never have to do it again ... but if I do...' He tapped the knob of the walking stick against his leg again. The thinly veiled threat was enough and the little fellow shifted nervously from one foot to the other, his eyes on the stick. Liam didn't have either the heart or the time for any more of this. He lifted the stick to his face in salute and Fergus flinched, then skulked away like a dog who has been beaten too many times.

When the Church of St. Mary's came into sight, Liam stopped, brushed as much mud as he could from his dirty feet, pulled the stockings on and put on the infernal shoes. He arrived at the church and, with his head up, his back straight and his shoulders back, he entered the sanctuary. He remembered something Mick had told him the day before. 'Make it look like you own the world,' he had said. Liam took a seat in a pew towards the back of the chapel, next to a very large woman. Although she was finely dressed, her clothes were well-worn and the smell of her cologne did a poor job of masking the aroma of wet bread that emanated from her. He nodded to her politely, seated himself and began to survey his surroundings.

The church was unlike St Patrick's in Gortalocca, where Father Grogan presided. It had been built from cut stone, undoubtedly looted from the old abandoned monastery at Killodiernan. The altar was of white marble, simple, but carved well, unlike the one in the Catholic church. The windows had leaded glass in them and the pews were solidly built from dark oak. An atmosphere of prosperity pervaded the building, and Liam's reaction was one of both awe at the architecture, and disgust at the oppression of his country's people. Nevertheless, he settled himself, ready for the service. Just then, a man approached him and whispered close to his ear. Liam had been invited to join the Johnsons in the first row. He nodded his compliance and allowed himself to be escorted to his new position.

CHAPTER 31

Michael Hogan knew the woods well and he made his own safe passage back through them to Gortalocca, whilst Roisin and the old priest accompanied Moira, who showed them a different path back to her cottage. If they used the same route each time, it could betray their intentions to anyone curious enough to investigate. Father Grogan and Roisin had to duck down in order to clear the branches overhanging the trail. As they made their way through the undergrowth, the old man thought about his future, also that of his companions, and the parish itself.

His thoughts turned to words. 'Many parishioners will be lost along the way, I fear,' he said, with a worried frown. 'Some will convert or defect to the Church of Ireland, some will remain Catholic in name only, and I'm afraid that some might lose their faith altogether.' This final prospect concerned him most of all because it had, after all, happened to him once, and he knew that it was only by the grace of the Holy Spirit, that he had returned to the fold. However, without a shadow of a doubt, it had changed him irrevocably. He still believed, of course, but his faith was different now. Previously, it had been a blind faith, an innocent faith, without question. Now, he lived his life and practiced his religion with a myriad of questions. There were times when he could meditate and find an answer that suited his immediate needs. Other times, too many than he cared to think about, his questions remained unanswered. Right now, he was placing all his faith in a simple carpenter, as the apostles had, more than fifteen hundred years before.

Roisin sensed the old man's unease. 'You must have faith, Father,' she said. 'Liam Flynn is the most determined man I know, as stubborn as a donkey.' The priest knew she was right. Any man who would walk across Tipperary to follow a dream was indeed a force to be reckoned with. He was the type of person who looked at an adversity, not as a stumbling block, but merely as time to change course in order to fulfill his goal.

'You're right, of course,' he said. 'Liam believes in himself because that's all he's ever had. Men like him turn out to be either heroes or scoundrels.' He noticed Roisin's quizzical expression, and began to explain. 'Take Cromwell, for example,' he said. Roisin and Moira glanced at each other, worried about what he would say next. To the Irish, Cromwell was not just evil, he was the very personification of the devil himself. The priest continued, 'To the devout Parliamentarians in England, Cromwell is a hero. To us Irish people, and to the Royalists, he is the most heinous villain who ever lived.'

'But he's a protestant,' she objected.

He smiled. 'Yes, my dear, but if he had been a Catholic, he would have committed the very same atrocities, if asked, in the name of the Pope. Sometimes religion is just a convenient excuse.' Roisin frowned. All this sounded too much like blasphemy, or even heresy, for her to be comfortable with.

Moira nodded her head slowly. 'It's all about power,' she croaked. 'power and wealth.'

The priest agreed. 'That's right, old mother. Those that have it, seek to keep it. Those who don't have it, desire it.'

Roisin's head was swimming with all this talk. The priest sensed her confusion and, as if he had read her mind, and was replying to her thoughts, he continued. 'You see, child, Liam Flynn is the unique combination of a worldly man and an innocent one. He knows the practicalities of life and yet he remains a dreamer. He is a bumpkin but, at the same time, his observations equip him with a level of sophistication. Some people learn from books. Our young friend sees the world and creates his own interpretations. He moulds himself to whatever situation he is confronted with and, despite what goes on around him, he remains one of the world's romantics.'

Roisin felt as if she should respond. 'If he is as practical as you say, why is he helping us?'

The priest smiled at her affectionately 'At first, his interests and ours were parallel. Now, however, our interests have become his. Now, if you were to trust that young fellow with your life, you could be sure it was in good hands.'

'How do we know he won't become just another greedy landlord?' she asked.

'Because he is modest, about everything except perhaps his work, and modest men don't seek power or wealth. Liam just wants his own piece of land and a place from which he can ply his trade.'

'But....' Roisin began.

'Trust me, daughter,' he interrupted. 'Liam Flynn is different to anyone you've ever met in Gortalocca,'

Roisin thought perhaps she was beginning to see the carpenter through the old priest's eyes.

'Can we help him?' she asked softly.

'We can simply be his friend,' Grogan replied, 'because he won't have any in the village before too long. He will need protection, not from the English, or even the Protestants, but from his own friends and neighbours. Liam's failing is that he doesn't watch his own back. He trusts people, you see. But make no mistake, when he is betrayed, he will bear a grudge. Just ask Sean and his cronies.' Roisin couldn't imagine anyone in Gortalocca who would behave in such a way. She nodded her understanding to the priest but she couldn't agree with him. As he had spoken the words, even in his own mind, he thought you could never be entirely sure of the intentions of another.

By now, Roisin's hair was plastered to her head by the rain and that same head was filled with so many questions. Father Grogan was the wisest man she had ever known and, if he trusted Liam with his flock, then that was all she needed to know. If she wanted the answers to any more of her questions, she would ask Liam himself. She was unaware of the nagging doubts in the priest's mind.

They arrived at the old woman's cottage and Roisin bade the others farewell and continued on to the main road. She was late starting her preparations for dinner. Inside the tiny cottage, the crone poured herself and the priest a dram each of the good stuff and lit the turf in the fireplace.

'There's bad times brewin, Father,' she said at last, 'and I don't think young Liam stands a chance. He's trapped between the English and the Irish and he can't confide in either one.' Grogan sat in silence as the words of the wise old woman hung in the air. He took a sip of the liquor and felt it burning the back of his throat and running down into the pit of his stomach. He had led Liam into this. It might get the young man half hung, drawn and quartered by the crown, or it could get his skull bashed in by the people he was trying to save. However, it was too late to turn back now and, even if it wasn't, there was now nothing left to turn back to.

*

Liam sat beside Mr. Johnson in the front pew. He smiled inwardly. Johnson no doubt believed that, since he had paid to build the church, that made him like the Pharisees in the Bible ... sitting a little closer to God. The carpenter didn't let his face betray his thoughts, however, and he followed the book by watching Johnson out the corner of his eye. He assumed his best pious expression and wished that the next hour would pass quickly.

The Anglican service didn't differ too much from those he remembered as a child, although the Homily was completely different. A prune-faced man raged from the pulpit in a contrived English accent, predicting hell and damnation for all the Papists, especially the priests who led their sheep to perdition. Liam instantly disliked the man. The service dragged on and the hour had begun to turn into two. This wasn't the Irish way, Liam thought. He received communion and, as he did so, he considered that the fires of hell must surely be like those of a forge, with the exception that they would never totally consume you, but would forever lap at your burning body. He had suffered small burns in his father's shop and his mind involuntarily imagined his whole body feeling that pain. He shuddered. I'll no doubt find out some day soon, he thought.

After the service, Liam attempted a hasty departure. Even though his body still ached from the previous day, he was eager to go and see Mick's horses. Johnson cornered him, however. He was more than cordial and insisted on introducing him to the vicar. Liam had no other option than to consent. The prune-faced man had softened his demeanour and he shook Liam's hand warmly, welcoming him to the congregation. Liam was astonished at the apparent transformation and began to think his first impression might have been wrong. Many years ago, in Thurles, he had known a priest to rant against the Jews, then go and do business with them. Some things, it would appear, were meant to be said from the pulpit. However real life, it seemed, was a different tale altogether.

Johnson invited Liam to eat breakfast back at the house with him, his wife, and the pastor, but Liam begged off, saying that he had something else planned. Johnson persisted but Liam stood his ground. He needed to get those shoes off his feet and he wanted to smell that musky aroma of horses again.

Finally, he successfully made his farewells and, when he was out of sight, he sat down on the fallen trunk of an old tree to remove his shoes and stockings. He sighed with relief as he closed his eyes and rubbed his sore feet. He didn't notice someone approaching him from the direction of St. Mary's until the person was almost upon him. Liam looked up sharply and was relieved to see the familiar figure of Mick Sheridan. He was dressed in a uniform of some sort, with highly polished boots. He sat down next to Liam and asked the young man to help him get his boots off. Liam turned his back and grasped the heel that was offered, with his fingers interlocked, and Mick put his other foot against Liam's arse and pushed.

The boot slid off and they repeated the procedure until they both sat, barefooted, on the tree trunk.

'It'll take more than clothes and shoes to take the bog out of the Irish,' Mick laughed. Liam knew that Mick had figured out he was no gentleman. Mick winked. 'Yer secret's safe wit me, boyo,' he said. 'I'm playin' d' same game as you. He makes all us workers dress like a bunch o' ninnies t' come t' services on Sundays. I stay long enough fer him t' see me and den I slink off back to me harses. Let's go down t' my place, an' I'll share a snort or two wit' ya.' Liam followed Mick, thinking that his secret must surely be the worst kept one in all of God's creation.

CHAPTER 32

Work was progressing nicely on Liam's cottage. The front and back walls were already complete and the gable ends were almost finished. Liam had cut the ridge beam for the roof but, at almost a foot deep, eight inches wide and eighteen feet long, he was going to need some help to move it from the grove of trees where he had cut the old oak. He would need six trusses to attach to it, and then the main framework would be complete. He used a carpenter's square to make his calculations. He worked out that if the trusses were each nine feet long, that would give him enough flexibility to cut them exact when he was on site. They didn't have to be pretty, so the work could be done with a hewing axe and an adz. He determined that, instead of cutting the tenons and mortices after the main beam was up, he would carry out the joinery work here in the forest. It was better to use a morticing chisel and mallet here on the ground, than when he was standing on a ladder, ten feet up. His hands knew what to do once the marks had been scribed onto the wood.

Liam had toiled all day on the preliminary work for the roof structure. He knew that once on site, he would have to make a few tweaks to get things to fit perfectly.

He numbered each of the tenons and corresponding mortices, because each would differ slightly. He dry fit them, there in the grove, and everything went well. He realised that when he got them to the job site, there could be glitches but, for now, he was satisfied and he was also as hungry as a wolf.

He dusted the sawdust and wood chips off himself, and made his way to Hogan's for a bite to eat and a beer. Three men were already gathered around the bar, two he recognised as local farmers, the other was a stranger. They seemed to be engaged in serious debate and it looked like the stranger was leading the conversation. Roisin hovered over them, listening but not taking part.

When Liam arrived, she gave him a weak smile and raised her hand in a gesture of acknowledgement. He settled himself at a table and took in the scene. Roisin didn't come to find out what he wanted, she was preoccupied with the debate that was going on. The stranger who was doing most of the talking turned to glare at him and Liam looked away. The men lowered their voices now, as if sharing a secret or a conspiracy, and quickly brought their conversation to a close. Liam couldn't help thinking his presence had a hand in that. They prepared to leave, settling their tallies with Roisin, and as they made their way to the door, Liam felt the stranger watching him.

Liam was the only customer now and, when Roisin brought a pitcher of beer to his table, she sat down opposite him, her expression sombre. Liam raised his eyebrows quizzically, waiting for her to speak first.

'The number of evictions out east of Nenagh are escalating now.' Liam waited. What did this have to do with Gortalocca?

Roisin continued, 'There's talk of resistance. The men

are starting to talk about burning out the landlords and killing livestock.' She had Liam's full attention, now. 'There's a new sheriff coming to replace the fat old drunk who's held the position for years. They said the banditry that's happening out on the roads into Nenagh is starting to affect business.' The young carpenter had heard that the old lawman had been a political appointee, someone of prominence's nephew or some such connection. It was well-known that he was incompetent and, indeed, seldom left his office at the gaol. A new sheriff would be welcome.

'What has all this got to do with us in Gortalocca?'

Roisin shook her head, 'Jeezus, Liam, you can be so thick.' Liam's face flushed. 'Listen to me,' she went on, 'Two of the men who were at the bar live on Johnson's land, and they saw you talking to him yesterday morning.'

'I only bid him the time of day, sure,' he protested.

'It doesn't matter what the exchange between you was,' she said, 'People see what they want to see and their thoughts turn to words and the word gets around and, before you know it, there's a plot. It's like a fire, it only takes a tiny spark to ignite it. That stranger who was watching you, he appears to be the ringleader in all this and he seems well able to rouse the rabble.'

'I'll get to the solicitor first thing tomorrow, and get things moving,' he said.

Roisin threw her hands up in dismay. 'Liam, my dear, that will make you the landlord here in Gortalocca and then you will be the enemy, no matter how good your intentions are!' Roisin thought back to Father Grogan's words yesterday. He was right, she thought. In some ways, Liam was like a child. He had only been listening to her up until she had called him 'my dear'.

Her voice was softer now. 'Listen to me, Liam. Your

land is safe now. You don't have to go any further with the old priest's plan.'

He sat up straight in his chair. 'I made a promise to him, Roisin. I never break a promise.' Roisin felt something unexpected stir inside her and it wasn't at all motherly. God save us from honourable men, she thought, they can be so damn stubborn and impractical. Liam continued, 'I will do as I said and let the wood chips fall where they may. Right this very minute ... my dear ... I'm starving hungry!' He grinned at her.

Roisin was exasperated. Here she was talking about life and death and all he could think of was his stomach. 'Grand,' she said, throwing her hands up again. 'God forbid I should tax your little brain with any more talk of this. I'll get you something to fill your belly, shall I?' With that she slapped a big spoon of mashed potato and a hunk of gammon onto a plate and almost threw it on the table in front of him. She made a gesture of dusting her hands off and went about collecting the empty flagons from the bar.

Liam tried to resurrect the conversation, 'What did they say about the new sheriff ?' he asked, stuffing his mouth.

Roisin didn't turn to answer him, 'They say he's a tough one, used to be a soldier in the European wars or some such thing. It seems he cleared up the problem in Wicklow in short order. It's said he presided over the hangings of twelve bandits all by himself and cut down a few more reparees single-handedly with his own sabre.' Liam raised his eyebrows and gave a low whistle.

'Howaya,' said Paddy, as he entered the bar. He sat heavily in the chair opposite Liam.

'Whatcha been about t'day?' he asked, jovially. The younger man had just taken a big mouthful of food. Isn't that the way of it, he thought. Just as you stuff your face, someone asks you a question. He held his hand up to Paddy and swallowed a lump of fatty gammon. It stuck in his windpipe and made him cough. He cleared his throat with a swallow of beer.

'Got the roof framing built.'

Paddy was surprised, 'Yu're after building' it today? Well den, we can hang it tomorra mornin', so.'

Liam shook his head, 'Maybe tomorrow afternoon, if you're not too busy Paddy. I have to go to Nenagh in the morning.'

'Perfect!' said Shevlin, 'I hafta go t' town wit Clancy meself, first t'ing in d' mornin'. Ya can ride wit us if ya don't mind sharin' d' back of d' wagon wit a pig.'

Liam shot a spud-filled grin at the old fellow, 'Fine with me,' he said. 'Pigs is good company,' and he held up a piece of gammon in Paddy's face.

'I hear dere's a smell o' treason in da air,' said the fat man. Liam opened his eyes wide and swallowed hard. If Paddy knew what he was up to, it wouldn't be long before the whole world found out. He shrugged his shoulders casually and Shevlin continued, 'Dere's a fella from down east who's tryin' t' instigate somethin'. Dem folks from da east are always up t' no good.' Liam was relieved. Paddy must be talking about the fellow who was just in the bar with the other two.

'It'll come t' no good, o'course' said Shevlin, 'It's bin done time an' again an' all dat happens at d'end of it is a good hangin'.' Liam wanted to change the subject. Ordinarily, the weather and a good hanging made for grand conversation in a bar, but right at this moment, the subject of the gallows was unwelcome.

'Do you know about tomorrow's weather, Paddy?' he asked.

'Ah sure, dere'll be wedder t'morra all right. I just don't know what it'll be.' Liam laughed, grateful for the diversion. When Paddy looked at him with surprise, Liam realised he had been serious and that made him laugh louder.

Roisin had overheard too, and joined in, 'Paddy Shevlin, you're either the daftest man I ever knew, or the funniest.' Paddy didn't get the joke.

CHAPTER 33

P addy had been right about the weather. There was weather all right and plenty of it. The day was cold and rainy and the wind whipped the low grey clouds across the sky. Liam waited by the open door of the rectory for Shevlin's wagon. He waited, and he waited, and was about to start walking to Nenagh when Paddy and Clancy finally showed up.

'I'm runnin' on Irish time today,' Shevlin called to him, in greeting, 'God loves time. Dat's why He made so much of it and I'm showin' me love of God by usin' as much of it as I can.' Liam had to agree. Paddy Shevlin never moved at anyone's pace but his own. 'Whatcha goin' t' Nenagh town fer dis mornin'?'

'Going to the tailor shop.' Liam told a white lie, although he did need to go to the tailor shop to change from the leine and trews he wore every day, to the costume which he assumed when he took on his alter ego. Liam hopped into the back of the wagon and the pig squealed.

Paddy looked back, 'Mr. Pig's after sayin' dat he doesn't like d' way ya' smell.' Liam scowled at the pig and Clancy chirped in,

'Maybe ya oughtta get in d' back wit' da pig, Paddy, you smell like his mudder.'

Shevlin's expression turned to one of indignation. 'Ben Clancy,' he said. 'ya shouldn' go roun' makin' jokes about people's mudders, even if dey are pigs.' Liam thought this was going to be a long trip.

The two farmers bickered as they drove into town, leaving Liam to his thoughts in the back. He was thinking about Father Grogan, he had to admit that he missed the old codger. An idea occurred to him, perhaps he could get the tailor to procure a set of clothes for Father Grogan. That way, he could travel without drawing too much attention to himself. It would free him to visit the sick and elderly, and to perform some of his other duties. The old priest had worn the grey frock of a Franciscan for so long that Liam wondered if he might object.

Clancy interrupted his thoughts. 'Have ya seen ol' man Grogan, lately, boyo?'

Before Liam could answer, Paddy jumped in, 'He ain't a man, ya stupid sheep, he's a priest.'

'Priests are men, ain't dey?' objected Clancy.

'No dey ain't, priests is priests,' snapped Paddy. Another one of their exchanges was underway.

'Well, once dey was men, an' now de're priests, so dat makes 'em men.'

'Jayzis, Mary an' Saint Joseph, next yer gownta tell me dat flies is maggots.'

Liam decided to step in before the two in the front came to blows over priests and maggots. 'No. I haven't seen him since he left,' he said. That satisfied Clancy for at least thirty seconds until Shevlin brought up the subject of the evictions and the new sheriff and they were off on another one of their exchanges. Liam drowsed next to the pig, who had also fallen asleep.

The wagon lurched to a halt and woke both Liam and the pig. The pig squealed and Liam yawned.

'Did ya have any dreams while ya was cuddlin' d' pig?' asked Paddy. Liam ignored him and jumped off the back of the wagon, right into a muddy puddle.

'Shite!'

Paddy and Ben laughed, 'See what happens when ya sleep wit' pigs? Ya start to waller in d'mud.' Liam shook a playful fist in their direction and walked off in the direction of the tailor shop. Perhaps he would find better conversation with the little man.

'Can I interest you in something today, my good man?' greeted the tailor, 'Or did you just want to use the changing room?' he added sarcastically.

'Maybe both.' This response improved the little tailor's mood immensely. He stepped back and looked Liam up and down.

Liam read his mind, 'Not for me, for a friend.'

'What size is your friend?'

After considering this for a moment, Liam held his hand up over his head, then opened his arms wide. He looked at each arm, then opened them wider. The little fellow looked aghast as he considered Liam's estimated measurements.

'Is your friend an elly-fant?'

Liam knew what an elly-fant was from a picture he had seen long ago in a book, in his old master's shop, and he tried to recall the story. Some general named Cannibal, or something similar, had crossed a river called the Alps, in Italy.

'No, he's a pr…,' he caught himself. '…he's a pretty good friend.'

'And what type of clothing were you thinking of?'

'The cheap kind.' Liam went on to describe the longshirted leine and the short-legged trews of a common man.

'I'm not sure if I have any that big in stock, but I'll see what I can come up with.' Liam went through to the back of the shop and changed his clothes. When he came out, a few minutes later, the tailor inspected him and sniffed. He wrinkled his nose.

'You have the slightest essence of pig about you today.' Liam's face flushed. The little man disappeared into the back of the shop and, when he reappeared, he held at atomizer and began to spray Liam with something that smelled flowery. It was Liam's turn to wrinkle his nose. The smell was sickeningly sweet and nauseating.

'I have something new to show you, Mr. Flynn.'

Liam looked at him with distrust. 'I'm not carrying that portable roof again. I looked like a horse's arse.'

'I agree, sir, it will never catch on with the public. No. This is called a raincape. It's a waterproof covering and I can sell it to you for a mere two shillings.' The tailor draped the garment over his arm and extended it to Liam.

Liam held it up. It looked like an oilcloth shawl with a hood that you could pull over your head in wet weather. Liam was loath to spend the money but, when he tried it on, it was not only practical but it looked surprisingly sophisticated.

'I'll give you a shilling for it.'

'One and six, and you can wear it out of the shop.'

Liam counted out the money and, dressed in his new apparel, he left the tailor's shop, trying in vain to dodge another spray of the offending cologne on his way out.

He walked briskly to the solicitor's office. He liked the way the raincape billowed and he imagined himself cutting quite a dash. He opened the door into the young lawyer's office and found him fast asleep, his head resting on his folded arms on the desk. Liam had heard someone say that if you wake a person too quickly, they could actually die. He didn't want to have to find a new solicitor, and so he coughed. The young man snapped awake and threw the powdered wig onto his head. It fell on the floor, and he retrieved it and put it on, backwards this time. Liam laughed and the young man blushed.

'I was lost in thought,' he lied. Liam thought he had probably been dreaming about a beautiful plump girl with a rich and generous father. 'I have some papers for you, Mr. Flynn, and some information that you requested.' Liam took the papers, they were the deeds for his property. The solicitor then crossed the office to where an oak cabinet stood, and he pulled out a large book. He opened it up on his desk and Liam saw that it was filled with hand drawn maps. There was a scrap of paper sticking out between two pages and the solicitor opened it there. It showed a map of Gortlocca. He turned the book around so that Liam could see the image. Liam studied the page and recognised the farms.

'How much per acre?'

'The crown is interested in disposing of the property as quickly as possible ... a shilling per hectare. That includes my fee, of course.'

The English are stealing the land and re-selling it, just to spite the Catholics, Liam thought with distaste. He knew he was probably being skinned on the price too, but he had neither the time nor the patience to argue. He indicated the area of land he was interested in, but purposely left out the land that Sean Reilly's family owned.

The lawyer noticed and pointed to it. 'You left out this parcel.'

Liam smiled and nodded. 'I'm leaving that one for you,' he said. 'You can use the profits from this transaction to buy it.' The solicitor gave him a mirthless smile and said he was grateful for the opportunity. Calculations were made and the purchase price came to a little under three pounds. Liam counted out the money, the lawyer signed a receipt, then handed it to the carpenter. They shook hands and Liam threw the raincape over his shoulders. The young man was visibly impressed and he asked where he could get one like it. Liam thought about selling it to him for five shillings, but decided against it. He directed the fellow to the tailor's shop.

Liam went back to the shop and changed his clothing. He told the tailor that he could expect a visit from the solicitor, with the intention of purchasing a raincape, but that he should charge him five shillings for it. The little fellow was elated. Although he didn't have anything to fit the young man's friend today, he might be able to find something for about a shilling later on in the week.

Liam thanked him and went in search of Shevlin and Clancy, to hitch a ride back to his land in Gortalocca.

CHAPTER 34

Paddy and Clancy were coming out of a pub, just off the market square, when Liam caught up with them. Clancy looked distressed and he was holding his belly.

'What's up, Clancy?' he asked.

'I can't get deese evictions outta me head, lad,' he said. 'and it's aytin' me guts up. Me, wit' so many mouths t' feed, dat I can't even save a farthin'. If dey evict me, d' kids'll starve, an' den me wife an' me. I wanted ta die before I buried me kids.' Liam felt sorry for the shepherd and he wished he could assure him that there was nothing to worry about.

'Agh, I'm sure everything will work out for you,' he said, but the sentiment sounded empty.

'Will ya promise me dat you'll take our Jamie, lad? At least den I know me name'll be carried on.' Clancy's eyes had moistened and Liam thought he was going to cry. It tore at his heart to see him suffer.

'You have my word on it, Ben.' Liam was unable to

say anything about what he had just done and, for now at least, he could only watch this man's anguish. Even Shevlin, who always had a smart crack for every occasion, felt deeply for his best friend and he put his hand on the farmer's shoulder to comfort him.

The journey back to Gortalocca was a quiet one. Ben Clancy was immersed in a deep depression and Shevlin knew when to leave his friend alone. Liam was lost in his own thoughts. He was thinking about the first day he had walked around Nenagh and the destitute family he had seen on the roadside, waiting for death to arrive. He had witnessed the same scene many times before but, now, he was picturing Clancy and his wife in that situation. No longer were the wretches he imagined, waiting in despair and praying for a miracle, nameless or faceless. It strengthened his resolve. Their future was in his hands now and he would not break his promise.

As they finally drew into the village, Shevlin was the first to speak.

'Lets go fetch d'ose timbers datcha made, Liam, d' shtones should be strong enough now t' support d' roof frames. Besides d' work'll take Clancy's mind off 'is troubles.' Liam wasn't sure if this was true but, sometimes, Paddy Shevlin was wiser than anyone knew. The three men put the trusses in the back of the wagon and dragged the ridge beam behind. In no time at all, it seemed, the pieces lay alongside the partly-built cottage.

Roofing was an occasion in the village, and people had already begun to show up. At first, Liam was apprehensive about placing the heavy beam. It was the only really dangerous part of building a house, but now there was plenty of help. Even the womenfolk and children had come. The household chores would have to wait.

The men wrestled the beam into the house and, when it was parallel to the long axis, they muscled one end up into the stone mortice left at one gable end. This proved easy, with all the manpower available. The dangerous part lay ahead. They moved to the lower end and, with poles precariously balanced, they pushed the beam onto the peak of the other gable. If it was to dislodge now, someone could easily be crushed within the confines of the walls. Liam's apprehension was unfounded, however, and it was soon done without a hitch. The beam was slightly too long, as Liam had intended. He straddled the gable end and hiked himself up the slope. Clancy passed him the bow saw. He marked the exact length, then took off an eighth of an inch more. The oak beam resisted but the carpenter had soon cut through it, and it fell into the mortice with such a thud that the whole structure shook. The next job was to attach all six rafters. The beams were brought inside, one at a time, to keep the men from tripping over them. The eave end of the first was lifted onto the wall and a rope was passed over the ridge beam and attached to the end with the tenon cut into it. Liam shimmied out along the main beam to where the mortice was.

'Watch yerself, boyo!' shouted Paddy. 'If ever dat wood pinches yer bollocks, it'll make a girl outta ya.' Liam shot a sheepish grin at the old fellow and the men hauled on the rope. The beam went up quickly and with a little juggling from a push pole below, it was in position. Liam gave it a little persuasion with a wooden mallet, and the first rafter was in place. The procedure was repeated five more times and the roof skeleton was now complete. Instead of climbing down, Liam grasped the main beam and hung down off it. His feet were still a long way off the ground but when he let go, there were plenty of hands waiting to catch him and those that didn't, applauded him.

Ben Clancy spoke for the first time since Nenagh. 'Jayzus! Dat's da fast'st roof I ever saw done'

'Many hands make light work,' shot back Shevlin.

No one had noticed the slight, hunched figure approach the assembled crowd. They moved aside now as Moira made her way towards Liam, with Roisin a few steps behind her. Some blessed themselves and some turned their heads away, as if they would turn to stone just by looking at her. In her hand, Moira carried a small branch from a pine tree and now she held it out to Liam. She instructed him to place it on the highest part of the framing, so that it would invoke God's blessing on all those who entered the house. She told him it was an old tradition, carried on by the Celts and, before them, the Druids. Liam didn't question her. He scrambled back up and placed a single nail through the pine bough, attaching it to the peak of the roof. The old crone now turned and whispered something to Roisin. She handed her something and then left as mysteriously as she had come.

Roisin walked over to join Liam. 'The house is coming along grand,' she said, lightheartedly.

He hadn't heard her. 'It's done,' he said.

'What's done?'

'It's done. I went to the solicitors this morning and now it's done.'

'Come over for a beer tonight, when this crowd has gone, and tell me about it so I can pass it on to the priest.' Liam forced a smile and consented. She handed him the little vial that Moira had given to her a few minutes before. 'Give this to Ben,' she said. 'It will help his bad stomach and allow him to sleep.'

'Why didn't she give it to him herself?'

Roisin smiled softly. 'Because he's frightened of the old woman. She said a few drops in his beer before he goes to bed should make him feel better.' He took the little wooden bottle from her and she turned and left. He wished she had stayed. He felt more comfortable among all these strangers when she was with him.

Clancy stood apart from the crowd, grim-faced, holding his stomach. Shevlin told Liam that now he needed to fill in the gaps between the rafters with interwoven hazel sticks ... 'sort of like a basket' he said ... before any actual thatching could be done. He assured the young carpenter that it was simple enough, but tedious. Liam nodded in agreement and headed over to where Clancy stood.

He told him about the potion that Moira had brought for him. Clancy looked at it sideways. He thought that old witch could probably turn a person into a natterjack or a fly if she wanted to, but right now his stomach hurt so badly that he would take anything that might give him some relief. He told Liam that he was in agony now with the cramps.

Liam knew that worry could make a man sick and he had even heard of cases where people had died from it. He remembered a fellow in Thurles who had borrowed money and couldn't pay it back. He had been threatened with debtor's prison, and told that his family would be sentenced to a work house. Liam had heard that he got pains in his gut too, and he had finally shit black stuff, like tar, and died. He shuddered to think of this happening to poor Clancy.

The crowd dispersed, some went over to Hogan's and some home to their labours. Many were disappointed that someone hadn't got crushed or, at the very least, suffered a broken leg. Raising a roof often provided as much entertainment as a hanging. Liam made his way back to the rectory. He would wait a few hours before going to Hogan's.

CHAPTER 35

Liam sat alone in the darkness of the rectory. He had lit neither fire, nor candle. He was thinking about the old priest and how he wished he was here now. He considered walking to Moira's but, in the dark, he might miss the turnoff for the woodland boreen, or even the little cabin itself, hidden deep inside the wood. The prospect of spending a night in the cold, dark gloom of a forest provided sufficient deterrent, tomorrow would be soon enough. The moment he had decided not to venture out, the door swung open and the old man himself stood there. His sudden arrival startled Liam and he leaped to his feet, upsetting the chair and almost the table too.

'You're a bit jumpy, aren't you, lad?' exclaimed the reverend, laughing. 'I just called in to see if you might have a nice gammon joint on the go, or a piece of mutton even. Moira's a wonderful hostess, God love her, but her dietary restrictions are killing me.'

Liam relaxed. 'Oh yes, Father, I can see that you're just a shadow of yer former self,' he laughed too.

The priest nodded, 'I am! Sure, I must've lost at least

three stone in the last week. Now, light a candle, will you, it's as black as pitch in here.' Liam struck a spark from a flint and steel into some tinder. He blew on it until the smouldering turned into a little yellow flame. He lit a candle and then pulled out his pipe, offering a twist of tobacco to the priest.

Grogan tore some off. 'And that's another thing. Old Moira smokes a bunch of weeds in her pipe. It could strangle a man to death. A wee pinch of real Indian tobacco would be lovely. This will serve me another pipeful later.'

Liam took back the twist and saw that the old priest had taken almost half of it. 'Hmmmm, sometimes my generosity surprises even meself,' he said, putting the pouch away.

The old padre began. 'Roisin tells me the deed is done, so.'

Liam misunderstood. 'I don't have the deed yet. It might be in next week.'

The old man laughed. 'Sometimes, Liam, you can be thick as shi......you can be a bit dense. I meant you've seen the solicitor and negotiated the deal for our land.'

'Oh, yes,' replied Liam. 'The deal is done, alright. I've bought all the land around the village, except for the Reilly property. I didn't have enough for it all.'

The old priest scowled, 'Liam Flynn, now that's just spiteful.' He knew that, even if Liam'd had a hundred pounds, he wouldn't have purchased land owned by a Reilly.

Liam shrugged. 'What will happen to them?' asked the priest. Liam shrugged again.

'Does that mean you don't know or you don't care?'

Liam stood and straightened to his full height. 'Both.' The priest knew that any amount of preaching the virtues of morality and Christian forgiveness was useless and changed course.

'What have you had to eat today, lad?'

'Nothing,' replied Liam sullenly. He was feeling a pang of conscience about not having included the Reilly property in the deal and was wondering if he had done the right thing.

'Go across to Hogan's and find out if Roisin has something in the pot. Tell her it's for a poor old mendicant, and tell her to include a bit of meat.'

Liam was still smarting from the priest's words. 'I'll light a fire and you can snuff out the candle,' he said. 'We don't want to attract any more attention than we have to.' The young fellow put some fatwood in the hearth and placed a couple of sods of peat on top. In just a few minutes, the fire was burning and the aroma of turf hung in the air. He picked up his walking stick and went over to Hogan's.

As he entered the bar, he saw the same stranger he had seen there a few days before, the one who had given the impression of being the ringleader. He was sitting alone at one of the tables and his face was as sullen as it had been then. His muddy green-brown eyes looked Liam up and down and his scrutiny was both unwelcome and uncomfortable to the young man.

Liam went to the counter and motioned for Roisin to come over to him. He whispered to her that the priest needed something to eat.

Roisin looked surprised and she whispered back, 'Where is he?' Liam didn't answer, but jerked his head in the direction of the church. When she had filled two large bowls with barley soup and some mutton, she walked towards the door, with Liam following. 'I'll walk with you,' she said. Liam didn't argue.

She was relieved to be out of the bar and, when they had walked a little way, she spoke. Liam spoke at the same time and they both giggled.

'You first,' he said.

'The fellow in the bar, his name is Connelly and I'm sure he's up to no good. I don't know whether he's a spy for the English or if he's trying to instigate some kind of rebellion but, either way, I'd say he's trouble.'

'That answers the question I was going to ask you, so. Just keep your eyes skinned and your ears open.'

Back at the rectory, Roisin related the story about the stranger to Father Grogan and he sat and contemplated silently while Liam and the girl talked about the land purchase. They had been deep in conversation and so were surprised when the old man suddenly slapped his hand hard on the table.

'He's both!' he said, emphatically. 'I'm sure of it! I'd say he's a spy for the English and that, if he can find enough Irish who are behind on their rents, he'll be looking to start something up. If he can incite some act of rebellion, no matter how small, it'll make the perfect excuse for mass evictions. And if he's gathering the names of those who are rebellious in nature, that could mean more hangings. Attracting too much attention could mean disaster for our plan. We have to get rid of him!'

Liam glanced at his walking stick which stood where he'd left it, next to the door. 'Oh no you don't, Liam Flynn!' said the priest. 'You're no assassin.'

Liam stood, 'I had never built my own house before either, but I'm a quick learner.'

'Ah now, stop,' the old priest said gently. 'Lies and deceit are one kettle of fish. Murder is quite another and I can't absolve you of that.' Liam was relieved. If the

233

priest had said to go ahead, he would have done the deed without a second thought.

'Anyway, I have a better idea,' the old man said. 'Conspiracy and intrigue is best performed in the dark. If anyone thinks Roisin is eavesdropping at the bar, they'll find a new place to plan their schemes.' He had turned his attention to the girl and it frightened her. Desperate men could be dangerous on so many levels. She looked to Liam.

'It's too dangerous for her,' he said. 'I would rather go and bash his brains in tonight than ask Roisin to take a risk.'

The yeoman and the girl walked back to the store in silence, each thinking their own thoughts. Roisin had heard about men sacrificing their wealth, even their lives, for someone but this fellow was willing to sacrifice his eternal soul in order to protect her. She felt something stir inside her again. Her hand brushed against his and, this time, she too felt it for several minutes afterwards. Liam had made up his mind that the stranger would be found on the road tomorrow morning with magpies eating his brains.

When they opened the door of the bar, the stranger had left.

'Good night, Roisin,' the young carpenter said to the golden-haired girl.

'God bless you, Liam,' she replied.

CHAPTER 36

T he cleric was waiting for Liam when he returned and he glanced at the holly stick as Liam put it back beside the door. Relieved to see no blood on the shillelagh, he said,

'At least you haven't killed the scoundrel. If he is indeed working for the authorities, that would have brought an investigation and we can do without that.' Liam shrugged. He didn't tell the priest that the miscreant had already left Hogan's because, if he had still been there, Liam had made up his mind that it would have resulted in bloodshed, regardless of the consequences.

'I have to speak with you, my son, and I must be gone by first light.'

'Well say whatever it is you've come to say, so,' replied Liam.

'Papers will be served by the sheriff's men as soon as the land sale is registered. That'll cause panic amongst the farmers, and frightened men can become angry and desperate. I've prayed about this, and the only way I can think to keep you safe is to hold a meeting here in the church.'

Liam interrupted. 'But that will put *you* in danger. You'll be arrested by the authorities if ever they find out where you are.'

'The risk to me is small. The powers that be have plenty enough to concern themselves with, trying to contain the banditry. One more insignificant priest isn't going attract too much attention until they have that problem under control.'

'When? And what is it you intend telling people?'

'Trust me,' said the old man. The barley soup had grown cold but both men gulped it down as if it was to be their last meal. They spoke no more that night. The old curate said his prayers and Liam tucked in next to the fireplace for a fitful night's sleep.

He heard the priest leave before dawn for the walk back to his refuge in the forest. He was as pleased to hear him leave as he had been to see him arrive the night before. The priest always gave him something new to worry about. Liam slept easier after that and it was full daylight when he awoke. He would get to work on his house. It would help to keep his mind occupied.

Shevlin was already waiting at the house and, as usual, had a smart crack.

'Ah, yer looking grand an' rested dere, boyo.'

The sun was well up. 'Sorry, Paddy. I didn't sleep too well last night.'

'Ah, no bother. Sure ya slept well d'is marnin' instead.' Liam had to laugh. Shevlin got down to business. 'Now den, dis is what ya have ta do next. Ya need t' tie d' sways … dem are hazel twigs. Ya haff ta tie 'em wit some tar and string to d' rafters, every foot or so. Dat oughta keep ya busy fer d' next day or two. When yer done, gimme a shout.' With that, Paddy left.

The carpenter spent the next few hours cutting the

hazel and, to his relief, Clancy's son, Jamie, arrived to help him with the task. When they were finished, they had a pile of the twigs ready for the work. Liam fetched a pail of the pitch he used as an adhesive in his carpentry work, and a ball of hemp twine. Jamie went to his house to get his father's twelve foot ladder, and he and his Da carried it back over to Liam's worksite.

'Well, Ben, how's your gut today?'

'It ain't all better, but it's better'n yesterday. I slept like a baby anyway, t'ank God.' Liam thought that Moira merited some of Clancy's thanks, as well as God, and he wished he'd had some of her remedy himself last night, it might have helped him sleep too.

Liam began tying the twigs to the roof, starting at the top, about a foot below the ridge. On the carpenter's instructions, Jamie cut the string, soaked it in pitch and handed each length to Liam, along with the hazel rods. He thanked the boy each time he took one from him, glad that he was there to help. By the day's end, the roof had begun to resemble a spider's web. A few more hours work tomorrow and he would be ready to send for Paddy. He put a farthing into the boy's tar-soaked hand. The child was shocked by the action and tried to give it back.

'No lad,' insisted Liam, folding the child's fingers around the coin. 'A man's labour must be rewarded. I couldn't have done it without you.' Jamie opened his fist and gazed wide-eyed at the coin in his hand. He beamed with delight at Liam, and ran straight over to Hogan's to buy himself some sweets.

As Liam had planned, the roof was prepared the next day and Shevlin came to inspect the work.

'Ye're fast workers, lads, I t'ought it'd take yuz at least two days.' Paddy looked at them and laughed, they were both covered in tar up to their elbows. 'All I need is sum fedders and I could tar and fedder yuz, like a couple o' scalawags. Agh sure, a bit o' lard will clean ye up.' He stood back and looked at their progress. 'It's a good time o' year t' t'atch, alright,' he said, as if someone had asked him. 'D' wheat's bein' harvested an' dere should be plenny o' straw t' be had.'

As Paddy had predicted, there was indeed plenty of straw to be had. The wheat was being harvested and thrashed, before the grain was winnowed, and ground into flour. Paddy showed Liam how to gather the straw so that the butt ends were all facing in the same direction. This would make it easier to tie the bundles, or 'wads', as Paddy told him they were called. Several wagon-loads would be needed for the roof. The straw was unloaded as carefully as it had been loaded into the wagon.

Paddy was a craftsman in his own right and Liam listened to the old man, keen to learn from him. 'Da shtraw is brittle, ya see? Ya have t' wet it, 'r it'll break when ya work it.' He left the two younger men to fetch bucket after bucket of water from the holy well. The well was only about thirty feet or so from the house but, again. Liam was grateful for Jamie's help. This would have been backbreaking work if he'd had to do it alone.

The beginning of the thatching process itself was left until the next day. It could not be rushed and, if the roof was to be made durable and watertight, there would be no shortcuts. Paddy arrived early and Liam and Jamie were already there, waiting for him.

He gave them their instructions. 'What ya do is dis, lads. Ya grab a wad. As much as yer two hands can hold. Give it a couple o' twists t' hold it t'gedder an' den ya pin it t'rough da middle under d' sways, so it won't slide off. Always keep d' butt ends down t' shed d' rain. When ye have one row done, ye overlap d' next row by a half. It'll look like shite at furst but don't worry, I'll show ya how t' make it a proper t'atch.' Liam thought Paddy's instructions were vague, to say the least, but he had never known a thatcher who was a genius, so it surely couldn't be that difficult.

Liam and Jamie began the work. Jamie would grab a bundle and twist and hand it up to the carpenter. Liam had a cloth sack, containing a bunch of hazel crooks, tied around his waist. It was slow going at first but, after a few days, they had the work choreographed and the process became smoother and faster. Shevlin had been right about one thing, it did look like shite, as if a big yellow hedgehog had perched itself on the roof.

They called Paddy when they had finished and he came to take a look at it. He seemed pleased with their work. 'That's grand, lads,' he said. 'Now do it again. It needs to be two layers thick.' He walked away and Liam and Jamie gazed at each other in stunned silence.

When the last bundle of the second layer was tied, Paddy was there. He was carrying what looked like a huge curry comb … row upon row of nails in a board, attached to a pole.

'Dis is what's called a legate,' he announced, grandly. 'Ya use it t' pound the bundles so dey make one, like dis, see?' He demonstrated for the two young fellows. Sure enough, the separate wads became as one. 'Ya do d' whole roof like dat an' it should end up lookin' like a mangy dog. If it looks like one o' Ben Clancy's collies, ya know you're doin' it right.' Liam wanted to know how the ridgeline would be waterproofed, but he was afraid to ask.

After two more days of shoulder-aching work, the roof did indeed look like a wolfhound's coat. Shevlin had been dropping by from time to time, watching from a safe distance and leaving Liam and Jamie to their own devices. This was how he had learned the trade and he considered it to be only way. When they had finished, he was there again, this time with a new device. This one looked like a common rake, the teeth set about three inches apart.

'Now den, dis here is a side rake. Ya comb d' straw down wit' it, like you'd imagine young Roisin wud comb her hair. Da roof'll start t' look a lot better when ye're done.' This process was a little quicker, but just as hard on the shoulders. Liam had to reach all the way to the ridge, work his way across and then down. At the end of the day, however, the raking was complete.

Liam realised that he had barely given a thought to his dilemma in the last two weeks. He thought the deed papers must surely be delivered soon and he began to fret again. He must try to put it out of his mind for now. There was still the ridge to get done.

The last part of the roof was the peak and it was crucial that it be done right or the roof would leak and the straw would rot. Paddy showed Liam how to build a lattice, sixteen feet long and nine inches wide. There would need to be two, one for each side of the roof. Tarred string was used to tie the hazel twigs together and more wads of straw were prepared. This time, they were well-soaked to render them pliable enough to wrap over the peak. It was tedious work but the result was attractive and it would ensure that the water stayed out.

One last task was to be accomplished. It wasn't absolutely necessary, but Paddy had insisted and he was the foreman on the job, after all. He had brought an odd-looking blade with him his time.

'I want ya to give it a little trim around d' edges, just t' neaten it up like,' he said. The eaves did look a little scraggly and, once Liam had trimmed it all the way around, he had to admit that it looked much better. In fact, it was beautiful. It shone like gold and, although he knew it would turn a grey-green soon enough, right now it reminded Liam of Roisin's hair. He realised he hadn't given much thought lately to the girl with those beautiful eyes that could melt him with a mere glance. Now, that was all he could think about.

CHAPTER 37

L iam hadn't give his appearance any thought at all in the last few weeks. Now, he took stock of himself. He looked a right mess. His clothes were filthy and his face unshaven. His hair hung down to his shoulders like a bird's nest. He went out to the back of the rectory and stripped off all his clothes, soaping up his head first. For a job this big, he would need to be organized. He would work from the top down. He shaved, it was a painful affair. The razor was sharp but it caught up in his coarse whiskers. He cut the skin several times and, each time, he felt the sting of a little slice of flesh coming off. He scrubbed right down to his feet, the soles of which were as thick as a shoe, from walking barefoot. The palms of his hands were almost as hard as his soles. His clothes, too, were a fright. They were filthy and dusty from working the thatch and they smelled like a funeral shroud. They needed a good scrub.

Liam stood in the rectory as naked as the day he was born. He really wanted to see the girl with the yellow hair who had been so much in his thoughts lately, but his clothes were wet and he certainly couldn't see her in his altogether. He shot a glance over towards where his gentleman suit hung. Well, it would certainly surprise her, he thought, and maybe even give her something to smile about. He wanted to see her smile again. The last time they had been together, neither of them had any cause for merriment. He dressed himself. He wouldn't wear those infernal shoes. They seemed to hate his feet almost as much as his feet hated them. Hmmm ... the necktie ... no. Only a fool would put a noose around his own neck. The trousers and the shirt were enough. He grabbed his walking stick and headed over to Hogan's.

As he approached the bar, he could hear no noise coming from inside. When he entered, he saw why. Sean Reilly and the sinister stranger were sitting together and, when Liam entered, they both turned as one. Sean stared at him and his hatred was so palpable that Liam could feel it. The dark-eyed man glared at him too. Liam cast a glance around the bar. Roisin was nowhere to be seen and Michael Hogan sat behind the bar, with a wooden bat next to him. Sean's former associates weren't there. Sean still had his right hand bandaged, but Liam noticed that the wrapping was much lighter now, also that his right arm was noticeably smaller than his left, from disuse. The two men stared at Liam for what seemed like an eternity, then Sean spoke.

'Did ya get dressed up to apologise?' He smiled mirthlessly. 'Well, I don't accept,' he spat. Liam instinctively grasped the walking stick with his right hand and the movement was not lost on the two at the bar. They both stood up and faced him. Sean was considering the odds and he didn't like them. Michael Hogan was behind him and Liam was in front, and both had weapons. When Sean leaned over and whispered something to the dark man, they both got up and made their way towards the door. They had to pass Liam and he moved aside but Sean made sure he knocked his own shoulder into Liam's on the way out.

Michael Hogan gave an audible sigh of relief. 'Dose two are worse fer business than a fire. Nobody's come in fer days since they've been hangin' around here.'

'The dark fellow has the look of a rough one,' said Liam.

'He does indeed, and he's bin comin' here regularly for d' last few weeks. Sometimes he has one companion but he's had as many as four.'

Liam asked, 'What do you know about him?'

'Nothing at all, sure. Roisin is so frightened of the man that she tries to keep to the back room when he's in, and she's not easily scared, as you know. He has the air of a ringleader of some sort, alright, but I can't find out what he's up to.' Liam wished he had acted on his first impulse and waylaid him on the road out of the village. He could have turned his pockets inside out as if bandits had done the nefarious deed, like had happened with the salesman at Knigh Cross.

Roisin came out from the back room. She looked pleased and relieved to see Liam.

'Ah Liam, it's you. It's well you didn't force a confrontation with that stranger. He carries a skeane under his left armpit, I saw it. It has a black handle of bog oak. With a knife like that, he could have cut you into dog meat.' Liam, too, was glad he hadn't pressed the encounter. A man skilled in the use of a skeane could slide it between your ribs and into a lung in one swift movement. Perhaps he had better give this fellow a wide berth. Sean Reilly was just a bully but this stranger seemed much more sinister and dangerous.

'Have you learned anything from him, Roisin?'

She looked dismayed. 'Not a thing. He's so guarded with his speech that, even when I've been here, I can hear nothing of what he's saying. I can tell you this, though. I've seen the scars on him of someone who has survived his fair share of fights.' Liam wondered if the stranger had been in the military and thought it wasn't unlikely. Many men had trained in martial arts on both sides during the wars, and had found themselves out of work when the wars were over. Now, for many of them, their business was any kind of trouble they could find.

'He could be a bandit or a highwayman,' speculated Liam, 'especially if he's consorting with the likes of Sean Reilly.'

'No,' replied Roisin. 'I don't think so because he's been in here with tenants from Johnson's property. I don't know what their names are, but McCormack and Gleeson have been seen with him. The others don't come in very often.'

So many thoughts spun around in Liam's head that he didn't even hear her when she commented on his attire. She repeated herself.

'I said you're a bit overdressed for Hogan's aren't you?'

Her humour was lost on him. 'Oh, I washed me shirt and britches and they're still wet so I put on what I had.'

'And it's very elegant you are, sir, but you forgot your shoes.' Liam's face flushed as he looked down at his bare feet.

'Agh, I'm just bog Irish, sure. You can dress a pig up but you can't take him to a dance.'

Roisin feigned indignation, 'Hey! You had better not say anything bad about my raggedy man.' She smiled and he smiled back. She had called him *her* man.

Roisin had ushered Liam to a table and was just

putting a plate of lamb stew in front of him when Paddy Shevlin walked in.

'Jeez, I just passed dem two rogues. Didya run dem out, Liam?'

'No Paddy, they left on their own account,"

Shevlin grinned his yellow-toothed grin. 'On account dey was afraid yu'd bang dem on d'eir heads wit yer stick.' Liam shook his head, Paddy never missed an opportunity.

The carpenter tucked into his supper and Roisin sat herself opposite him at the table, watching him.

'I haven't seen you for a good while, Liam.' He had just taken in a mouthful of food and shook his spoon at her while he chewed.

'I've been busy.' He swallowed. 'I almost have the cottage done. A bit of plastering on the outside walls to get rid of some of the bumps, some windows and doors and I can move in.' Roisin nodded and said she thought he should fit the windows and doors first. That way, he could move in right away and they would be neighbours and wouldn't that be lovely. He visibly blushed and tried to think of a reply.

'Liam Flynn,' she laughed, 'I am shamelessly flirting with you and you're so thick you don't even know it.' Liam was indeed ignorant when it came to any kind of interaction with an intelligent, beautiful woman.

'Sorry,' he said. 'I've never been flirted on before.'

'With! Liam. Flirted *with*. I don't think you would have recognised it if you had been.' Another epic flush threatened to redden him from the top of his head to his toes. Roisin was laughing and, as she re-filled his tankard with beer, some of it splashed on his good trousers. She gasped, instinctively reached for a cloth and started to wipe the spill off. She suddenly realised that she was wiping the front of a man's trousers, Liam's trousers, and now it was her turn to blush. She handed the cloth to Liam and hurried away.

CHAPTER 38

T wo days later, there was another incident involving the dark stranger.

Ben Clancy's wife, Colleen, had gone into labour and Roisin went to attend her. She had done this on several occasions before and all had gone well but, this time, the labour was troublesome and Roisin knew she was going to need help. She told Clancy to call for Moira. The old woman had delivered many babies over the years and Colleen was going to need an experienced midwife.

'I'm staying here,' replied Clancy. 'I'll send Jamie.' Jamie didn't wait to be asked and ran as fast as he could to the old hag's cottage. He was back in less than an hour but it was going to take the old woman longer to walk the distance to Gortalocca. Father Grogan arrived first.

Clancy's wife was covered with sweat and she was shivering one minute and burning up the next. She was lapsing in and out of consciousness and Roisin wiped her off with a damp towel, trying to make her as comfortable as possible. Colleen's legs had swollen to twice their normal size and her face was the colour of beetroot. The priest had seen this before, childbirth was a dangerous occupation. Ben sat by his wife's side, holding her hand and talking to her low and lovingly. Roisin heard him plead with her, 'Don't leave me. What would I do without you?'

The younger children didn't understand what was going on and just stared at their parents in silence, wide-eyed. The oldest, Jamie, had tears running down his cheeks.

The pregnant woman had now completely lost consciousness and her breathing was shallow and intermittent. Colleen Clancy was dying, and so was her unborn child. Father Grogan quietly began to administer the Last Rites.

Clancy tried to stop him. 'She's alright, Father. She'll be alright.' Roisin held Ben's hands and the priest continued. As he completed his ministrations, Moira crept in quietly. She put her hand kindly on Ben's arm and he turned his anguished face to her.

'She's gone to God and the ages,' she said simply. Then she kissed the dead woman on the forehead and left the house. Ben buried his face in Roisin's shoulder and wept silently. Jamie was heartbroken. With the single last gasp of his mother, his world had changed.

Colleen Murphy Clancy had been born on a farm in the township of Killadargan, about a mile from Gortalocca, and she had never travelled more than five miles from the place of her birth. She was a simple woman who adored her husband and her children. She was able spin yarn from the family sheep and turn that yarn into something useful and beautiful. She could create a tasty meal from very little and had never been heard to complain about the hard work that was her life. She had a patient warmth about her and an easy smile.

Now, she would smile no more. Her body would lie on the floor of the little cottage for two days, to allow the mourners to pay their respects, then she would be buried in the cemetery near St Patrick's Church here in Gortalocca. Her name would be scratched on a stone and the stone would be placed on her resting place, eventually to be forgotten. Colleen Murphy Clancy had been just 29 years old, but had looked much older. She left nothing behind her except her now motherless children and her grieving husband, who would never forget his sweet, beloved wife.

Clancy stood up and wiped his nose on his sleeve. 'I hafta go dig a hole,' he said quietly.

Roisin put her hand on his arm. 'Paddy and Liam will do that for you, Ben,' she said tenderly. 'You stay here with your wife.' With tears in her eyes now, she looked over at Paddy Shevlin and Liam Flynn, who had been hovering near the door.

'Show us where ya want it Ben and it'll be done,' said Paddy, trying to keep his composure. Liam left to get the shovels which had been used so recently to build his house. Now, those same shovels had a more sombre duty to perform. All of them knew that death, like birth, was just a part of life, but that held little consolation when they could do nothing but watch the agonising grief of their friend, Ben Clancy. The three men now walked over to the deserted church yard and Ben chose a spot that he could see from his cottage. Along with the other two men, he began to dig. He was inconsolable, empty and crushed.

Roisin had ushered the children outside, and now she began the process of washing and dressing the body of the woman who had been her neighbour. Father Grogan had gone outside with the children and he held the youngest in his arms as he watched over the Clancy brood. Jamie had gone off to sit by himself. He didn't want anyone to see him cry.

When she had finished, Roisin escorted the children back inside to see their mother. Her once rosy cheeks were now a bluish-white and her eyes still slightly open. That bothered Jamie and he said so.

'Sometimes the eyes do stay open a little, my son,' said the priest. 'Maybe she's taking a good long look at you all, just one last time.' This was more than Jamie's little heart could bear and now he wept in earnest.

Father Grogan and Roisin had a whispered conversation. The children had to be fed. The priest suggested that he remain at the cottage with the children and wait for the three men to return, and that she should go back to the store and prepare some dinner for the grieving family. Roisin agreed. She had done all she could do here now and she would rather be busy. She had hung a plump hen last night for today's dinner. Now, instead of feeding the usual inebriated men, the chicken would feed the children.

As Roisin prepared the food, she thought about Colleen. She had been just ten years older than herself and she'd had nine children and a loving husband. Now, it was her turn to let go of the tears she had been biting back, and she didn't know if they were for Colleen or for herself.

People came in two's and three's to pay their respects at the tiny Clancy cottage. Some shed tears, others were there merely because it was the custom and was expected. Some were cousins or distant family, others just people who had known the dead woman by sight. Roisin collected the flock of children and brought them back to Hogan's, where the younger ones played on the floor as if today's events were of no consequence. Jamie sat on a stool at the bar and stared into space with no expression, lost in his own world. Roisin handed him a piece of soda bread and he took a bite, then discarded the rest of it on the bar. His senses were dulled by grief and the bread had neither taste nor smell. It was about four o'clock in the afternoon when the door of the bar opened and the dark stranger walked in.

He stood inside the door and scanned the room, filled with children.

'What the hell is this?' he snarled. 'An orphanage?' Jamie leapt off the barstool and rushed at the dark man with the green-brown eyes. The man's right hand instinctively went for the long dagger which he had hidden under his coat. Roisin looked around for some sort of weapon.

'Our Mam died this mornin'. Me Da's diggin' a hole fer her.' Jamie cried out, caught somewhere between anger and grief.

The man's eyes softened perceptibly, 'I'm sorry to hear that, boyo.' Roisin joined Jamie with an iron pot in her hand and the man gave her a half smile. Roisin hadn't seen any expression at all on the fellow's face before and she relaxed a little. She told him the bar was closed to customers today, and he said that he had arranged to meet someone here. They heard the door open and they both looked towards it. Liam stood in the open doorway, with the holly stick in his hand. His feet were spread slightly and his blue eyes watched the dark man's every movement.

The man tensed. 'You're Flynn," he said, squinting his eyes and looking Liam up and down.

Liam stared back and their eyes locked. 'I'm Liam Flynn,' he said, 'from Thurles.' Roisin went to stand next to Liam now and the stranger laughed and turned his palms up in a mock gesture of submission.

'I seem to be outmanned here today.' He turned to Jamie and made a formal half bow. 'My condolences on the death of your mother, boy.' He looked back to Liam and Roisin and his half smile flickered about his face for a moment before it gave way to a scowl. He walked up to Liam and looked him square in the eyes.

'We'll meet again, Flynn.' He brushed past Liam as he walked out the bar and Liam felt a shiver go through his body.

CHAPTER 39

C olleen Clancy's death had cast a pall over the little village of Gortalocca and the whole atmosphere of the township changed. Clancy had changed too. Gone were Paddy and Clancy's lively discussions and banter. Ben's heart had been wrung out of him and he had become sombre and cheerless. He'd already had the threat of eviction hanging over him, and now he had lost his wife. Even his appearance changed. His once clean and neatly mended clothes were now filthy, and his eyes had dark circles under them.

When he was in Hogan's, what few conversations he did engage in became so dark that folk started to avoid him and, on occasion, even Roisin's patience with him was tried. He was always shouting at the children now and, sometimes, they could be heard screaming from inside the cottage. Jamie spent more and more time with Liam.

On the days that Liam went down to Matt O'Brien's forge in Ballyartella, he took the boy with him. Liam hadn't forgotten that he'd promised to help build the iron gates for the Butlers, in return for the stash of pine boards that were stored in Matt's barn. Jamie had an aptitude for building and the natural curiosity that was common in children went deeper with him. He was interested in the work the smith was doing too and, at first, Matt O'Brien just tolerated the boy's presence. However, after a few days, like Liam, he had developed an affection for the boy. It was easy to like Jamie. He would perform any task given to him, without complaint, and he asked questions which even the smith had to think twice about.

For a short time, at least, the two men and the boy were a team. Their days were spent forging the individual pieces of wrought iron and, after about a week of the two men hammering and the boy working the bellows, they were complete. The assembly process would be quicker. On one occasion, Liam overheard Matt telling the boy how much more rewarding it would be for him to work with iron than with wood.

'Hey! Trying to steal me apprentice, are ya?' Liam laughed.

His fellow yeoman looked up at him and winked. 'I could do worse.'

They were good days and Liam realised how much he missed the forge where he had grown up.

The gates were finished and it was time to hang them. The Butlers sent a large wagon, pulled by a team of draught horses, the biggest animals the young boy had ever seen. When the gates had been carefully loaded, Matt, Liam and Jamie climbed up onto Matt's wagon and followed. The journey to the castle took several hours and, when they finally arrived, they were met by the overseer. He was a tall man, impeccably dressed and with an air of authority. He regarded the yeomen distastefully, with the aplomb of a man used to looking down his nose at people. He was clearly annoyed that he had to watch as the gates were hung, but it was his duty to ensure that his masters were satisfied with the job. He asked far too many questions and finally, after numerous interruptions, Matt grew tired of it.

'If ya want me t' do d' work, it's one price,' he said. 'If ya want me t' teach ya, da price'll be double.' Irked by the boldness of this Irishman, the overseer directed his questions to Liam. Liam feigned ignorance, claiming he was just a carpenter invited to help.

The man immediately changed his demeanour. 'Oh really?' he said. 'Can you build furnishings?'

Liam stood up straight and looked the man directly in the eye as he had been taught.

'If it's made from wood, I can build it,' he said.

'Well then, I may need your services,' the man said. 'Where can I contact you?'

O'Brien smiled. Liam pointed at him and said officiously, 'You may reach me through my associate, Mr O'Brien.' The overseer just caught himself as he almost made a slight bow to Liam.

When the work was done, the three headed back to Ballyartella.

'Ya pulled dat ol' dog's tail, Liam, an' ya didn't even get bit,' Matt laughed heartily. 'He controls almost all o' da building being done dere. Ya might even get a commission out o' dis, sure.' Liam acknowledged him with a nod. Jamie was taking it all in. When they arrived back at the forge, Matt handed Liam five shillings. Liam was shocked. He hadn't expected any money in return, just the pile of wood.

'Take it,' said Matt. 'Dat ol' buzzard liked d' work an' he pro'bly stole 'is own share of 'is master's money. I'm only sharin' d' wealth.'

Liam handed Jamie five pennies. 'Well, in that case, I'm sharin' it too,' he said, smiling at the boy's delight. The two men shook hands and Liam said he would be back the next day to pick up the wood.

*

Sean Reilly was in Nenagh. He was back with his old associates and they were drinking as much beer and poteen as Sean's purse would allow. Today, his purse allowed for plenty. Mick Reilly had sent his son on an errand to buy a draught horse for the farm and had given him four pounds, a princely sum for a farm horse but the one Mick had picked out was well worth it. The draught was a gelding in his prime, four years old and seventeen hands tall. Now, with Sean's purse getting lighter and his belly full of whiskey, he thought he had better take stock of his finances. He cleared his head for a moment and counted the coins he had left. He was five shillings short.

He decided that, as he was always lucky at gambling, he would recoup his losses at a card table. It was a drunken man's idea and, as it turned out, not a very sound one. When he left the card table, he was fifteen shillings short. He only had a little over three pounds now and he couldn't possibly buy the horse with that. For that sum, the owner would never hold a note. He knew his father would be furious if he came home with no horse and less money than he had gone with. He wondered if he should tell his father he had been robbed by highwaymen and keep all the money for himself but, given his previous antics, he knew that his father wouldn't believe him. Sean Reilly formulated a plan.

*

It was getting dark by the time Liam and his young companion walked into Gortalocca. As they passed the Clancy cottage, Jamie hesitated and Liam said,

"C'mon, lad, let's go to Hogan's for a bite to eat.' The boy grinned and skipped the rest of the way to Hogan's. When Liam caught up to him at the door, he put his hand on the child's shoulder and opened the door of the bar, laughing. He pushed Jamie inside and announced,

'Does this establishment have any victuals for a couple of hard-working men?' Several locals who were sitting at the bar turned in unison and smiled at the sight of the grimy man and the broadly-grinning boy. Liam motioned for Jamie to sit at a table and he joined him. Roisin was pleased to see them and she immediately served them up a big plate of spuds each, with a hunk of greasy mutton on the side. She watched as they dug in.

'A beer and a buttermilk, is it?' she asked.

'No,' demanded Liam, jovially. 'This young fellow has worked as hard as a man for two weeks and he has a purse full of money to show for it. He wants a real drink!'

Roisin looked unsure but she poured a measure of beer anyway. 'If you ask for a dram of poteen for the boy, I'll throw you both out on yer ears.'

'Beer will be grand, thanks, we don't want him growing up too fast.'

*

The trio of miscreants left the gambling hall in Nenagh and, when they were out on the dark street, Sean presented his plan to the other two. They would go out onto the Lough Derg Road and ambush a traveller. If they got lucky, they might get someone with a good horse or a fat purse, or both. Fergus was enthusiastic but Seamus said he would rather take a nap. Sean gave Seamus a shove and sent him reeling and stumbling. He almost fell on his face and thought he would throw up. Sean prodded him onwards with his blackthorn stick. They had been walking on the road out of Nenagh for about twenty minutes or so when Fergus stopped. This location provided good cover for them to take someone by surprise and they had used it on several occasions before.

Sean shook his head. 'Not this time,' he said. 'There's a bend in the road another half mile on. We'll wait there.' The two lackeys knew where he meant and, as they set off, he walked behind, taking stock of them. Fergus was the faster of the two, so Sean would need to deal with him first. Seamus was fatter, so he would be able to run him down if needs be.

When they arrived at the point in the road where it changed direction, Sean looked around. There wasn't a farmhouse or a person to be seen. He waited until the little man turned his back, then he raised his stick and brought a mighty blow down on top of his head. The little fellow dropped as if he had been poleaxed. Now, Sean turned his attention to Seamus, whose eyes were wide. He couldn't believe what he had just seen and he was rooted to the ground. Sean lunged at him and the stout man held his arm over his head. The stick came down on it with a cracking sound and Seamus' arm dropped as he turned to run. Sean's next blow caught him a glancing strike but it was enough to stun him. The third hit him with a thud on the side of his unguarded head, and he fell to the ground like a sack of potatoes. Fergus rolled over and moaned. Sean raised his stick over him and brought it down like a sledge hammer. The job was done and the two men lay dead.

Sean's plan was almost complete. He had to give himself an injury that would at least appear plausible. He lowered his head and charged at a stone wall, his head taking the full brunt of the impact. He reeled back, blood trickling from his hair and down his face. He wiped his blood-smeared shillelagh off on Seamus' shirt and began the walk back to Gortalocca, planning his story. Maybe he could blame Liam Flynn. By now, everyone had heard how the carpenter had bested the trio before, so that would make a nicely plausible story. Perhaps even Roisin would believe it. That would stop her looking at that bastard with cow eyes. It would get him a bit of sympathy too and solve his money troubles, all in one stroke. Sean Reilly smiled with satisfaction at his night's work.

CHAPTER 40

The rumours spread like contagion around the eastern shores of Lough Derg. Two locals had been murdered and a third severely injured. The stories were tailored to the individual listener's ear. Most blamed outsiders, vagabond highwaymen who struck and then moved on. Others, particularly those who held the reins of power, believed there was a resident band of desperados. Ethough the victims were Catholic, the Papists would, of course, shoulder the blame. It was convenient for the fat old sheriff to believe that they were from Limerick or Clare, but his opinion was in the minority. His days as a lawman were numbered, and this would be the match in the powder barrel.

Sean enjoying being the focus of the stories, and he basked in the glow of attention. Even Liam and Roisin felt sympathy for the man who had lost his two closest companions in such a brutal way and was, himself, so grievously injured.

At first, Sean claimed his memory of the events was

muddled and that he couldn't name the perpetrators. In reality, he was taking time to work out the details of the story he would tell. Then, after two days, he said his memory had started to return and that he knew the culprit to be Liam Flynn. He doubted people would believe that one man could do so much damage to three, even if he had accidentally defeated the trio some weeks before, and so he said that Liam was the leader of a band of cut-throats. The problem with that story was that Liam had a perfect alibi. He and Jamie had been at Hogan's eating supper when the deed occurred, and there were corroborating witnesses to testify to it. Sean changed his story and now it was someone of the carpenter's height and weight who had led the gang. He even suggested it could be the dark stranger who had been loitering about. He said he was certainly of the correct stature and he knew that the man's presence already frightened many of the locals.

Because Sean Reilly had a penchant for hyperbole and because everyone loves a good story, the tale soon reached epic proportions. At first, he was merely one of the victims of a sneak attack by a few thugs. Soon, it became an epic struggle where Sean had fought valiantly to protect his comrades from a band of ruffians. According to him, he was holding his own and had most of them beaten when he was attacked cowardly from behind, and felled by the leader. Those that knew Sean, now had serious doubts about the veracity of what had occurred on the night in question. Those who didn't know him loved the tale of a hero who had courageously fought a losing battle against insurmountable odds. Whenever someone pointed out an inconsistency in the story, Sean would claim that his memory was still a little hazy.

Now, Sean Reilly was good for business in Hogan's and so Liam spent less time in the bar and more time preparing his house. He had built doors of thick pine. They were divided into two so that the top could be left open for ventilation, weather permitting, and closed to keep out the elements when it was not. The windows were built and installed. Roisin wandered across the road from time to time to check Liam's progress and to chat. Her father wasn't happy about it because not only was Liam a member of the Church of Ireland, but also it was unseemly for a unmarried woman of her age to befriend an unmarried man, unless there was some sort of agreement between the two families. On one occasion, Michael Hogan even suggested that perhaps his daughter might reconsider her relationship with Sean Reilly. After all, his family owned the largest farm in Gortalocca. By the time his daughter had finished telling him exactly what she thought of his suggestion, he wished he had kept his thoughts to himself.

Liam taught young Jamie the secrets and tricks of carpentry and let him help to build the sparse furniture for the cottage. The boy was eager to learn and a hard worker. Together, they built a table, three chairs and a dresser. The dresser was made of pine, washed over with a pale green milk paint, and it would hold his three earthenware cups and his three wooden plates. He had considered getting more, but he only had occasional visits from Roisin or Father Grogan. The Franciscan Friary in Nenagh remained intact, as long as no Masses were said there, and so the priest was becoming lax in his vigilance. He even considered moving back into the rectory but decided that, as a constable had placed a note on his door, it would probably be unwise. A low profile would be the most judicious course.

Sean's epic tale had reached the ears of those in power and the old sheriff had been sacked, because the spate of robberies and the mayhem was continuing unabated. The new sheriff had been installed and, so far, was an unknown quantity.

Liam's deed papers for the land around Gortalocca had finally been delivered. It had taken over a month, because the documents had to be registered in Dublin, and the backlog was immense due to the amount of Irish land changing hands.

The old priest came to Liam's cottage one night, along with Moira and Roisin.

'So, Liam,' said the priest. 'It's official. You own almost all the property in the township. What are you going to do now?'

'Me?' exclaimed Liam, 'I thought you had a plan!'

Moira and Roisin were both surprised at Liam's reaction. 'I have,' said the old curate, smiling. 'I was giving you your final test.' Liam looked puzzled. 'Sometimes,' said the priest, 'when a man acquires power, the temptation is too great for him to withstand. Now that the property is in your name, you could evict the tenants any time you wanted. I was testing you to see what your intentions were.'

Liam was furious and he let the old man know it. 'I risked my neck so that the people in your village could retain ownership of the land, and you still had to test me?' He paced around the room. If there's betrayal of any kind here, he thought, it rests on the priest's shoulders.

The priest looked down. 'I'm sorry, Liam,' he said. 'I'm old, and what I've seen of the world has taught me not to have great expectations from men.'

Liam shook his head. 'I trusted you, but you didn't

have any faith in me at all, did you? Alright, old man,' he fumed. 'tell me what the plan is, but I'm not going to trust you anymore, you old bastard.' He had been doubted by a man who he would have entrusted his life to and the priest's one question had changed things between the two men forever. It would be just business from now on.

The old priest gathered himself and looked up, although he still felt he couldn't look Liam in the eye because the young man's animosity was palpable. He began.

'I will call a meeting of the eight farmers involved and tell them that you are now their landlord, but that they will keep their land. I will explain the Penal Laws to them as well as I can. I'll tell them that you don't want any rent from them, but that they will have to pay the annual ten percent tithe to the Church of Ireland. It would not be fair for you to carry that burden. For them to have to pay anything at all to work their own land, will be a bitter pill to swallow, my son, but I will try to explain that it's what they must do to keep their land. Those who refuse, I will leave to their own devices and you can deal with them as you wish.'

Roisin interrupted. 'What about Clancy? He hasn't been right ever since his wife died.'

'I have thought about him too,' said the priest, 'and he's the fly in the soup. He's so bitter about his wife dying that it has disturbed his mind and I don't know what will become of him and the children. He even says that you stole his son, Liam.'

'What?' Liam interrupted, 'I stole his son? He gave him to me! In fact, the truth is he threw him at me!' Liam had had a bellyful of all this and was beginning to wish he'd stayed in Thurles.

'Well,' said the priest, 'you asked for my plan and there you have it. You will be hated by some, by those whose land you couldn't buy as well as those whose land you could, but that can't be helped.' Liam kept silent and went back to pacing the floor. The other three looked at each other and left Liam alone with his thoughts.

Roisin returned a few minutes later. 'You're not angry with me, are you Liam,' she asked softly.

'I'm angry at the whole world right now!' he snapped back at her, then relented when he saw the hurt on her face. 'I'm sorry, Roisin,' he said, with a sigh. 'I'm less mad at you than at anyone else but I'm angry with the whole situation and I'm angry with myself for getting into it.'

'Did you do this just for the priest, Liam, or did you have another reason?' she asked bluntly. He was taken aback by her boldness. Why could he never think of how to respond to her? He shrugged his shoulders and looked down at his feet and, this time, she didn't scold him for it but, instead, put her hand under his chin and tilted his head upwards.

'It doesn't matter, Liam. Whatever the reason, I think it's very brave of you.' Liam looked into her blue eyes and he couldn't utter a sound. She returned his steady gaze with hers and, after a pause of several long seconds, she laughed.

'I think I've struck you dumb again, haven't I, my raggedy man?' She flashed Liam a smile and winked before opening the door and leaving the cottage.

CHAPTER 41

F ather Grogan had notified the parish that he would be conducting a meeting in the old church. Most were overjoyed, thinking that things were about to get back to normal, and they had arrived, full of optimism, to hear what their priest had to tell them. As they listened to his words, their joy soon turned to anger and resentment and most of it was directed towards the carpenter.

The old priest tried to explain that nothing would really change for them, but the fact that they no longer owned their own land, and they had a landlord now, was enough to incite their outrage. As predicted, Clancy's reaction was the worst. He ranted on about how that devious Irishman had plotted with the English, whilst pretending to befriend the villagers. They had even helped the lowlife to build a house amongst them, he said, and he would see the carpenter dead before he would get an eviction.

Father Grogan made every attempt to bank the fires, but the hostility raged. The eight farmers who lived on the property that Liam had purchased, were furious that land which their families had farmed for generations, was now in the hands of a landlord. Those who lived outside Gortalocca were angry that their land had not been included. Even Paddy Shevlin harboured a silent resentment.

Liam had been warned that this would probably be the outcome from the very beginning but, back then, he hadn't really cared. He had been alone in the world for most of his life and he didn't need anyone's friendship or approval. Now things had changed. Liam himself had changed. He had shed his impenetrable shell and had begun to feel comfortable interacting with the local people. He felt he had made friends and had become part of the community, and he was surprised to find that he liked it. Now, however, he had become a pariah, an outcast shunned by almost everyone.

As he sat by himself in his cottage, he longed for the time when his life had been uncomplicated. He was glad he had his work, at least, it might help him to feel less isolated and alone. He wasn't alone for long. He heard a scratching noise at the door and, when he opened it, Jamie stood there. The boy had been battered. His left cheek was bruised, his eye was swollen shut and his nose was bloody. In his left hand, the boy held a rope which was tied around his dog's neck. The dog hadn't fared much better, his head hung low and he was shaking. The animal's fur was matted with blood, and the only thing that was keeping him on his feet was the love he had for the boy.

Liam picked up the dog and ushered Jamie inside the house. He pulled a blanket over from where it lay folded in a corner of the room, and laid the dog gently on it. He sat the boy down in front of the fire and pulled over a bucket of water he kept in the cottage. Dipping a rag into the water, he started to clean his wounds. The child stopped him.

'Could ya take care o' me dog first? He's all I got.' Liam did as he was asked and told the boy to clean his face himself. Jamie winced when he moved his arm.

'Take off yer shirt,' ordered Liam and the boy complied. His back was covered with bruise over bruise and, in places, his skin hung in shreds.

Normally, Liam considered himself to be an even-tempered sort of fellow and he prided himself on keeping his emotions in check. He had joked in the past about how it was the Presbyterian in him. Now, he saw red and his blood boiled.

'Who did this to you, Jamie? he demanded through clenched teeth.

'Me Da did it, but yer not t' take it out on 'im, because he ain't bin right since me Mam died.'

Liam inhaled and exhaled deeply. 'You clean your face, boyo, and I'll tend to the dog.' As bad as the boy was, it was obvious that the collie had been on the receiving end of an even worse beating. As Liam bathed the dog, uncovering its appalling wounds, he knew it would need more care than he was able to give, if it was to survive.

'I'm going to get Moira, for your dog,' he told Jamie. 'You put the bolt in the door and don't open it for anyone until I come back, do you understand?' The boy nodded meekly and looked anxiously at his dog. Liam stood outside the cottage and waited until he heard the bolt slide before he ran to the old woman's house.

When he arrived, he told her hurriedly what had happened. The twenty minute run in the cool air had helped to clear his head. When Father Grogan asked if he should come too, Liam snapped, 'No! You stay here, old man. You can't give a dog the Last Rites.'

Moira intervened before any more harsh words were spoken. 'Don't bury the poor beast until he stops breathing.' Liam acknowledged her and set out for the return trip. He jogged back along the road and, when he reached his cottage, Roisin was standing outside the door.

'Jamie won't let me in,' she exclaimed.

'He's only following my instructions. I told him not to let anyone in. I was afraid his father would come back to finish the job.' Roisin looked puzzled. 'Come in,' said Liam, 'and see for yourself.'

The boy was sitting on the floor next to his dog. The animal could no longer stand and its breathing was laboured now. The dog raised his head and wagged his tail in a feeble greeting when Liam and Roisin came in, then lay his head back in Jamie's lap. The boy looked even worse now. The bruising had twisted half his face into a purple mass and his eye had turned into a sightless slit. Blood trickled from his nose to his chin and onto his bare chest. The wounds on his back gave testimony to many beatings over a period of time. Roisin could hardly bring herself to look at his horrific injuries, and she could not imagine what the poor child must have suffered.

'That's right, boyo,' said Liam. 'You tend to your dog and I'll take care of your back.' He began to clean the lad's back and the boy winced with pain. Roisin took the wet rag from Liam, 'You're too rough, you clumsy clod,' she scolded. 'C'mere, I'll take care of the boy and you help him clean the dog.'

'I just don't understand.' Roisin directed her words to Liam as she bathed the boy's wounds. 'Why?'

'I don't know why. You'll have to ask the boy that.' Liam was bristling with rage and it festered inside him.

He scrubbed the dog a little too hard and it yelped in pain. Liam spoke softly to it. 'I'm sorry, fella.' The dog was too weak to even lift its head.

'Why did you get beaten like this, alannah?' Roisin asked the boy gently. Jamie looked at her and his one open eye brimmed over with tears.

'Me Da had too much poteen an' he said how Liam's sort was worse den Cromwell, an' I tol' him dat Liam's our friend an' dat's all it took t' get 'im started an' once he started he couldn't stop an' when he'd finished wit me, he lef' me on da floor an' he turned on me dog an' den he t'rew us both out da door an' said I w's never t' come back.' That was the most either Liam or Roisin had ever heard Jamie speak at once. The boy broke down and sobbed.

'You're staying here, partner,' Liam told him, softly. 'This is your home from now on.'

Moira arrived just then and, if she felt any surprise at what she found, her wrinkled face didn't betray it. She examined the boy quickly and said that he would be alright with time, but she still put some concoction she had brought with her on his face. The poor animal was another matter.

'I need some lard t' mix wit' me herbs,' she told Liam brusquely. He handed her a small tin and she looked at it. 'Dat's not enough,' she said. 'I'm going t' need much more. Go to Paddy's and get a big pail of it.'

Liam started for the door but Roisin put her hand on his arm. 'You stay here,' she said. 'If you ask Paddy for anything, he'll slam the door in your face.' Liam realised she was right. He sat back down on the floor with Jamie and tried his best to comfort the child.

When Roisin came back through the door, she was empty-handed. Shevlin followed her in, carrying a large bucket of lard. He took in the scene and was shocked at what he saw.

'Liam,' he said, 'I've bin tryin' me best not ta like ya, but ya make it very hard, lad.'

Liam looked up grimly at Paddy from his seat on the floor. 'I'm glad to hear you say that, Paddy, I was only trying to do what was right.'

Shevlin gave the carpenter a feeble grin. 'Ya wouldn' happ'n t' have a drop o' poteen around here, would ya?' he asked. Moira reached into her bag and produced a small flask of the good stuff.

CHAPTER 42

Moira stayed at Liam's cottage through the night and ministered to the injured animal, while Liam watched over the boy. Several times, Liam drifted off to sleep, only to be awakened by the ancient lady's murmurings. At first he thought she was just talking to herself, but then he realised she was saying some kind of prayers or incantations over the dog.

When he felt Moira touch his arm, he snapped awake. First light had just begun to appear through the tiny window.

'I've done everything I can, son,' she told him. 'Now it's up to the Almighty and the animal's will to live.'

Liam nodded and looked at the dog, who seemed to be resting peacefully. 'For the boy's sake, I hope your God has heard you.'

The old hag gave him her toothless smile. 'My God and yours are one and the same, but your faith is like

Thomas' from the bible story. You believe only what you see with your eyes. Sometimes, you have to look with your heart too.'

'I've seen a lot with my eyes, old woman,' said Liam.

She smiled again, 'I've seen much more, boy. When my sight dimmed, I began to learn how to put all my other senses to better use. Now, I gather the information I need with my head and I make my decisions here.' She crossed her hands over her chest. Liam thought the old recluse was mad and she read his thoughts. 'You and I aren't so different, my son. You have been alone too, for most of your life, at least alone in your mind, but that has been your choice. You have suffered losses in your life which have left you more damaged even than the boy sleeping over there. You have built up a wall to keep people out and you think, that way, you can spare yourself more pain.'

Liam became agitated. He was incensed that this mad old woman seemed to have penetrated his fiercely-guarded defenses so easily and seen into his very soul. He felt vulnerable and he didn't like the feeling.

'How could you know anything about me, you old witch, or anything about my life?'

She cackled. 'I know you are alone, my son, because I too am alone and I too have built my own defenses. Why do you think I live deep inside the forest? I live there to protect myself from all the chaos in the world.'

The voices had woken Jamie and he roused from his sleep. For a moment, he didn't know where he was and he looked around him. 'My dog!' he said.

Moira shuffled over to him and sat beside him, resting her hand gently on his shoulder. 'Don't worry, boy, I'd say he'll be grand. Your dog has a strong will and he doesn't want to leave you.' The boy was stiff from the previous day's beating and Liam helped him over to where his dog lay.

'He's in a bad way, isn't he, missus,' he said, his moist eyes raised to Moira.

'You have to believe, Jamie,' the old crone rasped. For all the good that will do you, thought Liam, cynically. Moira shot him a glance. He wished she would get out of his head and leave. The old woman stood unsteadily and Liam handed her her small walking stick.

'I'm afraid I have to be going now,' she announced, directing a gummy grin at the carpenter. 'But I'll be back if I think you need me.' She left the cottage humming an ancient melody.

There was a pot of cold porridge next to the fire and Liam felt his stomach growl. He realised that, in the excitement of the previous evening, he had eaten nothing. He hung the big iron pot on the crane and pushed it over the turf embers which still glowed faintly in the fireplace. He tossed an extra turf sod on the fire and blew on it until it caught. He fetched an apple and cut it in half with the little knife he always carried on his belt. He handed one half to the boy and they ate in silence, while they were waited for the oats to boil. Liam shot up out of his chair when he heard the sound of horses outside. Who could that be, this early? He stooped to peer out of the little window and was relieved to see Mick Sheridan, who had just dismounted from the big chestnut hunter. He had the hobby that Liam had ridden, in tow.

Liam went out to greet him. 'How's the horse coming along, Mick?'

'He's grand, sure. In fact, he's feelin' so much better dat when I returned 'im t' Harold Johnson an' da ol' buzzard jumped on 'is back, da horse t'rew 'im straight on 'is arse!' Mick laughed as he remembered the incident. 'He tol' me t' get him out of 'is sight before he made 'im intuh stew!'

Liam laughed too. 'A poor workman always blames his tools,' he said.

'An' a poor horseman always blames his horse,' responded Sheridan. Jamie had come to the door to see what was going on and Mick handed the reins to Liam. Jamie was standing in the doorway and Mick walked over to him and held his face in his big hands.

'I saw old Moira on d' road,' he said, looking at the boy's pitiful face with a pained expression. 'It's a bad business, dis. When ya feel up to it, boy, maybe yer master will bring ya down t' me and ya can try out a harse.' Jamie's one functioning eye opened wide in excitement and he looked toward Liam. The young carpenter nodded in affirmation.

Mick turned his attention back to Liam. 'Now dat Clancy has driven 'is sheep off yer property, is it alright wit you if I leave me hobby here t' graze? Dis big feller needs a lot o' grass an' I have too many mouths t' feed, an' not enough land t' do it on.'

Liam assured the big man that wouldn't be a problem. 'I have ten acres, sure,' he said, 'and the horse'll help to keep the weeds down.'

'Can I smell summt'n burnin'?' asked Mick. Liam sniffed and smelled the rancid odour of burnt oats. He realised they had left the pot on the fire and sent Jamie inside to see to it.

When the boy was safely out of earshot, Mick said, 'You'd better watch yer arse, Liam. Dere's been talk o' retaliation, wit you bein' a lan'lord an' such.' Liam looked surprised. 'I'm jus' sayin', boy, watch yer back.' Liam shrugged, he wasn't too worried. There were much bigger landlords around who had been the perpetrators of many evictions. It had become the way of things. He wasn't intending to evict anyone and he dismissed Mick's warning as just talk.

Jamie reappeared. 'I'm sorry, I let da oats burn.'

'There's no harm done, lad,' Liam assured the boy. 'We'll clean the pot and get some more from Hogans.' The boy was visibly relieved. He hadn't been sure whether he'd get another whipping and he was thankful.

'Don' t'row away d' oats, mind, boyo,' said Mick. 'Harses love oats 's much as dey love carrots, an' carrots costs money! Now open d' gate fer me, Jamie, an' I'll lead dis plug into greener pastures.' The big man led the horse into the field and slipped the rope halter from over her ears. The horse stood for a moment, then took off, racing around the perimeter and bucking every once in a while as she ran. The boy watched in wonder.

'Pretty ain't dey, boyo,' said Mick, putting his ham sized hand gently on the boys shoulder. Liam stood holding the chestnut horse. 'Ya can bring 'im over here, Liam,' said Mick. 'He's got legs, sure.' The young man walked the charger over to the other two and they all watched as the hobby ran amok, enjoying her freedom. The big horse snorted and he spat something at Liam.

Mick laughed. 'Ya got some horse snot on ya d'ere, boyo.' Liam looked down at his shirt in disgust and Jamie laughed for the first time since his mother died. The boy's laughter was infectious and they all shared it.

When Mick rode off, Liam and the boy stayed at the gate, watching the horse romp in the field. After a while, the animal settled down in her new surroundings and the boy went back inside the cottage to check on his dog.

Shevlin arrived and came to stand at the gate beside Liam. 'Ya have two new tenants now, I see.'

Liam didn't like the word. 'I'd prefer to think of them as guests, Paddy.'

'And am I a guest too?' Paddy asked.

'You are, o'course,' smiled Liam. 'and you're welcome in my house, anytime.'

Paddy's expression became serious. 'Are all yer *guests* welcome t' stay, in d'eir own homes I mean?'

Liam shook his head, 'I've already given my word,' he said. 'What more can I do?'

'Well, beauty is as beauty does,' responded Paddy. 'Anyway, whattid Mick have ta say?'

'Agh, nothing much,' said Liam. He was getting frustrated and wondered how long it would take folk to realise that his intentions were good. 'He just needed a place to board his horse and I gave him one.'

'You watch yer backside, Liam,' said Paddy. 'Dere's bin talk.' Not this again, thought Liam. Paddy continued. 'Clancy an' Sean Reilly have bin talkin' together.'

'I thought Clancy hated Sean. He busted his teeth out, didn't he?'

'He seems t' have forgotten dat. He hates you worse now and bad feelin's make fer strange alliances.' Suddenly, Mick's warning seemed like sound advice.

'Tell me what you've heard, Paddy?'

'D'ya remember dem fellers we seen in Hogan's wit' d'dark man? Well, dey've bin around again, only dis time, d' dangerous-lookin' feller wasn't wit'em.' Liam remembered that there had been been at least three of the men he'd had no previous acquaintance with. 'Dey come in when Roisin ain't aroun' an' Hogan serves dem d'eir beer.'

'Does Michael know what they're up to?'

'I can't say dat he does,' Paddy shrugged, 'an' can't say dat he doesn't. Ask 'him yerself, or ask Roisin.

Maybe 'er Da's said sumptin' to her?'

Liam wasn't sure if he could trust Michael Hogan any more or, indeed, if he could trust anyone any more.

CHAPTER 43

L iam walked over to Hogan's. He did need a bag of oatmeal and a twist of tobacco, but it was also an opportunity to test the waters. Michael Hogan served him, slapping the bag and the twist on the counter with more force than was called for. Liam handed him tuppence and the shopkeeper put it in his coin drawer, then turned his back on the carpenter. Liam opened his mouth to ask if Roisin was around and before he could speak, Michael turned on him.

'You're bad for business, Flynn,' he snapped. 'I'll thank you to take your commerce elsewhere from now on.' Liam was stunned. So the poison had even reached Michael Hogan. 'And you won't be seeing my daughter anymore either. I don't want you hanging around this establishment or around my Roisin.' Liam was so astonished that he could think of nothing to say. He simply thanked the man and left the shop.

He had been warned about this and, although he had known there would be some bad feeling towards him, he was surprised at the ferocity of the hate that now seemed to be directed his way. As he closed Hogan's door behind him, he exhaled deeply. He felt as if he had been punched in the stomach. He wasn't indignant or humiliated or even angry, just hurt. It seemed he had lost his friends but, worst of all, he would only be able to see Roisin from a distance. He would no longer be able to hear her voice or her laugher and that hurt him deep inside.

He had to try and shake off this darkness and so he would do what he always did, he would work. Liam Flynn always found an escape from reality in his work. He decided he would make himself a proper bed. Up until now, he had slept on the floor as was the custom but now he wanted a real bed and, by God, he didn't care if anyone thought it meant he was getting above his station. What did he have to lose that he hadn't lost already?

The cottage floor space was, to say the least, compact and Liam decided he would build a bed that he could stow, or fold up against the wall, during the day. Planning it and making it might serve to occupy his mind. Jamie was feeling a little better and the dog seemed more responsive than he had been the previous night. It never ceased to surprise Liam how resilient animals and children were, and he thought that a beating, like the one the boy had taken, would likely lay a man low for days.

'What will we build today?' asked the boy, when Liam returned to the cottage.

'It's funny you should ask that, Jamie. You and me are going to build a bed, or rather you'll build it and I'll supervise.' Liam had built some racks which he had joined to the rafters overhead to hold some of the pine boards Matt O'Brien had given him. Now, he took one down and inspected it. It looked straight enough. He took it outside and set Jamie to work, smoothing the faces with a jack plane. It was a good first tool to learn with, and the curls of wood that came out of it gave the boy a satisfaction, and a feeling that he was doing a man's work. Liam watched him for a while, correcting him from time to time, until he remembered that they had still not eaten.

'You keep working, partner, and I'll make us something to eat.' Liam put milled oats in the big pot and filled it up with water. They would make some thin beer from the extra water, later. He checked back on the dog and he checked on Jamie, neither one needed his attention for now.

*

Liam sat on a stump out the back of the cottage. The boy was writing the capital letter 'A' over and over on a piece of the pine board, with a bit of charcoal. They were both startled when they heard someone banging on the front door of the cottage, and Liam leapt up to see what all the fuss was about. Roisin stood there and she had her father gripped by the back of his collar.

'Well, tell him then, you old goat!' she demanded. 'You say it right now, or so help me…..!'

'Sorry,' Michael's tone was subdued.

Roisin cupped her other hand behind her ear. 'What did you say, old man? I didn't hear you!'

Michael looked at the carpenter and his apology was louder this time. 'I'm sorry, Liam.' She let go of his collar and he straightened his shirt, indignantly.

'Now you get yerself back to the bar and tend to business!" She gave him a mighty shove back towards the store and, in a vain attempt at manhood, he opened his mouth to protest. Roisin raised her hand as if she were about to deliver him a clout 'You mind your business,' she snarled, 'and I'll mind my own.' He scurried away and she lowered her hand.

Once she had seen that her father was back inside Hogan's, Roisin turned to Liam and raised her hand again. He flinched momentarily, then relaxed when he saw she was only brushing back the tresses of her hair that had escaped during the commotion.

She exhaled deeply through pursed lips. 'That auld sod told me what he'd said to you. He knows now that if he ever tries to tell me what to do again, I swear, I'll take half the savings and I'll move to Galway! He'd soon be on his arse then!' Now it was Liam's turn to exhale through pursed lips. He had heard about Roisin's temper but the stories didn't do justice to the reality.

'Calm yourself,' he tried to soothe her. 'It's alright, there's no harm done.' She glared at him and he averted his eyes, looking down at his feet. Roisin collected herself and touched his arm.

'I'm sorry,' she said. 'I was in Killadargan. I wanted to talk with Colleen's family about the children. Those babies shouldn't be in the house with that madman anymore.' Liam nodded his agreement. 'They're going to take the children between them. Colleen's cousins will have some and Clancy's sister will have the others. Anyway, when I came back, yer man there tried to deliver an ultimatum to me. Huh!' She made a gesture of dusting her hands off. 'He won't be doing that again in a hurry.'

Liam told her about the warnings Mick and Paddy had given him. Roisin was still incensed,

'Agh, sure take no notice,' she said, 'it's probably all talk. Talk isn't cheap, it's free. I think there's nary a one of them with the bollocks to do anything.' Liam burst out laughing and the girl relaxed.

'Why don't you and Jamie come over to Hogan's for dinner tonight?' she said. 'You'll be my guests and I'll show that auld so-and-so who's boss around here.' She flashed a grin at Liam, picked up her skirts and ran back to the store. He stood and watched, still watching even after she had gone inside and closed the door.

*

Ben Clancy's children were taken away. Even though he could no longer take care of the brood himself, he wouldn't give his babies up without a fight and he had to be restrained. He said he would rather kill them than let someone else take them. Ben was going out of his mind. He had sold off his sheep so that he could afford the drink, and he was seen all hours of the day and night, roaming the village street and the lanes around, raving. Sometimes he would talk to himself and answer his own questions, other times he would go into a screaming rant. Each of the locals had arrived at their own various explanations for his odd behavior. Some thought he was possessed by demons, others that he was being punished by God for some terrible past transgression. It was even suggested that an evil spell had been cast on him by a witch, perhaps Moira herself. The priest had tried to visit him on several occasions, but was driven off with a shepherd's crook and had to flee for his life. Paddy Shevlin tried to protect his best friend and watched out for him as best he could, but Ben's madness was without hope. He would spend hours talking to the hedgerows or shaking his fist at crows. He killed his own collie dog because he thought the dog was laughing at him. Ben's decent into the abyss was complete.

*

Jamie thrived under the guidance of the young carpenter. He learned his letters, one each day for a month, and now he had started to read. At their midday break from the work, Liam would listen as the boy read. Most of Liam's books just had illustrations of furniture design in them, but a few of them had writing and the boy read those over and over until he knew them by heart. Roisin also had some books and, when she shared them with Jamie, he devoured their contents too. She helped the boy with his handwriting, because Liam wasn't very good at it himself, and he had thought another professor would be advisable.

The boy changed in appearance too. His father was a tall lanky man and now Jamie had begun to gain height too. Regular meals and exercise soon saw him grow several inches and start to fill out. He became more talkative as his self-confidence improved and Liam even had to tell him to be quiet from time to time. With each admonishment, the boy's expression would turn to hurt and confusion and Liam would wave him on to say whatever was in his head. If the child had something to say, then let him say it.

*

Just before Christmas, Ben Clancy hanged himself.

He had finally lost his battle with the demons that tortured his mind and, in the end, the voices in his head had unhinged the shepherd. Paddy Shevlin had not seen his old friend for a few days and, when he went to check on him, he found Ben hanging from the rafters in his cottage. He had been there for some time and his neck was stretched to an almost impossible length. He was completely naked and Paddy's heart broke when he saw the emaciated body of his old friend dangling lifelessly in front of him. Months of drinking, without eating. had reduced the already thin man to a skeleton. His sunken eyes were not quite closed and his tongue protruded grotesquely from his mouth. Paddy knew that death had not come quickly for this poor soul.

With a heavy heart, Paddy went across to Liam's house and, when he saw him with Jamie, he whispered what he had found. They left the boy to his books and walked back to Clancy's cottage in silence. Between them, they cut the lifeless body down. Paddy held the legs, while Liam cut the rope around Ben's neck. The corpse was surprisingly light. Ben had been reduced to a shadow of himself by starvation.

They laid poor Ben on the floor of the cottage and thought about what they should do next. They certainly couldn't let Jamie see his father like this.

'I'll go and get Roisin,' said Liam, 'she'll know what to do.' He went into Hogan's, oblivious to a few accusing glares, and told the girl in a whisper what he and Paddy had found. They both hurried back to the cottage and Roisin gasped, before clapping both hands over her mouth, when she saw the bluish grey corpse, with the bloated tongue, lying there. She said she needed to go and get Moira and she left. When she had gone, the two men wrapped Ben's body in a ragged wool blanket. His clothes smelled rancid from not having been washed in months. The two men stood and stared at the pile of bones that had once been Ben Clancy, the sheep farmer.

'Ya better keep Jamie away until Moira works out what t' do,' said Paddy. Liam nodded. He would think up some project or other that would keep him busy for a few hours.

Back at his own cottage, Liam tried to be light-hearted with the boy. 'Here's an idea, Jamie,' he said. 'Why don't you go and start smoothing out those oak planks stored in the old church?'

The youngster could tell that something had shaken

Liam and he studied his expression with suspicion. 'I'll do it if ya want me to,' he said. 'but why are ya tryin' t' get rid o' me.' Liam damned his own countenance. 'It's me Da,' the boy said, 'ain't it?' 'I saw you an' Paddy go intuh me house an' den Roisin. It's me Da, ain't it?' Liam nodded. 'Is 'e dead?' Liam nodded again. 'He's wit' me Mam, so,' said the boy, his lip quivering. 'She'll look after her 'im now.' Liam nodded once again. He wasn't about to tell the boy that his father committed suicide, because then he would be damned to hell for all eternity. The boy tried to gather himself. 'I'm goin' to see 'im,' he said, making for the door. Liam stopped him and held him by the shoulders.

'No, lad,' he looked Jamie square in the eyes. 'Now, when you came to me as an apprentice, you promised to obey me without any questions and I'm reminding you of that promise now. Do as I ask.' The boy reluctantly acceded, and began to collect the tools that he would need to do the job his master had asked of him.

Moira arrived at the Clancy house with Roisin and Father Grogan. Liam wasn't far behind them. Paddy still stood gazing at the body and Moira wasted no time. She put powder on the dead man's face to cover his grey complexion and she pinned his eyes shut with a splinter of blackthorn in each eyelid.

'What about d' tongue?' enquired Paddy. 'Will we cut it off?' Moira shot him a withering glance and Paddy dropped his gaze, ashamed at his suggestion.

'He's startin' to go bad,' she said, looking at the others, 'so ye had best go fetch any family he has. We'll have to be getting' him in the ground soon.' Grogan mumbled something about not being able to bury Ben in consecrated ground, because he'd taken his own life, but Liam raised his hand for him to be silent.

'Listen to me, old man,' he said. 'The feckin' church ain't a church anymore. And anyway, I own the feckin' land. Ben Clancy gets buried next to his wife.' The old priest nodded and began to administer Extreme Unction.

CHAPTER 44

C hristmas morning came and went, Liam attending both the service at the Church of Ireland sanctuary and, later, the Catholic service in the woods. To him, the only difference was that one was in a dark stone building, with a well-dressed congregation, and the other was in a gloomy forest glade, with just the grey sky overhead and the parishioners dressed in rags. When he attended the Mass in the forest, he was still dressed in his finery from the earlier service and the only person who dared stand next to him was the other local outcast, Moira. Jamie stood next to Roisin, who wisely stood apart from Liam.

Back at Liam's cottage after Mass, the carpenter gave Jamie his own hammer as a gift, having bought himself a new one to replace it. Although the boy had handled Liam's hammer plenty of times before, he was transfixed by it now, fingering it and turning it over and over in his hands to examine it. It was the first Christmas present he'd ever had. Roisin came over a little later with what seemed like a feast of food, pork and lamb and, of course spuds. The three ate their Christmas dinner together at Liam's, much to the consternation of Michael Hogan, who ate alone across the road.

The day after Christmas Day, Liam and Jamie set to work on a job Liam had been given by Harold Johnson. They were to build an elaborate oak desk for him. He wanted something impressive to sit behind, which might serve to enhance his stature among the other gentry, most notably the Tolers and the Otways, who lived just outside of Nenagh in 'great houses.' Liam knew this job was important, because it might lead to other commissions, so it had to be the very best he could do. He had drawn up plans for a table, with a writing surface three feet wide and eight feet long, and ornately carved legs. They had only just begun work when they were interrupted by the sound of horses outside. Jamie's dog barked.

Liam had been half expecting Mick to call so, when he looked out the window, he was surprised to see two men in blue greatcoats, with white trousers and highly polished boots. Both men dismounted and one held the reins of both chargers. The first of the men was a tall grim-faced fellow and he held what looked like a piece of paper in his right hand. He rapped on the door with a leather-gloved hand, so hard that it shook the rafters. When Liam opened the door, the grim-faced man stood in the doorway and, without a word, handed Liam a sealed note. Liam looked down at it and then back at the man, expectantly.

'You will present yourself at the office of the sheriff in Nenagh tomorrow. If you do not, an arrest warrant will be issued in your name.' The man turned and took the reins of his horse from the other deputy. They both mounted in unison and headed back out of the village in the direction of Nenagh.

Liam stood and watched them go, then looked back down at the note. It was sealed with dark red wax and Liam was afraid to open it. Without saying where he was going, he left the boy to the work and, as he walked over to Hogan's, a thousand thoughts ran through his mind. Could his falsity have been uncovered? That was unlikely because he was still in Harold Johnson's good graces. Could it be about the murder of Sean Reilly's two companions? That was unlikely too because he had a cast iron alibi. What, then, could the High Sherriff want with a carpenter? When he got there, Roisin was dealing with a customer, a fat lady with a blue apron. When the large woman saw Liam, she quickly packed a cloth sack with her purchases and gave him a wide berth as she left. Roisin tried to dismiss the woman's actions, lightheartedly.

'What's it like to be a leper, Liam?' Liam shrugged his shoulders. He told her about his visitors and he placed the note on the counter. Roisin picked it up, examined it, and gave it back to him. 'Well, you'll never find out what's inside unless you open it.' Liam took it and slid his finger into the crease of the letter, cracking open the red sealing wax. He unfolded the paper and read it out loud. He was none the wiser. The letter gave no indication of why he had been summoned, just that his presence was required at the office tomorrow. It was signed in an elegant script, '*R. D'Arcy, High Sherrif*'.

Liam slept fitfully, knowing that tomorrow he would be on trial. He was wide awake long before dawn and so he washed and shaved. As he dressed himself in his gentleman's attire, he thought about how he should travel to Nenagh Castle. The weather was typical for a winter day, cold, grey and spitting rain. He thought about the long walk into town and knew that, even with his raincloak, he would be soaked to the skin and somewhat bedraggled by the time he got there. There was always the horse, he thought, the hobby which Mick had left in his charge. Mick Sheridan had left an old saddle for him and the boy to use, and Jamie had cleaned it carefully, blacking it with a mixture of soot from a candle and pig grease. He had polished the brass furnishings with the rouge that Liam used to polish furniture, as the final touch, and even Mick had agreed that it was looking as good as it possibly could. Yes, thought Liam, I'll ride into town.

He woke the boy and told him to saddle the horse but to wash the animal first. The boy hesitated for a moment, looking up at Liam as if he was seeing him for the first time.

'Just do as I say,' said Liam authoritatively and, without further hesitation, the boy put on his shirt and trousers and set about preparing the horse. When he had finished, Liam donned his hat and cloak and looked down at himself. This would have to be the performance of his life. His mouth grew dry.

Liam walked the horse at first and then trotted her. When he felt comfortable in the saddle, he pursed his lips and made a kissing sound. The horse responded by gathering herself and breaking into a canter as she had been taught. Within an hour, Liam had arrived at the gates of Nenagh Castle. The sentries crossed their pikes as the carpenter pulled up at the castle gates and they asked him to state his business. Liam told them he was answering a summons from the High Sheriff and, once they had examined the sheriff's note, they let him pass.

The sheriff had both his accommodation and his office in a two story stone building, inside the keep. A groom in uniform stood outside the door of the building and, when Liam dismounted awkwardly, the young fellow stifled a laugh before he took the reins off him. Liam was shown into a cavernous room, where another man in uniform asked him to state his business. When Liam told him, he consulted a large ledger book in front of him and ticked something off. He then escorted the carpenter to a big oak door, studded with iron rivets, and knocked on it. Without waiting for a reply, he opened the heavy door, ushered Liam inside and slammed it shut behind him.

Liam found himself standing in a sizeable room, with bookcases on either side, and a large desk in the middle. A man, in a blue uniform coat with gold braids at the shoulders, sat behind the desk in a tall chair, studying papers. Without looking up, he motioned for Liam to take a seat and, fighting the urge to tremble, Liam sat in the chair which had been gestured towards. As the man turned one page after another in silence, Liam took in his surroundings. On the desk, pointing at the chair which Liam now occupied, was a horse pistol, a huge dog lock with a bore so big that Liam thought he could get his entire head into it. He was still staring at the gun when the sheriff coughed and Liam flinched. He looked up at the man before him, and opened his eyes wide in recognition. It was the dark stranger from Hogan's, but now the man was transformed by his uniform into an even more forbidding sight. Liam's mouth fell open.

'It's quite a formidable weapon, isn't it?'

Liam couldn't speak. The man stood up and gave a half bow towards Liam. 'I'm Sheriff D'Arcy,' he said, 'and I expect you're wondering why I've asked you here.' Liam still couldn't speak. He felt as if his mouth was sealed shut as securely as the letter he'd been given and he simply nodded. He worked his tongue to pry his lips apart.

'I have a few questions for you, Mr. Flynn, and perhaps you might have some for me.' By now, he could see the young man's plight and he poured a glass of water and pushed it towards him. 'First, I want you to tell me everything you know about Sean Reilly. Don't hold back or lie because I will find out if you do and you will regret it.'

Liam drank most of the water down at once and, when he had regained his voice, he told the man everything he knew, from the first day on the road into Nenagh, to the incident of the fight at Knigh Cross. The sheriff took notes as he spoke.

'And the robbery where his friends were slain?' Liam couldn't tell him anything about that, except for the ever-changing rumours.

'And you will hold this interview in the strictest confidence?' It was an order more than a question. Liam nodded.

'Say It!' he shouted.

'I do ... I mean, I will,' said Liam and gulped down the rest of the water. The man stood up and Liam hoped this was the end of the interrogation and that he would be dismissed. The sheriff walked around to the back of Liam's chair, where Liam could no longer see him.

'There is one more matter, Liam Flynn from Thurles.' Liam thought he was going to wet himself. 'I know that your father was a Presbyterian blacksmith and that your mother was a Catholic.' Liam's secret had been uncovered. 'What's more, your brother was a rebel on the side of the Jacobites. That is treason. I deal very harshly with traitors and their families.' Liam closed his eyes and swallowed hard. He could scarcely breathe now. The man went to a cabinet at the side of the room and came back with two glasses of what looked like whiskey. He offered one to Liam.

'A man deserves a final drink before a verdict is rendered,' said the sheriff. Liam took the glass, closed his eyes again and took a gulp of the fiery liquid. The dark man sat in his chair again, placed his elbows on the desk and leaned forward. He looked directly at Liam and his eyes seemed to soften.

'It's good to see you again, Liam,' he said quietly. Liam knitted his brow. He had only ever seen this man twice before, in Hogan's, and it seemed improbable that the man would be so cordial, given the circumstances of the two encounters.

Sensing Liam's confusion, the dark man said, 'It's been a long time since I let you play in the blacksmith shop.' Liam frowned in bewilderment, then his eyes opened as wide as if he had seen a ghost.

'It's been a long time, Lum. Do you remember that's what I called you?' Liam had not let tears flow in many a year, but they flowed now, and he didn't give a damn if he was hanged, as long as it was by Robert's hand.

'I'm going to cancel the rest of the day's appointments,' said Robert D'Arcy, 'because you have a story to tell me and I have one to tell you.' He got up out of his chair, opened the big oak door and told his secretary to cancel his appointments, then closed the door and returned to his seat.

'I'll send my man out for some food in a while. This may take all day.'

CHAPTER 45

I t was the best day of Liam's entire life and, if he was to die right here in this room, he would die a happy man.

In his own way, Robert felt the same, and he reminisced about their times together all those years ago. For him, they had been times of innocence and idealism, when his business had been working with metal and not with the greed of men or the spilling of blood. He told Liam that the world, since then, had changed him and forged him into the man he had become. But, as he recounted the story of his life, here in this room today, to Liam he was the big brother with that same crooked smile.

Robert told Liam about the reality of life on the battlefield, of the mud and the blood and the carnage, of the desperate cold and the hunger. Both sides had been become war-weary. To the English, it was an expensive proposition and to the Royalists, it was a lost cause. The officers, and those high-born, were given the opportunity to go to France, Parliament considering it as good riddance to a rebellious lot, and the enlisted men were left to fend for themselves.

Robert Flynn had been serving in a regiment under the command of Robert D'Arcy, an Irish nobleman, descended from the Normans. It was Robert Flynn's good fortune that his commander died of a fever just before he and his fellow officers were evacuated to France. Robert had assumed D'Arcy's identity and arrived safely on French soil, where he became a mercenary soldier, fighting for whichever side was prepared to pay the most. Sometimes, it would be a skirmish between Baronies but oftentimes, he was involved in battles on a much grander scale. He learned well the craft of brutality and, whenever he loathed himself for doing what he did, he took solace in taking out his hatred on whoever was on the opposing side. He had abandoned his own idealism when he saw how the aristocracy abandoned the countless men who bled for them on numberless battlefields.

Robert travelled with the wars, following them and making a name for himself as being ruthless, cold and as brutal as the situation demanded.

When he had returned to Ireland, at first he thought he might take up his old trade and have his own blacksmith shop like his father. Instead, he found it easier and more lucrative to find employment as a lawman, where he used his experience to seek out and punish whatever predators afflicted communities. His reputation in Wicklow was legendary but, like most legends, was based more on flights of fancy than it was on fact. It was true that he had lopped off the occasional ear and, with repeat offenders, taken a nose or two, but he considered hangings to be a waste of time in that they left a family destitute, bitter and desperate, only serving to create more villains. He reserved capital punishment for traitors and murderers only and, with them, he took pleasure in carrying out the executions himself.

The afternoon went quickly and soon it grew late. The two brothers made every excuse to stay, relating remembered anecdotes and talking about family members long gone, but Liam knew that Roisin must surely think he'd been arrested by now and he wanted to be back in Gortalocca before dark. When the two men eventually shook hands, they gave each other a tentative embrace before Robert led the way to the door.

'You can tell the old priest that he's safe. I enforce whichever laws I choose and a fat old Franciscan is not high on my list of priorities.' He clapped Liam on the shoulder as he left and told him they would be seeing each other again soon.

When Liam stepped outside, he took a deep gulp of the cold air, it felt good. The groom handed him the reins of his horse and two large men on chestnut chargers informed him that they had been instructed to escort him to the village. Liam asked if they would kindly leave him when they reached Knigh Cross, so as not to unnerve the villagers.

'I'm sorry, sir, my orders are to see you home,' said the senior of the two men and so, in silence, they walked the horses through Nenagh, and then on to a gallop all the way to the Gortalocca. The two men on their great horses towered over Liam as he rode the hobby and he felt secure in their company.

As he had expected, the sound of horses galloping into the village caused some consternation among the inhabitants. Roisin poked her head out of Hogan's door and several men who had been drinking there, left in a hurry. Liam tipped his hat to the guards and they knuckled their foreheads in salute before expertly wheeling their horses around and vanishing into the night. Liam tied the horse at the gate and went into his cottage to switch his formal clothes for his more comfortable ones. He came back out, unsaddled the animal and took off her bridle. He put her in the pasture and watched her for a moment while she nibbled the grass.

Roisin had been worried that Liam had been detained by the sheriff, and she wasted no time in coming over. Although Liam hated lying to her, he had been sworn to secrecy by his brother, so he made up a plausible story as to what had kept him. Roisin wasn't satisfied but she saw no use in pressing him. They walked together back across the street to Hogan's, where Liam found Jamie sitting at a table. He and the girl had both been concerned about Liam and had kept each other company as they waited for his return. They were both surprised when Liam seemed to be in excellent humour, following his ordeal. It didn't seem logical. Whenever a person was ordered to appear before the authorities, it was almost always bad news. Yet here was Liam, as happy as a lark after his session with the sheriff.

'Did you work on the legs of Johnson's desk today?' Liam asked the boy.

Jamie averted his eyes. 'I...I did a little work but, sure, I was so worried dat dey t'rew ya in da dungeon dat I couldn't do much.' The boy still looked worried and searched his master's face. Liam's heart softened but he had to assume the countenance of the master.

'Never let anything or anyone come between you and the work, boy. That's what makes us professionals.' He ruffled the boy's hair to let him know he wasn't in trouble. 'We'll both get back to it tomorrow.' The child was relieved. He had been close to tears but now he smiled. 'Wipe your nose,' said Liam, sternly. 'men don't cry.' If the boy had seen his master just a few hours ago, he might have argued with this statement.

'Can I get you a bite to eat?' asked the girl, 'You must be starving with the hunger by now.' Liam shook his head. 'Well, how about a dram of the good stuff, so? Just to relax you?'

'No thanks,' said Liam. 'I've had enough to eat and drink for one day. I have to go and rub the horse down. She's had a long day, too.' Liam bid them both goodnight and left. As Roisin watched him go, her eyes narrowed. She wished she knew what was inside the carpenter's head but one thing was for sure, there was a secret there, and she would give anything to know what it was.

CHAPTER 46

L iam and the boy were up early and the boy hung a pot of oatmeal and barley porridge on the crane above the fire. While it was heating, the master carpenter marked out the design they would carve on the legs of the desk. Johnson had initially wanted 'ferocious lion heads' but Liam had shown him a pattern book which contained floral and leaf designs. Liam suggested that these were considered much more stylish and fashionable and that was enough to convince Harold Johnson, who must at any cost be considered in tune with the current trends. An oak leaf and acorn motif was chosen but the legs, insisted Johnson, would stand on lions' feet.

Roisin had been kept awake much of the night by curiosity, which could cause insomnia just as surely as worry could. She looked out of her window now and, when she saw the oil lamp lit in the cottage, she waited for a little while to allow the two men to get dressed before going over. On most occasions she would stroll across to the cottage demurely, in case Liam was watching, but this time, motivated by her inquisitiveness, she hiked up her skirts and flew there.

'Please, Liam,' she implored, flirtatiously, hoping this would add weight to her plea. 'You told me nothing last night. What really happened yesterday? I won't leave until you tell me.' Although Liam would have been happy for her to stay all day, he knew he would get no work done until he had offered Roisin at least a snippet of information.

'Alright, Roisin, you can tell Father Grogan that he's in no danger from the new sheriff.

'Well, how did you manage that?' she demanded.

'Perhaps I have a silver tongue,' he replied with a sly smile.

'Perhaps you're full of shite! Is that what took you all day?' Liam didn't answer her.

'You got safekeeping for the priest, you got fed and whiskeyed and you got an escort home by the new sheriff's men?' Liam shrugged his shoulders and his silence incensed the girl even more. The carpenter went back to drawing his design.

'What's that?' she snapped.

'Legs.'

'I never saw legs like that in my life!' If Roisin wasn't going to get herself enough information to warrant a sleepless night, an argument might make her feel better, but Liam's silent insolence seemed to indicate that she wasn't going to get her that either. She watched for a few minutes more, trying to think of something that would get a reaction. She found herself intrigued by the sketched scrolls and wanted to ask questions but instead, she said to Jamie 'That Liam Flynn is boring and he's teaching you to be too!' As soon as she had said it, she thought what an empty-headed statement it was.

Jamie smiled up at her. 'He is that,' he said. Roisin was exasperated with Liam and annoyed with herself.

Armed with the tiny morsel of information he had given her, and still spoiling for an argument, she stormed out.

'Uh oh,' said Jamie. 'I wouldn't want to be 'er Da when she gets home.' They shared a laugh.

Work on the legs took two days. Liam did most of it while Jamie watched with rapt attention as the raw wood was transformed into a thing of beauty. When the legs were scraped with a flat piece of metal, the whiskery wood began to shine in places.

'We need to get them all like this,' instructed Liam, handing the boy the cabinet scraper, 'shiny all over, front and back.'

'What about d' feet,' asked Jamie.

'You'll see,' replied Liam, 'in due time.' When the boy had finished, Liam laid out the pattern for the claw feet which were to go on each leg. He found the centre on the bottom and made a circle with a pair of dividers. Then he carefully traced the design for each of the toes. He cut between the toes with a back saw, staying well clear of the traced lines. Then, with a sharp chisel and a wooden mallet, he roughed them out. The boy was fascinated. To him, it looked like the feet had been in the wood all the time and that Liam was simply uncovering them. Liam then took a small skew chisel to refine them and, finally, a tiny gouge to cut in the hair detail. The boy told Liam he didn't think he'd ever be able to accomplish a feat such as this.

'Nonsense,' said Liam. 'Everything seems impossible or difficult until you do it once. Now, lad we have to carve our knees. Do you think you're up for it?' The boy looked down at his knees and back up at Liam, questioningly. 'Not *our* knees, ya daft lad. The ones on the legs, here look.' He pointed to the upper part of the table leg.

'Why do dey call'em knees when dey're at da top? Why ain't dey called hips?' Liam laughed, remembering how he had almost driven Mr. Bello mad with the same questions.

'They call them knees because... well, because that's what they are.' Liam knew from his own experience what an inadequate answer this was, so he changed the subject before Jamie gave him another opportunity to demonstrate his own ignorance.

'Do you remember when I drew the pattern the other day? Well, we're going to transfer it onto the work today.' The boy was mystified. How could they get a design from the parchment onto the curved surface of the table leg?

Liam made a mark, with a charcoal stick, down the center of each knee. He had already drawn one on the parchment drawing. He covered the back of the drawing with coal dust and blew off the excess. He put the markings into alignment and, with the point of a scratch awl, transferred the pattern onto the leg. He outlined the carbon marks with a chisel and began to remove the wood from the background. The leaves began to stand out from the leg. It was a tedious process and, although Liam found it rewarding, it wasn't captivating for a spectator. The boy lost interest after a while and started to fidget.

'If you can't pay attention, you'll earn your keep another way,' Liam told him. 'Sweep up the floor.' The boy was more comfortable with this, he understood how to use a broom.

The next day the carpenter had finished the legs, and Jamie was in awe of how realistic the oak leaf carvings were. He wished now that he had paid more attention to the process.

'Take a piece of scrap wood, boy, and carve the design on it until you get it right. You won't get anything to eat until you work out how to do it.' Liam surprised himself at how alike his tone sounded to that of his own master and he realised, with satisfaction, that Mr. Bello had passed on his knowledge to him, and now he was passing it on to another thick-headed Irish lad. It gave him a good feeling.

Things in Gortalocca had settled down a little, although Liam was still shunned by most of the local folk. Whenever he went to Hogan's to buy groceries, the women would walk around him, avoiding eye contact with him. Whenever he went in for a pint, the men at the bar would glare at him, slug down their beer and leave. Roisin called at the cottage from time to time, although not as often as she had and, once in a while, Paddy would drop in for a bit of banter. Liam was happy enough with Jamie for company. One day, the boy asked what would become of the house where he had grown up. The Clancy house had become derelict since the death of his father and the evacuation of his siblings. Liam hadn't given it much thought. The last time they went in had been weeks ago and there was still a faint putrid smell of death inside.

'What do you think we should do with it, Jamie? We could let an evicted family have it. That would be a good thing.' The boy's answer came as a surprise.

'I'd like to go and live there,' he said. Liam's first thought was to dismiss the idea out of hand, but then he realised that his motives were entirely selfish. He enjoyed the boy's company and it would be lonely in the cottage without him. He had come to appreciate Jamie as his old master had come to appreciate him. But he couldn't hold the boy back any more than he could have been held back himself before he began the journey across Tipperary.

'Let's leave the doors and windows open for a few days and get the.... musty smell out,' Liam said. 'Then, if you still want to stay there, that's grand with me.' It really wasn't grand at all but he couldn't admit it, not even to himself.

Jamie took up residence in his old house within the week and Roisin resumed her regular visits to Liam's cottage. Her calls had been scarce while the boy was there and she wasn't sure why. Perhaps the lad's presence had inhibited the conversation or perhaps she was just a tiny bit jealous of how much of Liam's time and attention he took up. Mick Sheridan would call in too, purportedly to check on his mare, but he usually had a bag of dominoes and he liked beating Liam in a friendly game. Liam wasn't keen on parlour games, he got bored with them and his mind wandered. Paddy Shevlin was still Paddy Shevlin. Even though he might have distrusted Liam's intentions initially, as long as he had his pigs and a roof over his head, he was perfectly content. He missed his friend Ben Clancy, but even that faded over time. Liam bought a milk cow.

An evicted farmer and his family walked through the town one morning as Liam had been checking the thatch on his cottage. They had stopped to admire the handiwork and told him they were heading to Galway, where the farmer's wife's family had a big farm. They raised dairy cattle, and already had enough head of livestock. The farmer had a milk cow in tow because he couldn't sell her in Nenagh. Liam paid him more than the cow was worth and, although the farmer thought he had skinned the young man, Liam shrugged it off as charity.

He planned his crop for the coming year. He would

keep the horse and the cow behind his cottage and put in a couple of acres of spuds and barley at the back of the old Clancy cottage. There were no sheep there now and the acreage was becoming fallow. Jamie could help with the farming, even though it held no interest for him. Life in Gortalocca passed at its slow, timeless pace with scarcely a thought for the events that were happening in the world around it.

CHAPTER 47

Despite the efforts of a carpenter, a priest and a barmaid, the events that were unfolding in the world outside Gortalocca couldn't be kept outside forever, and rumours about vandalism and violence began to seep in. It seemed that they mostly occurred on properties owned by absentee landlords, wealthy English aristocrats who had acquired vast properties in Ireland, and administrated them through their overseers, who collected the rents and ran the farms as if they were their own little kingdoms. The owners had no interest in their land, other than financial, and it was the duty of those left in charge to see that the estates were profitable. Many of the administrators were Irish themselves and most had their hands in the till. It was a downwardly spiraling cycle. More violence meant more paranoia, and that in turn led to more evictions. It didn't seem to be motivated by either politics or religion, but rather a class warfare, the kind not fought on fields of battle but in the debit and credit pages of ledger books.

It was a cold April morning and the fire had gone out

during the night. Liam could see his breath in the cold dark cottage, winter was refusing to leave this year. He put a sod of turf on the fire but there weren't enough embers to catch it, so he took some kindling and got it started. His first job was to go out to the back pasture and milk his cow. She seemed to enjoy the milking process, the pressure of several quarts of milk in her udders must have been uncomfortable.

He opened the back door and, although she was usually there waiting for him, this morning she wasn't. Liam cursed her because now he would have to walk through the mud to find the beast. It was still too dark to see clearly, the sun had barely pinked up the eastern sky, so he went back inside and lit a torch from the now burning turf. Back outside, he held the wooden milking pail in one hand and the flame of the torch high above his head in the other. The cold wet earth squished between the toes of his bare but he hardly noticed. He was becoming apprehensive, perhaps someone had sneaked in and stolen his cow. It wasn't the financial loss that would concern him as much as the violation of his homestead.

In the light cast by his torch, Liam spotted the cow lying on the ground. He thought that she had found a good dry place and was loath to leave it in the early morning chill but, as he walked towards her, he knew something wasn't right. She was motionless. As he got closer, he was overtaken by a sense of revulsion at what he saw. His cow had been hamstrung. The tendons in her legs had been severed, her udders had been mutilated and she had been left to bleed to death. There was a pool of blood in the grass around her. Liam felt his stomach move up into his chest and he retched. The agony the animal must have suffered was unimaginable. The ground around her was torn up as she had pawed it to try and raise herself up on useless legs. Liam stared at the scene, in disbelief at the violence towards a helpless dumb beast, and contempt for the type of individual that would do such a thing.

'Where's me horse?' Mick Sheridan's shout shook Liam from his thoughts. He was riding a little pony bareback, with just a halter and lead for reins.

Liam was so shocked by the carnage he had discovered that he hadn't given a second thought to the mare. The big man dropped the pony's lead and sprinted across the pasture towards Liam. The sun had just started to come up, and its faint yellow light was spreading across the field. When she had heard Mick's voice, the mare whinnied and the two men looked to where she stood, in a corner by a stone wall. Mick was relieved, at least until she tried to walk towards him, dragging a useless left hind leg behind her. Mick buried his face in his hands and wept shamelessly. 'She was d' first foal born on me farm.' he sobbed. Liam wished he could think of something to say to comfort the big fellow but all that concerned him now was how to put the poor horse of its misery.

Mick was thinking the same. 'You'll have t' do it, Liam, I ain't got d' heart t' do it meself.'

'Not me!' exclaimed Liam. 'You stay here, Mick, and comfort the poor animal and I'll get Paddy. He knows about such things.' Liam handed the torch to the disconsolate man and sprinted across the pasture.

Liam ran back from Paddy's, his feet splashing in the swamp-like grass, to stand with Mick. The horse stood on three legs, the other covered in congealed blood, hanging limp. Mick had buried his face in the mare's neck, hoping to remember her smell.

'Could Moira fix it?' said Liam.

Mick raised his tear-streaked face. 'Dere's sum t'ings dat even d' Almighty can't fix,' he said, lowering his head again. Paddy came running across the pasture, his big round body bouncing with every stride. In his hands, he carried a piece of rope, a sledge hammer and a long knife. The horse whinnied a weak welcome.

'Ya don't hafta be here t' see dis, Mick.' Paddy spoke softly.

'I was d'ere when she was born an' I'll be here t' see 'er go.'

Paddy slipped a loop around the horse's neck and told Liam to hold it. 'Mind ya don't get squashed when she falls,' he told him. Liam took a step back and Paddy raised the sledge.

'I'm sorry, ol' girl,' he said. 'we'll see ya on d' udder side one day.' With that, he swung a mighty blow and the horse dropped to the ground, senseless. He took the knife and cut her throat. Liam had never seen so much blood in his life and he dropped the rope, turned and threw up.

The three men walked back to Liam's cottage.

'I need a drink,' said Paddy. 'In fact, I need two.' Mick walked with his head down, trying to gather himself. Finally, when they were inside, he spoke.

'D' bastards got me too,' he said. Liam and Paddy both looked at the big man and waited. It took a while for him to speak again. 'Dey strung Rohan too.'

'But you're a tenant,' said Liam, 'not a landlord.'

'Dey musta t'ought d' big horse belonged t' Johnson, so d' bastards cut him too. Dat's why I come here dis mornin', t' warn ya. But dey beat me to it.' Liam poured whiskey from his jug into two big cups for Paddy and Mick.

'I'll not have one myself,' he said. 'I'm going to the sheriff.'

'Dat won't do ya no good,' said Mick, bitterly. 'He only answers to d' big shots.'

'I think he'll see me,' said Liam confidently.

'Well, we'll see,' said Mick and held out his cup for a refill. He had lost a member of his family and his grief was palpable.

Paddy and Mick sat talking and drinking, Mick recalling events that he and the horse had shared, recollections of better times, Paddy telling pig stories. Liam lost himself in his own thoughts.

'Who would do something like this?' Liam said, eventually, shaking his head.

'Dis has d' hand of Reilly in it,' said Mick, emphatically. 'Da rumours dat I tol' ya about a few months ago, dey all had him at d' centre, him an' dat dark feller. I could crush 'em both in me bare hands right dis very minute.' The other two looked at him in surprise. This was out of character for Mick Sheridan. He was an easy going fellow and, even though he undoubtedly looked capable of doing someone harm, it just wasn't in his nature.

Liam stood 'I'm going to Nenagh,' he said 'I'll see if I can get an audience with the lawman.'

'Good luck t' ya,' Mick raised his mug.

CHAPTER 48

Liam didn't bother to change his clothes but he did remember to take his walking stick with him. If the brigands were still around, he would make sure to take at least one of them to hell with him. He set out to walk to Nenagh to see his brother. The journey was like the first one he had made to Gortalocca. Every sound, every movement caught his attention, and the concentration made the journey seem longer than its five miles. As he approached the bustle of the busy market town, he began to relax.

He went directly to the castle, where the guards scowled at the commonly-dressed man and asked his business. Liam told them he wanted to see the sheriff. He even tried his best upper-class accent but it was met with mockery and they sniggered at him derisively. He wished he had worn his formal clothes. Finally, one of the men agreed to enquire about the possibility of a meeting with the head lawman. He went off and came back a few minutes later, saying that the High Sheriff was otherwise occupied and the man should try again tomorrow. There was nothing else Liam could do and so he left. He saw no point in staying in Nenagh, so he bought a boiled potato from a street vender and started the walk homewards. If anything, the journey back seemed longer. He was disappointed that his only brother couldn't spare the time to see him and he tried to make excuses for him, but he found it difficult.

The carcasses of the two animals they had left in the field this morning had been stripped of flesh now. One's loss is another's gain, thought Liam. As he walked close by, a few magpies and crows flew away from the dead animals but Liam knew the meat wouldn't be wasted. Tonight, at least, there would be quite a few pots filled with something other than spuds and cabbage. He would leave the carrion for the birds. Right now, he needed something to fill his own stomach so he headed towards Hogan's. He was angry about being snubbed by his brother and he was angry about the loss of the animals. He knew that hunger had allowed his anger to flourish and a bellyful of food always made the world a more tolerable place. Besides he would get to see the golden-haired girl.

When Liam entered Hogan's this time, no one left. They had heard about the loss of his livestock and they felt sympathy for him. It was one thing to talk about doing something like this but, in reality, the actual consummation of such an act was repulsive to them. Besides, if they stayed, perhaps they might hear some juicy gossip.

Liam sat himself at one of the tables and Roisin asked if he wanted a beer. 'I do, woman,' he said, 'and a plate of whatever you might have on the fire.' Roisin said she was sorry but the food had all gone. Hogan's had done brisk business that day, with folk coming to look at the carnage on Liam's farm, dropping into the store and bar in the hope of getting some spicy story that they could retell. After all, the usual conversation topics of the weather and who had died was never as good as a massacre, even if the victims were animals. Roisin put a plate of bread and cheese on the table in front of Liam and one of the men at the bar turned and asked if the carpenter had any idea who the criminals may be.

Liam was still in a sour mood. 'It could be any one of ye.' The men turned back to the bar. Flynn had an axe to grind and not one of them wanted it to be with him. Liam ate in silence and Roisin busied herself. Liam knew she didn't think it was the right time to talk to him and that was alright, he just liked her being in the same room. At last he stood up, left a penny on the table and left without saying another word. It had got dark outside.

Liam walked back his cottage and, when he opened the door, even in the gloom he sensed another person was there.

'Jamie?' There was silence for a moment, then a man's voice said quietly,

'No.'

Liam took a step back into the night and raised his holly stick. 'Come out here!' he demanded. 'Or I'll come in and bash your head in!'

'It's me,' said the voice

'Me, who?' Liam cocked the stick and got ready to deliver a blow.

'Robbie,' came the voice from the dark.

Liam relaxed. 'I tried to see you today.'

'I know. I heard about it after you left. I should have that guard flogged for assuming who I would, and wouldn't, want to see. A good caning would take some of the pretentiousness off the bastard.' Liam closed the door now and lit a candle. The house was cold. Robert sat in a chair at the table. Liam could see that he had blood on his clothes and a short sword unsheathed on the table. He opened his mouth to speak but the sheriff beat him to it.

'I met a few playmates coming into the village,' he said. 'They had flour sacks over their heads.' He gave a mirthless smile. 'One of them should be in Lucifer's company now but the others scattered.'

'Who did you kill?'

'One of your neighbors,' the sheriff said, enigmatically, and waited for Liam's question.

'Which one?'

'The poteen maker, Gleeson. He should have stuck with the whiskey, he didn't make much of a bandit. I heard about your horse and cow, Liam. I should have warned you that you might be a target, but all I had were rumours.'

'Do you know who's responsible for what happened to the animals?'

'I have a good idea,' said the dark man, 'but I'm not ready to spring the trap yet. I want to make sure I have all the scoundrels in one place, then I'll make sure they answer for what they've done.' Liam thought back to what had been said in the room earlier.

'Tell Sheridan to leave Reilly be,' said Robert, as if he'd read his brother's mind, 'and I'm giving the same advice to you. I have a flask of good Irish whiskey with me. Bring a couple of cups and we'll share a few stories.' That was all that was said about the subject. The two men drank together, just as brothers, sharing a few laughs and a few tall tales. When it grew late, Robert, the brother, became D'Arcy the sheriff once again.

'Remember what I told you earlier. Steer clear of Reilly and, if you have any regard for your friend Sheridan, you'll tell him to do the same. I've spent too long preparing my snare to let you two amateurs spoil my plans for him.' The Robert that Liam had known as a child was gone once more, and in his place, stood a man who was as cold as the steel he wore on his left hip.

'Walk me up to the church, brother, I have my horse stabled inside it.' He sheathed his sword in its scabbard, threw a dark greatcoat over his shoulders and the two brothers walked in silence to St. Patrick's.

CHAPTER 49

T he next morning was colder than cold, and the sky was as blue and crystal clear as a sky could be. Liam had been careful to put turf on the fire before he went to sleep. He was glad he had built a bed for himself because the floor of the cottage was icy. His head throbbed from the whiskey the night before and, through his window, he could see young Jamie toiling in the hard ground on the other side of the road, preparing it to plant seed. The boy was growing up, not because he chose to, but because he had to. Liam lifted the lid of the iron pot hanging on the crane. There was a small amount of porridge in it, so he swung the crane over the glowing embers and put on his shirt. He wished he had some milk for the porridge but he didn't even have a cow anymore. There was still blood on the table where Robert had laid his blade last night and, as he cleaned it up, he thought of all the animal gore he had seen yesterday. He tried to convince himself that blood was blood, wherever it came from but somehow, knowing that this blood belonged to an acquaintance, made it different.

He thought about Roisin. She was probably preparing breakfast for herself and her father right now. He should have wished her good night when he had left last evening. He would make his apologies to her later, after he had helped Jamie to turn the soil. He put on his britches and went outside. Putting his hands on his hips, he inhaled the frigid air and took a long look at the cottage he had built just months ago, admiring the work that he and the others had done. He went back inside and gulped down the porridge. It would do him until it was time for his evening meal. He walked over to the Clancy house and began to work next to the boy.

By the time the sun had got overhead, the frost had gone and it was warm, the first warm day of the year. Spring had arrived and the trees were beginning to show off their first leaves. The buds at the tips of the twigs were bursting open, one by one, to reveal the infant sprigs that would create Summer's canopy, and wild flowers were blooming in the meadows, the pinks and purples which would give way to the yellows of the warmer days to come. Liam took a moment to look around him and he was glad that he had made this place his home.

Roisin had been up with the sun, as was her habit. She had stayed up a little later than usual last night because she had seen the candle in Liam's cottage. The carpenter usually put his light out a few hours after dark, unless he had company, and she had made an excuse to her father, after the bar closed its doors, and had sat at a seat by the window, watching. At around midnight, she had seen Liam come out with a man in a greatcoat and walk towards the church. About ten minutes later, the carpenter had returned alone and, a few minutes after that, the candle was extinguished. Liam had aroused her curiosity yet again. Who was the mysterious figure with him? There was only one way to find out, she would ask him.

When Liam came in at midday for a beer, she did just that. She didn't try to flirt or be coy to extract the answer from him, but simply asked who the stranger was.

'Ah, it was just someone from my past,' said Liam, flippantly. 'Sometimes your past follows you.'

That wasn't nearly enough to satiate Roisin's interest. 'Was it someone from Thurles?'

'Yes.'

'Someone you worked with?'

Liam hesitated for a second. 'Yes.'

'C'mon, Liam, you're killing me.'

'Well, I don't want you to die from curiousity,' he said, smiling, 'but you might die of shock when I tell you something else.' Roisin leaned foreward and grabbed Liam's hand.

'It was my brother. It was Robert.'

Roisin gasped. 'But I thought he was dead.'

'So did I, until I was summoned to the sheriff's office.'

Roisin's eyes widened. 'So that's what took you so long,' she said. 'Had your brother asked the sheriff to find you?'

'No, Roisin, you don't understand. Robert Flynn and Robert D'Arcy are one and the same person.'

'What? I can't believe it, Liam.'

'And I have one more piece of information for you. Did you know Paul Gleeson is dead?' Roisin gasped again. She didn't know, and information like that didn't stay hidden for long. Liam continued. 'He and some other hooded men tried to waylay a traveller last night, and Paul didn't live to see the sun rise this morning.'

Liam had said it so casually that she was shocked.

'Where's the body?'

Liam shrugged. He had no idea but he had considered the question and thought it likely that perhaps the others had hidden the body to keep their own identities secret.

Liam finished his beer. 'Heard enough for one day?' Roisin just nodded and watched him leave, her head spinning with the revelations. Liam went back to finish turning the soil with Jamie, then he went home, washed himself and ate some meat that Paddy had provided. He hoped it wasn't the horse.

When Liam lay on his bed in the dark house, he thought of how he had teased Roisin with his answers, and he drifted off to sleep with a full belly and a smile on his face. He was awakened by a knock on the door. It was night now and he no idea how long he had slept. He wiped his eyes to chase away the sleep and got up to open the door. He hoped it was Roisin. If it was Mick Sheridan with his dominoes or a deck of cards, Liam wasn't in the mood. It was neither. As he opened the door, it was knocked out of his hand, and he found himself being dragged out of the house by a man with a flour sack covering his head. He was caught off balance as another man punched him in the face. Liam's head span as he was thrown to the ground, where someone with a familiar voice kicked him viciously in the ribs and then did it again. As if it was far off in the distance, he heard a voice shout.

'Fire d' house!' Someone kicked him in the head and he lost consciousness for a brief moment. He tried to get to his knees now and someone stomped on his back, forcing his face into the gravely soil.

'Strip him!' the familiar voice shouted. Now,

everything he heard sounded like it was coming down a barrel and he couldn't hear his own cries as he was punched, pushed, kicked and beaten. If this carried on, he knew he would be dead in minutes. He lay naked now and two men grabbed either arm and spread him out. He couldn't fight so many and so he resigned himself.

He heard 'Get d' tar!' and thought he would pass out again. His brain registered that the sun had come up now, but that couldn't be right, could it? It wasn't. The thatch was on fire.

'Cover 'im wit' tar. Don't cover 'is nose an' mouth, I don't want 'im t' suffocate. I got udder plans fer 'im.' Liam cried out in pain as the hot tar burned his skin. He heard a woman screaming and he knew it was Roisin. Paddy Shevlin was shouting something but was knocked silent as someone punched him in the face, and Jamie was kicked down the street by another of the masked men. Liam faded in and out of consciousness now, as he felt himself being dragged towards his burning house.

'Who's got d' fedders?' someone yelled. 'Ya can't tar an' fedder a man widdout fedders.' Liam was able to turn his head a little and, when he looked towards where Jamie was being beaten, he saw Mick Sheridan on his pony. Mick leapt off and struck the man who was kicking Jamie a mighty punch with his big fist. Two men left Liam and jumped on Mick, pummelling him with fists and feet. Liam struggled against the one man who was left trying to hold him down and he managed to get his feet under him. The fellow tried to push him into the burning house and Liam knew that he would light up like a candle if the man succeeded.

It ended as dramatically as it had started. Liam could barely see now, the beating had made his eyes swell and the hot tar had done the rest. The man trying to push him into the fire was thrown off by an unseen force. Liam tried to gather his senses, but all he could hear were shouts, screams and the sound of horses' hooves. The kick to the side of his head had rendered his right ear deaf. He tried to stand, stumbled and tried again. Then hands grabbed his arms from both sides and pulled him away from the now flame-engulfed cottage. His head lolled back and the last thing he saw before unconsciousness embraced him was a beautiful starlit sky.

CHAPTER 50

L iam heard voices, they seemed far off in the distance. He tried to open his eyes but he couldn't. He put his hand up to his face and it felt like bread dough. He was aware of people around him, touching him, but this time the touch was tender and he drifted back into nothingness. He dreamt of beautiful green rolling hills and of sitting alongside his old master, carving wood, a boy watching them work. He saw his Da and his Ma, and they weren't in a hovel in Thurles, they were in a beautiful cottage, his cottage. It was a good dream and he let oblivion envelop him once again.

When Liam eventually became aware of the pain, each breath felt like a knife being thrust into his lungs. He tried to move but hands held him, like on that starry night, and he tried to fight them off.

'Easy, Liam. It's all right. You're safe now.' It was a woman's voice and, in his delirium, he thought it must be his guardian angel and that he was in heaven. He relaxed again. And so it went, for what seemed an eternity, or perhaps it was just seconds. Brief flickers of consciousness were followed by nothingness, where he dreamt about heaven and angels and where heaven was like Tipperary, with green fields and woodland and streams with salmon, and where his angel had golden hair and the beautiful face of the sharp-tongued Irish lass.

He became aware of light and, as he lay in the dimness, he touched his face. This time, there were no hands to restrain him and he felt the slits that were his eyes and managed to prise one eyelid open. The sunlight stabbed his eye and he closed it again. Moira was talking to him and, although he knew it was the old hag, he couldn't remember her name.

'Don't worry, my son,' she said softly, 'you're not blind.' Liam tried to speak but his lips felt like raw liver and his throat was parched.

'Here, lad, take a sip of water.' He felt hands behind his head, raising it forward, and he drank from a cup that was held to his lips. He tried to lift his arms to hold the cup, but the pain in his ribs almost made him pass out again.

'Da bastards busted ya up pretty good, boyo.' Liam recognised Shevlin's voice and he knew by the way he spoke that Paddy must have received a God Almighty thrashing too.

'Paddy...?' Liam croaked in a low whisper.

'I'm here, lad,' said Paddy, and Mick's here wit me too. He almost killed Connor McCormack wit' a single punch.' Liam realised that McCormack's must have been the voice he had recognised. Liam held his palm up towards where the voice came from to tell Paddy to hush.

'Jamie. Is Jamie alright?'

'Ah, ya don't need t' be worryin' yerself about dat lad.

He's over at yer cottage now tryin' t' salvage what he can an' gettin' t'ings ready t' work.'

'…and Roisin?'

'Ah man, ya shudda seen 'er. Screamin' like a banshee, she was, an' she tried t' scratch Sean Reilly's eyes out, 'til he knocked 'er on her arse.'

'She's alright, so?'

'She's grand. Mick jus' left to go an' get 'er. She's bin here by yer bed fer d' las' two days an' she'd only jus' gone home t' freshen 'erself up.'

'I'm …? said Liam, feeling around him.

'Yes, lad, you're in a bed. Da boy made us get d' one from d' priest's house.'

Liam's brain was still woolly, 'Where am I?'

'Yer in d' Clancy house. Roisin wanted t' take ya home but her Da kicked up about it, said folk wouldn't go inta Hogan's if dey knew ya was d'ere and, with dem coming t' Gortalocca from miles around to see d' fire, he wanted t' make d' most of d' business. She put up an awful fierce fight until d' boy stepped in like a man an' tol' ev'ryone dat you're his family an' so ya were stayin' in his house.' Liam tried to smile but it hurt.

He heard someone come in and then Roisin, whispering to Moira.

'It's only one ear I can't hear with,' he mumbled, attempting a joke. 'And I'm not blind either, I just can't see.' He tried to prise open an eyelid with his thumb and forefinger so that he could see the golden-haired girl from his dream. He wanted to tell her about it but he was afraid that, even in his sorry state, she would have no mercy. His eye got used to the light and he saw her hovering over him, her beautiful blue eyes were moist.

'I thought we'd lost you a few times,' she said, her voice catching in her throat, 'but Moira prayed you out of it.' Liam tore his squinty gaze from Roisin to Moira and the old woman gave him her one tooth smile.

'Roisin's right, lad,' she said. 'Ya kept wantin' t' leave us but yer work here's not finished yet, so I wasn't lett'n ya go anywhere.' Liam was able to hold open his eyelid without the use of his hand now and so he tried to open the other.

Roisin came closer. 'Father Grogan administered the Last Rites to you,' she whispered. 'I thought I would die too.' Liam was touched and he had to swallow hard to get his voice back,

'My cottage?'

Paddy answered. 'D' roof's gone but, sure, d' walls is still sound. D' boy cut down a tree yesterday ... said he'd split a beam out as soon as you were well enough to tell 'im he cud use yer tools.' Liam could hold open both his eyes now and he viewed his world through slits.

'Why am I still alive?' he asked. 'With that many on me, I thought I was a dead man.'

'C'mere,' said Roisin. 'eat some broth and get some sleep. I'll tell you everything when you wake up.' Her tone was one that Liam was well aware he couldn't argue with, so he did as he was told.

He awoke with a start. He had been dreaming again. This time, a demon was pushing him into the fires of hell's forge and he had tried to resist, but it was no use. Down and down he had gone, the flames licking around him, getting hotter and hotter. The sweat was rolling off his body now and Roisin sat next to the bed, wiping his face with a damp cloth. A tall man in uniform stood at the foot of the bed, the same stern-faced guard that had accompanied Liam to Gortalocca some days before. He knuckled his forehead and said to Roisin,

'I'll be getting word back to the High Sheriff now.'

With that, he turned and left and, a few minutes later, Liam heard the sound of the dragoon's horse galloping away.

'Your brother sent him to guard you, Liam,' Roisin explained. 'He said he wanted to make sure no further harm came to you, he says he feels responsible for what happened.' Liam didn't understand. How could Robert bear any responsibility for the act of those thugs? Roisin continued. 'I'll tell you what I know, mo chuisle, and Robert can fill in the rest.'

'Paddy had been performing his usual antics in the bar and I was about to throw him out when we heard a terrible commotion coming from your cottage. We ran out and there were men, some of them with white flour sacks pulled over their heads. They had you on the ground, beating and kicking you, and Jamie ran from his house, right into the middle of the fray like a proper hero. He had no weapon and all he had on was his long leine, but he tore into the gang like a madman. One of them grabbed him and threw him down, then started to kick him. Paddy waded in, yelling at the top of his lungs but Sean Reilly punched him in the face and knocked him to the ground. I tried to gouge his eyes out but he clouted me and sent me flying too.'

Liam felt a pain in his gut, as if he'd been kicked again. Roisin carried on, she was in full flight now. 'Just then, Mick Sheridan rode up on his pony. He leapt off and punched the man on Jamie so hard that two others jumped him and then he had all he could handle. I was on the ground and I thought you were dead, but then you tried to get up and Gleeson's oldest boy tried to push you into the fire. I thought he would do it too, but just then four men on horseback came galloping in, as fast as the wind, from the direction of Killadargan, and the one in the lead had a sabre raised over his head. He swung the sword so quick and with such force that the Gleeson lad never knew what hit him, it just swept him away. Two more troopers arrived from the direction of Johnstown and two more rode in from Knigh and sealed the box. They killed two of the men and captured two more, Sean Reilly included, but one got away. Robert and Paddy dragged you away from the fire, just in time. Robert was so worried about you that he wouldn't leave you until Moira told him you wouldn't die that night. I went outside with him and he fetched a huge pistol from next to his saddle, said he was going to shoot Sean Reilly. Reilly begged him for mercy and, in the end, Robert said he wouldn't kill him, that he would rather see him dangle from the end of a rope, but first he knocked out his teeth with the butt of his gun, Then, he whipped Connor McCormack for being a treacherous coward and told him he would join Sean on the gallows. I didn't know that Robert was the dark man, Liam. You never told me that.'

Liam closed his swollen eyes. 'I gave my word.'

CHAPTER 51

I t hadn't even been an hour since the guard had left the cottage, when the hoof beats of a heavy horse could be heard coming in from the east. The horse skidded on the gravel as it came to a halt outside the Clancy home. Liam woke to hear the animal's laboured breathing and the scuffle of boots in the gravel, just before the door burst open. It was Robert Flynn, Liam's brother, not Robert D'Arcy, the High Sheriff.

'I'm sorry, Lum,' he said. 'I never meant it to come to this.' He sat on the side of the bed and Liam winced. The uniformed man stood up again with a pained expression. 'How bad is it?'

'As bad as it looks,' replied Liam. Robert shook his head. He knelt down next to his brother now and clutched his hand.

Liam gave him a crooked smile. 'You bear no blame for any of this,' he told him.

'But I do,' Robert replied. 'I investigated you. Not as a brother, but in my official capacity as sheriff, and I found out everything about you and what you were doing.' Liam watched his brother in silence as Robert continued.

'I interviewed the woman who owns the Inn, and the little tailor, and the solicitor. You'd be surprised how forthcoming they were when they found themselves sitting in a chair in my office, with a horse pistol trained at them.' Robert was smiling now but it was the smile of a predator. 'I was going to arrest you.' Liam drew his hand away from his brother's grip. 'And have no doubt, Liam, I would have done it. I've had to kill men in battle who were once close friends. Hanging a brother I no longer knew was no different.' Liam felt a deep sadness. The brother he thought he knew had changed beyond recognition. 'Arresting you, brother, was one thing. Tamping out a fire that could grow into a rebellion, now that will give a boost to my standing as High Sheriff.'

'I thought you believed in Irish freedom.' Liam's voice was low. The uniformed man stood up now and he held himself erect.

'I still do. It is my duty to enforce the laws, but I have a certain…,' he searched for the word, 'discretion… as to which laws I enforce.' He smiled again.

Liam's sadness has turned to anger now. 'So you used me,' he said. 'You used me as bait for your trap.'

'I did,' the sheriff smiled down at him, 'and I'd do it again. But I shouldn't have taken so long to spring it.'

'I almost got killed.'

'I know. And that's what I'm sorry about,' said the dark fellow. 'I was already on my way and, if I had arrived a minute or two earlier, we would be drinking a beer together now, instead of you having to sip soup.'

'And if you'd arrived a minute later, I would have been burnt alive,' Liam said accusingly. 'You played both sides. You're nothing but a hypocrite!''

Robert bristled at the word. 'I'm a hypocrite? Look in the mirror, Liam Flynn, common Catholic carpenter and gentleman Protestant landowner.'

Roisin had been listening attentively and now she spoke. 'But you're Irish, like us, and your job is to oppress your own people?'

Robert was still smiling. 'I'm sure it must appear that way to you. And sometimes I even have to ask myself whose side I'm on.'

Roisin looked at Liam, who shook his head. 'I don't understand,' she said. Neither of the two young people could grasp what Robert was telling them.

Robert shrugged. 'All you need to know is that this little community, here, that you call home will be safe, as long as I am sheriff. Any documents that make reference to Liam Flynn are in my possession and will go no further. Now, I will leave you young people to discuss what a scoundrel I am, but remember,' he turned to Liam 'I'm your scoundrel.' Sheriff Robert D'Arcy put on his greatcoat and straightened it.

'What of the raider who got away?' Roisin asked.

'I know who he is,' replied Robert, flippantly. 'He's another Gleeson boy. I could arrest him anytime I want, but I think his family has suffered enough for now, what with the loss of the father and now the older brother. I think this one will go back to making whiskey.' Robert gave a nod and a half bow and left.

There was silence in the cottage, while those gathered there thought about what had just taken place.

Roisin spoke first. 'There's no doubt that your brother is a callous man, Liam,' she said. 'He's ruthless and he's cruel, but he has compassion too. He showed mercy to the Gleesons, even though it would have added another notch on his pistol to kill the other son.'

'He already got the hangings he's been looking for,' said Liam, who was exhausted now.

'I'm just so angry that he put your life at risk, all because he wanted to put on a show.'

Liam was angry too. First the priest, a friend who he trusted, had used him and now his own brother. Both of them had put his life at risk. At least, with the priest, he had been a willing collaborator. With Robert, all he had been was someone to manipulate for his own ends.

*

The next morning, Liam tried to stand by himself. He stumbled and sat back down, then stood again with the aid of the holly stick. This time, he managed a few steps. The swelling around his eyes had begun to go down and he could see a little better now. There was a rushing sound in his ear, like running water, and whenever he put his hand over it, it seemed to get worse. Any movement at all gave him excruciating pain in his side. He was determined to try and get to his cottage and assess the damage. Jamie had told him that he'd already cleared most of the debris, and he'd given him reports and updates, but Liam needed to see it for himself. Paddy Shevlin saw him struggling to walk across the street and told him to go back, that it was too soon. Liam ignored the fat old fellow and hobbled to the house.

He stopped, putting his weight on the holly stick and looked at his home. All that remained of it was a shell. At the sight of it, a lump came to his throat. His home was in ruins and so was his battered body. He wanted to pack up and go back to Thurles. The thought didn't last long. Jamie had seen Liam coming and had run across the street to get a chair for him to sit on.

'There,' he said, proudly. 'Ya c'n watch from here. Ya c'n see if I do it right.' He helped Liam onto the chair and began to tell him how they would re-build his home together and the boy's eager enthusiasm chased away any thoughts of leaving Gortalocca.

Paddy and Jamie had already brought the main beam and the rafters from where the boy had cut the tree. 'You've been busy, lad,' said Liam. 'I couldn't have done it better myself.'

The boy's face flushed with pride and he grinned.

'You know you'll have to cut the tenons and mortices yourself this time. I'm useless.'

Jamie grinned and nodded. Paddy helped the boy and they moved the wood to where Liam could observe, and give advice to Jamie.

'How will we get the beam up without help?' asked the carpenter.

Paddy smiled. 'Mick Sheridan has d' strength o' t'ree men on d'eir best day,' he said.

'That's still not enough.'

'Well, we got da priest too,' laughed Paddy.

'Agh, Paddy, all he can raise is a flagon, sure.'

Paddy laughed again. 'Dat's true, but if he gives a plenary indulgence t' everyone who helps, we'll have d' whole o' Nenagh here.'

'What about the thatch? It's too late in the season for straw.'

'We'll cut river reeds. Dey make d' best thatch anyway. It'll be even more beautiful den it was before.'

'What about my tools?'

'Da box got a little scorched but d' boy an' Mick got dem out before d' roof collapsed altogether.'

'Help me up Paddy, will you, there's one last thing.'

'If it's yer purse yer lookin' for, it's safe, d' boy found it when he was cleanin' up.' Liam sat back in the chair.

Roisin had been watching all this from inside

Hogan's and had decided that her patient had exerted himself quite enough for now. She strode over, her head high and her face stern.

'You'll undo all my good work, Liam Flynn, if you don't get yourself back to bed.'

Liam smiled and grabbed her hand. 'I had to get out in the air to blow the stink off me.'

She shook her other fist at him, mockingly. 'I have something here that'll blow the stink off ya!' Liam pretended to cower and she laughed and whispered to him.

'I think me Da has something he wants to discuss with you.' She looked up and saw Paddy eavesdropping, 'IN PRIVATE!' she yelled, and gave Liam's hand a squeeze.

10525055R00199

Made in the USA
Lexington, KY
24 September 2018